EXCEPT FOR ME AND THEE

Jessamyn West

Except
for
Me and Thee

A COMPANION TO

The Friendly Persuasion

HARCOURT, BRACE & WORLD, INC., NEW YORK

Some of the stories in this book originally appeared in *Good Housekeeping, The Kenyon Review, The Ladies' Home Journal, Redbook, The Saturday Evening Post,* and *Woman's Day.*

CONTENTS

EXCEPT FOR ME AND THEE

The Wooing

Jess and Eliza Birdwell stood in the snowy twilight outside their own parlor window and gazed back inside like children at a peep show. The window, which was a farmhouse bay, was framed with lace curtains stiff and white as frost tracery. A lighted tree stood in the window, and around the tree was gathered a group of young people.

Little Elspeth, the grandchild, a Quaker like the rest of them, and as untaught as they in dancing, was dancing; a tiptoe step to touch a branch, then quickly back to her mother, as if she needed to offset the magic of the Christmas tree by the touch of something known and familiar.

The three young uncles were keeping their toes quiet; but their eyes were dancing, and their mouths were slightly opened as they gazed at the wonder. They had all seen Christmas trees before, but this was the first tree ever to stand inside the Birdwell parlor at Christmastime, "lit up," as Jess said, "like a bonfire."

Jess Birdwell was a nurseryman, raised trees and fancied them. "But," he had said, "I'd no more think of putting a tree in the house than of setting a sofa in the pigpen."

"Just at Christmastime, Papa," Mattie had pleaded. Mattie, having married a Methodist, had acquired worldly ideas.

"Christmastime would be the last time for it so far as I'm concerned. Fourth of July, maybe, when a little more hullabaloo one way or the other wouldn't cut any ice."

"I have to admit they are enjoying themselves," Jess told Eliza as he watched the circle around the tree.

The tree had been less of a hurdle for Eliza than for Jess. Like most women, Eliza was pretty literal-minded. "It's no more than a little woods-lot evergreen," she had told Jess, "with a few geegaws hung on it."

On the twenty-fifth of December, it was more than that. But it wasn't the tree itself Jess was wondering about now. It was the children around the tree; and the house around the children; and the acres of Maple Grove Nursery that surrounded the house. Standing outside his own window, he peered in with a stranger's amazement.

"Where'd it all come from?" he asked Eliza. "How'd we all get here?"

He gestured toward the clapboard house still white under the dark firs in the wintry twilight. "How'd we all end up here?"

Jess felt momentarily dizzy looking in the window, and beyond it, beyond it to beginnings in other states and years. He had felt that way sometimes reading a book; as if he were reading about himself, not a story about people who were total strangers. Only now it was the other way around. These people and rooms and acres were his own; but momentarily, they were storylike. All were strange. How did it happen that he wasn't an emir in Turkey? Or a black man in Africa? Instead of Jess

Birdwell, Quaker nurseryman, standing outside his own window on an Indiana hillside at the close of a December day.

"How'd we get here, Eliza?"

There are stories about himself, true ones, a man tells himself and never tells another soul. He tells these stories over and over again, trying to find the truth in them, for, as years pass, memories dim, and insights increase, the stories change. Jess had told himself a hundred times the story of how he came to be engaged to three girls at the same time. Eliza had been one of those girls, but in the twenty-eight years of their marriage he had talked with her but twice about what had happened. It wasn't just that he wasn't very proud of his actions, or that, in his opinion, a man has nothing to gain by talking to his wife about the girls he knew before he was married; it was more that he didn't himself truly understand what had gotten into him in those October days when he couldn't seem to stop proposing to girls.

The first two of the engagements, he felt certain, had less to do with youth, hot blood, and poor judgment than with his feelings about his father. He had had a fight with his father the night he got engaged to Georgia Harmon. He was six months past twenty-one that night. He was the youngest of nine children, the only one unmarried and living at home. His father was seventy, his mother sixty-five.

The other children thought that he should stay home and "look after the old folks." The old folks thought so, too. The only trouble was they didn't need looking after, didn't want to be looked after, and after almost fifty years of looking after others couldn't change. The one who got looked after was Jess. Jess, at twenty-one, was six feet two and weighed one hundred and ninety pounds. To his mother he was still eleven and weighed eighty-nine. She spoke to him about changing his underwear and purifying his blood with sulphur and molasses. Talbot Birdwell told his son when his horse needed shoeing and his buggy wheels needed greasing. Talbot and Hannah needed Jess, all right; they needed him to keep alive in themselves their long-possessed and deeply cherished conviction of being needed.

The evening Jess got engaged to Georgia began with an early supper at home. Because it was First Day, the table, which was set in the kitchen, was covered with a fringed white linen cloth. The food for First Day supper never changed. It couldn't. It was whatever was left over from First Day dinner, and *that* never changed. The evening he got engaged to Georgia there was, as always, cold chicken, leftover mashed potatoes made into potato cakes and served piping hot and nicely browned, a dish of corn relish, a dish of rosy watermelon preserves, an apple pie warmed up in the oven of the cookstove which had been lit to fry the potato cakes. The apple pie was served with yellow cream so thick it had been lifted in sheets from the milk crocks in the springhouse. There was hot black tea, which his father drank from his saucer, never noticing his son's frown as first he cooled it with blowing, then sucked it in with noisy satisfaction.

Everything on the table was rich, tasty, and repetitious. Jess thought he could lose his eyesight and never miss it insofar as First Night supper was concerned. The same food in the same dishes, and the dishes in the same places. The memory of identical past meals was so strong it scarcely seemed necessary to eat this one.

At twenty-one Jess hadn't understood the satisfaction elderly people take in seeing a thing, even if it is nothing more than First Night supper, remain unchanged. Everything else—the house they lived in, their children, friends, even their own bodies—was changing at a breakneck pace.

At twenty-one he had sat at the supper table and thought, as he looked out the kitchen window, Nothing changes but the view. And that change, from summer to fall to winter to spring, was also unchanging.

Once in a while Jess did seem to notice that his parents were aging, though he couldn't be sure. His father, for as long as he could remember him, had worn a beard about as long and as white as a tea towel. His father took good care of his beard; washed it with soft soap, combed it whenever he combed his hair, and trimmed it once a week in front of a mirror. It had occurred to Jess, watching him on these occasions, that his father was proud of his beard. Jess hoped this wasn't true. A man of seventy should have lost all interest in personal appearance; and particularly a Quaker who preached plainness and who should therefore practice it.

Now and then Jess had noticed that his father, lofty-browed, white-maned, and bearded, looked like Biblical pictures of God. The likeness was certainly one of appearance only. God, to judge by what He had done, was no Quaker. Only a wildly inventive un-Quakerish Creator could have called kangaroos, volcanoes, cannibals, ostriches into being. Quakers were far too cautious to have ever taken a chance on such creations.

His father would never even take a chance on his mother's having salted a dish properly. Before taking a bite he always asked for the saltcellar. After dipping the spoon in the salt, he would, in a never-varying fashion, tap the spoon with his forefinger. He always tapped it five times. Jess knew. He counted. Sometime, he was afraid, he would count out loud.

It was one of his father's many set and mechanical ways of doing things. The life of a coffee mill, Jess thought, or a corn sheller is just as adventurous. His father always peeled apples before he ate them; he salted them, too. His father wanted nothing raw, or unexpected.

Jess had eaten oak leaves in spring; love apples, muskrats, and crows in all seasons. Some with and some without salt. He intended to live, not to repeat a pattern.

The chief trouble with his mother was that she never found fault with his father. She sat at the table wearing, as she always did in the house, a white cambric cap which tied under her round pink chin. You couldn't hope for an elderly lady to look better: tidy, clean, and in good flesh. She had no interests that Jess knew of outside of her husband, children, and grandchildren; she attended the Religious Society of Friends, looked after her home and her prize flocks of chickens, geese, and guineas. To Jess's mind his mother could not properly be said to have lived. She had been born in Philadelphia, would die in Mount Pleasant, Ohio, and be buried under a plain stone which said only, "Hannah, wife of Talbot Pryce Birdwell." Jess loved his mother and pitied her.

At twenty-one Jess had thought that a painter could make a picture of them at the supper table called "Quakers Returning Thanks," and he had thought that the title would be misleading because he wasn't returning thanks, and because the thanksgiving his parents returned had become, he believed, a matter of rote. Later he wished that picture had been painted. He would love once again to see the three of them in the kitchen of that brick house in Ohio: his father and mother with heads bowed; he staring, wide-eyed and unthankful, straight ahead.

He was unthankful, for one thing, because of his name: Jesse Griffith, which was shortened by his parents to Jesse

G! He had as well have been called Billy Boy. Here were Quakers who made such a big thing of simplicity, but who decked their own son out with a two-handled name like Jesse Griffith. True, his friends called him Jess; but only when his parents weren't around to hear them. Counting his unblessings, Jess forgot and shut his eyes, and kept them shut, enjoying his anger long after his parents, finished with their blessings, had opened theirs.

"Jesse G," his mother said softly, "thee can look up now."

He should have told his mother that he wasn't praying. Instead he took a couple of crisp potato cakes.

He did tell his father the truth though. When his father said, "Don't dawdle, Jesse G, or we'll be late to Meeting," Jess said, "I'm not going to Meeting."

His father stopped in the midst of a tap on the salt spoon. He wasn't going to order a twenty-one-year-old to go to Meeting, but he did say, "Would thee mind telling me why not?"

Jess minded, but he told him. "I'm going with Joe Riordan to call on Georgia Harmon and her cousin from Indiana."

"Georgia?" his mother said. "Why in the world would a mother want to give her daughter such an outlandish name?"

"It's no more outlandish than Jesse Griffith."

"Why, Jesse G, *thee's* named for thy two grandfathers."

"Georgia's named for a whole state."

"Georgia's nothing but land."

"There's nothing wrong with land."

"How'd thee like to be called Ohio?" his mother asked. "Thee was born here."

Jess refused to be drawn into such a foolish argument. "She's no more responsible for her name than I am for

17

mine," he said. "Besides, what does that have to do with my seeing her?"

His father agreed with him. "Nothing. The point is, it's Meeting night. Don't the Harmons attend some sort of religious service on First Day night?"

His father knew well enough that the Harmons were Methodists and just as faithful churchgoers as the Birdwells were Meeting goers. No use talking about them as if they were savages; and Jess didn't intend to.

"That's a question thee can ask the Harmons. Georgia's not going to church tonight."

"Well, then," said his father, as if he'd hit upon just the idea Jess had been searching for, "thee could take Georgia to Meeting tonight."

The idea of Georgia sitting on the women's side of the Meeting House while he sat on the men's side, not a word being said, unless some elderly Quakers were moved by the Spirit to quote a Bible verse or offer a prayer, was ridiculous.

"A Methodist wouldn't know what to make of a meeting where nobody preached or sang."

"There won't be singing tonight," his father said, "but there will be preaching. There's a member of the Philadelphia Meeting going to preach tonight."

"I thought thee didn't approve of sermons in Meeting."

"I don't. But it might make a Methodist feel right at home. I hear this preacher's pretty lively."

"Lively for a Quaker," Jess said, and his mother, shocked, exclaimed, "Jesse G! That's no way to speak of a girl."

"Girl!" exclaimed Jess. "Why haven't I heard about her?"

"If thee'd been listening last First Day thee would have."

"How old is she?"

"Eighteen or nineteen. She's a friend of the Coxes."

"Now thee knows the Meeting won't be silent, there's no reason for not taking Georgia," his father said.

"No," Jess said obstinately. "When I get tired of silence, I'll go to the Methodist church."

"From the looks of things," his father replied, "that's the direction thee's headed."

Over at the Harmons' the Methodist direction seemed a pretty one. The Harmons, with the exception of Georgia and her Hoosier cousin Betsy, had all gone to evening services at the Methodist church. Georgia and Betsy were already feeling daring simply by having stayed home. Georgia had a pack of younger brothers and sisters, and furniture in the Harmon house wasn't, as in his own home, lined up as orderly as checkers in a checker game. There were signs of life in the Harmon house.

Joe Riordan had brought Jess along for Georgia because he, a former beau of Georgia's, had taken a shine to the Hoosier cousin. Jess had known Georgia all his life. He had pulled her braids at twelve and given her a kiss at a corn-husking when he was sixteen. The kiss was required; she had found a red ear, could choose any boy she wanted, and had chosen him, but he had remembered it. Georgia kissed like she meant it. She was an auburn-haired girl with brown eyes and freckles. Jess didn't have a thing in the world against her except that he had noticed that her hands were about as thick through as they were wide, a thing he didn't like in man or woman. Being fondled by Georgia might be something like being petted by a pony.

His own home was a prison compared with the Harmons'. A place for everything and everything in its place: that was his father's rule, and his mother kept it. There were no rules visible here—and the ones that did exist, the girls were breaking. Staying home from church and having young men callers had gone to their heads. Already bold, they decided to be bolder. George Harmon, like Talbot Birdwell, put horse-radish in his cider, hardening into vinegar, to discourage his hired men from sampling it. But the cider had already begun to bead, and George Harmon had yet to add the horse-radish. So the girls fetched a cut-glass pitcherful up from the cellar, set out tumblers, and prepared to entertain as stylishly as if they were Episcopalians.

It was the first hard liquor Jess had ever tasted, and he couldn't say he liked the taste or relished the smell. It smelled more like something to paint with or to rub on a sore joint than something to drink. But since drinking was expected of him, he drank. It agreed with him absolutely. With no effort at all, except swallowing, he became eloquent, gay, warmhearted, loving, irresistible. Quakerism was no handicap and Methodism nothing but a challenge. The Harmon household clutter, he saw, with the help of hard cider, was as inviting as a flower garden, and the coal-oil lamp shed light soft as moonbeams.

He never tasted hard liquor again. It was difficult enough to live in a world where he recognized things for what they were, where heavy hands were heavy, discarded socks dirty, and coal-oil lamps nothing but glass, oil, and wicks, without having them transformed into something that wasn't real: gardens lit by moonbeams.

Joe and Betsy took their tumblers and went into the parlor, which had a sofa, leaving the sitting room to Jess and Georgia. Jess sat in one rocking chair, Georgia in another, sipping. When they finished their drinks, Georgia came over and sat on Jess's lap. For a chunky girl, she was light as a feather. She stroked his hair and face, and her hands were delicate as moth wings. Jess rocked. When he rocked, the chair went up in a big arc toward the ceiling, paused there a second, then descended slowly and gently. He was so absorbed in these flights he might've forgotten Georgia. But she, for safety's sake, lay plastered close to his chest. She put one arm around his shoulders and the other across his thighs. Her hair was in his mouth. He told her how light, soft, warm, and beautiful she was. And rocked.

After a while she said, "There is one thing you haven't told me."

"What?" he asked happily.

"You haven't said you love me."

"I have, too, told thee," Jess said. He couldn't, in the state he was in, endure the idea of disappointing anyone. "Thee wasn't listening."

"I love you, too, Jess. We'll be married at Christmas."

Jess hadn't thought of marriage, but that idea also delighted him. That *would* give his father a start. Be married at Christmas with a Methodist whoop and a holler. Be read out of Meeting for marrying out of Meeting. That would be a comeuppance for his father, who still thought of him as a boy who needed advice about shoeing horses and greasing buggy wheels. He relished the whole prospect: the ruckus that would follow his announcement of his engagement and the consternation when they found him inflexible.

"Jess," Georgia said. "Jess?"

"Yes, Georgia."

"What're you thinking about?"

Too late, he realized that he should have said, "Thee," or, at least, "Us." But he told the truth. "Father," he said.

"Do you think he'll mind?"

"Yes, siree," Jess said, rocking high. "He'll mind."

*

He never found out whether or not his father would mind. He never got around to telling him. Next morning the idea of marrying a chunky hardhanded girl in order to rile his father seemed as preposterous as it actually was. What had that good old man ever done to deserve such treatment from an ingrate son? He had been drunk last night. That, he now understood, was the explanation for all his high rocking and hard kissing.

He lay in his bed noting from the way the leaves were coming down that there had been a killing frost in the night. They added to his melancholy and did nothing to relieve the heartburn the hard cider had given him. Maybe there *had* been a little horse-radish in that cider.

How could he have been so stonyhearted toward his father and mother, whose sole desire was his welfare? What lay ahead of him on the path on which he had set foot last night? Nothing but to become a hard-cider drunk on his way to becoming an applejack drunk with the falling-down fits. How else could a man endure seven brothers-in-law and sisters-in-law under fifteen, the extent of the Harmon clutter, and the din of Methodist worship?

He went downstairs for breakfast, despondent. When his father said, "Let us return thanks," he closed his eyes and prayed fervently. When his father tapped the salt onto his already salted eggs, the familiar sight filled him with pleasure.

"How was the Philadelphia preacher last night?" he asked.

"For a girl her age, she spoke to the condition of many there."

"Was she an exhorter?" Jess asked.

"An 'exhorter'?" his mother repeated. "Thee's been around too many Methodists lately. Quakers don't exhort."

If his father was anyone to judge by, they came close to it on occasion, in Meeting and out. But the point wasn't one Jess cared to argue, especially with his parents, who were about the only true friends, he now saw, he had in the world.

"This girl," his father explained, "don't preach, exactly. It's more like she just rises in her place and bears witness."

"She made the trip all the way down from Philadelphia to do it?" Jess said. "Don't they need witnessing up there?"

"Don't question the ways of the Lord," his mother said to him. "He's placed a concern for Mount Pleasant upon her shoulders."

"What's her name?"

"Eliza Cope. A fine old Philadelphia family."

"Is she pretty?"

To his parents, this was like looking a gift horse in the mouth. "Speaking the way she does," his father rebuked his son, "it's her words, not her looks, that command attention."

His mother understood a young man's interest in a young woman's looks better. "She looks like a good true-hearted girl."

About all this told him was that his mother thought Eliza Cope was a nice girl. For his mother, handsome actually was as handsome does. When she said a man was ugly-looking, she meant that he looked selfish, cruel, vindictive, worldly. He could be the handsomest man on earth and he would look ugly to her if she detected some meanness of spirit in him. Eliza Cope might be cross-eyed, hollow-chested, and bald, yet, with the right spirit, look comely to his mother.

His father, with some memory of a young man's viewpoint still lingering, said, "She's a little thing with black hair. Plump as a pigeon," he added.

"I might go to hear her," Jess said.

"Take Emily, why don't thee, Jesse G?"

Emily was another good, truehearted girl, but far from bald, hollow-chested, or cross-eyed. She was a biddable birthright Quaker, and the girl his mother had long had picked out for him. That was one of the reasons Jess hadn't gone out with her more often. This morning, however, he was of a mind to place a good deal of reliance on his parents' judgment.

"When's Eliza Cope speaking again?"

"She won't be back here until Sixth Day evening. She's staying with the Coxes, and they're taking her to Wheeling for the rest of the week."

"I think I'll drive over to Emily's this afternoon and ask her to go with me."

When he came home that evening, his mother, who was still up, laying the table for breakfast, said, "Georgia Harmon was over to see thee while thee was gone."

"What'd she have to say?"

"Why, nothing. Chattered on in Georgia's way. I was out in the yard feeding the chickens when she came in, and when she heard thee wasn't here, she didn't linger long."

"Did thee tell her where I was?"

"No," his mother said, "I didn't. I didn't think it was any of Georgia's business. And the minute she began prying as to thy whereabouts it struck me Georgia might be just the kind who'd try to come between thee and Emily."

His mother was taking a good deal for granted about his and Emily's closeness; but she did have Georgia figured out. He couldn't get up the courage either to face Georgia as her husband-to-be or to tell her that it wasn't his heart that had been speaking on First Day night, but hard cider. Daytimes he stayed out in the field shocking corn, and soon after sundown he was on his way to call on Emily. Emily, besides being truehearted, was pretty. She had wheat-colored hair, gray eyes, and a low voice. She wasn't as energetic about it as Georgia, but she was just about as loving. Besides, she waited to be asked, which was a more reliable way than Georgia's for tolling Jess on. So he asked her, too.

Even after more than twenty-five years he didn't know what his reasoning could have been; if reason could be said to have played any part in that week's affairs. Did he think one engagement canceled another? That being engaged to two girls at a time was the same as being engaged to none? Did he get engaged to Emily to please his parents? Just as he'd gotten engaged to Georgia in order to defy them? Was he trusting that Georgia's short temper would end her engagement the minute she heard about Emily?

But what would he do if Emily's good heart caused her to cling to him no matter what Georgia might say about his being a two-timer? If he had to be married to someone, and it looked like he had to, proposing at the rate he was, he preferred Emily to Georgia. But he didn't want Emily either. She had less rise to her than a buckwheat cake. After an evening with Emily he began to appreciate the merits of disorder and hard cider.

He couldn't remember sleeping a wink that week. The cornhusks in his mattress rustled all night long as he tossed and turned trying to figure out how in three short days a man could take such complete leave of his senses. He figured, meditated, cogitated. He didn't pray. He knew he was beyond the help of prayer. The Lord helps those who help themselves, and he wasn't willing to take the first step toward helping himself: tell at least one girl that he didn't want to marry her. He wondered if he was losing his reason. He had read of men who got into the habit of marrying women and who ended up with a chain of wives reaching from the Atlantic to the Mississippi. Was he at the beginning of a career of getting engaged?

What happened next didn't relieve his fears. He took Emily Pryce to hear Eliza Cope preach, and there in the old Sand Creek Meeting House he fell madly in love with the girl preacher. If he wasn't engaged to *her* at the end of Meeting, it wasn't his fault. He wanted to live and die with that girl preacher. Her preaching had nothing to do with his emotions. He hadn't heard her words, though the sound of her voice touched nerve endings all over his body. The engagements he had already contracted were as meaningless as Indian treaties. They had happened in a dream. This was real. What he felt must have had some connection with the girl's appearance, but he knew that he was his mother's boy and would have loved her no matter how she looked.

He wasn't a believer in heaven-sent visions. And if he had been, he would not have expected the Lord to send to a man engaged to two girls a vision of how much more desirable as a wife a third would be. Nevertheless, something extraordinary was revealed to him the night that Philadelphia girl preached. He understood what his father had meant in saying she spoke to the condition of many present. She spoke to his condition exactly; not by any of the words she used, but by being who she was.

After Meeting, Friends lingered to greet each other and to discuss the message they had received. Jess, with all of the authority of an Elder, sailed up to Eliza Cope. He backed her away from her other admirers and tried to tell her what was on his mind.

*

Once only Jess had asked Eliza for her version of their first meeting.

"Eliza?" he had said.

Eliza had looked up from her crocheting.

"Eliza, that first night I saw thee I surely didn't walk up to thee and propose on sight."

"Not that first night."

"Did I discuss thy preaching with thee?"

"From all thee said about my preaching I had as well never have opened my mouth."

"What did I talk about?"

"Thyself."

Jess laughed a little. "Well, thee can't say thee wasn't warned from the outset."

Eliza smiled. "Oh, I was warned. Thoroughly warned right from the beginning. The first thing thee told me was that thee was betrothed to another."

"Well, that was honest of me. Though considering I had the girl by my side, I didn't have much choice."

"The girl thee mentioned wasn't by thy side. Thee was engaged to be married, thee said, to Georgia Harmon."

"That was the truth, too. I was engaged to Georgia. And sorry for it."

"Thee made that clear."

"That was a pretty unmannerly thing to do. Tell a girl I'd just met I was engaged to someone else and sorry for it. How could thee put up with such talk?"

"I was sorry for it, too."

Jess heard Eliza preach again on Seventh Day night and on First Day morning. He spoke with her on both occasions. Emily was with him for the evening services, but neither she nor her family was at the Meeting on First Day morning.

After that second Meeting on First Day at which Eliza had preached, Talbot Birdwell, as was his custom, asked friends home to dinner. Hannah was accustomed to this unvarying hospitality and had enough food cooked for company. Three or four couples accepted Talbot's invitation that day. Except in body, Jess had not been present during much of that dinner. However, when the talk had been of that remarkable young preacher from Philadelphia, he had been totally present. If the talk, as it did more often than not, veered to crops, to health and the lack of it, to news from children moved west, Jess left the table in his imagination and had converse with that remarkable young woman herself.

The space he had been staring into as he sat at the dinner table took in the driveway that led up to the house; what he had been seeing there in his mind's eye was himself and the young preacher walking, arms entwined. This vision was suddenly replaced by a horse and buggy. The horse and buggy had reached the upping-block before it came to him that it was real, and that the two girls, Georgia Harmon and Emily Pryce, who occupied the buggy, were terribly real. Georgia was driving, of course. His muscles, at the sight of those two girls together, made all the preparations for leaping and running. It was odd to find himself, after all that knotting and flexing, still sitting, tablecloth over his knees and roast chicken in front of him. Then what he felt was relief: the relief of a man who has feared that he has a fatal disease, has been told that in truth he has, and is thus relieved of the burden of hope. He also no longer had to expect the worst; it had arrived.

The girls came in with all the dignity of wives hunting erring husbands in a saloon. Georgia wasn't fuming, and Emily wasn't moping. Their bearing was sorrowful, but proud, women who knew their rights and had the courage to ask for them. Jess couldn't help thinking as he sat, paralyzed, watching the girls go to the head of the table, where his father sat, that if he had to get mixed up with two girls at once, and those two girls the wrong ones, he could've done worse. They didn't endear themselves to him, however, by addressing themselves to his father instead of to him, as if he were a schoolboy incapable of speaking for himself.

Georgia, naturally, did the talking; and she didn't mince words. Jess had asked both girls to marry him and both had said yes. Now he obviously couldn't have two wives; perhaps one or the other had misunderstood him, though it didn't seem likely. In any case, he would now have to make his choice. The girls would abide by his decision, and there would be no backbiting or faultfinding because of the misunderstanding—if that was what it was.

Both girls were especially dressed for the occasion. Jess seesawed between feeling that he was a groom at a wedding and a corpse at a funeral.

What his father undoubtedly felt was that he was a judge, and that court was in session awaiting his judgment.

"Jesse G," he asked, "is this true? Did thee ask both these girls to marry thee?"

"Yes, I did," Jess said.

"What possessed thee? Two at a time?"

"I don't know," Jess answered, truthfully.

"Which one did thee ask first?"

"Me," said Georgia.

"How long has thee been Jesse G's promised wife?"

"A week," said Georgia. "He proposed last Sunday night."

"And since then thee broke thy word to Georgia and asked a second girl to marry thee?"

"I'm the second girl," said Emily, meekly. "He asked me Third Day evening."

"Jesse G," his mother said, "has thee been feeling feverish this past week?"

"Yes," said Jess, "I have."

His father would have nothing to do with any attempt by his mother to excuse her son's actions on the grounds of brain fever. Immorality certainly and insanity possibly were the only explanations acceptable to him. Here were two girls both claiming to be his son's promised wife. Since he couldn't marry both, Jesse G would have to choose one.

"Though why either of thee would want him, after these antics, is beyond me. Well, which one is it, Jesse G?"

"Neither," said Jess.

"Neither what?" asked his father.

"Neither girl," said Jess. "I don't want to marry either girl. I will not marry either girl."

It was easier on the girls to be turned down by two than be turned down singly. It seemed less personal. Emily cried. Georgia tossed her head. "I pity the woman you do marry, Jess Birdwell, from the bottom of my heart."

Consternation reigned at the Birdwell table after the girls left. Jess added to it by saying, "I didn't want to say so before the girls, but the reason I can't marry them is that I'm going to marry Eliza Cope."

They didn't think they had heard aright. Mixed up not with two, but with three girls. And the third a preacher!

"What did thee say, Jesse G?"

"I said I was going to marry Eliza Cope."

Jess knew that his father would not, in spite of what had just happened, call him a liar, not in front of so many people. But he didn't understand his father's feeling that the neighbors would like some proof of the authenticity of his latest engagement. His father, under the circumstances, put it very delicately.

"Does thee think Eliza Cope would care to call on us this afternoon?"

Whether she would or not Jess didn't know. But if she wouldn't, he didn't want to be kept on tenterhooks. He hitched right up and drove over to the Coxes'.

The Coxes, like the Birdwells, had had friends home from Meeting for dinner. By the time Jess got there, all had left the table and were in the sitting room rocking and chatting. Jess asked if he could speak with Eliza Cope alone. The Coxes, taking for granted that Jess, who had become so faithful an attendant at Meeting since Eliza had arrived, had a spiritual problem, gladly excused her.

Jess walked Eliza out of the house into the bright windy afternoon. Maria Cox had a little side garden where asters were bending and quivering in the breeze. Jess was much too agitated to stand still. He walked Eliza up and down the one short graveled pathway.

"Eliza," he said, "I have just told my family that thee is going to marry me."

He was prepared for shock, anger, refusal. He was not prepared for calmness.

There was a little pause before she spoke, but all she said was, "I hope this has thy parents' approval."

Jess was shocked himself. Didn't she know she hadn't really been asked in so many words? Could she actually read what his eyes had been saying to her? Didn't she really need protestations and vows of everlasting fidelity?

Or did she think that, coming from him, such things were useless? It was then he noticed for the first time how beautiful she was. The wind couldn't budge her black hair, anchored by her Quaker cap, but it blew her skirts about her, and Jess thought she was lovelier than any of the wind-blown flowers.

"How did thee know I wanted to marry thee?"

"Thee told me the first night we talked."

"I told thee I was engaged."

"Thee said thee was sorry. I didn't think thee would tell me that except for a reason. Nor that thee would keep on with an engagement thee was sorry for."

Jess was too weak-spirited to confess to her how the engagement had ended. Or how many engagements there had been to put an end to.

"Thee is free now, Jess?" she asked with a smile that was somehow saucy as well as sweet.

Once, after Jess had asked Eliza about their first meeting he asked her another question.

"Eliza?" he said.

"Yes, Jess," she answered.

"How did thee get those two girls together?"

"What two girls, Jess?"

"Thee knows. Georgia and Emily."

"Oh," said Eliza. "Georgia was the girl thee was engaged to, wasn't she? Before me?"

"Thee surely hasn't forgotten that."

"It's not been easy, but I've tried."

"How did thee get her and Emily Pryce together?"

"Thee's never told me they *did* get together."

"Well, they did, and thee had a hand in it, or I miss my guess."

"All I did," Eliza said, "and it was for Emily's own

good, seeing how she doted on thee, and how useless it was, considering thee was promised to another, was to tell her about thy engagement to Georgia."

Jess stared for a while at his wife.

"Thee never told me this before."

"Thee never asked me before."

Eliza rolled up the sock she was knitting, put it on the center table, came over to Jess, folded his paper, and put it beside her knitting. Then she sat on his knee. Now they had come to that part of the story they had repeated to each other often.

"When I got home to Philadelphia," Eliza said, "and told my news, Father said, 'Eliza, I've put up with thy gallivanting about the country preaching. But when it comes to a lifetime of missionary work reforming and educating and likely supporting some O-hio backwoodsman, I put down my foot.'"

"He did, too," Jess said, delighting, now that it was overcome, in his father-in-law's inflexibility. "A whole year before he gave in."

"Thy father was just as bad."

"Pa never had anything against *thee*," Jess said. "He was always proud as a peacock of thee. I was the chancy one, he thought. 'Jesse G,' he once said to me in all seriousness, 'has it ever occurred to thee that the Lord perhaps designed thee for a Mormon?'"

Eliza laughed. "Thee had subjected Father Birdwell to a number of shocks."

"Shocked or not, Pa was wide of the mark in his ideas about the Lord's designs for me."

"Well now, thee's still a young man, Jess," Eliza had said. "Don't whistle till thee's out of the woods."

Heading West

For five years after their marriage, Jess and Eliza lived with Jess's parents in Ohio. There couldn't have been a daughter-in-law anywhere easier to get along with than Eliza. She accepted her in-laws' ways, kept her children as quiet as was humanly possible, did more than her share of the work. And she shushed or tried to shush Jess when he felt like berating his father for his highhanded, old-fashioned ways.

In spite of this, or maybe because of it, a lot of whispering went on in the Talbot Birdwell house. Not that anything underhanded was ever plotted, or even uncomplimentary said. But a son has things to say to his wife he'd just as lief his father didn't hear. And a daughter-in-law has even more things to say to her husband that she'd be uneasy saying in front of her mother-in-law. The older Birdwells were more forthright. What they had to say they *wanted* the young couple to hear. "When I was a boy, I got up at four o'clock in the morning and never gave it a second thought." "That child will never learn to use a knife and fork if they keep feeding her." Critical remarks like these by the old couple were the cause of whispering between the young couple.

Jess and Eliza, with three children, weren't actually a young couple any longer except in the eyes of Jess's father and mother. But to Talbot Birdwell, now seventy-seven, and his wife Hannah, seventy-two, Jess and Eliza would always be "the children."

"When I'm fifty years old," Jess whispered to Eliza, "I'll still be a boy to my father."

Jess and Eliza were upstairs in bed whispering. Talbot and Hannah were downstairs sleeping. And even if they had been awake there was no real need for whispering. The Birdwells' home was a big two-story farmhouse, and Talbot and Hannah had taken the parlor bedroom downstairs in order to leave the entire upstairs to their son and his family. The two boys occupied the room next door. Little Sarah, aged two, slept in a trundle bed beside Jess and Eliza. Whisper or not, she was liable to rouse up at any time of the night and clamber into her parents' bed for a little talk. The real reason for the whispering was their feeling of guilt; or Eliza's feeling of guilt. She knew that Talbot Birdwell was a good old man, and she kept shushing Jess. She wasn't able to shush him into a complete whisper, but she was able to hold him down to a growl.

"Eliza, I don't intend to keep quiet while Father tells a tableful of visitors that thee was too busy talking to help with the dinner."

"Preaching *is* talking," Eliza reminded him.

"It's a special kind of talking, and Father can give it its right name."

Eliza understood her father-in-law better than his son did. Talbot, a dyed-in-the-wool Quaker, believed that in the Society of Friends women had every right men had,

which included, when the spirit moved them, the right
of preaching. But till now he had never had to put up
with having a female preacher in his own family. The
principle of male and female religious equality he sub-
scribed to. He'd put up overnight many a gallivanting
female Friend from Philadelphia or London, England,
come down to the Ohio country with a concern placed
upon her by the Lord for the redemption of frontier
society. He had put up these ladies, gone to Meeting to
listen to them, and remembered them in his prayers. But
he'd never before lived with one in the house, never had
to weigh his own regard for spreading the Light against
his conviction that as soon as Meeting was over the
women of his household would be, would *want* to be,
home at once preparing the food that made it possible
for him to keep open house after Meeting. "Come home
to dinner with us; no trouble at all; Hannah'll be put out
if thee doesn't come." This was Talbot's sermon, and he
preached it every First Day.

Hannah might be put out with no visitors for dinner,
but not Eliza. Eliza hadn't even walked in the dining-
room door that noon until the meal was half over. Lis-
teners, moved by what she had said during Meeting,
had lingered for prayer and talk with her afterward.
Prayer and talk of salvation were not occupations Talbot
Birdwell was prepared to fault. On the other hand, nothing had prepared him for a daughter-in-law who put
praying and talking ahead of getting the food on the
table for his expected guests. And a man who finds that
his lifelong principles don't hold up when faced with a
little home practice of those principles is, if he's an honest
man (and Talbot Birdwell was honest), a miserable man.
Eliza understood this. Half of her father-in-law was saying, "Why ain't that girl home helping Hannah lay the

36

table?" The other half was saying, "What's thee come to, Talbot Birdwell, putting dinner before salvation?" He'd voiced the first half of these feelings at the dinner table. Later on he'd confess the second half, and with contrition, to Eliza.

Eliza whispered all this to Jess. But what his father had said about Eliza was the small half of what was irking Jess. Eliza guessed this but she wouldn't have brought it up at this hour of the night herself.

"I've about had my fill of Brother Amos, too," Jess said, forgoing whispering entirely now and rearing up to press his broad back against the headboard of the bed.

Brother Amos, ten years older than Jess, was a Philadelphia pharmacist who took an occasional rest from pill-rolling to come down to the farm bearing agricultural advice. The advice, intended for his father, who held the farming reins firmly in his own hands, was addressed to Brother Jess. "Brother Jess," Amos had said at the noon-day dinner table, "I wonder thee hasn't adopted Pennsylvania practices of fertilizing."

Jess held his tongue, though he resented this beating the Devil round the bush. Amos knew as well as he did that their father was the man to be talked to if he wanted anything besides barnyard manure used on the place.

"In Pennsylvania," Amos told the backward Ohioans, "we have increased our output of corn ten bushels per acre by using modern methods."

Jess knew as much about modern methods as Amos did. And Amos knew as much about old-fashioned fathers as Jess did. "Tell Father," Jess had said, "about any changes thee wants made here."

"Changes, changes," Amos had spluttered, "who said anything about changes?"

"Amos was just bringing us the news, Jess," Talbot Birdwell said. "No use flaring up about it."

Well, there was no use flaring up about being held responsible for results without having a free hand to change methods; and there was no use flaring up about his wife's being considered a table-setter first and a preacher second. Not as long as he lived under his father's roof and his father was the kind of man he was.

He gave the headboard a shove that made the whole bed creak. "Eliza," he said, "we are getting out of here."

Eliza wasn't sure whether he meant bed or house.

"Out of this house, out of this country, out of this state."

"Where are we going, Jess?"

"We are heading west, Eliza."

Jess, who had never before voiced this determination, though he had been thinking about it for almost five years, felt such a surge of accomplishment at the sound of the words that he took a flying leap out of bed. It was a February night, the bedchamber was unheated, and the rag carpet under his feet was stiff with cold. He scorned to notice it. A man who would flinch at a cold rag carpet was no likely candidate for the prairies.

"Heading west, and five years late getting started."

His walking and his talking roused up little Sarah.

"Papa," she said, "I want to walk with thee."

She was capable of it. Though only two, Sarah was no toddler. She had been walking at nine months. Now she was striding, running, and trotting. At nine months she had looked out at the falling snow and, Jess's own daughter, had said, "Pretty flowers." So Jess had understood anyway. Now she talked in complete sentences, made rhymes, and remembered Bible verses.

Jess picked her up in his arms and wrapped the tail of

her bedgown around her tiny feet. "Thee'd freeze thy toes off walking on this floor."

"Won't thee freeze thy toes, Papa?"

"My toes are old and tough."

"How old, Papa?"

"They'll be thirty before I know it."

"Ten," Sarah said.

"Ten?" Jess asked. "Oh, yes. Ten old toes."

Sarah was as round as a gooseberry in his arms, light as a dandelion fluff. She had Eliza's black hair and the Irish-blue Birdwell eyes. She seemed overly warm to him, but then she always did. It was a part of Jess's belief that persons were born to be different. Sarah didn't have to be as cool to the touch as his boys. This belief of his was one of his reasons for wanting to get out from under his father's roof. Sarah should be treated like every other child, in her grandparents' opinion. In their opinion, walking the floor with her now in his arms would spoil her. She should have been left in her trundle bed, otherwise she would demand that her father walk the floor with her every night. Sarah was not like other children; not like the two he knew, anyway, his boys, Josh and Labe, who might well enough test their power by commanding nightly walks.

Each happening was singular to Sarah. Tonight's walk was a gift. She would not expect the same walk tomorrow night. She tasted her pleasures like fruits of a particular season. Jess did not believe that he loved the warm fold of Sarah's small body in his arms more because she was a daughter. He loved her more perhaps because she was Sarah. Or love was perhaps the wrong word. He didn't love Sarah any more than he loved his boys. But Sarah gave him more pleasure. He was not unfair to his boys in receiving this pleasure; nor were his boys at fault in

39

not giving it. The world had been put together with this possibility in it. And Sarah hadn't all the advantage. Her grandparents found more pleasure in happy-go-lucky Labe and earnest Josh than in their precocious grand-daughter.

"Where are we going, Papa?"

Jess, who had been thinking about his daughter, not destinations, repeated, " 'Going,' Sarah?"

"When we head west?"

"I don't know the exact place yet."

Eliza said, "Jess, is this a nighttime dream to make up for what thee couldn't say at the dinner table?"

Jess said, "Thee's got every reason to suppose that, Eliza. I've postponed and postponed. But today's talk didn't pull my trigger. I've laid plans."

"Can thee bring thyself to leave the old folks?"

"I hope so. I'm banking on it. I'm a hired man here. Father can hire ten as good and better any day in Belmont County. It's bad for us both. Me taking orders at my age and his handing them out to a grown son."

"Can thee tell him that, Jess?"

Jess tucked Sarah more snugly into her gown. "I could, but I won't have to. Not in so many words. In the last five years fifty people must've left Belmont County to move west. No other excuse than cheap land and better land. It's all the reason I need to give Father. I've got Ioway fever!"

"He won't think it a good reason."

"I plan to put it to him in a good light."

"Will Grandpa and Grandma head west?"

"No, pet. They're too old."

"Will the boys?"

"Of course."

"Where is the west?"

"It's a direction," said Jess. "It's where the sun sets."

It's where the sun rises, he thought. It's out from under this roof, where my brothers can't point out that on the one hand it's my duty to stay with the old folks and that on the other I lack the get-up-and-go to make my own way. It's where I can raise my children like my children, not like their grandchildren. Where Sarah won't be squeezed down pea-shaped to fit in a pod with every other pea-shaped child. Where my wife can preach, not set table. Where I can get up in the morning and plan my own day.

"Is it better than here?"

"Far better."

"Prettier?"

"Much prettier. The wild flowers are still blooming out there, and the wild animals aren't afraid. Nobody has lived there yet, and the land hasn't been plowed."

"Won't thee plow, Papa?"

"No more than I have to."

"Am I going?"

"Does thee want to go?"

"Yes, Papa."

Jess gave his daughter a toss, caught her, a live warm ball, and hugged her. "Thee can go with us. Thee can grow up to be an old maid and live with thy father and mother the rest of thy days. How does thee like that?"

From her bed Eliza said dryly, "That's the life thee is presently trying to escape from thyself, Jess."

"I got married anyway," Jess reminded her.

"Thee had better let Sarah know thee doesn't regret it."

Jess kissed Sarah and tucked her under the covers of her trundle bed, then he got in beside Eliza.

"Jess, I'd rather have the whole of thy feet at once to warm than one cold toe at a time."

41

Jess took her at her word. "I'm so happy," he said.

Eliza didn't speak for a while. Then she said, "Thee knows what's to come won't be pleasant? Or easy?"

"I know that."

Eliza thought Jess was asleep. She herself had been thinking of the sorrow, and anger, likely, of the old folks; of the hardships of travel and homesteading. It would be easier in many ways to put up with known drawbacks and inconveniences than to face what was new and unknown.

Jess, in a voice untouched by sleepiness, said, "After ten years, headed the right direction at last!"

Jess was so closemouthed about his plans, if he had any, that Eliza began to think that no more would come of "heading west" than had come of other proposals of Jess's to escape. He suffered from his father's highhandedness; but he would suffer now, and he knew it, if any harm came to his father and mother through his absence. And, leaving his parents out of it, he was attached, as most men aren't, to the hills and streams of the farm where he had been born. Morning and evening he was tramping around to what he called "overlooks" to see how the light of a spring morning or of a fall sunset touched woods lot, grain stubble, or sliding water. He seemed as dependent upon these moments of solitary viewing as another man might be on prayer. He had not much hankering for travel and new sights; he was able to make so much of what there was at hand. The prairie lands, Eliza knew, promised a man double and triple the crops of the worn-out East. Still, she pitied Jess torn away from the rolling countryside, the great stands of hardwood, the clear creeks he loved, and set down on land as flat as a table top, and that top hid from sight by grass growing high as a horse's shoulders.

Eliza was as surprised as she supposed Talbot and Hannah were when Ben Tappan and his young brother-in-law, Eldon Dukes, stopped in after supper on a raw blustery evening toward the end of February.

Talbot Birdwell, hospitable as always, seated his guests by the sitting-room fire, provided them with Rome Beauties and a bowl of hickory-nut kernels and offered them cider, hot and mulled.

"Ben, Eldon," he said after the men had warmed themselves, "what brings thee out on a night like this?"

"We have come to talk migration," Ben said.

"You two planning to pull up stakes?"

"The three of us," said Eldon.

"Three?"

"Me and Ben and Jess."

Talbot and Hannah, taken aback as they were, were also, as Jess had undoubtedly foreseen, far too mannerly to make any kind of a to-do with company in the house. Whatever their feelings were about Jess's heading west, they had to listen to some very good reasons for making the move, and without much opportunity—Eldon Dukes had a tongue that wagged at both ends—for talking back.

Jess couldn't have chosen partners harder for his father and mother to fault. Ben Tappan was a steady forty-year-old, the father of six children, a sanctified double-dipped Baptist, as strait-laced as any Quaker. He had married a Quaker, Eldon Dukes's oldest sister, Amy. Amy had been read out of Meeting for marrying a Baptist and had become a Baptist like her husband. That persuasion had never seemed to agree with Amy. She had ailed since she was sprinkled, though the children had come along just the same, and were still coming.

If ever a man had an excuse for coming down with a case of the Ioway fever, it was Ben Tappan. He had a stony hillside farm, where the seed corn slid off and the stones stuck. What little bottom land he had was liable, if he was lucky enough to get a good stand of corn, to be flooded by spring freshets. He worked hard. He never complained. He finished a day in the fields by coming home to cook up something nourishing for his ailing wife and hungry children, who, for all his efforts, looked bedraggled and underfed.

Amy's young brother, Eldon, showed what a Dukes who stayed Quaker, and didn't have to have a new baby every two years, could look like: fine as frog's hair. Eldon's family had been Quakers when they landed in Pennsylvania, and for a hundred years before that in England. But they hadn't been able to put their mark on Eldon. Plain speech and plain clothes told you Eldon's religion, but they didn't hide his mettle. Not that he wasn't as sensible in his way as his brother-in-law. He was engaged to be married in the summer to Amelia Jessup, a niece of Talbot's and Hannah's, forming a Quaker union any Friends Meeting would heartily bless.

"But before I settle down," Eldon said, "I want to do a little adventuring. I don't plan on any footlooseness after marriage. So I figure now's the time for any roving I have in mind. I'm not land hungry the way these two fellows are—and with good reason. Ben's farm is nothing but rock with a dusting here and there of soil. And Jess is landless. I've got as good a farm as there is in Belmont County, and Amelia is bringing me another. I don't make any bones about it: adventure's my aim in this jaunt."

No one said anything for a while. Then Talbot Birdwell spoke up with an old man's authority. "I don't consider Jess landless."

Eldon, smooth, polite, and to the point, said, "Has thee deeded over the place to Jess?"

"No," said Talbot.

"Some of it?"

"No," said Talbot. "But he'll inherit."

Everyone in the room could see the word "when" slide up Eldon Dukes's gullet and then slide back down again as he thought better of it. After all that swallowing, something had to come out, and he said, "Along with eight others."

"The other eight will take into consideration the work Jess has put in here."

"Maybe they will and maybe they won't," Eldon said. "I've known it to work out otherwise."

It was maybe only a fraction of an inch, but heads in the room tended to nod in assent. Who hadn't known a hardworking son come out the little end of the horn when long-absent sons and daughters gathered with broken hearts round a deathbed? The old father had had many an argument—fallings-out, even—with the son who'd stuck with him. These returned wanderers had never spoken aught but words of love to him. What had ever made him think that he could deal with his children on any other basis than that of share and share alike?

Eldon, considering that point won, went on to another. "Men with pretty fair farms here are moving west. To Ioway. As far as Nebrasky. How can they resist? It's like trading a worn-out nag for a fresh two-year-old."

Talbot said, "This farm's no worn-out nag."

"How long has thee been here, Friend Birdwell?"

"Fifty years. It's fifty years since I left Pennsylvania." Talbot Birdwell spoke as if he expected someone to deny it. The way a woman says, "I'll never see forty again," waiting for someone to exclaim, "That can't be true."

No one exclaimed. The farm had had a half-century's use. It was no longer in its prime.

"Why did thee leave Pennsylvania?" Eldon asked.

There was a long silence. Eliza felt pity for her father-in-law. He had left Pennsylvania, from all she had ever heard, for reasons exactly like Jess's: a big family, an old farm, and rich land farther west practically for the asking.

Eliza looked at her father-in-law. He was a handsome old fellow. He had grown old in ways that didn't give young people qualms. He was upright, well-fleshed, and with skin that had stayed anchored to the bone. He had a head of white hair that flowed upward, a white beard that billowed downward, and in between the two a nose imposing enough to save his face from appearing to be mostly hair. And when his head was lifted, his blue Birdwell eyes dominated both. But Eldon's question had caused him to lower his head.

"Father Birdwell," Eliza told Eldon, "came to Ohio to better himself."

There was no good way of contradicting that. So Talbot enlarged upon it. "Fifty years ago the countryside round Philadelphia was beginning to fill up. The best land had long been taken. A man hardly had elbow room for himself, let alone for a growing family. It wasn't a place I wanted to bring up children. Start playing, they'd be trespassing before they knew it."

Nobody said it, but Talbot denied it anyway. "Things are quite different here in Ohio for Jess."

Nevertheless, he made Jess's leave-taking easy. "Go and have a look," he said.

A look, he implied, would be enough. Jess would discover what wiser men already knew: you couldn't beat Ohio. Talbot was careful not to argue with Jess, not to make it a question of "Who knows best, father or son?" If he did *that*, Jess, having discovered for himself what Talbot believed to be true, that Ohio *was* God's country, might feel honor bound, and just for the sake of winning the argument, to settle down on some piece of sun-baked prairie. Talbot, by his meekness, took some of the wind from the sails of Jess's departure. He spoiled Jess's picture of himself as a man defying a father's tyranny to break the bonds that had been thirty years in the weaving. If this was all there was to pulling up stakes, why hadn't he done so ten years ago?

They breakfasted on leave-taking morning long before daylight. Jess had packed his gear the night before, for he intended to be saddled and waiting when Ben and Eldon came by. The candlelight flickered across three bowed heads; Jess alone sat upright and with eyes open. God would be with him in the wilderness, but these three he would not see again for some time. His father departed from his habit of silent grace and prayed aloud, "Father in heaven, watch over the traveler and bring him safely home."

Jess felt pretty sure that, silently, his father had added, "Safely home and with no encumbrances of out-of-state land." He couldn't be positive, and aloud his father continued, "Strengthen us here at home to manage the burdens younger shoulders have long carried."

Talbot could hoist a sack of wheat that buckled the knees of younger men from the ground to wagon bed, but in the candlelight he looked his years and condition, an old man abandoned by the last of his children.

"Make our departing son the object of Thy continuous care and mercy."

Jess felt a botheration to God himself.

Eliza was putting plates of fried corn-meal mush,

maple syrup, and bacon in front of them. Had she ever
complained about table-setting or the curtailment of
her ministry? The two boys upstairs sleeping, had they
ever found fault with the lack of elbow room in Ohio?
Little Sarah, maybe she *wanted* to be a pea in a pod.

Little Sarah, who had ears in her finger tips, opened
the door from the back stairway that led upward from
the kitchen. She had come down the stairs in the dark
and, being a careful little girl, had held up a corner of her
bedgown to keep her from stumbling. It could have been
four in the afternoon instead of four in the morning. She
was wide awake. The early breakfast didn't startle her,
or the candlelight make her blink. She knew about drafts,
came down from the last step and closed the door behind
her.

"Is thee heading west, Papa?"

"Yes, Sarah."

"I want to go with thee, Papa."

Talbot was not pleased with children who put in an
appearance after their bedtime, or before their rising
time. During their bedtime hours he wanted to be able
to depend upon children's being in bed.

"Eliza," he said, "take that child up to her bed."

That command put some wind back in Jess's departure
sails.

"Come here, Sarah," he said. He took Sarah, a bundle
of tiny bones and soft flesh, in his arms. "Thee can't go
with Papa now, pet. But Papa is going to find a home for
us out west. Then we'll all go there together."

Jess didn't put Sarah down until Ben and Eldon rode
into the yard. For the sake of holding Sarah he had given
up his plan to be standing foot in the stirrup and hand
on the pommel when they arrived. He had fancied himself in this pose of a traveler long packed and impatient

to go. But he fancied Sarah more. He put her into Eliza's arms reluctantly and hugged them both together.

"Don't come out with me," he told Eliza. "Thee'll hear from me every chance I have means of sending a letter."

He kissed his parents. Nothing more was said of "going to have a look." At some minute between sitting down to the breakfast table and rising from it, "going to have a look" had become, in everyone's mind, "going."

"I'll meet you at the Wheeling pike," Jess told Ben and Eldon. They understood what he meant. He wanted a final look at the home place. Ben had felt that way himself. Eldon, who was not settling out west, was less sentimental about his farm. It would be there when he got back.

Jess headed, when he left the men, for one of his favorite "overlooks," a rise above the south branch. From there he gazed back at the farm buildings. The sun was not yet up, but its light had run ahead, and the old brick house was luminous and rosy. Around it clustered the buildings in which he had worked all his life: sidehill barn, carriage house, smokehouse, tool shed. Smoke from the kitchen fire he had started was still rising gray-blue in the early-morning light.

Below him, the branch, as the sun neared the horizon, took on its true water color. On the bank above it dogwood frothed amidst the transparent yellow-green shimmer of its leaves. Redbud, half-opened, looked as hard as rubies. It was the best of a spring morning. Jess could smell grass and water, and both flavored with the smoke of home. The sky rang with the songs and cries of birds.

He had plowed every plowable acre in sight, sowed wheat, dropped corn, planted potatoes. He had mowed, ricked, shocked, husked. He knew those rolling hills with

the muscles in the small of his back and forearms. His
sweat had run off him onto those acres. He was leaving
more behind than a half-section of land. The young Jess
Birdwell, the man who had been a son, was being left
behind.

He did not expect to find another combination of land
and water, of light and shade, so beautiful. He did not
suppose he could become so attached to any other house
and cluster of outbuildings. He did not know that he
would make discoveries every day—and that among them
would be Jess the traveler, the letter writer, the assayer of
human personality.

Either Ben and Eldon were changing with travel or he
had been blind all his life to their real natures. He already knew he relished letter writing, but except during
the two years that he had wooed Eliza by mail while she
lived in Philadelphia he had lacked correspondents. His
brothers and sisters wrote to his parents, not to him. His
ideas of what a love letter should be, all romanticism
and yearning (which in his case was true), had prevented him from writing to Eliza of anything but the
farm's more flowery aspects, and in language as high-
flown as he could command. Eliza had kept his letters, a
stack tied with a blue ribbon. It was Jess's intention that
this stack be lost someday. He did not care to be reminded of the fool who had written them.

Since marriage he had never had occasion to write to
Eliza. Now there was no longer any need, or any possibility either, of persuading her that he was a fellow who
spent his time sniffing apple blossoms and watching the
flight of hummingbirds, a fellow who never laughed
when the old sow got her head caught in the slop pail
or shed tears when his mare Dixie died foaling. A sweet-

heart, to judge by his experience (limited though it was), couldn't hold a candle to a wife as a person to write to. Marriage had taught him that Eliza had not married that flower-sniffing boy; she had married the man she expected that boy to grow up to be. She had married the man who laughed and cried and wanted to tell her about it.

The trouble with writing Eliza now (though he burned to have her see every sight he saw and to puzzle with him over the unexpected unfolding of the natures of Ben and Eldon) was threefold: scarcity of writing materials, and of time, and the difficulty of getting the letters back to Mount Pleasant.

They were traveling through sparsely settled country on horseback. They were in their saddles by sunup and ready for their blankets by sundown. As long as they were in Ohio, they found United States post offices here and there. They ran out of post offices when they hit backwoods Indiana. From there on they had to depend upon backtracking travelers to get their mail east.

Because of the scarcity of paper and time, Jess couldn't make full reports. He thought paragraphs and wrote sentences. He crosshatched his pages, of course, and Eliza was so good at reading these that she said he could write a third message diagonally across the page and she would make that out, also. But two were enough. He didn't want to come home to a blind wife.

There was still a springtime flush of rose in the sky, though the sun had been down nearly a half hour, when Jess took out his writing materials. He was close to the fire, for the sake of light rather than warmth, and was using the bottom of an upturned frying pan as a writing board. He'd put too much water in his ink mixture, and his pen strokes were pale. Though he had learned to write with a quill, he was writing with what he called his "iron" pen. He could not make with metal the flourishes by which he was accustomed to convey his feelings. He could more easily leave his own mark in a stubble field with a plowshare. He tried to bend the iron pen to his will, but it resisted him. It was iron and it was new—and it had to be broken like an unridden horse. And Jess, with much to say, hadn't the time or the patience for the breaking that was needed.

"My dear wife," he began in pale ink and with the pen that fought him.

He tried to resist geography. "Thee needn't waste time," Eliza had often told him, "on up hill and down dale, on hardwood and softwood, on the creeks thee has forded and the creeks thee has swum. Or on how far south or how far north thee has fared. I haven't much sense of direction. Just tell me how *thee* is."

How *he* was was the sum of these things: of up hill and down dale; of the hardwood forests; of the Little Miami, the Big Miami, the White Water, East and West Fork, the mighty Ohio; of the little glades, the patches of marshland; of wild turkeys courting, spotted fawns trying to straighten their too easily folding knees.

He reminded himself this was not what Eliza wanted to hear; and that if she had wanted to hear of such things, there wasn't the paper for it. And even with paper, he would himself be asleep before a tenth was told.

She wanted to know how he *was*. He told her.

"I am in good health and spirits after a fair day's travel westward through the southern part of Indiana." (This, he knew, was about as much geography as Eliza was prepared to stomach.) "I am camped by a nice little creek, a good fire burning to write by. I can hear over the sound of the water and frogs, which are very numerous at this season, a fiddle playing at Meeker's tavern a quarter-mile or so upcreek. Now thee may wonder why I am not taking advantage of a home-cooked or at least a woman-cooked meal and a night on a good cord bed and under a roof when they are so near at hand. I had every intention of doing so and am surprised to find myself, when this may be our last chance for some time to put our knees under a table and our heads on pillows, eating corn pone of my own baking and sleeping on the usual makeshift bed of blankets and boughs. I am not overloaded with money, as thee knows, but with a supper of pork or beef for 25¢ and a bed if shared for 50¢ I thought I could for one last night (perhaps) afford the luxury.

"However, Friend Eldon changed my mind. Yes, thee heard me aright: Friend Eldon.

"We knew this tavern, run by a respectable widow, lay ahead of us, and Ben and I at least had spoken of enjoying once more the civilized pleasures of eating at table and conversing with a lady. As thee knows" . . .

And here, though Jess had just dipped his pen in ink, he broke off. He had, he thought, a good and surprising story to tell Eliza. There were few things he enjoyed more than having, or, with a little help from his imagination, making, a good story, keeping the best to the last, putting Eliza on tenterhooks. But the good story he could now tell Eliza would have to be toned down. First of all, he didn't have the space for it in a letter. Second, the letter would be read by all and sundry, certainly by his parents, and possibly by the Dukeses and Tappans as well. And while Eliza needed to be reminded of Ben's and Eldon's natures to fully appreciate what had happened, certainly Ben's wife and possibly Eldon's betrothed wouldn't care for the information being made public.

Jess looked over at Eldon Dukes, stretched out straight as a lodgepole pine under his blankets, sound asleep since sundown, tavern music falling on closed ears, husbanding his energy for the morrow's travel. He had intended writing to Eliza, "As thee knows, we all had it in mind that Eldon would be the gay blade of this expedition." Eliza would understand what he meant by "gay blade." A *Quaker* gay blade. Which didn't imply downright roistering, but did envisage a little heel-tapping and flirtatiousness from a rich young man out for a last fling before settling down to the confinements of life as a married farmer.

He didn't know how that hint of gay-blading would set with Eldon's intended or with Eldon's parents. Besides, there wasn't room for saying it in the letter, no matter how it set. But it was the point of his story. Or at least fifty per cent of the point. If Eliza didn't recall that Eldon had embarked on this journey as an adventure, that he looked like a young Turk and had enough brass in his pockets to buy out the Birdwells and throw in the Tappans as change, where did his story go?

Nor could he write, "As thee knows, Ben Tappan's got no brass at all. And after twenty years of daytime farming and nighttime nursing he surprised us all by having the get-up-and-go to make this trip."

He hoped Eliza remembered these facts about Eldon and Ben. Without them, what happened didn't make much of a story. When the three of them reached Meeker's, he had planned a good wash-down in hot water, a home-cooked meal with maybe a side dish of greens to go with the meat, and a sweet cake and fruit sauce to finish off with. He and Ben had been speaking of it all day.

About a mile before they reached the tavern, Eldon said, "I can't see the point of laying out hard cash for a bed and food. In a tavern."

Neither Jess nor Ben said anything. Eldon was the one who had the hard cash to lay out.

"Well," said Jess finally, "it would make a pleasant change and not set us back any considerable sum."

"Thee do as thee likes, Jess," Eldon said. "Thee's a free agent. Thee knows thy own mind. But I didn't take this trip for the purpose of lining the pockets of innkeepers."

"This'll likely be our last chance for some time," Ben ventured.

"Thee take the chance then, Brother Ben," Eldon said. "I'm not stopping thee. But my experience has been it's not so much the income as the outgo that makes the difference between the well-to-do and the hard-up."

That silenced Brother Ben.

"What does thee plan?" Jess asked.

"Plan?" Eldon asked. "It don't take much planning. I'll do what I've been doing. Find a creek and bed down by it. It's a mild spring night. Be a pleasure to sleep under the stars."

"It might prove handy," Jess said, "to talk with somebody who's covered the territory we expect to be passing through."

"Talk," Eldon said. "I've got nothing against talk. I'm as hungry for information as the next man. But talk's free. If talk's what thee wants, I reckon the inn's running over with it. And all free. Go sit on a bench and thee can hear as much talk as the man who drinks five glasses of rum and eats two plates of hog meat. And thy pocket won't be any the lighter because of it."

Eldon was riding a big stiff-legged gray, and his words had the emphasis of the animal's jouncing gait as well as his own conviction.

Ben, on a plow horse with an amble soft-footed enough to qualify him for riding, said, "I wouldn't think of sitting down without buying something. Be a sponger."

"Thee's just the one who should think about it," Eldon said. "Thee's got six hungry children and a wife who's poorly back home. While thee's buying information by the plateful and the mugful, what does thee think they'll be doing?"

Ben answered in a quiet voice, unaccusing, with the tone of a man who's been asked if the mail's come in or if the cow's been milked. "I think they'll be whining and crying and puking," he said. "That's been my experience most evenings."

This was said to a man about his own sister, about his own blood nieces and nephews. Eldon reined in his horse. "Don't thee go blaming Amy for being poorly, Ben Tappan."

"I ain't blaming her," Ben said, "now or ever. Amy's got my entire sympathy, and always had. You asked me what they'd be doing, and I give a straight question a straight answer. 'Whining, puking . . .'"

"Shut up," said Eldon. "Thee keep quiet about my sister."

"You asked me a question, and I gave you a truthful answer. Now, Eldon, you answer me a question. How're they going to feel any better if I sleep on creek bank tonight, bit by mosquitoes and kept awake by bullfrogs?"

"They'll feel better when thee comes home with enough money left to buy them a little corn meal and sugar."

"Eldon," Ben said, "I ain't ever in twenty years put

foot inside a tavern, let alone set down there. I ain't ever once in twenty years not nursed somebody in the night. I ain't never in my life bought a tavern drink or heard a fiddle played in a public place. I ain't ever slept in a bed Amy wasn't in, and she most usually in no shape to be slept with. Most nights I've cooked, and many a night did the washing up afterward. Now tonight I'm going to sleep in a bed by myself, I'm going to eat somebody else's cooking, and if the dishes are still unwashed in the morning, I don't give a hoot. I'm going to buy me one drink and I'm going to hear fiddle music, and if somebody'll dance, I'll clap hands. I'm going to do this, and in the long run I don't think Amy and the young'uns will be any the worse off. But even if I knew they was, you couldn't stop me. I've known I was going to do this since I started."

Both men now had their horses pulled up side by side. Eldon glared at Ben, and Ben let his brother-in-law's glare melt off him like snow off a warm south bank.

"I begin to think thee had this trip planned from the beginning as a little holiday from wife and children."

"I never did think of taking them along," Ben admitted.

Eldon turned sharply to Jess. "Jess, is thee going to spend the night drinking rum and clapping for dancers?"

"That ain't exactly what I heard Ben propose," Jess answered. "I was planning on sleeping under a roof tonight, if that's the question. But if Ben will be there and keep his ears peeled for word about what lies ahead, I reckon I can occupy the creek bank with thee."

He thought that Ben would likely enjoy himself more without somebody from Mount Pleasant there to count claps and mugs. "And," he went on, "since Ben will be saving me money by doing my listening for me, I'll add what I would have had to spend on a bed."

He put a fifty-cent piece in Ben's hand.

"I'll listen for both of us, Jess," Ben said. "I'll give you the news in the morning." Ben turned upstream in the direction of the tavern.

Eldon watched him go. "A fool and his money," he told Jess.

Jess made no answer; couldn't very well. Amy was Eldon's sister, and Ben his brother-in-law. A man feels free to run down his own family, but let someone else chip in and he takes it amiss. Jess couldn't even write Eliza what he thought: that while Ben's electing to spend the night in the tavern was the last thing in the world he'd have expected, it seemed, once Ben had done it, the most natural thing in the world to do. The only question was: Why had he waited so long? And that wasn't a fair question either. Up to now, when had Ben had a chance?

Given sufficient paper and time, and some assurance of Eliza's privacy in reading, Jess had another idea he'd like to try out on her. Had the Dukeses always been shy spenders? Did that, as much as anything else, account for the size of their farms and bank accounts? Get it, of course—but then hang on to it? Was that the royal road to riches?

Eldon looked royal, a long plank of a fellow with a Norman king's flaxen hair, bright in the firelight as clover honey. But a shy spender, nevertheless; a nickel pincher. And plodding Ben, shaped like a churn, but equipped with the instincts for kingly behavior—given half a chance.

And where, Eliza, Jess thought, does that leave me? Ruminating, Jess thought, that's where it leaves me. Figuring things out, sitting by a dying fire in a strange land. He looked down at the last line he had written, the last part of a line: "As thee knows." He finished that sentence: "our plan was to bear north from here through northern Indiana and Illinois. Then to cut west across Illinois to Iowa. All are agreed that the bargains in land are to be found in the plains country. However, I talked with an Ohio man homeward bound from Iowa yesterday. He is returning to Iowa with his family, but he spoke of farmland in southern Indiana that had the very look of Belmont County. Land likely not as fertile as Ohio land, but costing nowhere near as much. It is my present plan to leave Ben and Eldon as they head directly north toward the Illinois plains and have a look at this section before joining them. In that way we can report the prospects of various sections to each other without need of each making the trip.

"There is no present means at hand for sending this on to thee, so I will save the overleaf for future news. I am spending the night with Eldon on the banks of a pretty little creek. Ben is at a nearby tavern for the night, picking up some useful information for our further travels. Thee is still at this hour, I expect, busy with children and kitchen work. I see each of thee with perfect plainness, the old house lit by the same quarter-moon that shines on me, and the kitchen lamp shining out on the blooming forsythia. I will save good-bye for when I finish this letter and for now say only good night and a fond kiss for all my dear ones."

When Jess next sat down to write Eliza, with the same sheet of paper, same frying pan, and a duplicate of the fire that had lit the writing of the first page, he was alone. He had been sitting, back against his saddle and pen in hand, for half an hour, and not a word was yet on the paper. He could and would send Eliza some statistics:

twenty, thirty miles west of Madison. Five, eight miles beyond a village called Vernon. Off in the morning to join up once again with his two companions in Illinois, and with them to press on to the Iowa plains. But he was a man to tackle the hard job first, and the hard job was to write about now. And he didn't know any figures to explain now, any of the four directions that would convey to Eliza or even to himself the place to which he had now arrived.

He got up, put his paper on the ground, set the skillet on the paper, and pen and ink in the skillet. There was a sweet little blade-bender of a breeze blowing through the grass at his feet, and he didn't want it sending his sheet of precious paper off to float down the branch that circled the knoll on which he was standing. There was enough late twilight and early moonlight blended to show him the occasional petals of wild plum, he supposed (for he could smell the tart fruity smell of that blossoming) carried along by that full-running, night-colored water. He could hear Charlie grazing nearby, the slow easy chomp of a horse which knows that his day's work is over and sees that there's food to last the night. Frogs celebrated the plenitude of water. At the top of the rise behind him the night air that stirred the grass at his feet was blowing through the treetops with the sad whistle that only pine needles give.

Jess walked down to the stream and looked back toward his fire, and, beyond it, at the higher stand of trees. He returned to his fire and gazed across the stream to the shallow valley walled by a gentle ridge.

"My God, my God," he said. Not praying. And certainly not cussing. Conversing, rather, there being no one else at hand with whom he could talk. And not wanting, even if his iron pen were up to the job, to set Eliza all atwitter with his feelings about a place he had come upon four hours ago and would leave before sunup.

He had first seen that gentle slope, that circling stream, that ridge of trees in the deepening light of the late-spring afternoon. He had sat his horse for a long time without dismounting. He was responsive to landscapes. They stirred him more, he thought, than faces. He could not be sure whether this was a place he had searched for all of his life, gazing out from many an overlook in the hope of seeing it, or whether it was a place remembered, a place lost, yearned for, and rediscovered.

Both he and his horse had many more miles left in them at that early hour. But he could not leave. He dismounted, threw Charlie's reins over his neck, planning then no more than a fifteen-minute look around. What he saw sank into his heart. He was a farmer, a builder, a father. (If he was more than that, he didn't know it.) He began, as unconsciously as he breathed, to set down buildings, to plant apple trees on the slope, and to turn the bottom land into cornfields. He was not looking for a rich wilderness, or hunting for a good place to locate a sawmill. He had seen a thousand sawmill sites and enough wilderness to last him a lifetime. What he saw was beauty; but it was a homestead beauty, and in his mind's eye his children dabbled in that stream and Eliza's pesky geese muddied the clear water. He saw himself age there: a beard sprouted from his chin; the beard grew white and long like his father's. He died there, was buried under a tree he had himself planted; bees hummed above him in summer, and in the fall wasps ate the windfalls that rolled across the flattening mound that had once marked his grave.

It was all a dream, and he knew it. He was searching

for land richer than Belmont County, and he doubted this equaled it.

He took his writing paper from under the skillet and, cross-legged by the fire he had recruited, wrote to Eliza.

"I am camped alone tonight by a fair spot reminiscent of Ohio—but less fertile. I aim to press on with all speed in the morning for my reunion with Ben and Eldon at Swalesville in the deer prairie of Illinois. I will write thee more when I reach there. I am in good health. Thee and the children have been much in my mind tonight."

Jess did not expect to find Ben or Eldon in the tavern at Swalesville. Ben surely did not have the money for continuous tavern life, and Eldon, who did, intended to hang on to what he had.

He inquired at the land office. The two men, the last the government agent had heard of them, were camped about ten miles west of town. The younger man had bought a second horse and a tent.

"What for?" Jess asked.

"What for ain't any of my business," the agent, who obviously had had his fill of Eastern folks, said. "But my guess would be the horse is to work and the tent to sleep under. Might be the other way round, though. There's no telling what a greenhorn'll try."

Jess didn't plague him with further questions. A tent ten miles south of town ought to stand out in this uninhabited land plain as a cuckoo egg in a wren's nest.

It wasn't quite that plain, though. There were more than one habitation—tent, shack, sod house—west of Swalesville, each one as pitiful-looking as the next. The ride out depressed him. Except for these pitiful-looking abodes, there was nothing to rest the eye. Sky and grass, sky and grass. And the grass so high the horse had to

forge through it like an animal fording a stream at high
water. An overprovision by nature was as bad as under-
provision. All sand was a desert; and all grass was a kind
of desert, too. A man took pleasure in good pasture land
and prided himself on a fine stand of rye or timothy. But
a man who could pride himself on this unending stretch
of green could feel something personal about the ocean
and its tides. It was a sight to be seen, all right, and five
miles out from Swalesville Jess had seen it—and was willing to turn back.

He didn't have any trouble locating the tent. Eldon
wasn't a fellow to do things by halves, and he had cleared
off a considerable space around his tent. And in the clearing Traveler, his big gray, was easy to pick out. Jess rode
toward the tent with a feeling of apprehension he couldn't
account for. Would he find both men down with malaria?
Or milk fever? Had somebody died? Did they have some
word from back home he hadn't received?

It was getting on for suppertime, and a suppertime sight
greeted him when he pulled up in the dooryard, if that
was the name for it, of the tent. A steaming kettle was
hung over a tidy little fire; Eldon, shirt off and galluses
down, was bent over a washbasin placed on as steady a
wash bench as graced the back porch at home in Mount
Pleasant. How Eldon had come by such a civilized piece
of furniture in this howling wilderness, Jess didn't know.
Or if he proposed to carry it all the way to Iowa and
back. Eldon, huffing and puffing, with his ears full of
water, didn't hear Jess at his first call. When he did, he
said, "I'd about given thee up, Jess."

"I got held up, back in Indiana."

"Anything there?"

"Nothing like this," Jess answered truthfully.

Eldon dried his face, and put on his shirt, pulled up his

galluses. He threw out his wash water and pulled the wash bench toward Jess. "Have a seat," he said.

"I been sitting all day. Feels good to stand up. Where's Ben?"

"In Ioway. Or headed that direction anyway."

"Why didn't he wait for us?"

"Well, thee didn't show up. And I'm not going."

"Thee's decided to turn back without seeing Ioway?"

"I'm not turning back. But why go on to Ioway?"

Jess didn't take in his meaning for a minute.

"I've bought land here."

That was hard to take in, too.

"Here?"

"Right here. A section."

"I thought thee was after adventure."

"I am."

"Where's the adventure in buying up a section of grassland?"

"Money," Eldon said. "There's adventure in money, Jess. In two years this'll be worth twice or three times what I paid for it. It'll raise wheat that'll put Belmont County to shame."

"I don't have much faith," Jess said, "in land that won't grow trees."

"I don't want to grow trees."

"What does thee plan to do about Amelia?"

"Go back this summer and marry her."

"Then move out here?"

"Likely."

"What'll thee do with thy Belmont County farms?"

"Sell them. I can get ten acres of land here for every one I sell in Ohio."

"This don't look much like Ohio."

"It don't, for a fact."

"Does thee like it?"

"Like it? It's made to order for farming, and that's the business I'm in. If I'd sent in specifications on the day the Lord made Deer Prairie, I couldn't have been handed anything more to my taste. No trees, no streams, no hills, no stones. The land all cleared and waiting for the plow. And I've got the plow."

"Thee bought one already?"

"This, Jess, is no place for a man who's willing to let the grass grow under his feet. It don't stop, as thee's maybe noticed, with under thy feet. It's over thy head before thee knows it. Jess, has thee heard how rabbits escape dogs out here? They jump on top of the grass and run across it, not through it. This is God's country, Jess."

"Why didn't Ben stay?"

"Ben's got an itchy foot, Jess. He'll be back here, I warrant. He seen this couldn't be bettered, no matter how far west he went. But we'd set out for Ioway, had announced it to one and all, so he had a good excuse to keep going. He's in no hurry to get back to tending those six children. Seven maybe by the time he gets there. And Amy likely in worse shape than when he left her. So when he said he felt like he ought to see Ioway before making up his mind, I sympathized with the poor fellow. He'll likely never have another letup from Amy and the young'uns in his lifetime. So I didn't discourage him. Get the itch out of his foot once and for all, I thought. I didn't say this to him. 'Have a look' is all I said. 'Jess will likely want to join thee.'"

"I've got no itchy foot," Jess said. "I'm a homekeeping body myself."

"Thee's a man who once he's put his hand to the plow don't want to take it off."

"What plow've I put my hand to?"

"A plow named Ioway. Thee said thee'd go there, and I reckon thee will before thee makes up thy mind. Ben'll be waiting for thee at Cedar Falls."

That night Jess, who had spared Eliza, up to this time, a lot of geography, gave her some. He felt he had more than an excuse, a real need to explain to her why he wasn't throwing in his lot with Eldon. The Dukeses were known for their long heads when it came to farming and money-making. Eldon would have written home about the rich land to be had for a song in Illinois. "What's the matter with Jess, passing up a chance like that?" the Dukeses would be asking.

Jess let Eliza know what the matter was. Eldon had a table as well as a wash bench. Jess wrote in style that night, sitting on the bench with his paper spread out on the table before him.

"Eldon, as thee perhaps knew before I did—I only reached his place late this afternoon—has decided to locate in Illinois. This came as a great surprise to me, since he had announced no intention of buying on this trip, and already he owns two fine farms in Belmont County. Nevertheless, he has bought here and plans to sell his Ohio land as soon as may be, convinced that this land is more productive—as well as being so much cheaper.

"True, there is a great deal of productive land hereabouts—beautiful tableland, if that is what thee is looking for. But the trouble is, at least as I judge it, that there is too much prairie, too little woodland, and but little or no water supply except by digging. There is nothing in any direction to see except an apparently boundless prairie, dotted here and there by a small clump or grove of what appears at a distance to be fine large timber but nearly always proves on reaching it to be but little better

than what we would call a thicket or underwood from
the size of riding switches to trees a foot in diameter.

"It is a rare occurrence to see a tree in this country
away from a running stream large enough to make more
than one rail cut, and the largest portion that I saw would
have required to have been spliced to do that. I inquired
one place how far they had to haul their firewood. They
told me seven miles! With our love of open fires, this is
not the country to move to, that's certain.

"Ben has gone on to have a look at Muscatine County
in Iowa, though Eldon thinks he will find nothing there
to equal this and that he will be back shortly. I will be off
early tomorrow to join him. Should I find a place there
rolling, well-watered, and healthy, with excellent timber
at hand and rich bottom land for corn, I may come home
with the Ioway fever. And it may take such a deep hold
on me as to carry me off before a great while. However,
this is to be proved yet, so thee need not get frightened
at once."

Jess sat at the table, pen in hand, but not writing, for a
considerable time after he had finished that sentence.
Eldon snored, a young man's quiet deep-chested breathing. The wind off the plains sucked the tent sides in and
out with a sound, Jess supposed, of canvas at sea. The
candle flame he wrote by wavered so that the shadow of
his hand shifted uneasily across the paper. There was
more to tell Eliza, but he could not put into words for her
what he was not yet able to state to himself. A place he
already knew wanted to tell him something. A knowledge
he was not yet ready to accept had been revealed to
him. He did not think that his trip to Iowa would make
this revelation clearer. But it would justify it. "I went
everywhere. I saw everything." When he had done
that, he could listen to what was being said by the sound

of water, by a hillside curve, by a cresting lift of hardwood.

He was wasting Eldon's candle. The horses had stopped grazing. Even the wind had died down.

He wrote a few final lines to Eliza. "I will mail this in Swalesville tomorrow. Thee will not hear from me again until I reach Ben in Iowa. I will send thee a full report from there, and thee can judge if I've fallen prey to the Ioway fever. I send my best love to thee, dear Liza, and the little ones. Kiss them all for me. Thy loving husband and father, Jess Birdwell."

Ben, without his brother-in-law's restraining presence, might, Jess thought, have had another fling at tavern life. He asked after him in the nearest to such a place Muscatine boasted, a kind of combination livery stable and boarding-house run by a kind of combination hostler and cook, a fat person, round in the bosom as a woman, but heavily bearded. Jess talked with the man in the kitchen, where he was washing up after the morning meal, the dishwater thick enough with scraps to serve as the evening soup.

"Has a man named Ben Tappan been staying here?"

"Are you Jess Birdwell?"

"I am," Jess said.

"Ben left a letter for you."

"Left? Isn't he here?"

"If he was," the dishwasher said, "would he leave a letter?"

"I reckon not."

The letter, with others, was on the mantel over the kitchen fireplace, the packet of them wedged in place behind a clock that had surely come from Connecticut. There were plenty like that in Mount Pleasant. The man's wife had likely carted it all the way across the plains, cradled from jolts in bedquilt. The tavern owner dried his hands on his apron, which was also his dishcloth, and sorted through the mail.

"Some of these 'bout as well be thrown away. They ain't never going to be picked up. But then, you can't tell. I kept one eighteen months. The writer passed through again, added a P.S., and a month later it was called for. If there's one thing I hate to do, it's to burn a letter. Like silencing a fellow in the midst of a speech. Before I burn, I always read. I do it for two reasons. First, if someone does turn up asking for it, I know the gist of what was said and can give it to him. Second, some of these writers have put a lot of time and words into their writing. Seems a shame to throw such a job away without its ever seeing the light of day, so to speak. I'd rather somebody sampled a bowl of gravy I made than have it thrown out because the man it was made for didn't show up."

"Does thee ever read a letter thee isn't going to burn?"

"Once in a while. If it looks interesting. I ain't read this. Tappan didn't have the look of a man who'd have anything very catchy to write. He wasn't much of a talker."

Jess took the folded sheet, when he finally got his hands on it, outside to read. The morning was sunny, meadowlarks were calling, and the sky here, as in Illinois, stretched, as far as he could tell, clear to the Rockies without let or hindrance. The tavern had an uppingblock for the convenience of lady travelers, and Jess went out and sat on it.

"Friend Jess," wrote Tappan. "I know we had an understanding to meet here, and I wouldn't like you to think I was running out on you. I figure I am doing what you did in looking at the Indiana prospects without tying me and Eldon up for the trip. An outfit passing through here Texas-bound needed a cook. As you know, I've had considerable experience in that line. I was offered the chance to see land they claim can't be equaled for richness or climate—without its costing me a red cent. Iowa, according to them, is the North Pole in winter for snow and coldness. I don't think Amy could stand a winter of that kind. She has a weak chest, as maybe you've heard. I figured I owed it to her to try to find a climate more suited to anybody delicate as she is—no matter how many miles I had to travel to do it. The prospects for cheap land and balmy climate are higher the farther south you travel, everybody says.

"I have written Amy my reasons, but I am leaving it to you to put my case to Brother Eldon. He is so Illinois-crazy he likely can't be reasonable about a man's settling anyplace else. I have banked on your coming this far, whatever you decided about Illinois, since you are a man of your word. This looks a good deal like Illinois, as you likely noticed, but I hear there's prettier, more wooded land south of here.

"I wouldn't think of leaving Amy at a time like this except for her own future good. And she's got so many Dukes relatives in the Mount Pleasant neighborhood she will never be allowed to suffer for want of anything. In case of any talk, I trust you to explain that this was all done for Amy's sake, hunting her a good climate and so forth. With best wishes, your friend Ben Tappan."

Jess folded the letter and put it in an inside pocket. He took off his hat so that the spring sun could shine down on, maybe warm up, his brains. They felt tired. Off in the distance there was what appeared to be a grove of goodly trees. If he rode out to it, he knew he would find a thicket.

The tavern owner came out of the kitchen carrying his dishpan of water to the pigpen. He threw the slop into their trough and watched them eat with a smile of pleasure. "Soo boy, soo boy," he said as they gulped down the mixture. He came around to the front steps, where a striped cat heavy as a young shoat lay sunning itself. Jess had been watching the cat bat down and eat blowflies. The tavern keeper picked up his big cat, which sagged across his arm like a sack of grain, and wrapped his apron-dishcloth around it carefully.

"You going to want dinner, Mr. Birdwell?"

"No, I don't think so."

"You going to spend the night with us?"

"I think I'll be pushing on."

"Heading west?"

"No. I've gone west far enough."

"Going south to join your friend?"

"I thought thee didn't read that letter."

"What makes you think I did? Tappan didn't talk of nothing else. And it would've showed he was lighting out if he hadn't said a word. His feet wasn't hardly touching the ground a good part of the time he was here. 'Off and away. Off and away.' That was the tune he was piping."

Jess got down from the upping-block. "Thee'll notice my feet are on the ground."

The tavern keeper wrapped the cat a little more snugly. "Heading home, I take it?"

"Depends on what thee calls home."

"Why, where thee lives, I reckon."

"I been living in Ohio. On my father's farm."

"You single?"

"No, a family man. Three children."

"And a wife?"

"They're not wood's colts. My wife's a preacher."

The tavern man said, "I've seen preachers in my time, plenty of them. This is the first time I've ever seen the husband of one."

"Look thy fill," said Jess.

"You look a little past the age for living with Papa. *And* with a preacher wife. *And* three young'uns."

"Thee hit the nail on the head," Jess said. "I'm past the age."

"Where you going to light now, may I ask?"

"Thee may. Indiana. Southern Indiana."

"Indiana? I don't see many settlers who've seen this who are willing to turn their backs on it."

"Thee's seen two curiosities in one day then, I reckon."

"Well, one thing you can say: that you seen the Promised Land and turned your back on it."

Jess laughed. "Yes, I can say that."

The hogs whomped about in their pen trying to shoulder each other away from the already empty trough. The hairy, bosomed man rocked his apron-wrapped tom in his arms. Away west where the green earth met the blue sky some domed white clouds held steady as mountains. From the blacksmith shop back in the village came the smell of burning horse hoof. Meadowlarks were calling. A small level wind, never having known an interruption in its life bigger than the tavern itself, blew steadily by.

"I can say I seen Ioway and turned back," Jess said.

On his last day homeward bound Jess saw that by pushing hard he could make Mount Pleasant by midafternoon. If he did so, he would run into the whole household, father, mother, children, hired man, hired girl, before he had a chance to talk with Eliza alone. There was nothing he was going to tell Eliza the others couldn't hear, but he wanted Eliza to hear it first. He had more than news to give Eliza; he had his feelings. He didn't know how on first telling he could separate the two; and for the others the news alone would be best. His father and mother and the children went to bed with the chickens. Eliza, once the children and old folks were tucked away for the night, settled down in their chamber to lead her own life, to do things she never had time for in the day. She studied her Bible and made notes, she wrote letters, she sewed for the children and read the Philadelphia papers sent her by her father, who feared that his daughter, married to a backwoods farmer, might, without his help, become an ignoramus.

So instead of pushing hard, Jess took it easy. He dallied through the May afternoon. He gave himself a chance to have regrets, to see what he had turned his back on.

It was close on nine before he turned into the lane he had ridden down more than six weeks ago. As he had hoped, all lights downstairs were out. Only in his and Eliza's room did a lamp still burn. He couldn't stop the horses from nickering a welcome to Charlie, but he himself entered the house noiselessly, shoes in hand. He went upstairs carefully, avoiding the steps that squeaked.

Eliza, when he opened the door, didn't spring from her chair. She looked at him very contentedly, but calmly, as though he had just left the room. Then she came to him.

"Something told me thee would be here tonight."

Jess held Eliza close. It was a clasp of more than homecoming after absence. When he had first held her as wife, he had held more than a girl in his arms. The family to come was in his arms also. Now along with Eliza he clasped for the first time a home of their own. It was a kind of second wedding.

"Did Tom Donohoe get my letter to thee?"

"He brought it to Meeting First Day."

"I hope thee didn't have thy heart set on the Western prairies."

"Now, Jess, thee knows better than that."

"The next state to us—that's not much of an adventure."

It wasn't true. Eliza wouldn't have turned a hair if he had told her that the next step for them was beaver-trapping. She might've suggested reasons against it for the children's sake, or the beavers', but for herself she wouldn't have been daunted.

"Eliza, there's things I forgot to tell thee about the place."

Eliza said, dryly, "I can't imagine what it could be, Jess."

Jess laughed a little, but went on nevertheless. "The spring back of where our house will be. I didn't tell thee about the spring. I don't know how I missed it as long as I did. It comes out of limestone rocks up in back of the knoll. There'll be no trick at all to piping into the house."

"The same as here," Eliza said.

"I suppose so. I hadn't thought of that. It's got a bigger flow, though, and is colder. Coldest water I ever tasted. Then south of the spring and farther up the knoll, but not to the top of the ridge . . ."

"Jess," Eliza interrupted, "I'm willing to listen to thee, but thee knows as well as I do I've got no head for the lay of a piece of land. All these souths and wests, up the rise and over the ridge and down in the hollow, I just can't picture. I know they're plain to thee as looking out the window. But thee had as well save thy breath and wait until I get there."

"It's not the same to me," Jess said, "unless thee can see it, too."

"One thing I can see," Eliza said. "It's the nearest to this place thee could find."

Jess, who had been holding Eliza, stepped away from her. He scanned her face as if her eyes might mirror the two places—the old home and the new one.

"Is that what I was doing?"

"There's nothing wrong with it, is there?"

"I told myself I was looking for rich prairie land."

"Well, Eldon told himself he was hunting adventure. And Ben that he was looking for a better farm."

"All I've found is Mount Pleasant with another address?"

"Thee never had anything against this place, did thee?"

"This place? No, I never did. I was born here. Everything I've learned, I've learned here. The shape of its trees and the sound of its water and the taste of its dust'll never leave me. The Western fever never hit me."

Eliza didn't ask, "Why are we going, then?" She knew why.

Jess was up before break of day next morning. Eliza was an early riser, and Sarah a light sleeper, but once again holding his shoes he was able to creep out without rousing them. He planned to have a look at the old home place. Had he fallen in love with the new the way a man who loves his mother is drawn to girls who have the look and bearing his mother may have had when young?

When he reached the kitchen, he found his father sitting by the fire, the kettle already steaming.

"Don't thee feel well, Father?"

"Feel fine," Talbot said. "I heard thee ride in last night and I was anxious to hear thy report."

"Hasn't Eliza told thee?"

"She's a young woman keeps her own counsel. Said thee'd likely want to tell me what thee'd found thyself."

"Well, she'd got no head for remembering the lay of a piece of land, that's a fact," Jess admitted.

"She did say thee'd located something in Indiana that suited thee."

Jess sat down on a chair and began to shove his foot into a boot.

"Well, the pull's west," Talbot said. "Everybody feels it nowadays. I'm surprised it didn't take hold of thee earlier."

"I didn't get pulled very far west."

"What's the point of keeping on going when you find what you're after? Flat grassland with no clearing to do. Cheap as dirt in the bargain. Prairie and no timber wouldn't suit me, and the place'll probably look strange to thee for a while. But thee'll get used to it. It'll look like home to thee before thee knows it. A man nowadays can't seem to resist the West any more than a fish can the tide. I didn't resist it myself when I was young."

Jess, boots on, stood and faced his father. His father, looking into his face, seemed to be talking more to himself than to Jess.

Light, not sunlight yet, but darkness diluted enough to see by, filled the room. Jess walked the length of the long kitchen, opened the door into the big cold dining room. In the sitting room the embers from last night's fire were still alive. The parlor, dark at all times, with its blinds pulled to keep horsehair and plush from fading, was like a part of another building. It didn't have a human smell.

"It's a big house," he told his father when he came back to the kitchen. Big, and going to be empty, he thought.

"With nine children, nothing else would have served."

"Will thee and Mother make out all right with me gone?"

"It's a fine time to be asking a question like that," his father said.

It was, for a fact. Where would he be if his father answered, "No, son, we can't spare thee"?

His father said, "I've got a second hired man coming. My understanding is he can husk two bushels of corn to thy one."

Jess smiled. "He ain't here yet," he said. "I'll take care of the feeding and milking as usual."

He had wondered, when he made the down payment on the Indiana place, if compunction would choke him when he got home. Would homesickness at the thought of leaving the only home he'd ever known twist his heart? He gave compunction and homesickness their chance now. Halfway to the barn he turned to look back at the weather-worn house. He sniffed the smoke rising from the well-known hearth.

What he felt was elation. Oh, my own place, wait for me. Creek and knoll, cold spring, and ridge with the big hardwoods. Earth that has never borne cabin or house before. Wait for me, wait for me. I've been slow to claim my own, a long time coming. Wait a little longer.

His eyes were so filled with the sight of the road he would build to cross that Indiana branch, then wind up the hillside to his unbuilt house, that he didn't see his father standing in the open kitchen door until he turned toward the barn.

He saw him then with, between them, the years and miles that were to separate them. What a fine old man he is, he thought, how handsome and upright. What a life he has lived. He rejoiced that he wasn't, like some children, unable, until his parents died, to appreciate their good qualities.

The New Home

When Jess, Eliza, and their three children left Mount Pleasant for Indiana, you might have thought their departure had been Talbot Birdwell's idea. Since Jess didn't think his father capable of play-acting, he could only believe that deep in his heart Talbot was proud of a son who had finally showed enough get-up-and-go to strike out on his own. In any case there had been no tears; no expressions of "What will we do without thee?" Only smiles, "God bless thee," "Write often," and many last-minute gifts of kitchenware and farm gear from the old homestead which Talbot and Hannah thought would be needed on the new.

All this had made the leave-taking easy. And they had been fortunate in settling and building. Their house of squared logs wasn't as elegant or as large as the home they had been accustomed to in Mount Pleasant; but every inch of it was their own. Jess went to sleep at night relishing this fact and when he opened his eyes in the morning his pleasure hadn't dimmed.

Jess roused up before daylight and listened to the far-off crowing of a cock. A cock in his own barnyard answered, and Jess stretched himself on his good cord bed with pleasure.

"Summer's come," he said. He whispered the news to himself, lightly. He would not think of awakening Eliza, sleeping soundly by his side. Still, if she overheard him and awakened of her own will, that would be a different matter. It was neither day nor night. Some place in between. The sitting room of the log house, which was also his and Eliza's bedchamber, had the darkness of a roiled stream when the mud first begins to settle. There was less and less blackness. Jess could pick out here and there the shape of a piece of furniture, slats of a chair back against a window, curve at the top of a secretary, knobs of brass on the firedogs where the broad mouth of the chimney let down a shaft of morning grayness, unbleached-muslin curtains straight hanging in the motionless air. The air itself was scented with hay and ripening fruit and the cinnamon pinks under the window.

"Summer is here," Jess said, a little more loudly though still privately and to himself.

Eliza opened her black eyes. "How does thee know?" That was one of the things Jess liked about Eliza. She was awake or asleep, one or the other, no in-between states.

"Can tell by the way the cocks are crowing."

"Have they crowed?" asked Eliza.

"Yes," said Jess. "Didn't they waken thee?"

Eliza plumped up her pillow and from the extra height looked across at her husband. "Thee knows what wakened me."

Jess often marveled at the way Eliza sleeping was diminished. Rising to speak in Meeting, lifting a child in her arms, she was good-sized, commanding even. Asleep, she was near to nothing. One of his legs from hip socket to toe would like as not outweigh her. She lifted the two heavy braids of black hair away from her neck and shoulders as if in the growing warmth she did not like their weight.

"Thee knows well enough what wakened me, Jess Birdwell," she repeated. "Thee whispering to thyself. Can't thee make out to speak without whispering?"

"Don't seem so," Jess admitted. "There!" he said. "Hear them?"

Eliza listened. In the distance could be heard the broken scratching of roosters' voices, young roosters growing toward a Fourth of July skillet. "Sounds as usual to me."

"Listen," said Jess. "When roosters wake crowing hoarse, summer is here," he explained.

Eliza often wondered at the relish her husband had for the seasons. As another person ticks off the hours of the day, saying, "It's sunup," "high noon," "lamplighting time," Jess kept track of the year's changes. He would appear suddenly before her as she straightened up from making a bed or buttoning a child's drawers, put a leaf into her hand, and say, "Fall's here." He appreciated it if she answered, "What makes thee think so, Jess?" But whether she did or not he told her.

"Seems I recall thee saying summer had come when flies buzz before sunup. Or when there's morning thunderclouds."

"There's more signs than one," Jess admitted. "But cocks crowing hoarse—that's a sure sign."

Eliza liked weather herself: sun and a brisk wind on washday, warm weather when her Plymouth Rocks hatched, a mild spell for Yearly Meeting. She liked to hear weather busy doing its duty: sending the windmill around, distributing a leisurely rain once the corn was in, snapping the nails in a hard frost when fall fruits needed a touch of cold for mellowing. But Jess relished weather, it seemed, for its own sake. Hailstones big as pullet eggs cutting the corn to shreds, and Jess in the thick of it gathering up bucketsful like diamonds. The wind so strong the log cabin, low as it was, quivered like an old dog beat down to its haunches, and Jess out, hat off, mouth open, gulping down draughts of air like a doctor's prescribed medicine. Unless death changed him more than it seemed death *could,* Jess might have a tedious time hereafter: no unseasonable spells, no high-water marks, no snowdrifts to keep track of. Poor man! Eliza reached over and laid a hand on his shoulder.

Jess placed his large hand upon her small rough one. "Thee glad to have it summer, Eliza?"

"Summer for us, too," she said unexpectedly.

"Summer," Jess repeated, startled. Said that way, the word shook him. He felt himself no more than started in life, a few steps taken on a journey of miles. He heard one of the cows in the pasture speak, she also saying "summer." The bull replied with a sleepy rumbling. Saying "cow," I suppose, not "summer," Jess thought. In the loft overhead, the boys, moving into the shallows of sleep, spoke a word or two. "Play," "swim," "good time," something like that, Jess imagined. Though who could tell? Here was Eliza near to him as one of his own ribs, her hand in his, thinking a thought he would never have credited her with: that they had come to a halfway mark. The boys stirred again, saying, for all I know, Jess concluded with dismay, "I hate the world."

"Three children," Eliza said.

It was a fact. Laban and Josh in the loft; in the trundle bed by their side little Sarah. One minute a man was riding off to go courting, no responsibility in the world but keeping his horse fed and his hair cut, and the next he was as patriarchal as Abraham, his offspring and flocks gathered about him.

"Past twenty-five," said Eliza. "Half of life gone by."

It was true. A quarter of a century. More than that for him. Through the imperfect chinking, an eye of light fell on the moving pendulum of the clock. A few more swings and he'd be a grandfather. In the loft the boys, now wide awake, began to talk outright. Sarah sang to herself, "Icy, icy, icy, icy all the world" was her song, as far as Jess could make out. The house was full of life.

"We're crowded," Eliza burst out. "We need more room."

Jess made a movement away from his wife, and she said, "I mean in the house. We're all bunched up together."

"Bunched up?" said Jess. "Why, we got four rooms." That was stretching it a little maybe, calling the porch a room. But kitchen, sitting room, and loft were real rooms. He could remember when there had been only kitchen and loft, and Eliza content as a queen.

"We've outgrown them," said Eliza. "Us sleeping in the sitting room and the children in and out and company having to double up. It's not dignified."

Dignified! So now they would live with dignity. Jess tried on the word like a new shirt, and it fit him fine. "For dignity," he asked, "what does thee figure we need, Eliza?"

Eliza didn't need to figure a minute. "We need to add another room," she said. "A chamber of our own."

Jess sat up in bed and looked about. It was full day now, the morning light rosy on the chinked walls, the puncheon floors, the exposed rafters. Clad in his new dignity, his life half spent, Jess looked at the room with a stranger's eyes. Chinking falling out here and there. Beams darkened with smoke. Puncheon floor scarred and splintered. Plainly the main room of the house, parlor and sitting room in one; and bedroom, too, a man and woman bedded down there. Man's breeches hanging catty-cornered by one gallus on a peg. Woman's petticoats, neater, across the back of a chair. Child in another bed. This stranger, this dignified middle-aged man, did not see the room as Jess had, as a young man starting life, lucky to have raised himself such a fine and weatherproof house in the midst of his clearing. *He* saw it against houses left behind in Ohio and Pennsylvania, houses where the sitting was done in one room and the sleeping in another; houses where no daylight came in except through the windows, where the floor boards were so slippery with wax a man had to clench his toes to stay upright. Why, this was a makeshift place, a camp in the woods, a building a man could make do with while young and getting a start but one he'd want to get shut of by the time he'd reached the summer of life!

Jess put a long, rusty-haired leg out of bed and picked up Sarah, who was now wide awake. With Sarah on his shoulder, he took the poker from the hearth and rammed it through a weak spot in the chinking. "House falling down about our ears!" he said. Sarah put her fingers through the opening. "Falling down," she said with pleasure.

"Our children exposed to the elements!" lamented Jess, making the dried clay fly. "A chamber of our own! A single room!" He was scornful. "What we need's a whole new house."

Before breakfast Jess did the chores and surveyed the landscape. The sun was still low, and its beams came coasting in without much slant. A kind of bluish haze hung above the pasture's clover. Where the light touched the silvery upturned undersides of the grass, there was a sheen like that from winter's hoarfrost. The shadows of the trees were long, stretching away, it seemed, from the sun's heat. Butterflies were already running their tongues deep into Eliza's morning-glories, and cows walked the shady way to grass.

Josh said, "Labe slipped his pig a handful of corn when thee wasn't watching, Pa."

Labe's pig was the last of a litter, a runt, a salmon-colored weakling. He was trying to build it up.

"Thee old tattletale," Labe said. "Thee old spill-it-all."

Josh was not hurt by these words, or surprised. Name calling was but part of his brother's general want of principle. "It's not fair," he said, "for one pig to get more than another."

"Joseph needs it," said Labe. "He's the littlest."

"Joseph!" repeated Josh. "Pa, Labe's calling a pig after a man in the Bible."

"Could call thee after one," said Labe, darkly.

"Thee better not," said Josh, having a good idea he would not be called after anyone nice.

Jess, roused from contemplation by the hullabaloo at his side, said, "Boys, we're going to build us a new house."

"Logs?" asked Josh.

"No siree," said Jess. "White clapboard."

At breakfast Jess raised the house before their eyes: laid the foundation with one motion of his hand and built up the walls with another; traced a lacy line with his fingers, and there was gingerbread galore around the gables, rich and intricate; lifted his eyes, and there was a weather vane on the roof, lightning rods, and a bell in

84

a little house of its own to call the men in from the fields.

"Kin I ring the little bell?" asked Sarah.

"The very first ring," said Jess. "I promise thee."

"Thee can't reach the rope," said Josh, looking with distaste at the dribblings on his sister's chin.

"I'll hold thee up, Sary," said Labe.

"Will we have a dining room to dine in?" asked Josh.

"We will have a dining room to dine in, a sitting room to sit in, a cooking room to cook in, and sleeping rooms to sleep in. For everything we do there will be a special room to do it in."

"What'll we do in the parlor?" asked Josh.

Jess looked at Eliza. "In the parlor," said Eliza, "which comes from the French word *parler*, meaning to talk, we will talk."

"Yes," said Jess, "in the parlor we will *parler*, meaning to talk."

He spooned deeply into the cold dewberry cobbler left over from the night before. Eliza had given him a strange setout for breakfast: leftover cobbler, new potatoes cooked in their jackets, and cream gravy. She had kept her head bowed so long when they returned thanks that he'd considered giving her a little tweak to bring home the fact that the gravy was getting cold. Cold cobbler was one thing and cold gravy another. But when she had lifted her face, shining with thankfulness and pride, and said, "Children, thy father is going to build us a new house," he was glad he had thought better of it. Now she said, "When does thee plan to start?"

In Jess's mind the house was already so thoroughly built that the word "start" sounded strange. Start? Why, there it stood! Weatherboarded, shuttered, windproof, snowproof, the storm howling around outside and they inside, snug and warm and not in the least bunched up.

"Today?" asked Eliza, not one to loiter in a dream house.

Jess emerged into the log cabin. "Certainly," he said. "Postponement never yet raised a rooftree."

"What's the first thing to be done?" asked Eliza.

"Go to Vernon," said Jess, "and get Joe Kimball to figure on the building. Pay him a down fee and get him to come out, see what timber'll need cutting. Put in an order for windows and hardware if he says so."

"Thee have money for all this?" asked Eliza. "All this feeing and ordering?"

"I got enough to show honesty of intent, anyway," said Jess, "and after harvest, more. Oh, this ain't no card house, Eliza. No leaping without looking. This is something I've had in mind for some time. Just hadn't dawned on me the day for it had come."

"What I would like," said Sarah, squinting into the distance, "would be a little window. A little tinsy window to peer through."

They could all tell that she was peering through it that very minute, but what she saw, none of them could say.

By noon Jess and the two boys were in the buckboard, halfway to Vernon. Eliza had packed them a noontime snack and seen them off. "Thee just hold things down here," Jess told her in high spirits, "and by nightfall we'll be back, Joe Kimball's receipt in my pocket and the cornerstone as good as laid."

The June sun was directly overhead as they drove along. Heat waves shimmered across the ripening corn, and shadows squatted at the base of trees and shrubs. Old Dolly wore a second set of harness outlined in sweat around the set used for pulling. Once in a while she twisted her head sideways, as if trying to catch Jess's eye.

Failing to do this, she would let out her breath in a long damp weary snort. Labe inspected the fleck such a snort deposited upon his bare forearm.

"Horse breath," he concluded, and no one contradicted him.

The sky was deep blue, quite empty except where on the horizon great clouds rose up like distant snow-covered mountains. A hawk flew out of the woods, then hung overhead inspecting the travelers and screaming with energy.

"Could a hawk eat a man?" asked Labe.

"Of course not," said Josh.

"If the man was hawk-size," said Labe, "and the hawk man-size?"

"They ain't any man-size hawks," said Josh flatly.

Labe hung for a time over the edge of the buckboard watching the right front wheel pick up the soft dust, carry it upward, then let it fall back in two soft downward-falling runnels.

"My stomach's agrowlin'," he said, as if this were news to anyone.

"When a hog's stomach growls, the weather's going to change," Josh told him, his mind still on swine.

"You boys hungry?" asked Jess.

"I'm hungry," said Labe. "That's why my stomach's agrowlin'."

"Thee keep a sharp lookout," Jess told him, "for a likely place to stop, and we'll pull up and have a bite to eat."

Labe saw a likely place almost at once, the sandy curve on the far side of the ford at Bee Crick. They were at the top of the hill that led to the crossing when he pointed out the spot and the man who had already stopped there. "It's dinnertime," he said. "There's a man already eating." He was out of the buckboard before its hind wheels left the water, and while Jess took Old Dolly out of the shafts, he spent the time inspecting the traveler.

After a little of this the traveler said, "In case you're wondering, I'm a man."

"Thee is a very neat man," Labe answered politely.

He was. On the ground in front of him and held down by four stones was a piece of white goods which served him as a tablecloth. On this cloth were crackers, cheese, and a dish of stewed pieplant. A cup and saucer awaited the coffee which was just coming to the boil in a pot supported by a little trivet.

"I try to be," said the traveler. "The wilderness round about me, least I can do is tame myself."

Labe looked up and down Bee Crick. It was not his idea of a wilderness, though the man before him was so orderly he made the festoons of wild grape, the peeling sycamore bark, the ragged clusters of elderberry look wilder than he had ever seen them before. The traveler was a small man, peak-nosed, lantern-jawed, with dark furry hair. In the heat of midday he wore a cloth coat, a collar held up close to his overhanging chin by a wide lapped-over tie. He was not sitting in the sand any which way, but on a smooth little box, painted yellow, and over by his light spring wagon his two horses, bays with black switch tails, ate their oats from a larger box, also yellow.

"That your pa and brother?" he asked Labe.

Labe nodded, his eyes still too busy to give his tongue much chance. The traveler, he thought, looked like a raccoon: shiny, black, bright-eyed, point-nosed. Labe almost expected to see him dip his sliver of cheese in the crick, raccoonlike, before he ate any of it.

"Going to town?" he asked.

"To Vernon," Labe said, giving his eyes a little rest. "Picked a hot day for it."

"We're in a hurry."

"Yeh?"

"We're building a house."

"Yeh?"

"White clapboard," said Labe, "with diamond-shaped windows."

"House," repeated the stranger, and he got to his feet as Jess approached. "Be a pleasure if you'd join me in a cup of coffee," he said.

"Thanks," said Jess. "I'd appreciate it. It'd help wash down the ham and light bread."

"I'll fetch a cup. I take for granted these two chaps won't be drinking?"

Labe tried to look like a coffee drinker, but Jess said, "Warm milk's their strongest tipple."

When the traveler returned with the cup, he said, "My name's Leutweiler, Herman Leutweiler."

Jess held out his hand. "I'm pleased to meet thee, Friend Leutweiler. I'm Jess Birdwell, and these are my two young'uns, Joshua and Laban."

"Mr. Birdwell, boys, it's a great pleasure," said Mr. Leutweiler. The boys stood pushing the warm sand up between their bare toes. Jess brought forth their spice-cake, bread, and ham; Mr. Leutweiler poured the coffee.

Jess rolled up a piece of driftwood, nowhere near as fancy as Mr. Leutweiler's painted box, but just as comfortable for sitting purposes. After he'd filled the boys' hands with meat and bread and had a sip or two of Mr. Leutweiler's black coffee, he said, "Thee from hereabouts, Friend Leutweiler?"

"Nope. Just passing through."

"What does thee think of our country?"

"Too ambitious," said Mr. Leutweiler.

"Ambitious?" asked Jess.

"Climbing. Where I come from there ain't so much perpendicular."

"Where's that?" Jess asked.

"Ohio."

"Ohio? Thee know Belmont County?"

"Like the palm of my hand. Ain't a crease or crevice I can't trace."

"I was born there," Jess said.

"Well, well," said Mr. Leutweiler, "and me passing through less than two weeks ago."

"Thee happen to see the Grubbs? They're kin of mine."

"Nope. But the Milhouses next door I did see."

"Know them well," said Jess. "How did thee find them?"

"In sorry case. Very sorry case." Mr. Leutweiler shook his head without saying more.

Jess took out his pocket knife and divided the spicecake into four substantial slabs. He handed them around, balanced delicately on the blade of his knife.

"Have some sauce to dampen it," urged Mr. Leutweiler. He piled half the stewed pieplant on his own slice, pushed the saucer with what was left toward Jess.

"Thanks," said Jess, "it'll be a treat."

"Can we swim, Pa?" asked Josh, swallowing the last lump of his cake.

"Thee can wade," said Jess. "Don't see how thee can make out to swim in water not knee-deep."

"Have to lay down and roll over to wet yourself on both sides," said Mr. Leutweiler.

Josh stepped modestly behind a bush, divested himself in a twinkling of shirt and breeches, then lunged into the knee-deep, dapple-lighted stream.

"Young Adam," said Mr. Leutweiler. "Naked and un-ashamed!"

"Adam never was that age," Jess reminded him.

"You're right, Mr. Birdwell, you're right. I was disre-membering Adam's lack of a childhood."

"Always thought Adam might've handled his boys bet-ter if he'd been a boy himself," said Jess. "Worked under a handicap, as it was."

"Ain't you swimming?" Mr. Leutweiler, plainly unin-terested in Adam, boy or man, asked Labe.

"Yes," said Labe. But he didn't move from the smooth birch against which he was leaning or chew any faster on his cake.

"Little pitcher," observed Mr. Leutweiler.

"Only way to get filled," said Jess. "Stomach and mind at that age both agrowlin' for something to chew on."

A time of stillness settled on the bend at Bee Crick. Josh lay in the sun-flecked water like a scrawny log, his head on a boulder and the water moving across him like a shifty coverlid. Jess and Mr. Leutweiler had their second cups of coffee and let them wash down content in knowing that it was all the coffee there was, and that it was enough. Labe swallowed the fine-grained cake, crumb at a time, relishing the balance between sharp and sweet. Trees grew close about them, so that to see the sky, Labe had to tilt his head backward. It was as if they had fallen to the bottom of a well, deep and green, quiet and hot. Now and then in its need to pass around or over some rock, Bee Crick made a watery sound: glup, glup. And the men drinking their coffee seemed to be imitating it: glup, glup. Labe shut his eyes for a minute to see if his ears could tell Bee Crick over rocks from coffee swal-lowed.

"Asleep on his feet," observed Mr. Leutweiler, motioning to Labe, and took the rest of his coffee in one swallow. Labe, unsleeping, said to himself at that sound, "Coffee."

Jess slapped at a mosquito. "When mosquitoes give over stinging for biting, it's a sure sign summer is here."

Mr. Leutweiler put down his coffee cup. "Lucky for the Milhouses, it *is*," he said, but said no more.

"The Milhouses' misfortune kind of private?" Jess ventured after a while.

"Least private misfortune a man could have, I reckon," said Mr. Leutweiler.

"Death?" asked Jess. "A death in the family?"

"Nope. I left them all well. Downcast, but in good health."

"They're all Friends," said Jess. "Not likely any of them's made a misstep."

"Misstep?" said Mr. Leutweiler. "What the Milhouses are suffering from is the lack of a step."

Jess scraped a thread of pieplant from the saucer; a steel-colored darning needle flew low over the creek, stitching air to water; Josh rose from the creek bed, dripping; Labe explored with his tongue the spaces nearest his mouth for a missed crumb.

"Reckon we ought to be pushing on," said Jess, trying his knees for bend.

Mr. Leutweiler spoke, and he straightened them once more. "The Milhouses' house burned."

Jess was taken aback at the news. "It was a brand-new house."

Mr. Leutweiler agreed. "Less'n a year old. White clapboard."

"A total loss?"

"Total. Burned to the ground, including barn and outbuildings. Nothing left to show the place was a site of human habitation except two brick chimneys and privy pit."

"A new house," Jess said, thinking. "What was the cause?"

"Lightning. Line storm."

"Most dangerous kind."

"All lightning's dangerous," said Mr. Leutweiler severely. He gazed overhead so searchingly that Labe, following his glance, half expected to see a blue-white bolt launch itself downward. "Chain, sheet, ball. Each able to kill and burn."

"Ball lightning ain't usual."

"Fortunately. A man who looks on ball lightning is not the man he was before he seen it."

"Thee ever see it?"

"Once," said Mr. Leutweiler. "Age ten. Summer evening of a day like this. Me on the upping-block. Distant storm, but nothing near. Or so I thought. Then there it was, knee-high, a traveling ball of light."

"How big was it?" asked Jess. "This ball thee seen?"

"About as big as a good-sized gravy bowl."

"What color?"

"Green and blue. Some yellow. Quivering and wiggling like a mess of maggots."

Josh came up out of the stream and leaned against the tree Labe had been leaning against. Labe leaned against his father and looked over his father's shoulder at what Mr. Leutweiler seemed to see.

"Rolled along knee-high like the Devil's head escaped from Hell. I watched it, shivering in every limb. Moved like it was guided by a string straight in the open door of our house."

Mr. Leutweiler paused, and Jess said to Labe, "Stand back, stand back. Thee's pushing me over."

"And there," said Mr. Leutweiler, "it exploded."

"Inside the house?"

"Inside."

"Do any harm?"

"Bodily, no. Mentally, yes. It sent my poor mother out of her mind."

Jess was shocked. "A pity," he said, "a great pity. She recover?"

"Don't know her own name to this day," said Mr. Leutweiler. "But ball lightning's uncommon. What does the great harm is chain. Chain reaches down for you. Chain reaches down for your house. Your new house. Just built. Everything you value in it, to say nothing of the money tied up in it. Wife and children asleep. One bolt. Then you're alone in the world like Adam here, and no spare rib to start over with."

"Well," said Jess, "there's misfortunes in the world, there's things that can't be avoided, acts of God."

"Acts of God! It ain't God's acting so much as man's not acting causes most trouble. With a lightning rod, lightning ain't anything but Fourth of July in Heaven. When God made lightning he expected man to make rods."

"Milhouses have rods?"

"Not a rod. When Amos Milhous was planning his building, I said to him, 'Order your rods! Before you fell a tree or drop a plumb line, order your rods!' But not Amos. He had plenty of other places for his money, as who ain't? So he would raise his house first and buy his rods second. I was on my way with them when his house burned."

"Thee sell lightning rods?" asked Jess.

"Sell!" said Mr. Leutweiler. "Mr. Birdwell, at the age of ten I dedicated myself to the saving of life, reason, and property by means of the lightning rod. Whenever I see a fine white two-story or two-story-and-a-half house sitting amidst its fields, untouched by lightning, family in full possession of its senses, the meat on their bones unscorched, the whole shebang protected by one of my gilded ball-topped rods, *that*, Mr. Birdwell, is my reward."

"I don't reckon thee gives rods away," Jess said mildly.

"For the company, I collect certain sums."

"Thee have some rods with thee?"

"I have."

"Thee have any objection to my looking at them?"

"Yes, sir, Mr. Birdwell, I do. Your boy here by chance let drop you were building a house. Now my rods are all spoken for, and there's no use your seeing them and hankering for them for nothing."

"Needn't hanker," Jess told him, "being forewarned."

"No, sir," said Leutweiler, "you couldn't help yourself. You'd see these rods and want a pair, and I'd have to turn you down. Then your house'd burn, as is more than likely, this hilly country breeding thunderstorms the way it does, and who'd you blame? Herman Leutweiler. No, sir! I don't want the burden of your burning on my shoulders. Not your white clapboards curling up and your lace curtains blazing and your wife and child like as not trapped in an upstairs bedroom. No, sir!"

Mr. Leutweiler in the heat of his feeling rose and gave his yellow box a solid kick. He turned his face away from Bee Crick as if it ran flame and not water. He looked up toward the sky, the source of the lightning he was sworn to defy and circumvent. "No, sir," he said.

Labe felt like plunging into the crick, clothes and all, so real was Mr. Leutweiler's storm and flames. He could see the red tongues licking up the lace curtains, hear his mother and Sarah trapped upstairs and crying for help.

"I'd appreciate looking at the rods purely as ornaments," Jess said, "and with no thought of their chief use."

"Purely as ornaments, and if they had no more use in the world than a firefly in Hell, my rods are to houses what tails are to cocks: an end-all and a come-see. There they stand! There they flash! Saying to passers-by, 'This house is complete'; and saying to the Lord, 'I'm working with You.' Since I've put it that way, Mr. Birdwell, I don't see why you *shouldn't* have a look at them."

After Mr. Leutweiler, his yellow boxes, his trivet, his coffeepot and cups, his bay team, with their black switch tails, and his lightning rods, minus two sets, one each for house and barn, had left the bend at Bee Crick, Jess and Labe took off their clothes and had a roll in the Bee Crick waters. Josh dressed again, sat on a stump and watched them. It was midafternoon, or a little past; midges hung in clouds above the shallow pools; birds skimmed low to eat them; shadows crept out from under trees.

"It's going to be dark before we get to Vernon," Josh told the swimmers.

Jess rolled over, face up. "We've given that trip up," he said.

"Thee told Mama," Josh said reprovingly, "thee'd have the receipt in thy pocket."

"Haven't got the wherewithal at the minute to buy myself any more receipts," Jess admitted.

"It was going to be a cornerstone," Josh, who had a good memory, said sadly.

"Going at it the other end to," Jess informed his son cheerfully. "Going to build up to meet the lightning rods."

"How can thee do that?" Josh wondered.

Jess didn't answer, but Labe could see it being done, the beautiful, golden balls high against the blue sky, and beneath, progressing upward to meet them, the shining white house.

"Pa can do it," he said confidently.

Josh was unconvinced. "Mama'd like a cornerstone better."

Jess rose from the stream, and the air, warm as it was, struck a little cool on his dripping body.

"Thee's more'n likely right," he said.

Jess awakened with the feeling that he had slept only a minute or two, but the moon, which did not rise until past midnight, was already shining, a mild, spent moon which laid yellow beams across the floor boards. He awakened slowly, feeling a little heavyhearted and lonely and not knowing why. Then turning toward Eliza he found that she was not beside him, and he sat up and looked about the room. It, too, was empty of her, and he swung his feet out of bed, stood noiselessly, stepped into his pants, and walked out into a world lighted by so small a segment of the moon it seemed more a private lantern lit for him and Eliza than the public moon.

Only where *was* Eliza? He walked barefooted down the front path between the rows of bleeding hearts, little colorless clots, they were, in the dim light. The smell of woods and fields came to him strongly after his half-night in the house, and he realized anew how wild the earth was and how far out on its edge he and Eliza lived. He did not want to call out and awaken the children, so he walked on, silent and peering, thinking what if, as in stories he had heard, Eliza had simply vanished, disappeared without a sign, proved to be a dream. What would he do? He did not know. In such a case he would need Eliza to advise him, tell him how in the world he could get on without her. An owl dropped out of the Juneberry tree, fell softly, like a lump of snow, then suddenly whooed. There was a movement, at the sound, across the road against the trunk of the yellow poplar, and Jess walked across the road to the tree and put his hand on Eliza's warm arm. She had on her nightdress, and was leaning against the tree facing the log house and crying.

"Eliza," Jess said. "Eliza."

Eliza turned away from him, tried to burrow her face into poplar bark.

"Eliza," Jess said, "it's the smallest kind of a setback and no waste of money. They're A-1 rods, pretty to look at and useful. A month more, two at the most, and the money'll be on hand to go ahead just as we planned."

"I don't care about thy old lightning rods," said Eliza. She was leaning against Jess now, not the tree. "I wish thee'd bought a thousand."

"Why, Eliza," Jess said, "Eliza."

"Whatever were we thinking of, Jess," she asked, "planning to leave the log house we just built so lately?"

"Thinking of?" Jess repeated. "Thinking of how it'd had its day. Thee said so thyself. Thee was the one suggested building."

"I was wrong," said Eliza. "This is our home. When we first built it, I'd walk out at night to this tree just so I could look back and see how pretty it was, lamplighted and shining. I was proud of it, Jess. And it's been a good tight house to us. Other people've had trouble with their houses: chimneys smoke, doors stick, roofs leak. But *our* house never did give us any trouble, Jess, and I never can leave it."

"Ain't so weather-tight," Jess reminded her.

"Thee go on, Jess. I don't blame thee. Thee put up thy big clapboard house. Lightning rods, diamond window-panes, whatever strikes thy fancy. Thee can live in it, and Sarah can keep house for thee. But I can't ever leave the log house. It wouldn't be right."

Eliza's tears were so plentiful they went right through Jess's nightshirt to the skin. When they lessened a little, he folded down his nightshirt collar and wiped her cheeks dry.

"Beautiful night," he said, putting his collar back. "Beautiful, mild, balmy night."

"Is it, Jess?" Eliza asked, lifting her head to look about.

"Hasn't thee seen?" Jess asked. "Beautiful summer night."

Katydids, ever so far into the night, were still sounding. "Listen," said Jess. "Hear them? Katydids sounding at midnight, that's a sure sign of full summer."

Eliza did not answer. "Summer coming for us, too, like thee said," Jess reminded her. Eliza gave a few more sniffs. "Don't hear any Rome Beauties crying because they ain't apple blossoms, does thee?"

"No," said Eliza.

"Don't hear any little hoot owls hooting to get back in their eggs?"

"No, Jess."

"No little oaks scrunching down trying to be acorns again?"

"Was I scrunching down," Eliza asked, "trying to be an acorn?" There was a little sound of laughter in her voice, but Jess was serious.

"Thee *was* when I came out and found thee. Scrunching thyself down mighty low. No house is our home, Eliza. A house is just a makeshift place at best, a place to fit our

99

size and be comfortable in. The earth's our rightful home. And the sky. And after that a house to suit our size as we grow. Why, men have faced the prospect of leaving their earthly home, Eliza, with less taking-on than thine over leaving a log cabin. Babies grow tall. White clapboard takes the place of log. Nothing stands still."

Jess started back across the road, Eliza leaning on his arm. Overhead the sky was garlanded with stars, and underfoot the earth was dusty but soft and warm.

"Jess Birdwell," exclaimed Eliza, "is thee barefoot?"

Jess looked down at his feet. "I was too anxious about thee to take time for shoes."

"Thee'll have to wash thy feet before thee can get back in bed," Eliza told him.

"Well water's going to be mighty cold, this hour of the night," Jess objected.

Eliza didn't reply, and when they reached the house she fetched him the washbasin. But as Jess recoiled from the first dipperful of water, she said, "If thy feet are cold afterward, Jess, thee can warm them on mine."

First Loss

Jess was in what Eliza would call a swivet. It was a mild swivet, and Jess smiled to himself as her word came to his mind. The word meant, as Eliza used it, a kind of sweating impatience with a situation you wanted to change, but couldn't. It was a word she reserved for him. He had never heard her tell anyone else, "Now don't get in a swivet." He didn't think he was any more inclined to swivets than other people. But he did think that Eliza herself bordered on a swivet whenever she foresaw him having one.

All that was troubling him now was an overabundance of delight in what he saw—and no one to share his pleasure. It was dinnertime. Sun overhead in a May-blue sky. He had spent the morning hoeing corn and had come up to the house when the dinner bell rang. In mid-yard he had been struck in his tracks by the beauty of creation, his own and the Lord's combining. When he first saw it he had fallen in love with this knoll and circling creek and the overhang on the ridge above of hardwoods; fallen in love the way some men fall in love with a woman. He

had to have it. And to get it he had left home, turned
down richer land farther west.

Everybody might not agree with him, but he believed
that what he had added to the knoll had bettered it: the
clapboard house still awaited building. Clearing land
and planting crops had come to seem more important.
But a room had been added to the log house they had
which was now whitewashed and well caulked. The rail
fence that ran round the yard was covered with blue
morning-glories; and outside the fence young apple trees
were in blossom. Even the hog houses looked good to
him. The tail feathers of the Buff Orphington roosters
glinted in the sunlight. Daisy, the calf, shut away from
her mother, had given up bawling. You could argue that
Eve was a better-looking woman before she added the
leaves. But after she ate the apple, the leaves became her.
It was the same with earth. Homes and blossoming trees
and cows with big bags became it since man had left the
garden. "And all in three years!" he wanted to marvel
with someone. Eliza, preferably, since she had seen it as
it was and had had a hand in the transformation. But
Eliza had rung the dinner bell and was a stickler for eating dinner when it was dished up. The two boys were in
school. Two-year-old Mattie wasn't yet much of a con-
versationalist. That left Sarah, who *was* a conversational-
ist. The dinner bell had rung as much for her as for him;
and if he knew Eliza, Sarah was at this minute seated,
knees under the table and knife and fork in hand.

"Well, Snip," Jess said to the little short-haired dog
which lay by his feet, "that leaves thee and me."

Snip was an obliging dog, eager to agree with anyone.
"It's a sight to behold, wouldn't thee say?"

Snip, who was under two and had never seen the farm
without the log cabin, fence, and flowers, was in no posi-

tion to say. But he knew what he was being asked and beat the earth with his stubby docked tail.

"Wouldn't know it was the same place, would thee?"

Snip, along with his brother, Snap, had been the gift of a passing settler who had found the addition of three pups more cargo than his western-bound wagon could bear. They had been destined for drowning in the creek at the bottom of the hill, but Jess, softhearted when his children cried, accepted two of them as gifts. They were the last thing on this earth he needed. Old Pedro, smart with livestock and a good watchdog, was plenty of dog for them.

The dogs, little brown-and-white-spotted animals, some mixture of terrier and hound and possibly bull, might've been twins for looks. Their names grew out of their natures. They were never named insofar as Jess could remember. They were Snip and Snap the same way dog is dog and cat is cat. They were born that way. Snap was snappy. He was strong, cheerful, and pugnacious. Snip, bark and body, was more fragile. For a little dog, Snap had a full-chested big-dog bark. Snip made a sound more like a pair of scissors cutting calico. "Snip, snip" was the sound that came through his sharp white teeth when he opened his mouth. He ate less than Snap, and what he did eat agreed with him less well. Eliza was always having to cook up invalid mixtures for Snip —corn meal and milk or bacon-rind soup. Snip never complained when sick, was never feisty; he ate what he could, puked when he had to, and kept as close to Snap's heels as possible, his "Snip, snip" like an echo of Snap's big hearty bark.

When Neil Ricketts, over in the next draw, lost his dog in his own bear trap, he asked Jess if he didn't find three dogs one too many. "I know you wouldn't think of parting with Old Pedro, but you'd never miss one of the twins, would you?" Jess would never miss Snip, but he didn't have the heart to wish off a cull on a friend. "Take your pick," he said.

Snip had his own appealing ways. He was more affectionate than Snap. While Ricketts was making up his mind, Snap was busy digging a hole, more interested in what he thought he smelled than in the visitor. Snip sat at Ricketts' feet, gazing up at his broad red face. If Ricketts chose Snip, Jess was prepared to part with him without tears.

Sarah wasn't. Snap would thrive anywhere, and Sarah knew it. He was his own dog, and any master would serve. Snip was more particular. He'd never had the toe of a boot in his belly, however playfully, the way Ricketts' boot was nudging him now. Sarah picked up Snip. Snip laid his head against her shoulder and rolled his eyes around, to see what the men made of this.

"Don't thee want to part with Snip, Sarah?"

It was a poor question, Jess realized the minute after it had left his mouth. Sarah, a truthteller, would as likely as not give her real reasons for wanting to keep Snip— truth ranging from Snip's sickliness to the rough play of Ricketts' boot.

"No," said Sarah with surprising restraint and tact. "He is my dog, and I don't want to give him away."

Jess didn't know how Sarah had come to the conclusion that Snip was hers, but he accepted it.

Ricketts, who had already picked out Snap as the better dog, was happy to be able to bow to a little girl's preference.

"Jess, I wouldn't think of robbing your little girl of her pet," he said. "That digger back there may lack something her dog has, but I'll be thankful to have anything that barks to take my Brewster's place."

"Brewster?" asked Sarah.

"That was my old dog's name."

It was then that Sarah showed herself to be the child she was. "Brewster is a strange name for a dog."

She hadn't been rude, hadn't said, "Why did thee call thy dog Brewster?" But Ricketts didn't mind telling. "He was named after my wife's father," he said. If he expected Sarah to ask the why of that, he was disappointed. She said not a word, but went over to Snap, and with Snip still in her arms bent down and talked to him in a voice too low for the men to hear.

Sarah and her father together watched Snap ride off on the wagon seat beside Ricketts, upright and without a farewell glance for friends or brother. Jess wondered what Sarah thought about losing Snap. All she said was, "Brewster's bark was worse than his bite."

Snap had departed six months ago; only to meet Brewster's fate, death in one of Ricketts' traps. Snip, still fed on messes of gruel, had prospered. He waited now at Jess's feet for more conversation, his tail thump-thumping an agreement with whatever might be said.

"No one's got more reason than thee," Jess said, "to appreciate this place. Thy brother was the better dog, and he's dead and gone. And here thee lives on, pampered."

Snip's answer to this was his little clickety bark. He raced toward the house, barking as he ran. Sarah, closing the door behind her, had come into the yard.

"Papa," she called.

Jess beckoned to her before she could get the rest of her message, which would be "dinner's waiting," out.

It was the wrong thing to do, and he felt guilty about

tolling her away from her own meal and preventing her from delivering a message her mother had told her to deliver. But he longed to have the delight of seeing her, light-footed, run up the rise toward him. He sometimes wondered if he would have found her movements so pretty to watch if she had been someone else's child. He supposed not. Though on the other hand, he could admire the gait of another man's horse as much as one of his own. And he had stood, head thrown back, half an hour at a time watching the great soaring loops of turkey buzzards, which were truly free as a bird and no man's possession whatever. Sarah was his little girl, and he loved her; but he would surely have watched with pleasure any five-year-old who could manage so skimming a flight.

She had on her red dress. This was one of Eliza's real concessions to Sarah and a slap in the face, as one of the Meeting's Elders had said, to Quaker belief. Eliza herself held to the principle of plain colors. Jess had never been able to square the Quaker belief in the colorless with the Almighty's plentiful use of what was vivid and bright. Eliza had tried to explain it to him. Red birds and orioles and peacocks were content to remain as the Lord had made them. Human beings by putting on bright colors changed themselves.

"Changed themselves by putting on clothes at all," Jess said.

"They did that to hide their shame," Eliza reminded him.

Jess himself didn't feel that he had any shame to hide. But accepting the fact that Adam's problem was peculiar, he contented himself with saying, "Shame is shame and cover is cover. And cover don't have to be any particular color insofar as I can see to do the job."

"It don't have to call attention to itself either," Eliza replied.

In spite of all these convictions, and of Eliza's need as preacher to be a little more strait-laced than any of her flock, she had made Sarah her red dress. Sometimes Jess thought she had done so because she recognized that Sarah was different from her other children. Taking color from Sarah would be like asking a jay bird to give up blue, or a cardinal to masquerade as a crow. Not that Sarah was in any way wild or gypsylike. She was willful, maybe, but not wild.

She had been willful that very morning. She had put Eliza's sewing basket, a present from Eliza's father, an ornate silk-lined affair, on the floor. Then she had mounted the basket, which was barely able to hold her weight, and stood there like some statue or sentry.

Eliza, explaining mildly enough that she would ruin the basket by standing on it, had asked her to step off.

"Daughter don't feel able to stand on the floor," Sarah explained mildly in return.

Jess didn't admire such behavior, but he was tempted to laugh. Sarah, when she had done something she knew to be wrong, often referred to herself as "daughter"; a person known to both her parents and herself, but over whom neither had any control.

"I think daughter'll find she's able to stand on the floor if she steps off the basket."

Sarah made no move to step.

Jess was willing to play the game of "daughter," the third person, whose behavior lay outside his jurisdiction, for a very short time.

"Sarah," he said, "thee step off that basket and step fast."

"Daughter don't feel able to stand on the floor."

"Papa feels able to whip daughter. Maybe that will help her."

"Oh, don't have to whip me."

Jess hoped he wouldn't have to. He had never known anyone who suffered more from a spanking or who profited less. A whipping wasn't for Sarah, as it was for the boys, a reminder to obey or a punishment for disobeying. It was a call to something deep within her, which had no kinship to daughterhood, or to him, to endure and resist. It was as if, Jess thought, some dark power whispered to Sarah, "If thee gives in, thee'll die." There were those in the Meeting who had a name for this power, and believed that Jess and Eliza encouraged Him by treating Sarah as gently as they did. Dark power or Devil, Jess didn't feel ready that morning for the ordeal of a struggle, with Sarah's small body as the battleground.

He snatched her off the sewing basket without gentleness, carried her up the stairs to the loft, and sat her down on the floor with a thump.

"When daughter feels able to stand on the floor, she can come downstairs."

He thought he might not see her for the rest of the day, but she was downstairs before he went out to work.

"Daughter feels able to stand now," she announced.

"On the floor?"

"Yes."

She went to her mother. "I'm sorry I stood on thy basket."

"My father gave that basket to me, thy grandfather. He is dead now. I would like to keep the basket as long as I live as a keepsake."

"I will keep it as long as I live, too," Sarah said.

As Jess watched Sarah run toward him, he saw the edge of her white drawers beneath her full red skirt. Her black braids swung first to one side, then the other. A rooster crowed, shrill as if he had just discovered daylight. The shadow of a cloud passed slowly over the green slope and over Sarah running. Jess knew as he watched that this was a moment he would always remember. Great occasions were forgotten while the mind clung to small things observed in some period of quietness. This moment, even as it occurred, seemed to be already a part of eternity, destined to go on and on, he forever waiting, the child forever running toward him.

He didn't hold out his arms to her. Sarah wanted to choose her own times for being caught and held. She was like Josh in that. Mattie and Labe were always ready for a squeeze; their bodies were shaped for hugging. But Josh and Sarah had flesh that found touch comforting only when emotions of their own had prepared it.

"Dinner is on the table, Papa."

"I know it. I'm playing hooky."

"When Labe played hooky, thee spanked him."

"That's why it's better to be a man than a boy."

"Is it?"

"I don't know. I hope so. We're men so much longer than we're boys."

Another cloud crossed the sun. "The firmament on high," Jess said, "His Glory doth declare."

"Are the clouds God?"

"God? Whatever gave thee that idea? No, God made the clouds."

"Which did He make first? Us or clouds?"

"Clouds."

"Why?"

"I don't know," Jess said flatly. He could've said that, before He made people, God had to have a place for them to live. But he dreaded the turn the conversation was taking. Either Sarah was too imaginative or too literal for the usual ideas of God. Maybe not for God Himself. But for him, anyway. She asked questions that Jess had never thought of, let alone knew the answers to.

She had learned from listening to her brothers and looking at their books to read when she was three. She read everything that came into the house—and the better the motive of the writer, the worse the effect on Sarah. Temperance tracts, with their pictures of fathers in gutters while their small children cried, and abolition tracts, with their pictures of slaves with their backs laid open by whips, made her cry for hours. How could such things be? Why were they permitted?

"Dear heavenly Father," she had prayed, "I thank Thee for turning my papa's mind from drink."

Jess hoped she never made that prayer in public. It had very much the sound of a child's concern for a father whose mind might not be very permanently turned in the right direction.

There were prayers every night at bedtime, silent or spoken as the Spirit led the prayer. The Spirit frequently led Sarah to pray aloud; and her prayers at these times, Jess sometimes suspected, were intended for her family's ears as much as for God's. "Help the poor drunkard to repent" was all she needed to ask God. But her brothers were more impressed when she petitioned God to cause all who made or drank rum, brandy, gin, wine, whisky, alcohol, or arrack to repent. Jess knew just the tract this list of words had come from. But he didn't know any good way to prevent her from learning big words; or to persuade her that little words were more suitable for prayers. If they were. He was far from certain about this himself.

She had recently lost some of her interest in big words.

And in prayer, too, for that matter. Or perhaps she had prayed herself through to such a closeness to God that formal prayer was unnecessary. In the evening prayer time she no longer prayed aloud. Eliza, missing Sarah's voice on these occasions, had asked her, a fortnight or so back, "Sarah, don't thee want to pray tonight?"

"No," Sarah had answered quietly. "I don't feel prepared."

She hadn't felt prepared either, Jess had noticed, to bow her head or to close her eyes. But he said nothing. Prayer came from inside or it was meaningless. That was the whole burden of two centuries of Quaker belief, and he didn't intend to disavow it on his own hearth.

"Does thee want to see Snip and me play a game?" Sarah asked.

"Yes," Jess said. "Though we are being very bad to thy mother. She has spent the morning cooking us a good dinner and we don't come when she calls."

"I'm not hungry," Sarah said.

"I am," Jess said. "Famished."

"Appetite," Sarah told him, "is the best sauce."

"There's no such thing as too much sauce." But Jess followed Sarah and Snip up the hill to the barn. Inside the barn was a wooden box with a hinged lid which Jess used for storing grain. The lid was to keep the mice out.

"Now in this game," Sarah said, "I get in the box first. Then I call Snip, and he jumps in with me."

"What's the name of this game?" Jess asked.

"Afraid."

"Who's afraid?"

"I am."

"What's the idea, playing a game like that?"

"After I play it, then I'm not afraid. I play every day the weather's not bad. Bad weather excuses me from coming to the barn. But if I don't play it in good weather, then I'm afraid all day."

"What's thee afraid of?"

"Afraid of not being able to get in the box."

"Is Snip afraid, too?"

"Oh, no. Snip likes to get in the box. I'm there."

"The game he plays is not Afraid then, is it?"

"Oh, no. The game Snip plays is Trust. Come on, Snip, let's play Trust."

"Is thee afraid with me standing here?" Jess asked.

"Yes."

"What if I got in the box first?"

"Then I'd be no better than a dog. I have to get in alone."

"Why is thee afraid?" Jess persisted. "It's just a tight, good-smelling box. Thee could sleep there every night and come to no harm."

"It makes me afraid."

"What if I forbade thee to play this game?"

"Thee would make me disobedient."

"Let's get it over with, then. Come on, Snip," he said, for Snip was backing away. "Thee get up here ready to do thy part."

"I told thee Snip's not afraid."

Sarah looked peaked to Jess. Perhaps he hadn't taken a good look at her for a day or two. Her hand, as she reached for the lid, trembled, but Jess knew better than to try to help her. The lid was heavy, but she managed to hold it up until she was inside. She was inside, Jess supposed, about a minute, though it seemed longer to him. When she opened the lid, she was smiling. The bad part was over. Now for the fun.

"Come on, Snip."

Snip had retreated to the far side of the barn. He faced

Sarah but he looked at her as if he had never seen her
before.

"Snip, Snip, come on, Snip," Sarah urged.

Snip pushed himself against the wall.

"My being here has likely spoiled the game for Snip."
Sarah called him again.

"Shall I put him in with thee?"

"No," Sarah said. "That's not the game. Any more than
if thee put me in."

Jess held the lid open while Sarah climbed out. Snip,
as soon as Sarah was out of the box, came to her, trustful
again, but hunched over a little with shame because of
his failure. Sarah knelt and held him to her.

"Snip's about half-human now," she explained to Jess.
"He's been with me so much he gets afraid when I'm
afraid."

"He never was the bravest dog in the world."

"Papa, if Snip got sick, thee wouldn't put him out of his
misery, would thee?"

"More likely we'd sit up nights with him. Thy mother
would make a nightcap for him and serve him floating
island and cambric tea."

Sarah laughed. "I'd like to see Snip in a nightcap!"

"Thee can sew. Make him a nightcap."

"Mr. Ricketts wasn't very good to Brewster and Snap."

"Brewster and Snap were unlucky."

"Papa, carry me to the house, will thee?"

This was an unexpected request. Usually when Jess at-
tempted to carry her about she was impatient or wriggled
free. "I'm not a baby. That's Mattie."

Sarah, when Jess picked her up, held onto Snip, so that
he carried the two down the slope to the house.

"Everybody's carrying something," he told her.

"What's Snip carrying?"

"Fleas."

"Do fleas carry anything?"

"Yes."

"What?"

"Little fleas."

"Did thee ever see a little flea on a big flea?"

"No. I never did."

"I would like to see that."

Sarah, Jess noticed, was much warmer than Snip. If a child's health, like a dog's, was to be judged by coolness, Sarah was less well than Snip.

At the house he said, "Eliza, this child feels a little feverish to me."

"She always has," Eliza said, "compared with Mattie and the boys. And if she's feverish, thee hasn't helped her any keeping her away from her food. It upsets Sarah not to be regular in her eating. Thee knows that, Jess."

"I do know it. I got carried away playing with her. I'm sorry."

He was truly sorry then. But he was never afterward sorry remembering the red dress flying up the hill, the white pantalets, the crisscrossing black braids.

When he came in for supper that evening Sarah wasn't at the table. The two boys were there: spindly, wiry Josh; Labe, blunt and square. And Mattie, round as a cabbage rose.

"Where's Sarah?" he asked.

"She seemed a little dauncy this afternoon. I put her to bed early with a dish of custard."

After supper he went up with Eliza to the end of the loft that served as a bedroom for the two girls. Eliza carried a lamp. Though it wasn't yet full dark outside, the loft, with only two little windows, was dusky even at midday. Sarah lay straight on her bed, eyes closed. The dish of custard, untasted, was on the floor beside her.

"She's asleep," Eliza said. "That's a good sign."

Sarah, at the sound of her mother's voice, opened her eyes. For a second she seemed to be trying to remember something. Then she said, "How's Snip?"

"Snip?" Jess repeated, surprised. "Snip's fine as frog's hair. Thee's the one we're worried about."

"I dreamed he got in the box and wouldn't come out."

"Snip's too smart to even get *in* the box. Remember?"

"He was afraid, wasn't he?"

"I can't read a dog's mind."

Eliza put a hand on her daughter's forehead, then turned back the top quilt.

"The minute summer comes," Jess said, "this loft's an oven. I've got to figure out some way to get more windows in here before this summer's over."

"Sarah," Eliza said, "let's say our bedtime prayers."

"Thee pray for me, Mama."

"I always remember thee in my prayers."

"Will thee ask God to make me well?"

"Yes, I'll ask Him."

"Will He do it?"

"If it is His will."

Jess smelled the May-night sweetness drifting in through the loft opening, the vanilla-nutmeg scent of the uneaten custard; and over it all the odor of fever and sickness.

Eliza knelt by Sarah's bed. Jess knelt, too. "My God, my God, make this child well," he prayed, without any mention of God's will. How could he pray to a God whose will it was for a little girl to suffer? His little girl? Sarah?

Next morning Sarah had broken out. There were speckles of red on her chest and hands. Jess and Eliza both felt much relieved. Measles! Measles had been flickering around the neighborhood all spring. Sarah was not a robust child, but measles was not a fatal disease and, with care, a week should see her as good as new. The two boys had had measles before they left Ohio, and neither had been in bed for more than two days. Mattie would no doubt come down with them, too. But Mattie was sturdy enough to throw off anything short of lockjaw.

Eliza sent Jess off on two errands as soon as the morning work was over. "Get word to Dr. Sutro, in Vernon, and ask him to drive out." Measles was no life-and-death matter, but Sarah was delicate, and they could go inward, settle on the lungs, and cause lung fever. The other errand was to fetch Mrs. Sarah Leverett. Mrs. Leverett was a widow, past middle age, who helped in times of sickness. If Mattie came down, too, Eliza would need more help. Mrs. Leverett was not a woman Jess would care to have tend him on a sickbed. Even so, he supposed, she would be better than no one. She, like Eliza, was a recorded minister in the Friends Meeting, a gaunt and forbidding woman who had never been reconciled to the death of her husband, or perhaps to God's will in taking him from her. Like many another sinner, she was overeager, in Jess's opinion, to make up for her own lapses by missionary work among her neighbors. Eliza respected Mrs. Leverett's beliefs and sympathized with her troubles. And as Jess himself admitted: Who else was there?

It was getting on for evening before Jess returned to the house with Mrs. Leverett. The doctor had come and gone and had pronounced Sarah's sickness, as he and Eliza had guessed it to be, measles. Keep her in bed, bathe her body with a weak solution of lye water, and put poultices of slippery elm on the blisters that had come out around her mouth.

Mrs. Leverett had her apron out of her satchel one minute after she entered the house, and in two minutes she had taken charge of the kitchen. Supper was on the table at suppertime, the children had washed their feet and sat quietly while Mrs. Leverett dished up.

Jess found Sarah much changed after supper. The morning's pinpricks of red had become threatening splotches of a darker color. Her eyes, because of the fever, he supposed, were big and owl-bright in the half-lighted loft. He sponged her body gently with the cool lye solution. The blisters around her mouth made it difficult for her to speak. It pained Jess to hear his precise word-loving little talker have to fumble to get her words out.

"Papa, I could drink a pail of water."

He poured her a glass from the pitcher, but she was unable to swallow the mouthful she took. He dried her lips and chin.

"What did thee do with the pail?"

It was the first hint Jess had had that her mind was wandering.

"I thought the glass would do."

Next minute she was reasonable and pondering. "Yesterday I was well. This morning I was some sick. Tonight I am very sick. How will I be in the morning?"

"Better," Jess said.

"If it's God's will."

Jess wanted to contradict her, to say, "Better, much better. It is my will." How could a little girl be told one day, "God is love," and the next, "It is God's will that thee suffer"? How could a grown man believe it?

"Sing me to sleep."

"Which song?"

"'There is a river.'"

117

Jess sang:

> "There is a river flows forever
> With trees on either hand.
> There is a tree that grows forever
> In the white white sand."

Sarah was sleeping quietly when Mrs. Leverett came up the steps. Jess met her with a finger on his lips.

"Your dog puked on the kitchen floor," she whispered.

"The little one?"

"Yes."

"I'll clean it up."

"I've already cleaned it up. I thought thee might want to dose the dog."

"I'll have a look at him. Thee sit by Sarah."

Eliza was in the kitchen getting Mattie ready for bed. "Mrs. Leverett says Snip is sick," he said.

Eliza motioned to Snip stretched out under the table. "He's no sicker than usual. How's Sarah?"

"I left her asleep. Mrs. Leverett is going to sit by her. Thee get some rest while thee can. I'll take Snip out to the barn."

"Jess, what does thee think?"

"I think there is nothing we can do but wait and hope."

"And pray."

"And pray."

Outside, the night was as sweet as the day had been, fragrant, still, and warm. A big lopsided moon was in the sky. Snip's body felt hotter to Jess than it had the evening before when he had carried Snip and Sarah to the house. It was likely his imagination. With one person sick, it was easy to imagine sickness everywhere. When he put Snip down, the dog curled up in the hay in his accustomed sleeping spot.

Jess spent most of the night by Sarah's side. She was very restless, throwing off the covers and moaning. She spoke one word over and over again, very low, almost under her breath. By bending close, Jess caught it. The word was "Hush." "Hush, hush, hush," she said. To whom did she speak? To "daughter," Jess thought. Sarah was telling willful daughter to be quiet, to rest, not to disturb others.

When morning light came, Jess and Eliza, standing by her bed, saw at once that Sarah's sickness was not measles, but scarlet fever, something far more dreadful. Jess's heart pinched together with the same sick pain he had on seeing a deep wound or the burn from a scald. He was looking at something he could not bear to see, his daughter suffering, her face swollen and empurpled, her eyes half-open.

"The doctor promised to be back this morning." Eliza said this to Jess as if she understood his pain.

Jess did the morning feeding and milking as surely and deftly as ever. He was surprised at himself. How could a man who felt what he did manage these jobs as if nothing had happened? Snip was still sleeping where he had left him the night before, but when Jess set a pan of new milk before him, he sat up and lapped it. While Snip was feeding, Jess closed the barn door and latched it from the inside. When Snip finished, Jess picked him up, then settled himself on the floor, back braced against a wall with Snip in his arms. He closed his eyes and rocked Snip back and forth. His feeling at that minute was that whatever happened to Snip would happen to Sarah. If he could nurse Snip back to health, Sarah would get well, too. It was what Sarah had had in mind with all her talk about the dog and sickness the day before. He could do Sarah no good standing at her bedside. He might help Snip. He needed to prove to someone that all suffering concerned him, not his daughter's alone. It was dark in the barn, not hot yet, smelling of hay and animals. He cradled Snip as Sarah would have.

Josh's voice at the barn door roused him.

"Pa?"

"Yes, son."

"Mama wants to know where thee is."

"I'm in here. Does she need me?"

"No. She wanted to know if thee was well."

"I'm all right. Tell her I'm looking after Snip."

"Is he sick?"

"He's getting better."

He heard the doctor's trap drive in and wondered how Eliza would explain his absence. He could say to himself that he was proving that he cared for all God's creatures big and small, animal and human. But when he imagined Eliza saying that to the doctor, he heard the words as the doctor would hear them, the words of a weak-kneed fellow, not strong enough to stand at his wife's side when their child was sick. Nevertheless, he did not stir. He had even less power to move when he heard the doctor drive out. Then he might hear the doctor's verdict, "There is no hope."

Sometime after the doctor left, it came to him that Sarah might get well if he could bring himself to say, "Not my will but Thine." He was so distraught that God's test of Abraham came to his mind. This was surely a lesser test. He was not asked to kill his daughter as Abraham had been asked to kill his son. He was only asked to say what up until now he had always been willing to say, "Thy will be done." "Thy will be done on earth as it is in Heaven." He had said those words an uncounted number of times, believing that he believed. God moves in a mysterious way. Was Sarah's sickness God's way of bringing Sarah's father closer to God? He struggled for a long time with these ideas, sweating, rocking the poor dog, unaware of Snip's efforts to free himself. If someone said to him now, "Eat straw, worship cows, pray to thy little dog, and thy daughter will be cured," would he not do it?

He put Snip down, got to his knees, clasped his hands, and prayed, "Thy will be done."

Afterward he sat with his head on his knees. What kind of a prayer was that? What kind of a God wanted to hear a prayer like that? "Do what Thee wants to, God. If it is Thy pleasure, kill my child. I am willing." What kind of a God wanted worshipers like that? Wouldn't He rather hear, "Never let a child die. Mine or anyone's. If Thee wants my worship, spare children. If Thee wants my love, love little ones."

In the midst of his continuing prayer, if that was what it was, it took him some time to become aware of Mrs. Leverett's voice. When finally he recognized it, he thought for some time of not answering. He was afraid to hear the message she might be bringing.

"What is it, Mrs. Leverett?"

"Open the door, Jess." It was Mrs. Leverett's voice at its most commanding. Jess didn't think she had come to tell him that Sarah had died in a voice like that.

"Open the door, Jess, or I'll pry off the lock."

She was a big, strong-willed woman, and could likely do it.

Lame from sitting, Jess hobbled to the door. When he opened it, he was surprised to see that it was already late afternoon. He could not say a word to Mrs. Leverett. If she had bad news, he couldn't ask for it. She stared at him for a second, then said, "Jess, I've been talking to Sarah."

"Can she talk? Is she better?" He was filled with a rush of hope, a premonition that he would wake up and find that the past two days had been nothing but a terrible dream.

"No, Jess, she's not better. The doctor says she won't last the night. With the time so short, there were questions I thought should be asked."

"Questions? What kind of questions?"

"I asked her if she was saved."

"Of course she's saved."

"That wasn't what she said. She said she had no reason to think so."

"Mrs. Leverett, what does thee want me to do?"

"I want thee to come pray with her mother and me for the renewed state of her heart. Prayers offered before the throne of grace for the unsaved are heard. Her soul will be washed in the blood of Christ which cleanseth from all sin. A child's heart, even the heart of a good and obedient child, is not saved unless she accepts Christ as her saviour."

"What is thee talking about, Mrs. Leverett?"

Mrs. Leverett backed away from Jess as if he were a lunatic. "Jess, I think this sickness has unsettled thy mind. Out here with a dog when thy daughter is dying. I am talking about thy daughter's soul. Doesn't thee hope to meet her one day among the redeemed in Heaven?"

Jess started on the run for the house. Halfway there he turned around to call to Mrs. Leverett, "Stay away from my daughter."

❖

They had carried Sarah downstairs, and she lay now on the trundle bed in his and Eliza's room. Eliza sat in a low chair by her child's side. She held out her hand to Jess.

"Does *thee* want me to pray, Eliza?"

"I think thee has never stopped."

It was true. Every kind of prayer he knew: because I ask it; if it be Thy will; save her, save her.

Sarah's face was less disfigured than it had been that morning. The welts were less livid, her lips less swollen. She was sleeping or unconscious. About every three breaths, she caught her breath and held it. Then, until she breathed again, Jess held his breath. Her hands, dry and feverish, were still Sarah's hands with Sarah's life in them.

They sat by her bedside through sundown, the deepening dusk, and first starlight. In the kitchen they heard Mrs. Leverett cook supper and feed the children. Eliza went out to see the children into their beds.

Between nine and ten the pauses that came between the quick, sharp-drawn breaths became longer and longer. One pause was so long that Jess and Eliza, bending their faces close to hers, thought she had gone. But she began to breathe again, and as she did so she opened her eyes. There was no sickness in her eyes. It was any morning's awakening.

"Sarah," Jess said.

He had never expected to look into her eyes again. As he gazed, Sarah tried to say something. It was something she wanted very much to say, something she wanted them to understand, and that she thought might amuse them.

She was able to say only one understandable word: "Daughter."

Then she closed her eyes and didn't open them again. But Jess understood her word and her expression. "This is daughter," she was telling them, "who is sick and causing all this trouble, and dying. The one who stands on sewing baskets and is afraid of boxes. Not Sarah."

She died Wednesday night. They buried her Friday morning after services in the Grove Meeting House. The children of course went with Jess and Eliza.

Many were moved by the Spirit to speak at that Meeting before the burial. Sarah Leverett quoted Gospel, "Our light affliction which is but for a minute, worketh for us a far more exceeding and eternal weight of glory."

Many of the words Jess did not hear. He heard those. He did not want a weight of glory paid for by Sarah's death. He heard Sam Templin's words, "Man is born to trouble as the sparks fly upward." There was more comfort in that. Eliza was able, as she was expected to do, to read from Scriptures. She chose Psalm 103. Her voice did not break, but Jess saw tears fall onto her opened Bible as she read.

"Like as a father pitieth his children, so the Lord pitieth them that fear Him.

"For He knoweth our frame: He remembereth that we are dust.

"As for man, his days are as grass: as a flower of the field, so he flourisheth.

"For the wind passeth over it, and it is gone; and the place thereof shall know it no more.

"But the mercy of the Lord is from everlasting to everlasting upon them that fear Him."

Eliza and Jess were silent on the ride home through the May woods and fields. In the beginning of the ride the children were silent, too. As they neared home they began to squabble, and their voices were as sweet as bird song to Jess.

Neighbors had brought in many dishes of cooked food, so Eliza's suppertime duties were light. Jess thanked God that the usual suppertime chores had been left to him.

"I'll take the children out with me," he told Eliza.

They were standing hand in hand in the kitchen doorway. Eliza could not speak, but she nodded.

The three children and the two dogs walked with him to the barn. Mattie and the dogs frolicked as usual. The two boys were silent. After he had fed the animals, but before he had started milking, he stood in the barn door for a minute and tried to see Sarah once again in her red dress.

Behind him he heard Labe say, "I wish they hadn't put her in such a deep hole."

"It was only her body," Josh said.

"It was Sarah."

"Sarah is in Heaven now."

"Is she an angel?"

"Yes," Josh said. "She is an angel."

"Can she fly?"

"Yes."

"Why do you have to die to fly?" Labe asked.

"Angels fly," Josh said. "That's why."

By the time Jess had finished milking, the children were playing hide-and-go-seek. It was their usual evening game; they were playing more quietly than they ordinarily did, but they were playing. Josh had his eyes closed and was counting. Labe and Mattie were trying to find hiding places. Labe covered Mattie, huddled into a corner, with a sack. Then he, casting about for a hiding place, lifted the edge of Jess's grain-storage box. He was half in before Jess snatched him out.

"Never do that again. Does thee understand? Josh? Mattie? Does thee understand me? Never get in that feedbox again."

"We always have."

"No back talk. Never again. If that's not plain, I can make it plainer. Thee understands that, don't thee?"

Jess's outburst seemed to free the children from the heaviness of the past few days. Things were more home-like. Papa was more like Papa. Sarah was gone, but everything hadn't changed. They ran down the slope ahead of him toward the house. Halfway down Mattie stooped to pick up Snip. He was a sizable load for a two-year-old, but Mattie was sturdy. The words "Put that dog down" were in Jess's mouth, but he clamped his jaws shut, and they never came out.

On the porch Eliza awaited them with milk pans and strainer. Jess wanted to smile at her, but if he moved his mouth at all, he was afraid he might cry.

"Look, Mama," called Mattie. "Snip's my baby."

Over the heads of the children left to them, Jess and Eliza looked at each other, but were unable to speak.

Mother of Three

After Sarah's death Jess began work at once on his often postponed plan to replace the log house with one of white clapboard. It seemed to him almost providential that he hadn't built the house earlier. Without the hard, demanding—and often absorbing, too—work of getting the house built, he thought he might have been felled by grief. As it was, he would stand motionless, plane or saw in hand, minutes at a time remembering his lost child. Eliza, he knew, suffered as much as he. But she was less selfish than he, and for his sake and the children's was better able to keep up an appearance of cheerfulness.

The house was finished in six months; and it was in many ways a relief to be in rooms that had never heard Sarah's laughter or footsteps; to see steps she had never climbed and windows from which she had never waved him good-bye or welcome.

The second spring of their occupancy of the "big" house had never been springlike. Then, after months of rain, wind, and even sleet, summer arrived overnight. The white clapboard house rose like a lighthouse above the froth of leafing and blossoming orchards, above the white surf of dogwood which was cresting late in the woods lots. In the upstairs bedchamber that Jess and Eliza occupied, it was still dark as night at four-thirty in the morning. But warm, warm as day. Eliza usually awakened at five when Jess got up, and followed him downstairs only after he had started the kitchen fire and lighted the kitchen lamp.

She had been awakened by a dream, for in her mind as she came out of sleep were the words "Eliza Birdwell, mother of three." Someone had spoken these words in her dream; and in a sense they were true. She *was* the mother of three; if Sarah had lived, she would have been the mother of four. But she had never imagined herself being so characterized—"mother of three." In her own mind she had remained Eliza Birdwell, the girl (at her age, this was, of course, untrue), the wife, the Quaker minister. Had someone in her dream, identifying her to a stranger, said, "There goes Eliza Birdwell, mother of three"? She was filled with a strong desire to look at the three who had thus transformed her.

She began slowly and carefully to turn back the bedcovers. She did not want to awaken Jess, who, toiling from sunup to sundown trying to catch up with the work a wet cold spring had delayed, needed his rest. In the full dark she could not make out even his big beaked profile, let alone whether or not his eyes were closed. But his steady breathing told her he still slept.

At the first seepage of light across the window sill Jess would rear up, wide awake, and step from their bed into his pants, singing, rain or shine, summer or winter, as he hoisted galluses and buttoned buttons, "The sun is up and shining, shining; all the world is bright and gay. The face of nature smiling, smiling, glad to greet the dawn of day."

This song took the place, with Jess, of morning prayer. It *was* his morning prayer, she thought; and even in the days when he had lain ill with typhoid, if his mind wasn't wandering, he had sung that song each morning, in a sad weak whisper. Only in the mornings of Sarah's sickness and death had Jess arisen songless.

The warmth of the morning made it a luxury to walk barefooted, with no covering over her long full bedgown, out of their chamber into the hall which connected their room with the children's rooms. There were four bedchambers on the second floor: the large front room where she and Jess slept, the hired girl's room (when they had one) tucked in at the top of the kitchen stairs, and the two end chambers where the children slept.

She went to the boys' room at the north end of the hall first. She needed no light to tell her how they were sleeping. Joshua would be lying, straight as a string and not much wider than a string, on the bedrail next to the wall. He would be on his back, arms by his sides, mouth firmly closed, and long bony toes lifting the covers.

Labe would be on the outside, the middle, and a good part of Josh's inside half of the bed. Labe might be lying in any number of ways, none of which took into consideration the comfort of his bedfellow. Labe went to bed happy and distributed himself like an octopus. Legs and arms sprawled out from his pumpkin-shaped center in every which direction. He opened his mouth, breathed deeply, and was asleep at once. If he was a bother to anyone, he would be told, wouldn't he?

No, he wouldn't; not by Josh anyway. Josh needed proof of his own superiority; and lying on one-tenth of the bed, while a selfish inconsiderate brother hogged the other nine-tenths, gave him proof of this night after night. But how was it, Josh asked his mother occasionally, that people were so taken in by someone like Labe, lazy, dirty, and thoughtless? What was a boy brought up to believe that "as ye sow, so shall ye reap" to make of someone like Labe? Labe sowed nothing, just lounged around with his hair in a mat and his feet, even after he washed them at bedtime, grimy, but still he reaped a rich harvest of loving glances and friendly words.

Eliza, of course, loved both her sons equally, though both were so different from her and Jess. They were strangers, she and Jess often agreed, given to them by God to bring up. And since God had chosen them as their parents, they had to believe that, unlikely as it sometimes seemed, they, out of the whole world, were best suited to the task.

Mattie slept alone in the room that faced her brothers. Sometime, Eliza hoped, Mattie would have a sister to share her room and to take the place of the lost Sarah. Though no one would ever be really able to take beautiful Sarah's place.

Mattie was about as pretty as a weanling calf. She might grow up to make a good and handsome woman, but now she was no one's baby doll—which was undoubtedly a very good thing. Plain as she was, Mattie, as the only girl and youngest child in the house, with two brothers to wait on her, had all the airs of a beauty. She had yet to see anything she thought too good for her. She accepted her brothers' homage as natural and found fault when there were occasional lapses. Eliza could never remember being like that herself. She had been a shy, quiet, undemanding child, speaking only when spoken to and thankful for small favors.

The "mother of three"! And the three stranger to her than many a towhead who faced her on the benches at First Day Meeting! She went, marveling, still barefooted and luxuriating in the unaccustomed warmth, down the back stairs to the kitchen.

She hadn't needed a lamp to inspect faces as well known as the three upstairs. But she couldn't start breakfast in the dark. She lit the big glass-bellied, unshaded kitchen lamp. The lamp, its circle of yellow light her partner in secrecy, pleased her. She had left the kitchen in beautiful order, the table set for breakfast and every chair ranged squarely in front of a plate. The room was a joy to behold, but her nose didn't take the same pleasure in it her eyes did. First of all, no one, expecting the night to cool off, had opened the kitchen windows. And added to the smell of last night's cooking was the almost barnlike smell of the straw on the sitting-room floor. She had had the rag carpet taken off the floor yesterday and hung on the line for airing and beating. But the straw which cushioned it had been left in place, its removal a fine Seventh Day chore for the boys. There was no use tying up Jess or the hired man in a small job like taking out old straw and putting down fresh when the boys had all the strength necessary for such light work. But whew, the smell! All last winter's odors of wood smoke, frying sausages, and drying boots had been absorbed by the straw and now, with the carpet up, were filling the house all over again. Eliza opened the kitchen windows and the door to the back porch wide before she started the fire.

When the corncobs, soaked overnight in coal oil, had started the stovewood to blazing, Eliza stepped out onto the back porch. It was the time of change from night to morning. Birds were not yet singing; stars were still shining. But the dark of night was being diluted. Daylight was coming down from the eastern sky. The birds, as she stood there, began their first reluctant waking songs.

A star winked out. She held the folds of her bedgown away from her body so that she could have a morning bath in the warm air, which smelled of blossoming orchards and the sweet river water.

Jess, in his sock feet, carrying his boots, was beside her before she heard him.

"Thee got the cows milked yet, Eliza?" he asked.

Eliza lifted her bedgown to show him her bare feet. "It'll be later in the summer before they're toughened up enough to be barefoot outdoors."

"Thee planning on a barefoot summer?"

"No, thee knows not. The warm morning tempted me."

"What roused thee so early?"

"I had a dream. I was called the 'mother of three.'"

"That's pretty near a fact."

"Does thee think of thyself as the 'father of three'?"

"Father of fifteen sometimes, when the three of them get to racketing around."

Eliza said nothing. "Did it seem a comedown to thee?" Jess asked.

"A comedown? Of course not. Strange. A time I didn't know I'd reached."

"Oh, we've come to it, all right. And more than three, I hope."

The darkness was lifting now, like dregs rising instead of settling. Jess said, "I remember when first I set eyes on this hillside. The branch winding around the foot of the slope that leads to the house, and the dogwood and redbud blooming then as now."

"There wasn't any house here then to see."

"In my mind's eye I saw the house. I kept on seeing it when I went on to the plains of Illinois. I couldn't settle on that rich prairie land for the pull this slope and branch and white house had on me. Traveled all the way from Ohio through Illinois and on west of that, to come back to this stony hillside."

"I remember a letter thee sent me. 'Land that won't grow trees bigger than buggy whips and without running water is no place for us.'"

"I don't remember saying that. But I do know they're making money hand over fist out there on those prairies while we scrabble away."

"We'd neither one be happy out there on that tableland. No hill higher than a prairie dog's mound."

"We?" Jess asked, for the pleasure, Eliza knew, of hearing her say it again.

"I'm not of a turn," Eliza said, "to call things beautiful simply because they make money. Or because they're mine. If they're mine, I tend to underrate them."

"Me?" Jess asked. "Thee surely don't underrate me?"

"Yes, even thee. But this is the best homestead and the best site for a house I ever saw. If thee had chosen another place for us to live . . ."

Eliza didn't finish her sentence. Jess did. "Thee would've come with me all the same."

"Yes," Eliza agreed. "I would have."

The horses, who had heard their voices, were nickering for breakfast. Jess sat down on the wash bench to pull on his boots.

"Thee didn't have anything planned for the boys today, did thee, Jess?"

"Hauling that straw for thee. If thee can keep them at it."

"I can keep them at it," Eliza declared. "I'll be in the kitchen all morning where I can keep an eye on them every minute."

Every other minute was more like it.

The plan was for Labe to carry out one basket of the

133

soft trodden-down straw while Josh filled the second. Thus the boys would be kept apart most of the time, and the chances for horseplay, or, worse still, dogfights that could send chaff flying over an entire quarter-section, would be, Eliza hoped, lessened, if not prevented. Eliza was a planner, more so than Jess, she often thought; and she had planned the straw removal to a T. She didn't have Labe carrying out baskets and Josh filling them by chance. Josh was careful, Labe rambunctious. So she had given Labe a chance to spend his energy tramping back and forth, and Josh a chance to prove his care in filling the baskets.

Mattie she had settled in her little rocking chair in the kitchen; out of the way of Labe, who had to pass through the kitchen with his baskets of straw, and near enough the stove, where Eliza was cooking, so that she could supervise Mattie's work. Mattie was piecing her first quilt blocks, a simple four-patch of the kind Eliza herself had made at five. At seven, Mattie was beginning late; but she took to sewing like a veteran and was proud of turning four little squares into a block which would someday be part of a quilt of her very own.

At the stove Eliza was preparing food for tomorrow's First Day company dinner. Jess was like his father. He couldn't shake hands after Meeting without saying, "Won't thee come home and have dinner with us?" When the prospective guests, a family of seven, like as not, said, "Well, now, Jess, we don't want to be a burden to Eliza," Jess would turn to his wife and say, "Thee's all prepared, isn't thee, Eliza?" And knowing Jess, she would be.

On the back of the stove a large shallow pan of clabber was gradually becoming smearcase. Two sweet cakes were baking in the oven. And on the front lid of the stove Eliza was stirring with great care a large kettle of boiled custard, which, after cooling in the springhouse, would become the base for tomorrow's floating-island pudding.

All was going as planned. There was even a quiet rhythm in the work. Eliza, stirring her custard with a long wooden spoon, felt like a bandmaster, conducting her musicians. There were pleasant sounds, steady regular movements. Mattie's needle went in and out of the cloth. Labe carried his baskets with no undue stamping or jouncing. He was losing a little straw each trip, but that was to be expected. Eliza could hear from inside the sitting room the soft snurr of Josh's broom as he went about his careful gleaning. There was nothing, Eliza felt, to compare with the satisfaction of plans that worked, or the contentment a mother took in the harmonious industry of her children. And here she had, on one summer morning, the two combined.

She pushed her custard kettle gently to the back of the stove so that she could test her sweet cakes with a bent broom straw. While she was still leaning over, head in the oven and straw in a cake, Mattie screamed. Eliza was a pretty good judge of all the sounds her children could make. Mattie's scream was one of outrage rather than physical pain. Straightening and turning quickly, Eliza saw no signs of violence; only Labe, standing beside Mattie's chair, with one of her quilt blocks in his hands.

"Mama," cried Mattie, "Labe blew his nose on my quilt block."

"I didn't," Labe declared.

"What is thee doing with thy sister's quilt block?" Eliza asked.

Labe dropped the block like a hot coal. "Nothing," he said.

"He blew his nose on it," Mattie wailed.

Josh, coming to the door to see what all the ruckus was

135

about, supported his brother in a kind of backhanded way.

"Labe don't ever blow his nose on anything," he said. "He wipes it on his sleeve."

"I don't either," Labe yelled to Josh. And Mattie supported Labe. "He blew it on my quilt block!"

"Labe," Eliza ordered, "thee take that quilt block of thy sister's and wash and rinse it. Then thee hang it up to dry."

Labe grabbed up the quilt block and brought it to his mother.

"Look," he begged. "There's not a drop of snot on it."

In the doorway Josh recoiled with horror. "What a nasty word to say before thy little sister and while thy mother's cooking."

"What word?" asked Labe, genuinely puzzled.

"Thee knows," Josh told him, too nice to repeat the word himself.

Eliza knew it shouldn't, but somehow Josh's nasty-niceness grated on her more than Labe's nastiness.

"I'll take care of Labe," she told Josh tartly. To Labe himself, using the very word Josh had acted so fine-haired about, she said, "Snot or no snot, thee wash out that quilt block, Labe, and hang it up to dry. And hereafter keep thy hands off thy sister's sewing."

Thereafter there was some peace. Quiet, anyway. Labe washed and hung up the quilt block. Josh, acting put upon, both filled and carried out baskets. No straw dropped now. Mattie sewed two-inch squares of calico together like a famous needlewoman engaged in a series of French knots, feather, chain, and satin stitches. Eliza's custard had only a few lumps in it.

At ten o'clock, time to be thinking of something for dinner, she gave the children a rest from their tasks. Labe and Mattie went outside; Mattie carried her china-headed doll, Harriet Ann. Josh sat down at the kitchen table to memorize Bible verses to say in First Day school tomorrow. Eliza felt that there was likely as much show-off as piety involved in all this memory work of Josh's. But she didn't feel it was suitable for a mother, let alone a preacher, to urge a boy to slow up on Bible study. Josh could memorize about as fast as he could read, and by tomorrow, give him a chance, he'd have more to say than she and all the Elders combined. And maybe better, as well as more, she tried to console herself.

Some of her earlier pleasure in the warm morning returned. The house already smelled fresher for the removal of the straw. The vanilla pungency of sweet cakes and boiled custard filled the room. Josh said his Bible verses under his breath. An oriole, gold as sunlight amidst the furry green quince leaves, sang his low song. She went to the opened kitchen door to have a closer view of this summer world newly returned to them. This time she saw with her own eyes, as soon as did Mattie herself, what was causing Mattie to scream.

Labe, holding Harriet Ann by her long petticoats, was swinging the doll, head down, in swoops that just missed the stone well-curbing. He was being pretty careful, Eliza concluded, to miss the curbing; still, the sight could not, for a mother, as Mattie considered herself, be very reassuring. Mattie continued to scream, but Eliza, for fear any word from her might bring Harriet Ann's head a fraction of an inch too close to the stone, said nothing.

Her silence didn't save Harriet Ann. Labe, to judge by his face, was as astounded as anyone to see Harriet Ann's china head explode into bits, black curls in one direction, dimples and blue eyes in another. He let Mattie take the headless body from him without protest. Mattie, holding her mutilated child close, ran to her mother.

"Harriet Ann's dead," she said, "and Labe killed her. I hate Labe."

Labe, as serious as Mattie, but quieter, also ran to his mother. "I didn't mean to, Mama. She slipped."

"I hate thee," Mattie said. "Thee killed Harriet Ann."

"She slipped," Labe insisted.

Josh, Bible in hand, said, "Thee didn't have her in a very good place for safekeeping, swinging her by her skirts over stone, did thee, Labe?" Josh patted Harriet Ann's headless body sympathetically. "Poor little Harriet Ann."

Mattie sobbed. "I hate Labe."

Labe, half sobbing himself, said, "She slipped, Mattie, honest she did."

Josh said, "Thee had her in a good place for slipping, didn't thee, Labe?"

Eliza said, "Josh, thee go back to thy Bible reading," as sharp as if *he*, not Labe, had been the killer of Harriet Ann, the snot-blower, the troublemaker. She was sorry at once, but it was too late to make amends to Josh. Josh went back to the kitchen table, Bible in front of him, but with his eyes, black as his mother's, not on the Bible but on his mother, accusingly.

Mattie continued to sob, Labe to protest. Eliza put her arms around the two of them and led them together into the kitchen. She put Mattie in her little rocker, where she could rock and comfort her headless child. Eliza seated herself in her own kitchen rocker. Labe she pulled down onto a footstool.

With a hand on the shoulder of each, she said, "Mattie, will thee stop crying while I tell thee a story about when I was a girl?"

Mattie didn't say "yes" or "no," but her sob became a sniff.

"Thee has heard me talk of thy Uncle Will, hasn't thee? When I was just thy age and Brother Will was eleven, Will made himself a bow and arrow."

"How did he do that?" Labe asked.

That wasn't the part of the story she had intended telling, but it all came back to her so clearly and was so strong a reminder of her favorite brother's ingenuity that she told it, too.

"He made it out of an old umbrella," she said. "He took one rib and, by tying a cord to each end, bent it into a bow. Then he took another rib, sharpened one end on the grindstone, and had himself an arrow. So then he had a bow and arrow."

"What did he do with it?" Labe asked.

"That's the story I want to tell thee and Mattie. I had a pet hen, an old Plymouth Rock named Becky. I loved her more than any dog or cat."

"More than a doll?" Mattie asked.

"More than any doll, because Becky was alive. And I think Becky loved me. She let me put clothes on her. She would wear a sunbonnet. If I set her on a fence post or the upping-block, she would stay there until I came for her."

"Did she lay eggs?" asked Labe.

"I don't remember that she did. I believe she thought she was a little girl. I didn't have any sister, so Mama made me and Becky matching sunbonnets and pina-fores."

"What's a pinafore?" Mattie asked.

"We'd call it an apron now. It was kind of a dress with-out sleeves. I wore a blouse with mine, but Becky just put her wings through the armholes. She was a great big fluffy hen, and I was a skinny little girl. People even said we looked alike."

Labe and Mattie looked her over. "Thee don't look like a hen now, Mama," Mattie said.

Eliza put one arm around Labe, one around Mattie. "I feel like a mother hen sometimes, and want to take my chicks under my wings."

At the table Josh closed his Bible with such a slap that Eliza looked up at him.

"Is thee finished, Josh?"

"Yes," said Josh.

"Did thee really love Becky, Mama?" asked Mattie.

"I think I still love her. Becky was the first thing, outside my own family, I ever loved. We don't forget our first pets."

"Like Harriet Ann."

"Harriet Ann can be brought to life. All she needs is a new head. But Becky was dead forever."

"What killed her?" asked Labe, more interested in how the hen died than in what she wore or looked like.

"Will killed her," Eliza said. "He wasn't really aiming at her—just teasing me. Becky walked in front of him just as he let fly with his bow and arrow."

"Did she die right away, or did she kick around some?" Labe wanted to know.

She had kicked around some, but that wasn't a memory Eliza wanted to recall. "She died," Eliza said.

"And you blamed Uncle Will?" asked Labe, getting that point easily.

"Yes, Labe," said Eliza, and this *was* the point of her story, though a point she was intending for Mattie, not Labe. "I knew very well it was an accident. Will wasn't aiming at Becky. The arrow slipped out at the exact wrong time. And I knew it. But I told my father and mother that Will killed her on purpose, and they believed it. I've never forgiven myself for doing it."

Mattie's face was still tear-stained, but she no longer clasped Harriet Ann to her breast.

"Does thee want me to punish Labe?" Eliza asked.

"No," Mattie answered. "Thee mustn't do that. Labe didn't mean to hurt Harriet Ann."

Mattie leaned over to Labe and kissed him on the cheek. "I'm sorry I said I hated thee, Labe."

Labe squirmed but had the good sense not to pull away from forgiveness. Eliza, her arms around both children, looked up at the table to share with Josh this moment of love and reconciliation. Josh was no longer in the kitchen.

Jess came into the kitchen late for dinner, apologizing as he wiped his face on the back-porch towel.

"I got so carried away talking to thee this morning I had to work late to make up for it."

"It's just as well," Eliza said. "Dinner's only just ready."

Jess sniffed the air. "Smells like something special."

"It is," said Eliza.

Jess looked at the table. "Two places? Where are the children?"

"Upstairs. In their rooms."

"They been up to some mischief?"

"I don't know for sure."

"Then why?"

"Jess, don't badger me. They weren't good; no one could say that. But they're having bread and milk in their rooms because I couldn't bear the sight of a one of them any longer."

Jess took his place at the table without a further word. But when Eliza put a platter of fried chicken before him, he said, "I can understand the children's eating bread and milk. But why are we having fried chicken?"

"Because a chicken died," Eliza said.

Jess looked startled. "What did she die of?" he asked interestedly.

"A bow and arrow—to begin with."

"I didn't know we had any bows and arrows around here."

"We didn't until an hour or so back. Josh made himself a bow and arrow out of umbrella ribs."

"Thee don't mean Labe?"

"No, I don't mean Labe. I mean Josh."

"Josh made a bow and arrow! And shot a hen dead? Well, that's hard to believe."

"He didn't shoot it dead. He wounded it. I had to chop its head off."

"Why in the world would he do a thing like that?"

"Because he heard me tell Labe and Mattie a story about Will's killing Becky that way."

"Becky?" Jess asked.

"Thee knows about Becky."

"Well, I do for a fact. But I tend to forget her now and again."

Eliza put the mashed potatoes and gravy on the table. "Why was thee telling Labe and Mattie about Becky?"

"It's a long story," Eliza said.

Jess pulled out her chair. When she had seated herself, he said, "What's the gist of it?"

"The gist of it is, first Labe blew his nose, or acted like it, on Mattie's quilt block. Then he broke her doll—by mistake, I think. To get her to forgive him, I told her how I'd blamed Will for shooting Becky, when I knew it was an accident."

"Then Josh goes out and shoots a hen?"

"A pullet, really."

"A pullet, then. What's he want to shoot a pullet for? That don't make sense."

"It makes sense."

"Not to me."

"The bad ones—Mattie screaming she hated Labe, and Labe, at the very least, teasing Mattie—were getting all my attention. And there was poor old Josh sitting at the table all alone studying his Bible while I hugged the two bad young ones."

"Well, did thee hug him when he was bad, if that's what he wanted? Mother love?"

"By that time, Jess," Eliza said, "I had run out of mother love."

She thought maybe she had run out of love of every kind. She didn't even feel much affection for Jess.

Jess reached an arm over and encircled her shoulders.

"Thee'll feel better when thee's had something to eat," he said. He passed her the platter of browned chicken.

"It reminds me of Becky," Eliza said forlornly.

"Now, it's not Becky," Jess told her firmly. "That hen died years ago. It's a pullet who'd have ended up on the stove sooner or later anyway. Now eat."

Eliza looked at the pieces, then took the part of the breast Josh had wounded with his arrow.

Jess saw what she did, shook his head, but didn't say a word. He took his own favorite pieces, drumstick and wing, put gravy on his potatoes, and ate with relish.

After a while he said, "Thee ought to lock those three upstairs oftener."

Eliza looked up, surprised but still mournful.

Jess reached his fork over, removed the wounded breast from her plate, and replaced it with a well-browned drumstick.

"It's nice, the two of us being alone once in a while," he told her.

143

Neighbors

Enoch Miles, the Birdwells' twenty-year-old hired man, carrying two milk pails, stepped out of the white clapboard house into the cold grayness of a November morning. He paused on the slope that led up to the barn to look back over his domain. He thought of it as "his" in the way a sailor considers the ship he serves on as his. Though Enoch knew well enough he wasn't even first mate here. Jess Birdwell was the captain, and Jess's preacher wife, Eliza, was second-in-command. Nevertheless, Enoch felt a possessive pride in the Maple Grove Nursery, its buildings, livestock—and owners.

It was nothing but pure chance that had brought him to work for the Birdwells; but Enoch thought that he was the kind of a man chance looked after: gave him a couple of Quakers, peculiar as Dick's hatband in some ways, to work for, instead of some run-of-the-mill farmer who didn't know or care what was going on outside Bigger Township. Jess and Eliza took a Philadelphia paper and a journal that crossed the seas from London. Bigger Township was a dot on the map to them. Even Jennings

144

County and the whole state of Indiana were too small to hold them. They knew and talked about what was going on in Richmond, Virginia, and Charleston, South Carolina. It was an education just to listen to them, and he had listened well enough to be able to put in an oar himself sometimes. He himself was a Methodist and didn't hold with all their Quaker turn-the-other-cheek doctrines. And he sometimes wondered if, put to it, Jess and Eliza could really practice what they preached. Neither one had any overload of meekness.

The smoke from the chimney changed color as he watched. He had started a corncob-and-kindling fire in the cookstove before he left the house. Now someone— Eliza, he hoped—had added oak and pine: the last to blaze up, the first to give out heat. Enoch, who didn't always beat Jess to the barn, but should, hurried toward the two cows he had to milk, milk pails swinging.

While he milked the first cow he thought about breakfast. He hoped it would be buckwheat cakes from the stone jar of buckwheat batter that always stood, working, on the back of the stove. But Eliza prided herself on providing her household with a variety, and this might be the morning for fried bread or corn-meal mush or soda biscuits and sausage gravy.

By the time he got to the second cow, Enoch had stopped thinking about breakfast and was thinking about Eliza herself. It wasn't a nice thing, and he knew it, to think about the matrimonial arrangements of people old enough to be his parents; though at thirty and thirty-three, this wasn't actually the case with Jess and Eliza. But while he was away from home and working for them, they stood in the place of his parents. In spite of this, he let his mind, heated maybe by the pressure of his forehead against Bossy's warm flank, think what it would be like to kiss a Quaker minister lady.

Without that title, there would have been nothing to wonder about. Eliza, past thirty and with three children, was still pink-cheeked, round-faced, and black-haired. But a preacher!

The mere idea of a lady preacher was enough to make a Methodist mind boggle. He knew that Eliza didn't, like their own Reverend Godly, mount a pulpit every First Day, as the Quakers called Sunday, and preach a two-hour sermon. Nevertheless, she was a woman chosen of God; not in the same class, of course, with Biblical women like the three Marys or the Queen of Sheba, but still very special. And it always amazed him the way Jess didn't seem impressed by the fact. Gave his preacher wife a hug or a piece of his mind as freely as if she'd been some nonpreaching Methodist woman.

Jess and Eliza, when he finished milking, were out on the slope between house and barn doing what he had done earlier: admiring, in the brightening morning, their domain. And having a talk. That meant, likely, that there'd be biscuits for breakfast, something that didn't take the care of fried bread or buckwheat cakes.

Enoch set his pails down when he reached them, opening and closing his hands to simulate a numbness he didn't really feel, and waited for an opportunity to take part in the conversation.

Jess, understanding about such matters, opened the conversational door for him. "Eliza and I were talking about the Cincinnati news," he said.

Enoch, who needed more information than that to put his oar in, nodded sagely, but said nothing.

"A mob in Cincinnati," Eliza said, "caught a man who

was trying to help a slave escape and split his head open. They don't know whether he'll live or not."

"They don't own slaves in Cincinnati, do they?" Enoch asked before he thought. He knew they didn't, and asking a question like that would make Jess and Eliza think he was a complete dunderhead. "What I'd do," he went on quickly, "is march south and give every man jack south of the Mason-Dixon Line a round of musket fire."

"Thee'd hit a lot of good men that way," Jess said.

"Those that run with foxes had 'bout as well eat chickens," Enoch said.

"Not as far as the chickens are concerned," Jess told him. "Most men in the South aren't slaveholders."

"What're they doing to stop it?"

"Same as we are, I expect," Eliza said. "Working where they can, and praying for better days all the time."

Talking back to a lady preacher was almost as unthinkable to Enoch as kissing one. He picked up his milk pails and started down the slope toward the house.

When he was out of earshot, Jess said, "What work do *we* do, Eliza?"

Eliza turned to face her husband. She had to tilt her head to get a good look into his Irish-blue eyes.

"What *can* we do, Jess?"

Jess didn't reply.

"Musketry isn't the answer," she persisted.

"I never thought that for a minute."

"But thee isn't happy."

"Oh, I am, I am," Jess said. "That's the pity of it."

Enoch, looking out of the kitchen window, saw Jess and Eliza pacing down the hill toward the house as far apart and solemn as a sinful Methodist couple at a protracted meeting. The morning, which had started out so cheerfully, was already clouded over with the prospect of troubles that were none of their making.

By First Day evening the troubles that had been only a prospect to Enoch, watching Jess and Eliza come up the path, were real enough to Jess and Eliza themselves. Swan Stebeney brought them the news.

After Swan left, Eliza, who was in a rocking chair in front of a small November fire, essayed to take up rocking where she had left off when Swan arrived. She found she didn't have a rock left in her. She had as well have been sitting in a straight-backed kitchen chair. Her muscles were as stiff as bones, and her bones ached.

"Bad things go by threes," she said to Jess.

Jess, after seeing Swan to the door, was standing by the window looking out toward the pike which ran in front of their house. It was a mild evening, not yet dark. The days were already drawing in, but the trees that embowered the house had lost most of their leaves, so that the sitting room, which was in a green shade all summer, was now lit to its far corners.

Jess couldn't help smiling at his wife's inconsistency. After the first two of the "bad things," of which Swan Stebeney's visit was the third, Eliza had rebuked him, as was suitable for a Quaker minister, for calling those happenings a "coincidence." "Jess, thee does wrong to say 'coincidence.' Coincidence is hapchance. What happens in this world is by design of the Lord. And if two happenings are alike, it's the Lord's way of trying to make sure we get His message."

Jess, remembering that rebuke, couldn't help saying now, "About hapchance, Eliza, I was willing to agree with thee. But the Lord tapping out messages by threes is something else again."

Eliza had been caught mixing backwoods superstition and Gospel truth, and she knew it and would have admitted it if that had been the point. The point, as she reminded Jess, was, "This is no joking matter."

Jess had no trouble agreeing with that. "Nearer to crying than joking," he said. "And that's a fact."

He left the window and came over to stand by the hearth, facing Eliza. Hapchance or hand of God, it was strange that within twenty-four hours three events all bearing so closely on the same matter should have occurred.

The first of the three had been Sam Templin's visit the night before. "Sam, at least," Jess said, "would agree with thee."

"About threes?"

"No," Jess said. "About *his* coming being no hapchance. He's never had any trouble seeing himself as an instrument of the Lord."

"He may be," Eliza answered. Though truth to tell, she herself was able to see Sam as an instrument of the Lord only as the result of considerable prayer. Sam was one of the least-favored men, as far as looks go, she had ever laid eyes on. He was a speckle-faced, small-eyed, high-stomached fellow, and bald-headed, with his speckles extending up onto his skull as thick as mildew on spoiled clabber. When he smiled, and he did so often, his upper lip ran up to the base of his nose and stayed there in a firm pleating. None of Sam's lack of beauty mattered in the sight of the Lord, and shouldn't have mattered to her. Eliza knew this and struggled to overcome the domination of her eyes.

In addition to this un-Christian feeling about Sam Templin's looks, Eliza had to struggle with her feelings about Sam's ways. Sam was an enthusiast, filled with many laudable Quaker concerns which he tried to forward in Meeting. Eliza hoped that her disapproval of Sam's harangues had nothing to do with *her*, not Sam, being the recorded minister of the Grove Friends Meeting and the one of whom sermonizing, if any, was expected. With Sam's concerns Eliza was usually in agreement. As long as Sam had talked against slavery she was ready to say "Amen." But since the passage of the Fugitive Slave Act, Sam had come out against something more than slavery: now he was defying the law of the land. The law said that runaway slaves must be held wherever found and turned over to their owners. Eliza wasn't yet ready to set herself up against the law of the land; nor was the Grove Meeting. Though she well knew that there were some members, Sam Templin among them, who were doing just that.

She had been sitting the day before exactly where she was now when she saw Sam turn in their lane. It was around four o'clock, early quitting time for a farmer. But it was the slack season, and next day being First Day the inclination among Quakers was to stop work a little early. Jess was still busy at the barn with chores. But Eliza was in her sitting-room rocking chair, table already set in the kitchen for supper, and supper itself keeping warm in the oven. It was an in-between time of a sort that didn't happen often. In between seasons, harvest over and winter not yet settled down on the land; in between weekday labor and First Day worship, and, sweetest of all, maybe, the hour between daylight and nightfall: enough light to see by, but dusky enough for the wood fire to show up. Eliza was rocking and relishing the peace (the three children were out gathering hickory nuts), the house so quiet she could hear the kettle in the kitchen, the clock on the mantel, and the soft snurr of the fire in the grate. It was just then that Sam drove in; and that was the end of quiet.

She had hoped that whatever Sam had to say would be said to Jess at the barn. But either Sam wanted to talk to both of them or Jess thought the sitting room would be a more cheerful place than the barn to listen to Sam exhort. In any case, the two men came in.

Sam, as affable as he was ill-favored, urged Eliza not to rise.

"Don't trouble to get up, Eliza. I know it's supper-getting time and I won't keep thee more than a few short minutes. I've got a couple of newspaper clippings I'd like thee and Jess to read."

He refused a chair, trying to give the impression that, for a man staying no longer than he planned, sitting would hardly be worth his while. Standing in front of the window where the fading light was still strong enough to read by, he said, "The first piece I'd like thee to hear is from the *Carolina Advocate*, date, August 30th, 1856. It begins, '$1000 Reward.'"

Eliza knew what was coming: notice from some slave owner of a runaway. Friends circulated such clippings from Southern papers pretty regularly as proof of what was going on down there. Eliza had read many a one, and thought it her duty to do so. Whatever she did or didn't do, she wasn't going to plead ignorance for an excuse. But she didn't have the stomach this quiet evening to listen to Sam's trumpeting, "I told you so" voice proclaiming, she couldn't help thinking, his own rightness in fighting the law, more than his sympathy for the suffering of slaves.

"Let me read it, Sam," she said, holding out her hand.

"Whatever thee likes, Eliza," Sam told her. "Jess can

read the other piece while thee reads this one. It's about
the same family."

The clipping began as all such did:

Ran away from subscriber on Saturday the twenty-ninth day
of August my servant woman Daffney, about nineteen years
old, medium-sized, bright gingerbread color, has rather a down
look. When spoken to replies quickly. Brand S on inside both
legs. Recently cobbed for stealing.

Believed to be traveling with her husband, Nate, who
calls himself Nate Amboy. Nate is dark chestnut color, about
six feet high, has full suit of hair. Large scar on side of neck.
Independent in his speech.

Carrying with them a male child of one year or thereabouts,
very light color, might be called a yellow boy.

I will give the above reward for them if taken out of the
state and lodged where I can get them again. If taken in the
state of Carolina, $500 for the two, or $250 for either alone.

Perry Dade

Eliza, when she finished, didn't look up, but moved her
fingers across the paper as if they might come at facts
about Daffney and Nate more truly than her eyes. A
small item in these notices, small anyway as compared
with human ownership itself, troubled her greatly: the
identification of runaways by color. This was nothing but
a womanish quirk, maybe. She had never mentioned it
even to Jess. In the face of what colored men and women
put up with, they might laugh at her squeamishness. But
the matter-of-fact labeling of men and women by shades
of color like domestic animals: "strayed, my claybank
mare," "runaway, my brindle cow"—no, that hurt her
more than accounts of whippings. She had on more than
one occasion taken a gad to her own boys. But to call
human beings chestnuts, gingerbreads, yellows, as if skin

were more important than heart and soul, was worse than use of the rod, which could be cruel but didn't deny humanity.

Thinking about this she spoke without intending to, "Every color but black mentioned."

"Eliza," Sam said, "thee underestimates the bleaching power of the great Southern Patriarchal Institution. It beats soap and sal soda all holler."

Jess, finishing his clipping, which was longer than Eliza's, folded the paper slowly. "So it's struck Indiana," he said somberly.

"This isn't the first time, Jess," Sam said. "The news don't always get in the papers."

"What's struck?" Eliza asked.

"The marshal in Vincennes jailed the runaway couple thee's been reading about."

"Daffney and Nate? And their baby?"

"Little yellow bird didn't make it that far, Eliza," Sam said. "Ships leaving Carolina ports nowadays have to be smoked to drive out stowaways. The father and mother stuck it out. The baby suffocated."

No one said a word. The light that had lasted long enough for reading suddenly darkened and thickened. The log in the fireplace broke up in ash. The clock stroked steadily on. Eliza handed her clipping back to Sam. Jess continued to fold his. It would soon be the size of a button.

"Vincennes," Jess repeated. "That's pretty near at hand."

"Might as well be Vernon," Sam agreed.

"Are they still in jail?" Eliza asked.

"Oh, no. The owner's agent picked them up. Started south with them. Chained to the axle of his buggy."

Eliza said, "Not Daffney!"

Sam appeared to be thinking. "Eliza, Southern gentle-men take slave women into their beds sometimes. But they don't set them down on the front seats of their buggies."

"But chained," Eliza said. "Didn't they have to run to keep up?"

"When last seen they were running," Sam said.

Jess suddenly, without appearing to know what he was doing, fired his ball of newsprint into the fire. It glowed red for a second without flaring up. "How'd they come to be caught?" he asked.

"You know that big wash down south of Vincennes on the river? They were hiding there and had run out of anything to eat. Hadn't run out, actually. Didn't have anything to run out of. Daffney was half-sick, so Nate came into town to steal something. He was caught, didn't have free papers or a pass, so was put in jail."

"How did they get hold of Daffney?"

"Nate told them where she was."

"Told them?" Eliza asked, shocked.

"He had some persuasion. Besides, his wife was going to starve to death, if she didn't freeze first, laying out there in the wash."

"How did they dream they could get all the way to Canada?"

"Slaves do it all the time. And Nate and Daffney had gotten more than halfway there before they were caught. And they wouldn't have been caught if they'd known to stop at my place."

Eliza had heard stories, but had never known for sure. Now she asked outright. "Sam, does thee hide runaways at thy place?"

"I don't, because it's not safe—for them. I'm watched. I'm a conductor. I go down into Kentucky sometimes. I meet the packet at Madison. Sometimes Cincinnati. I keep a pair of fast horses and a closed carriage always ready to take runaways to the next station. If I'd known about Nate and Daffney, I could've saved them. I could've picked them up at night, taken them to a hiding place where underground people would've cared for them and fed them. Then they would have passed them on to the next station."

Eliza said, "What thee does is against the law, isn't it, Sam?"

"It is. Same as if I took some man's abused runaway horse and hid it, so he couldn't find it. They'd call that horse-stealing. Even though I never worked the horse a lick, never made a cent of money out of it, did nothing but care for it and feed it out of downright goodheartedness. But the law would call that horse-stealing. And the South and the law they've got passed call helping runaway slaves 'nigger-stealing.' That's where the law and I part company. I can't see treating human beings as horses. Less good than horses. The law takes care of horse abuse. No, I'll choose jail any day if I can keep folks like those two from being chained to buggies and headed south."

Eliza said, "Sam, I'm not afraid of jail."

"What is it thee's afraid of, then, Eliza?"

It was hard to put into words. She was afraid of setting herself up to know more than the lawmakers of her country. She was afraid of spiritual pride. The Friends Meetings in Indiana disowned members who preached abolition. She believed in the wisdom and godliness of the Elders. If she set herself up in opposition to them, Grove Meeting would have to join those other Meetings disowned and cut off from the main body of Quakerdom and practice their own unsanctioned brand of religion.

And be outlawed as lawbreakers by their country, too.

"I can't set myself up as being holier than Yearly Meeting, Sam. I can't claim to be wiser than the Congress of the United States."

"Oh, pshaw, Eliza," Sam said. "That's the way Friends got their start. Set themselves up as holier than the Church of England and defied English law when it said they wasn't. Thee knows that. They broke laws left and right. Wouldn't pay tithes. Wouldn't take oaths. Wouldn't be married by the church. Wouldn't fight. Wouldn't take their hats off to any man. And thee worries about helping a runaway who's had his back laid open by a whip. There's no call for thee to be so meechin', Eliza."

The children came into the kitchen just then with their bags of nuts. Eliza called to them that supper was in the oven and to feed themselves. She didn't ask Sam to have supper with them because, without appetite herself, it was hard for her to think of anyone else (except children) as being in any mood to relish food. One of the children, Josh likely, had lit a lamp in the kitchen. They needed one in the sitting room, but darkness suited her frame of mind better than light.

Sam moved to the door. "I'm keeping thee from thy supper, Eliza. I'd better be on my way."

Jess stood. He was less burly than Sam but half a head higher. "Before thee goes, Sam, there's something I've had on my mind to say to thee for some time. I don't have Eliza's responsibilities. I'm no minister, and where I go the flock don't have to follow. I can break the country's laws and defy Yearly Meeting in a way she can't. For some time I've been convinced that if I thought slave owning was wrong, it was wrong for me not to do something to help put a stop to it."

"What did thee have in mind, Jess?"

"I don't know. That's what I wanted to ask thee."

"Want to buy some stock in the underground?"

"Make a contribution? I can do more than that. I'm not going to ask Eliza to put up runaways here. She's uneasy in her mind about the rights of the matter. But hearing thee talk's set me to wondering about conductoring. I've got good horses—and a couple of fast ones. I've got stout wagons and carriages. I know the country clear over into Kentucky like the palm of my hand from delivering nursery stock. Thee knows better than I do what kind of help's needed, and I'll abide by thy decision. But I'm volunteering."

Except for a slice of light coming into the sitting room from the partly closed kitchen door and the faint glow of embers in the grate, the room was in darkness now. Eliza heard rather than saw Sam pat Jess on the shoulder.

"Jess, thee's a born conductor. I've thought so for a long time. The first of the week, we'll talk about this. I don't want to keep Eliza from her supper work."

Jess saw Sam out the kitchen door, then came back to Eliza, still sitting alone in the dark. "Best recruit the fire, hadn't I, Eliza?" he asked, willing for advice in matters that didn't count.

"Thee do what thee thinks best," Eliza said.

Jess threw on some logs, and the fire blazed up, sending long prongs of light across the rag-carpeted floor.

"I didn't have any choice, Eliza, feeling the way I do."

"There's a man down in Georgia, Jess, who's been in jail seven years for trying to help a slave escape."

"That's where he belongs, if he's against slavery."

Eliza turned sharply toward Jess as if taking a long last look at him.

"I don't plan going to Georgia," he said.

"The law's the same in Kentucky."

"I know my way around Kentucky pretty well."

"Jess, I believe thee relishes the idea of a set-to with agents. Then thee whipping up thy horses and leaving the Southerners to eat thy dust."

"If I have a set-to, that's what I'll relish."

"It's the next thing to fighting."

"Now, Eliza, thee knows better than that. Fighting's to kill. This is to save life."

"Jess, don't it seem strange to thee that we should know what's right and everyone else be wrong?" When Jess didn't answer, she said, "How could the country and all its lawyers and lawmakers—the president, even—be so wrong?"

"That's a question I often ask myself, Eliza."

"And the Meeting? The Meeting is against this, too."

"The Meeting gets what light it has from people, Eliza. That's all it is. Its members. And its members are people. As times change it needs more light, and the only place it can get it is from its members."

Eliza said dryly, "Thee feels thee has some light to shed, Jess?"

Jess chuckled a little at that. "I know I'm an unlikely source, Eliza, and I don't claim to be doing anything now but reflecting the light Sam shed. But he shed some, and I plan to stand in it as square as I can manage."

That ended for Eliza the matter of Jess's being a conductor on the underground. He had received some light she hadn't; and even if he ended up chained to the stone floor of some Georgia prison, that would be better for him than staying home against his convictions because of his wife's doubts and fears.

It was well on into the night before Eliza again spoke to Jess about Sam's visit. It seemed to her that she had been awake for a long time. It also seemed that she might just have awakened from a dream of being awake. She felt neither sleepy nor sleepless. It was a clear night of cloudless skies and star shine. A light wind was blowing, and through the windows of their upstairs chamber she could see the interlaced branches of the leafless maple and Juneberry trees moving together silently in a giant spider-web pattern. She didn't make a sound, didn't, she thought, alter her breathing; looked and pondered was all she did, she believed. But Jess knew she was awake and spoke as though answering a question she had asked. "I didn't have any other choice, Eliza."

She accepted that and slept. When next she awakened the wind had died down and the thermometer was falling. In the growing frost, clapboards were creaking. The windows in their unheated bedchamber were closed, but enough air seeped around their frames to tell Eliza that there would be a skim of ice on the horse trough by morning. There was a cold rim of air under her edge of the covers, and Eliza moved nearer to the unfailing warmth of Jess's big body.

"Jess?" she asked.

"Yes, Eliza."

"What does cobbed mean?"

"Where'd thee hear that?"

"I read it. That notice about the runaways. It said Daffney'd been cobbed."

"Cobbed is belabored with a wooden paddle."

"Why would a slave owner admit to a thing like that in the public print?"

"He wasn't writing for us. Cobbing's nothing out of the way down there. And since the poor girl like as not was too blistered to sit, it was a way of identifying her."

There was one more thing Eliza had to say before she could sleep.

"Jess, how could they keep quiet while their baby was dying?"

"Likely they didn't know it was dying."

"Maybe they did. Maybe they knew it and said to themselves, 'Better dead than a slave.'"

Jess put his arm under Eliza's head.

"Heard it choking," Eliza went on, "and let it die rather than all of them come out, get caught, and be sent back to what they'd run away from."

"Go to sleep, Eliza."

"I've heard colored people love their children more than we do even."

"That feeling's about the same, world over, I'd judge."

"I wonder where they are tonight?"

"Go to sleep, Eliza."

When they headed for Meeting the morning after Sam's visit, the surrey left tracks in the hoarfrost on the dead grass by the carriage house where they turned around. The horses, dapple-gray Diamond and coal-black Dandy, had resisted having the cold bits put into their mouths, and they still breathed plumes of smoke.

It was the first day Josh and Labe hadn't complained about their long underwear; and the three children snuggled closely together on the back seat without their usual bickering as to who had more than his rightful share of space.

Eliza loved First Day worship, and this prelude to it of the family together, riding in harmony, well-dressed and clean after the night before's bathing, was a part of the pleasure. She looked forward all week to the hour of silence in the Meeting House. At that time, in the general silence, all weekday frets excluded from their minds, an exultation clear as light, fresh as bells, filled her. It was an experiencing, she never doubted, of the presence of God; and once experienced could never be forgone on First Day without a sense of emptiness and deprivation.

The Meeting House was filled, men and boys on one side, girls and women on the other; Eliza and the Elders on benches at the front. All of the common places of seating arrangements, of the plain walnut pews and plain white walls, of drab clothing and coal-scuttle bonnets and worn Bibles pleased Eliza because they were what she was accustomed to leave behind when she went during the silence of worship into the presence of God: they were the last things she saw, the shore line from which she launched into the everlasting.

Silence did not continuously prevail for the hour of worship. Out of it revelations came to some worshipers: questions, testimonies, prayers, and exhortations to others. Sam was an exhorter. Alone, Sam may have sought God in silence. If so, he used Meetings as a place to make known what in silence he had learned of God's will. It was God's will, according to Sam, that the Grove Meeting take up the fight against slavery. God wanted the Grove Meeting to oppose slavery by "underground or overground," "by hook or crook," by "the legal if possible, but the illegal if necessary."

Sam wasn't at Meeting this morning, and Eliza couldn't suppress the relief she felt when she saw that he was absent. She had spent a sleepless night thinking of that poor couple headed southward and she longed for the release from those thoughts that silent worship would bring.

Eliza herself was the one who, by bowing her head, gave the signal that the meeting for worship had begun. Usually no one, no matter how deep his concern or pressing his insight, broke the silence that followed for at least fifteen minutes. This morning, no sooner had Eliza bowed her head than John Shelby, Patriarch of the Meeting, rose to his feet.

"Friends," he said, "I cannot delay my report to you of the action taken by the Green Plains Meeting."

John Shelby's voice was Southern, even by southern Indiana standards, for he had not left South Carolina until he was a middle-aged man. It was a voice suited in its softness and slowness to a recital of sorrowful happenings; not the voice of a man easily angered, or of a man, once his mind was made up, who backed down easily. He did not speak often in Meeting, and Eliza, disappointed as she was to lose her time of silence, listened attentively.

"I have here," John Shelby said, lifting his hand, "a letter from a friend in Clark County. A week ago the Green Plains Yearly Meeting adopted a resolution condemning the Fugitive Slave Law. Our friends in Green Plains declare that they will continue to aid escaping Negroes as they have done in the past. They declare that they will continue to comfort the enslaved and to do all in their power to help them break free of the chains that bind them. And they say that they will do so in defiance of all the enactments of all the governments on earth. They say that if it really be a constitutional obligation that all that live under this government shall be kidnappers and slave catchers for Southern tyrants, that they go for revolution. The means to be in keeping with God's will."

Old John Shelby lowered the sheet of paper from which he had been reading, and Eliza was glad to have it out of sight. The paper, while Friend Shelby held it, had trembled like a poplar leaf. John Shelby was old but not infirm. What that trembling had shown was the state of John Shelby's emotions.

"Friends," he went on, "as most of you know, I left South Carolina twenty years ago with my slaves so that they could be freed from slavery and I could be freed from slave keeping. I will not be overtaken by it once again here in the free state of Indiana. If slave catching is what my government requires of me, I will have to turn my back on my government, for I have already turned my back on slavery. If this Meeting continues to support the law, then I must transfer my membership to Green Plains. I do not 'go for revolution,' but I will accept it as the lesser of two evils if I am required by my government to help men forfeit their souls by enslaving other men."

Moses Hiatt, a Quaker of the old school, rose when John Shelby sat down. "The world is filled with much that is sinful," he said. "Many people suffer unjustly. Nevertheless, this is a Meeting for worship. We are not met here to discuss the constitutionality of congressional acts."

Maria Stout, a young matron, her four sons sitting in order so that the flat brims of their hats formed the descending steps of a stair, was on her feet before John Shelby's carefully bending knees had let him touch the bench he had been sitting on.

"By our acts," she said, "we worship God. This includes congressional acts."

That was the end on that November morning of silent worship in the Grove Meeting House. Eliza was not sure whether it was not also the end of worship, silent or spoken. In any case, she herself did not recover the First Day calm she had anticipated all week until nearly nightfall. Now in her rocking chair, soothed by the rhythm of its gentle up-and-down, by gathering darkness, by the fire's rosy diligence she was beginning to recover what she had lost in that morning's contention at Meeting. And it was just then that the third of the bad things "that go by threes" occurred. Sam with his clipping had been the first. John Shelby with his news of the action taken by the Green Plains Meeting was second. Now Swan Stebeney arriving with his message from Sam was the third.

Swan Stebeney was a Negro, a neighbor of Sam's and a farmer. The bleaching power of the Southern Patriarchal Institution had not worked on Swan. Here was a man, Eliza thought, when Jess brought Swan into the sitting room, who couldn't have been advertised, if he had been a runaway, as being of any shade of chestnut, coffee, or gingerbread. Swan was black. Eliza had heard Swan called "black as the ace of spades." An ace of spades was something Eliza had never seen, but it obviously was, if Swan was anything to go by, something pretty dark indeed.

There had been times in the past when Eliza hated to see Swan and Jess get together. They were two of a kind: horse lovers, music lovers, fruit growers, talkers. And when they got together their conversations were long-drawn-out. Eliza had spent many an hour waiting in the buggy at Stebeney's for Jess, who on leaving her had said, "I won't be gone but a minute." Neither she nor Swan's wife, Susan, would make things easy for Jess and Swan by visiting each other while the two men talked. The men would then have excused themselves by saying, "We knew you women had a lot to talk about." So Eliza would sit in the buggy listening to Swan and Jess, who were both jokesters as well as talkers, laughing at each other's witticisms out in the barn while Susan went on with her work in the house.

But this First Day afternoon, not yet knowing the purpose of his call, she was glad to see Swan. She needed to hear someone laugh, and if he and Jess could tickle each other's funny bones, she'd be the last one to begrudge them the pleasure.

"Good afternoon, Eliza," Swan said in a voice which, if you had your eyes closed, you would believe to be John Shelby's. Swan took after Shelby in a good many ways, which was not surprising considering that he had been raised in the Shelby household and had been brought to Indiana twenty years ago as a boy of fifteen by the Shelbys.

"Swan Stebeney," Jess used to say, "has all a Southern gentleman's virtues and none of his faults."

Eliza didn't know about that—and doubted Jess did either—though she would be the first to admit that Swan Stebeney could give most Hoosier farmers lessons in parlor manners. Eliza felt herself respected as a woman and honored as a preacher by the men of the neighborhood. But when Swan Stebeney lifted his hat and bowed, she got an inkling of how Southern men, rascals though they might be in every other way, made their women feel with their politeness.

"Well, Swan," Jess said, "I'm glad to see thee. Have a chair. I hope all's well with thee and Susan."

"Nothing wrong with Susan or me," Swan said. "But Sam's in bed sick. That's why I'm here."

"Sick?" Jess asked. "He was here not more than twenty-four hours ago, rambunctious as usual."

"He was trying to hold up," Swan said. "But Sam's been feeling dauncy the past week. When he got home from your place last night, he had to give in."

"Nothing serious, I hope," Jess said.

"At his age it could be."

Jess and Swan, Eliza thought, those two conversationalists, could spend an hour on Sam's sickness and never name it.

"What's the matter with Sam?" she asked.

Given a direct question, Swan could come up with a direct answer. "Sam's down with the mumps," he said.

Now Swan knew as well as anyone else that the idea of Sam Templin swelled up with the mumps like any twelve-year-old, and maybe with a bandanna tied around his swollen jaws, was laughable. But Swan never cracked a smile, and Eliza respected him for it. If Sam had broken his leg or even come down with the measles, she would have been properly sympathetic. But for a paunchy over-forty-year-old like Sam to swell up with the mumps was ridiculous. Both her boys had been finished with the mumps by the age of eight.

"Doc Henning says Sam's not to put a foot out of bed for a week. Mumps can take a bad turn with a man Sam's age." Swan was far too delicate-minded to say what everyone knew: that mumps in a grown man who didn't take care of himself could "descend."

"Only thing to do," Jess agreed. "Mumps are nothing to trifle with."

"I'm here with a message from Sam," Swan said. "He said you and him had a talk yesterday."

Eliza's heart sank. There was more to come, and on the subject she dreaded.

"Sam's expected to meet the Louisville packet in Cincinnati Wednesday afternoon. It's plain to see he'll never be able to do it. He said you told him you'd like to give him a hand now and then with the work he's doing."

166

"I did," Jess said. "The truth is, though, I had no idea anything would be coming up this soon."

"No more did Sam. It was the furtherest thing from his mind. He said to let you know that. He no more expected to swell up with mumps than he did to cut teeth. But mumps is what it turns out he has, and there's going to be two disappointed passengers in Cincinnati Wednesday if they're not met."

"Sam told me thee does some driving for him on occasion?" Jess said, questioningly.

"I do. But I'm not the right color for this occasion."

"What's your color got to do with it?"

Swan looked at Jess humorously, or as humorously as he could under the circumstances. "Just about everything." Then he amended that. "It's got more than usual to do with this trip. Color and shades of color. Mine, yours, the couple that's coming, the woman's father, her father's wife's color. If we'd all been the same color, Sam wouldn't have been making this trip at all."

"How do you know so much about this couple?" Eliza asked.

"Sam's the one who knows. And he knows because he's got a friend in Louisville, a Mr. Wistar Jones, who puts the runaways on the packet for Cincinnati at Louisville. Mr. Wistar Jones wrote Sam who was coming and when. And Sam told me to tell you. You've got to know a good deal about them before you can help them."

Eliza didn't understand how it was possible to listen to a conversation in two such different ways: sometimes as if to news she'd been waiting for half a lifetime; then, turning away from what she heard, as if from something she'd spent half a lifetime trying to avoid. What she heard was not new. But hearing about it with the persons named, and with those names ones Jess would be saying in two days' time, if he accepted the undertaking Sam was proposing, took the happening out of some distant slave state and set it down on a First Day evening by her own sitting-room fire.

The couple Wistar Jones was putting on the steamer at Louisville were young and married—in the only way slaves could be married in the South: they lived together. The woman, her name was Lily—oh, all these slave girls, Eliza thought, named after flowers by their poor owned mothers, Daffneys and Roses and Violets and Lilys—the woman, Lily, was white. Or as near, Swan said, "as makes no difference." She was the daughter of her owner, and her owner, on remarrying, had been told by his new wife that she found the sight of offspring of his by slaves offensive. Newly married and biddable, the father had sold such offspring, Lily among them. Lily had been sent with a coffle of slaves to Louisville, there to await passage on a steamer making downstream for New Orleans. But in Louisville, Lily's husband, Burk, runaway from *his* master, had spirited Lily out of the coffle and had taken her and himself to an address known to runaways: that of Wistar Jones. There, for a month, Mr. Wistar Jones had hidden them. Now the agents had given up searching for them and gone home; and Mr. Jones had booked a stateroom for them on the *Southern Queen* for Wednesday.

While Eliza wondered how parents could sell their own children (she understood somewhat better how a master could sleep with his slave girl), Jess was wondering about practical matters.

"How does Jones get runaway slaves into staterooms on boats like the *Southern Queen?*"

"It's done all the time," Swan said. "They don't smoke the boats at Louisville. There's a lot of hubbub when a boat comes in and leaves. A lot of baggage is carried on.

A lot of freight. Slaves do the carrying, and some that come on stay on. But this case is easier than most. Lily can pass for white. She's been outfitted in fine clothes by Mrs. Jones. She'll be wearing a veil, in case anybody remembers her description from the runaway notices, so that her face can't be seen too plain. She'll have a slave, carrying her trunks and bags, her husband. Since Burk ran away he's grown a beard and he's had his hair and beard stroked with white paint. He looks fifty now, not thirty. Lily will have the key to her stateroom when she goes on board. She'll open her door, and Burk will come and go depositing her luggage. He'll come and go into and out of the room. Nobody'll notice that finally he does not come out. Lily'll then lock the door and keep it locked until the boat reaches Cincinnati."

"Well, that gets them on," Jess agreed, "if they're lucky. How do I get them off?"

"Your part's easy," Swan said.

Jess laughed.

"Easy compared with what Mr. Jones has done," Swan explained.

"And with what Burk and Lily will have done," Eliza put in.

Jess and Swan both gave her surprised looks. "Thee's right, Eliza," Jess agreed. "But easy or not, I'll need to know what to do."

"First of all," Swan said, "get there a day early. These Southern boats don't keep to any schedule as we know it. Slaves do the work, and to a slave tomorrow's just as good as today and more than likely better. Get there a day early and be prepared to stay a day late. Go on board when there's the most coming and going. Burk and Lily will be in stateroom seventy-four. Knock on the door four times and say, 'Lily.' Lily will unlock the door, step out, and take your arm. You start yelling orders to Burk. 'Step lively. Watch what you're doing. Mind that trunk, you black rascal.' Then with the young lady on your arm, and Burk doing the carrying, you go to your carriage. You and the young lady will sit on the back seat. Burk will do the driving."

Jess said, "A Quaker with a slave for a driver and a young lady in fashionable finery for a companion will cause some attention."

"I forgot to mention that," Swan said. "Thee won't be a Quaker in Cincinnati on Wednesday, Jess."

Quaker talk tickled Swan, and sometimes when he was with Jess and Eliza he dropped into it without knowing it.

"What's to change me?" Jess asked. "Between now and Wednesday. Two days."

"Clothes," Swan told him. "Sam said, 'Tell Jess he can't go meet that boat in Quaker garb.' "

"Quaker garb's all I've got."

"How's Jess supposed to look?" Eliza asked. "If he's not a Quaker."

Swan rubbed his big jaw. "Sam didn't say. But since he's meeting a young lady of fashion, I reckon he should look like a man of fashion."

Jess laughed again. "Something easier said than done."

"Enoch," said Eliza. "Borrow from Enoch."

"Your hired man?" Swan asked.

"He's Jess's size," Eliza said. "He'd loan Jess an outfit."

Swan was doubtful. "This young lady, the way Mrs. Jones is dressing her, wouldn't be met by a hired man."

"Thee's never seen Enoch dressed up?" Jess said.

"Not that I remember."

"Thee hasn't seen him then."

"Dressed up," Eliza explained, "Enoch looks more like a

senator than a hired man. He'd be proud to loan Jess his clothes."

Jess said, "I don't misdoubt that Enoch will loan me an outfit. Whether it'll transform me into a man of fashion's another question. But, Eliza, does thee know what thee's advocating?"

"Lawbreaking," Eliza said.

"I thought thee was against that."

"I am. But thee's going, isn't thee?"

"I don't see how I can say no."

"That's what I thought. Since thee's going, I'd like to have thee come back alive. And that young couple, too."

But after Swan left, with word for Sam that Jess would make the trip in his place, Eliza sat unmoving, gazing into the dying fire. Lamps should have been lit long ago. Upstairs, the children were racketing around with bedtime play in the attic. Enoch came into the kitchen, hungry after a buggy ride way out Rush Branch way to visit his girl. Ordinarily Eliza would have gone to the kitchen to rustle up something for his supper. Now she told herself he wouldn't starve without her help and sat on, not even calling out to him what was left over and available.

Jess put some corncobs and a couple of new logs on the coals and coaxed a fire back into being. Eliza was sorry to see it blaze up. It asked for a cheerfulness she didn't have. So long as Swan had been there and the trip to Cincinnati had been nothing but talk, something to plan for, like a pie supper or a Quarterly Meeting—what time to go, what to wear, how many knocks on the door—she had been able to plan with the men. But with Swan gone, the talk finished, she and Jess alone together, the meaning of the plans made settled heavily on her heart. The Meeting over at Green Plains could say, "We go for revolution," but she had as well face it: revolt had been left out of her make-up. She wasn't ready to see Burk and Lily chained to a buggy axle and she was ready to do what was necessary to see they weren't. But if "revolt" was the right word to name her acts, someone else would have to say it. She couldn't. She named herself by what she was for, not what she was against.

There was only one thing she was sure about. Jess had to do what he thought was right. She knew well enough what he risked. Over in Cincinnati persons who had done no more than preach abolition, not practice it, had been shot at, pelted with rotten eggs and tomatoes, tarred, feathered, and ridden on a rail out of town. If Jess was caught, a pair of slaves in his carriage, eggs and tomatoes and feathers would be nothing but love pats compared with what he'd get.

"Bad things go by threes," she said once again to Jess.

Nothing had improved by next morning. She was in the kitchen stirring up a boiler full of white clothes before washing when Enoch came down the back stairs into the kitchen.

"Mrs. Birdwell," he said, "Jess wants you to come have a look at him."

Eliza's first thought was that Jess was ailing, coming down with the mumps like Sam Templin and wanting her to examine his jaws for swellings.

"Is he sick?"

"No, no. Nothing's wrong with Jess's health. He just wants you to see him. You won't hardly know him," Enoch warned her.

Eliza dried her hands on her apron and followed Enoch up the steep stairs to the upstairs room. Enoch led the way to her and Jess's bedchamber, opened the door, and said proudly, "Well, Mrs. Birdwell, what did I tell you?"

Enoch was right. She would hardly have known Jess. He was turning from left to right, head high and tail over the dashboard, as he himself would have said; and was, Eliza thought herself, as proud as a dog with two tails. She also thought, but didn't say, that it didn't take much to bring out a streak of worldliness in Jess. He was wearing Enoch's clothes like a peacock that feels he has too long been disguised as a turkey buzzard.

"Stand still," Eliza said. She was obliged to pass judgment on how he looked, but not to watch his preening.

Enoch's taste in clothes, while jaunty, was also rich. He liked strong colors, but also good fabrics. Jess was enough heavier than Enoch to give Enoch's suit a tight fit; the bulge of his calves and the taper of his body from shoulders to waist showed as they never did in Quaker garb. Eliza knew Jess too well to think of him as a disembodied spirit. But neither was she accustomed to being reminded of this fact by the clothes he wore.

"Fine as frog's hair," Enoch said admiringly.

The cravat Jess wore was of silk in Roman stripes, enough material in it to cover a lady's bonnet. His collar had outspreading starched white wings, and Enoch had lent Jess his flashy gold watch chain. Jess's stomach was too flat to provide the chain the curve it deserved, but Jess, thumbs in his vest pockets, was giving it what prominence he could.

"Nobody would ever believe there was a Quaker inside that outfit," Enoch declared.

"I half doubt it myself," Eliza agreed.

"Eliza," Jess protested, "thee's the one suggested this."

"I never thought thee'd *enjoy* it," Eliza said.

"No reason not to relish a little play-acting for a good cause," Jess said.

"Play-acting!" Eliza exclaimed. "One thing leads to another."

Jess took his thumbs out of his pockets and came over to Eliza. "Say the word, Eliza, and I'll wear my own clothes to Cincinnati."

"No, no, Jess. This is just what thee needs. It looks fine. It becomes thee. But seeing thee in it, I can't put it out of my mind how much our great-grandfathers suffered for the right to put off such clothes and dress plain. And here we are going back to what they suffered to be shut of."

"We're going back to exactly what they believed," Jess answered sternly. "We're dressing whatever way we figure'll do the most good. That's all they were doing. Our great-grandfathers weren't settling on some uniform Quakers were to wear like an army of soldiers till kingdom come. They put on plain clothes to save themselves, and anybody who cared to join them, from a slavery to fashion. It was a kind of peculiar garb they chose, but it served the purpose. This is a kind of peculiar garb, if thee'll forgive me for saying so, Enoch. But it will serve the day's purpose."

"It's acting a lie," Eliza insisted mournfully.

"It's not," Jess disagreed flatly. "Being a Quaker is more than wearing a certain kind of clothes, and folks ought to know that. For those that don't, this may open their eyes."

Jess took Eliza by the shoulders. "I'll do what thee says, Eliza. I've never misdoubted but that thee comes a lot nearer knowing right from wrong than me. But the right and wrong here's not in what I wear; it's in choosing what's best calculated to save a man and a woman from being taken back into slavery."

"Save them," Eliza said resolutely, "if thee can."

Then she added, speaking slowly and somewhat shame-facedly, for jesting never came easily to her, even on light subjects, "But try to remember, Jess, thee's a sheep in wolf's clothing."

Jess laughed, dropping his hands from Eliza's shoulders to her waist. "This is the first, and I hope the last, time, Eliza, thee's ever going to be kissed by a man of fashion. Best make the most of it."

Enoch didn't suppose she would, Monday morning and the wash already on. But he was gentlemanly enough to tiptoe out of the room.

Jess had driven down the graveled driveway under the arched limbs of the leafless maples wearing his own clothes.

"I'll change in Madison," he told Eliza. "Too many people between here and Madison know me. No use rousing up the curiosity of the countryside any sooner than necessary."

Eliza regained some composure seeing him leave looking like himself instead of some worldly stranger. But it was disturbing to see him drive an empty carriage out onto the pike. Jess, alone, used the two-wheeled cart for quick business trips into Vernon; the buggy on more dignified occasions. When he delivered nursery stock, he took the spring wagon. The carriage was the vehicle for family travel, the three children on the back seat, she and Jess together up front. Jess was wearing his First Day clothes, and Eliza couldn't help thinking he looked like a man bound for a funeral and planning to pick up his mourners elsewhere. It was a foolish thought, and she tried to put it out of her mind. But a man driving away from his home in the family carriage, his carriage empty, was a mournful sight. What had gone wrong?

The weather was miserable for waiting. Overcast without rain, warmish without sun, useless flurries of breeze with no more leaves to fall. It was weather to mark time in, a hollow gray empty space, mists rising off the Muscatatuck, and crows listless among the ragged corn shocks. November in Indiana was capable of weather that could keep you thinking: sleet, wind, rain, snow; even out-of-season twisters. Eliza, for her own sake, would have welcomed all. Her mind would have been occupied with keeping the stock fed, the house weather-tight, the fires up. As it was, she had plenty of time for thinking: Where is he now? Where are they now? Did they meet as planned? Will Jess get back safe?

With Jess gone, everything slowed down. The weather stood still. The cows gave less milk. The hens slacked off in their laying. When Josh and Labe brought in a half-dozen eggs fewer than usual, Eliza was short with them. "The minute thy father leaves, thee starts scamping thy work. With him gone, thee should do more, not less."

She made Josh cry. Labe, with a less tender conscience, was sassy. "Can thee work miracles, Ma? Put the eggs in empty nests?" For this she boxed Labe's ears. Then he, too, cried. Mattie, seeing her two brothers in disgrace, put on airs as the household's one good child. This irritated Eliza even further.

Enoch, in the midst of all the strife, tried to take Eliza's mind off Jess's absence and her children's misbehavior by imitating Jess conversationally. The only likeness Eliza could see was in quantity. Jess was a talker, but Enoch was downright long-winded. At noon on Fourth Day, deciding that she had been rude to Enoch, whose only sin had consisted of trying to keep her spirits up, she cooked one of Enoch's favorite meals: beans with dumplings, a sweet cake with a boiled custard to pour over it.

Enoch repaid her for her kindness by talking about the subject he supposed was uppermost in her mind: Jess and his whereabouts.

"We ought to see Jess driving in any time now," he said.

"The *Southern Queen's* not due until today," she reminded him. "And Swan said not to count on any definite time. It could get in a day or two early or a day or two late."

"Them Southerners are not very reliable people."

"Swan said the cause was slave labor."

"Niggers can't be depended on either."

"Don't call them that."

"Darkies," Enoch amended. "What I'd like to see," he said, trying to get off a touchy subject, "is Jess walking the streets of Cincinnati in that suit of mine."

"What I'd like to see is Jess walking in that door."

"Don't you trust in God?" Enoch asked, this being his idea of the kind of religious conversations he'd heard Jess have with Eliza.

"I trust Him. But good men before this have died doing God's work."

"Do you think helping runaway slaves escape is God's work?"

"I don't think God wants our brothers bought and sold like horses and mules."

"Do you count a darkey your brother, Mrs. Birdwell?"

"I do. In the sight of God."

"Does that mean right here, eating with us?"

"We're in the sight of God. I'd as lief have Swan Stebeney at my table as any man I know."

"Swan's more than half white."

"Thee doesn't know what thee's talking about, Enoch. Swan Stebeney's as black as the ace of spades."

Enoch considered this pretty plain talk for a woman

and a preacher but refrained from commenting on it. "What I mean by half white is that he's got white ways. He was brought up by whites."

"So was thee, Enoch Miles, and I don't take credit from thee for the fact. God made our skins. Is thee going to fault God for his handiwork? Say birds should be without feathers because we haven't got them? And everybody in the whole world the color He happened to chance on for us? Is thee ready to tell God He made a mistake? And to start over again?"

"No, ma'am," said Enoch, the conversation fully as interesting as any he'd heard between Jess and Eliza, but one he decided he'd rather listen to than be in. Jess could handle these sharp sayings of Eliza's in a way to make her laugh. But Enoch couldn't think of anything funny, or that Eliza would think of as funny, that could be said about God's choice of colors for the human race. As a matter of fact, he had never thought of darkies as being God's handiwork at all. White people were God's handiwork, and darkies had just somehow slipped in. One thing he did know: best get off the subject of God altogether. Whatever else he might set himself up as being, he didn't fool himself that he was any equal in a debate on religion with a lady minister. Quakers had silent meetings for worship, but when they got out they made up for all that time of quiet by letting their tongues wag at both ends. Not that he would say this of Eliza. But he would say she wasn't tongue-tied. And even a mite feisty when it came to talk about God and the darkies.

Eliza was a woman, however, who knew the value of a dollar. She ought to understand what an owner lost when a slave ran away.

"Every time a man loses a slave he loses one thousand dollars," he said.

"Sometimes more, sometimes less," Eliza answered calmly.

"Don't you think the owner's being robbed when people keep him from getting his property back?"

"No," said Eliza. "The slave owner's property was stolen in the first place. The slave was stolen. Then his freedom and his learning and his earning were stolen from him. The law of this land says it's not legal to possess stolen property. Thee knows that, don't thee, Enoch?"

"Yes, ma'am," said Enoch.

"If thee was stolen, chained in a cellar someplace and whipped if thee didn't work, and if thee did work, no money given thee, wouldn't thee want me and Jess to rescue thee?"

Enoch started to say, "But, ma'am, I'm not black," thought better of it, and said, "Yes, ma'am, that's what I'd hope for."

"That's what we'd do," Eliza assured him.

She felt much better. Convincing Enoch, she had convinced herself. And for ten minutes she had not worried about Jess. In the heat of the discussion she had forgotten to give Enoch the cake and custard she had made especially for him. She put a double helping in front of him. At twenty Enoch was still enough of a boy to think the sweet the best part of the meal.

"There, Enoch," she said, "that's to thank thee for keeping my mind off Jess for a while."

"Don't worry about Jess," Enoch said. "He'll prove a mighty hard possum to tree, or I'll miss my guess."

When dinner was over, Eliza asked Enoch about his work for the afternoon. She treated the hired man much the same as she treated her own boys: let him know she was keeping track of him. Enoch's plan for the afternoon was to take the wagon down to the bottom land along the river, strip the corn from the shocks there, and bring a load or two up to the barn. Eliza approved. "Rain's overdue," she said. "That corn ought to be under cover."

As Enoch was driving out of the barnyard, Eliza ran out with a message for him. "Tell the children as they come by from school that they can wait and ride up with thee. It'll be a treat for them, and maybe thee can get a little work out of Josh and Labe."

Enoch grinned at that joke. "I won't count on it," he said.

Eliza nodded understandingly. "They're both big enough to throw corn in a wagon. Don't be too easy on them."

She stayed out in the yard until the farm wagon pulled by old Duke disappeared from sight over the rise past the apple orchard. She was able to keep her mind off Jess so long as the housework lasted. But when the noon dishes were washed, the table set for supper, the churning finished, the kitchen brushed out, a fire laid in the sitting room, she was back exactly where she had been before dinner. Seeing in her mind's eye pictures of Jess. Boarding the boat? Hand raised to knock on the stateroom door? In the carriage with Lily and Burk? Followed by agents? Caught before he set foot on the ship? In jail? Whipped? Stoned?

Pictures of all this, and more and worse, she could see more clearly than her home and its furnishings. She stood in the opened kitchen door and looked out into the November afternoon. The day, which had been gray and heavy as an iron skillet, was opening up a little now. There were streaks of yellow above the dark hills on the far side of the Muscatatuck. Against the lightened sky the bare-limbed trees of the woods lots made a strange black tracery. While she stood in the doorway, a rooster crowed and another occupation suggested itself. She could gather the eggs. It was early for it, but the boys, waiting to ride home with Enoch, would be late, and if Enoch *had* been able to get any work out of them, tired. She took her shawl off the coat rack in the kitchen, got the egg basket from under the wash bench on the back porch, and went out to the chicken house. The day was cooling as it drew toward its close. Eliza put her shawl over her head and fastened it closely under her throat. She discovered that the boys had been right. The fruitful season for hens as well as trees and vines was past. She came out of the chicken house with fewer than a dozen eggs in her basket.

Halfway to the house she heard the sound she had been waiting for all day: the fast hard clop of galloping horses. She spun about to scan an empty road. Whoever was coming could not be seen until he topped the rise. She ran, carrying the egg basket, which she should have put down, toward the road. She could recognize the sound of their own team, and, though she longed to believe that what she heard was Diamond and Dandy, the sound was not right. She stopped at the edge of the pike, waiting to see.

It was not their horses or their carriage, though until the turn was made into their driveway she was unable to make out who her visitors were. A Negro was driving, and though the horses were not Diamond and Dandy, but a pair of matched bays, heavily lathered, she thought for a second that it might be Jess after all, with a change of teams and carriage. The driver didn't pull up until he came abreast the upping-block. Eliza, running, carrying her egg basket carefully, caught up with them there. The man on the back seat was not Jess, but Sam Templin, his face still swollen but bleached white now, like a piece

of salt pork left in water overnight to freshen. He was
leaning against a young white woman, who herself looked
as if she had just risen from a sickbed, and since then had
been in a runaway, been dragged and run over. Her dress
was muddy and torn, her long brown hair uncombed,
her eyes filmed with the glass glaze of fever. The driver,
the healthiest-looking one of the three, was not undam-
aged. His brown skin was light enough to show bruises;
his mouth, split and swollen, was shapeless. In the November afternoon he wore no coat, and his shirt was mostly
neckband and armholes.

"Jess?" asked Eliza, ashamed of herself in the face of
so much misery.

Sam Templin, though he couldn't sit up without help,
could speak. His words came out of his mouth but were
not shaped by his lips. They were breathed or sighed from
deep inside, emerging whispery and sick. "We don't know.
He missed them. The boat was early. Somebody . . ." Sam
closed his eyes. "Somebody . . ."

Burk, on the front seat, picked up Sam's words like a
man helping a friend with a valise too heavy for him.
"Somebody had another key to the stateroom. We run for
it, and the deck hands helped us. It was near night. Tuesday. We hired a skiff to take us across the river. We knew
how to get to Mr. Templin's. We hid by day and traveled
by night."

"Where are you going now?"

"Here," Sam said. "Here, if you'll have them. My place
isn't safe."

"We're followed right now," Burk said.

"Enoch's . . ." Sam began. "We talked to him. He's
keeping a lookout."

Lily, on the side of the carriage next the upping-block,
reached into the egg basket with a snake-quick hand,

grasped an egg, cracked it against the wheel rim, and began to suck the meat.

Burk apologized. "She's pretty near starved."

Eliza had never seen a person suck an egg. "Eat, eat," she urged. "Eggs are strengthening. I'll have thee something warm in a minute."

Sam whispered, "Eliza, I know thee's against this."

Eliza denied it. "I'm not against the hungry and hunted."

"Let's get inside," Burk said. "If they find Mr. Templin's rig here, they'll tear your house apart hunting us."

"What'll thee do, Sam?"

"Drive," Sam said. "Lead them a pretty chase."

"Can he drive?" Eliza asked Burk.

"He don't look like it. He can't properly sit up. Look out," he yelled. "They're coming."

It wasn't the agents, but Enoch, riding Duke bareback, coming up through the apple orchard.

"That buggy," he panted with excitement, "it took a wrong turn down toward the Bethel Church."

"They'll be back," Sam said, "when they find we ain't there. Enoch, take Lily down to the river. Head back toward Ohio. Nobody will hunt that direction. Hide her in a thicket."

Sam's face, which had been pale as boiled meat, was becoming flushed. He leaned forward, hands on knees, head hanging forward, but thinking and planning.

"Eliza, will thee ride with us?"

"Ride with thee?"

"Take Lily's place. We'll change horses at Swan's, and Swan'll drive us from there. Burk, thee'll head downriver at Swan's and join Lily. Thee wait for him, Lily. When he comes, both of you lay low. You'll be picked up tonight by friends."

"What if the agents catch up with *you*, before you get to Swan's, Mr. Templin?" Enoch asked.

"We don't aim to let that happen. Afterward, no great harm'll come of it. Swan's a freedman. Eliza's white, and a preacher to boot."

"What about thee, Sam?" Eliza asked. Sam, a known helper of runaways, was on no such safe ground.

"Oh, I'm sick with the mumps," Sam said. As if that would cut any ice with an agent within reaching distance of a five-hundred-dollar reward.

Lily leaned forward from the back seat, her arms across her husband's shoulders.

"Get out, Lily," Sam said. "There's no time to lose."

"Run for it, Lily," Burk told his wife. "It's our one chance. We made it this far. Three, four hours more, and I'll be with you."

For a minute Eliza thought that any more running was going to be beyond Lily, that she was going to lean back and say, "I can't take another step." But when Burk repeated, "It's our one chance," she flung herself out of the carriage and, except that Enoch caught her, would have fallen.

"Take the eggs with you," Burk told Enoch. "See that she eats."

Eliza unwound her shawl. "Thee'll need this," she told Lily.

"First road on the right," Sam told Burk as they drove out onto the pike. "Then straight on till Swan's. I'll tell thee when."

Sam leaned back and for the first quarter of a mile kept his eyes closed. "Thee should've kept thy shawl," he said finally to Eliza, eyes still shut. "Hide that black hair of thine. They're following a light-haired woman."

Eliza took off her apron and wrapped it around her head like a turban.

Without opening his eyes, Sam said, "Let 'em have a taste of the whip, Burk."

Sam's team, heavily lathered, was already extending itself. Whipping a trier was something Jess could never abide. Eliza drew away from Sam in disapproval.

Sam understood why. "The choice is between Burk and the horses, Eliza. Once we get to Swan's and Burk heads downstream, the big danger's past. Meanwhile, my poor boys will have to suffer. Touch them up, Burk."

Sam's poor boys let out another notch of speed. Sam said, "I could do with a glass of cold buttermilk."

It was the fever working on Sam, Eliza supposed. She herself was trembling with cold, chilled by the rush of air past her face. The running horses pulled the carriage in a series of swoops. They were traveling like a bird that alternately flies and soars. Farms, ordinarily familiar to Eliza, passed by, strange as the landscape of a dream. Flicks of foam blown from the horses touched her, white, like snow, but warm. She could name the fields they passed by ownership: Trueblood's, Stanton's, Grubbs', Burdg's, Griffith's; and by what they contained: corn stubble, corn shocked and pumpkins piled between the shocks, pumpkins still attached to the frost-touched vines, orchards of leafless trees, dried mullein and milkweed stalks like crops of unharvested walking canes. Dead grass along the roadside was like sun-bleached lifeless hair. She knew it all, and all was strange. Oh, the change in the countryside when you're fleeing: nothing familiar, nothing welcoming. Mrs. McConnell, sweeping her front steps, turned, broom in hand, and stared without a gesture of greeting, as if she had never before laid eyes on the Birdwells or the Templins.

Now and then Eliza peered over her shoulder at the road behind them. She was afraid to do so and afraid not to. She saw nothing. But Burk, better trained than she in watching for followers, said in a steady voice, "There's a buggy topping the far rise, Mr. Templin."

Sam raised himself. "A roan?"

"Too far in this light to tell."

"Touch 'em up," Sam said.

"What if Swan isn't home?" Eliza asked.

"We ain't come to that bridge yet." Then, more reassuringly, "Swan's a clockwork man. He'll be doing his chores this time of night."

Swan was just where Sam had said he'd be when Burk, after turning into Stebeney's land on two wheels, pulled the team to a stop in front of Swan's barn. Swan was on a stool, milking his cow—with a squirt now and then into the mouth of a ten-year-old girl who stooped beside him.

Eliza judged that Swan had been interrupted like this before. He needed no explanations, no instructions from Sam. He rose unhurriedly, looked over the carriage and its occupants, then said quietly to the girl, "Run get your mama."

To Burk, to whom he handed the milk pail, he said, "Drink." To Sam he said, "You taking a pretty big chance, out of bed this soon, ain't you?"

"My chance was a better one than Burk's," Sam said.

"This Burk?" Swan asked. He had Sam's team half unhitched already.

"This is Burk," Sam said. "His wife is already down by the river below Jess's place."

"Who took her there?"

"Jess's hired man, Enoch."

"He safe?"

"I pray," said Sam. "No choice there either. We're followed close."

Swan, by the time Susan came out from the house on the run, had his own team harnessed.

"Sue," he said as he worked, "get this man to the river. Head him downstream toward Alder Island. You keep going, Burk, till you catch up with your wife. Lay low. We'll pick you up tonight."

"Rose," he said to his daughter, "you drive Sam's horses away from here. Head them away from the river. Hide them in the woods lot if you can."

Swan's wife, when Swan picked up the reins, didn't make any long farewell speech. She said, her voice as quiet as for any ordinary good-bye, "I'll be waiting, Swan."

"No telling when I can get back."

"I know that, Swan."

Behind them as they pulled out, the lamplight in the kitchen was showing a clear yellow in the deepening dusk. On the stove, Eliza thought, there was a skillet of food that would dry out uneaten.

Swan's team was as fast as Sam's and fresher. And Swan, unlike Burk, was driving horses he knew on a road that was familiar to him. Eliza clung to the edge of the seat. She tried not to jostle Sam, who looked barely able to hold himself upright, let alone anyone else. Swan gave the main road a miss, driving down his own back lane and onto the little-used river road. On that rough road, and the way he was driving, all four wheels weren't often on the ground at once. Eliza's mind was filled with questions she wanted to ask Sam; but he appeared to be dozing, resting, at least, with eyes closed, and she didn't have the heart to rouse him up. Like as not he didn't know the answers any more than she did. What would happen to Swan's wife if she was caught helping Burk? What would happen to Burk, she knew. What was likely to come of Enoch and Lily? If Burk wasn't caught, what were his chances of finding Lily? And, above all, Jess. Where was Jess? What was keeping him? Had he been caught? Was he hurt?

Without knowing she did so, she must've spoken aloud. Sam hadn't heard, or, if he had, was too played out to talk. But Swan, speaking over his shoulder, answered her questions.

"I figure Jess is still hunting Burk and Lily. Threading his way homeward and looking into every crevice and cranny. He gets word of their being first here, now there. And not being an easy man to give up, he's still looking. But he'll turn up in one piece. I give you my word for that. He never so much as laid eyes on Burk and Lily. So they can't hang anything on him even if they catch him."

"Does thee think he'll be back by the time we get home?"

"Be waiting for us. I guarantee it."

Eliza knew Swan couldn't guarantee it, but his words reassured her.

"How's Sam?" Swan asked.

"Sick," Eliza said. "Sam's sick. This jaunt could be the death of him."

"It won't be," Swan said; but didn't add, and Eliza was glad, "I guarantee it." Too many guarantees would take away from the guarantee he had given her about Jess. "Sam was never born to die of the mumps."

The first rim of a big moon, yellow as the coal-oil lamp they'd left behind at the Stebeneys', was lifting itself up from behind the dark hills to the east. Once it cleared the hill, it seemed to float in its own light. The dust their wheels turned up was visible now. An owl, squatting on the top rail of the roadside fence, before beginning his night's work, followed them with round eyes which mirrored the moon's yellow. A cow staked out on the river side of the road was startled by their clatter, and Eliza saw her stop in mid-chew and saw the green slaver around her mouth. Before the moon had come up, when they had been running away but invisible, Eliza had felt strange, but safe. Who could find them in the dark? Now every time they breasted a rise or came into a clearing they were as plain to see as in daytime. That big moon shone down on them like a watchman's lantern.

"Now the moon's up," she said to Swan, though Sam could hear, too, if he was awake and listening, "we can be seen for miles. No use trying to hide now."

"Hiding," said Swan, "never was the idea. The moon's on our side, not theirs. It shows us up. And if they don't see us, they can't follow us. And the whole point of this trip's to keep them following."

Eliza knew that. She didn't need to be told, yet it kept slipping her mind. The point of running away was surely not to be seen. That's what she kept thinking in spite of what she knew.

"We don't want to be caught, do we, Swan?"

"The later the better, anyway," Swan agreed. "The longer they chase us, the more time Burk and Lily's got."

"Has thee seen any signs of the buggy lately?"

"Not lately."

"Does thee think they're still following?"

"I hope so."

"Could they have stopped to search the riverbanks?"

"They might've. They're more likely to have taken a short cut, racing us to someplace where they'll try to cut us off."

"What'll happen when they catch up with us and find we've fooled them?"

"That's a bridge we won't cross till we get to it," Swan, like Sam, said. "And maybe we won't ever have to cross it. My horses still got a lot of run left in them."

Swan let his horses have what Sam had recommended for his own team: a taste of the whip. The creak and swing of the carriage increased; the clatter of the horses' hoofs came so close together it was like the sound of a hard hail on the roof of an upstairs bedroom. Sam, asleep, or saving his strength for whatever might lay ahead, lurched heavily against her as Swan swung his team around a bend in the road. Eliza linked her arm through Sam's to steady him.

Sometime, or maybe many times, she must have dreamed she was running away, pursued by people who would do her harm, guilty of she knew not what. She had taken hold of Sam's arm for his sake, but she held onto him for her own. He was sick, worn out, maybe didn't know what he was doing, but if the worst came to the worst, if those who were chasing her caught up, Sam would stand between her and them. No one's chasing *thee*, she reminded herself, but she had dreamed it too many times. Or else with an apron wrapped around her head, crouched down beside a man who in the South had a price on his head, driven through the night by a Negro who whipped his running horses, she had become a slave and a runaway, too? In the pretending to be Lily had the pretension become real? But if she was Lily, why did she feel like a wrongdoer? Lily had done nothing wrong. She was sinned against, not sinning. Her only sin was running away. But when you had to run, did a feeling of guilt come over you? So that you said to yourself,

Sometime when I didn't know it, I must have committed a crime?

"Sam, Sam," she said.

Sam groaned a couple of times and lifted his head.

"I didn't mean to waken thee, Sam."

"I've never been asleep."

Swan, hearing Sam's voice, said over his shoulder, "I figure it would be a good thing to cross the river at Jessup's bridge and head back downstream for a ways from there."

"There been any sign of them lately?"

"Not that I seen. They may have crossed the river themselves at the ford. They maybe found your horses and are searching the riverbanks. We ain't doing anybody any good pounding along here if we've lost them."

"Cross over," Sam said.

Eliza knew Jessup's bridge well. It was a one-way plank affair with cracks between the planks, so that you could watch the gray creek waters sliding along beneath as you crossed. Swan slowed his team to make the turn into what in summertime was the tunnel of green that led to the bridge. Now in November they drove under a fretwork of bare limbs. The moon shining through them made Eliza feel that they had entered a ruined and deserted building, and the feeling of fear and a conviction of wrongdoing came back. Off to the right, through the tree trunks, she saw glimpses of the river, which with the moon on it shone like a cast-iron skillet filmed over with grease. She noted, with time to marvel that she did so, the lighted ridges that marked the passage of water bugs; and she breathed in the heavy funky smell of riverside pools and rotting leaves and of fleshy watery growth, and was glad she lived on high ground.

As they came out of the raftered tunnel onto the sandy

stretch that led up onto the bridge, Swan said in a quiet voice, "They crossed at the ford, all right."

Eliza looked toward what she hadn't wanted to see: a buggy facing their way and stationed mid-bridge. Swan pulled his team to a stop.

Sam, sitting upright said, "Swan, don't mix in this any more than thee has to. Thee let me do the talking."

"You better spare yourself, Sam."

"I been sparing myself just for this. A man thy color could speak Holy Writ and do nothing but rile those two. Eliza, take that covering off thy head."

Sam, who had been too weak to hold himself upright, climbed out of the carriage and, leaning against it, waited. He didn't have long to wait. The buggy was driven abreast the carriage and so close that Eliza's first thought was that Sam would be ridden down. The two men— one bearded, the other white-faced in the moonlight but with heavy dark burnsides narrowing his wide face—remained seated. They talked down to Sam like passing travelers to a boy waiting to hold their horses.

"You're under arrest," said the bewhiskered older man, "for helping two runaway slaves escape." Then turning to Swan and Eliza, he said, "You two light down." As he said this, the younger man, a blocky fellow in a light-colored suit, jumped out of the buggy.

Sam said, "Stand back. The arresting, if any's done, will be of you two."

"On what charges?"

"Holding up the passage of citizens on a public road."

"Citizens? Two slaves and a slave stealer?"

Sam said, "You've got the wrong people. My driver is Swan Stebeney, a freedman who has lived in this township for twenty years. The lady is Mrs. Eliza Birdwell, a

Quaker minister and a long-time resident of Campbell Township. My name is . . ."

"We know your name, Sam Templin. Lafe," ordered the bearded man, still seated in the buggy, "get the buck Negro out of the carriage."

Swan was too fast for Lafe. He was out of the carriage before Lafe could reach in and grab him. Facing the man in the buggy he said, "You've got no claim on me."

"He's not the one, Lafe. We've been tricked."

Lafe said, "He may not be the man, but the woman may be Burk's wife."

Eliza didn't have Swan's chance to jump. Lafe hauled her out, then caught her as she fell forward.

"She don't feel like a preacher, Mr. Burritt."

Mr. Burritt said, "She's not the one. She's got black hair."

Lafe said, "Black skin, too, maybe," and ripped Eliza's close-buttoned bodice open. Underneath was Eliza's high-necked shimmy, so there wasn't much skin to be seen. Swan moved to strike Lafe, but before he could do so Sam stepped between them.

"Mr. Burritt," said Sam, "thee admits thyself that these are not the runaways thee is after. Mistakes have been made before—and we'll overlook this one. But I warn thee, mishandle these two, and thee'll call the whole state of Indiana down on thy head."

Mr. Burritt said, "We don't claim these two. But we claim you're a known lawbreaker and that these two were helping you. This wasn't any moonlit drive on your part to court a married lady preacher. It was a staged race to lead us away from catching the two runaways we've been following. Now if you were leading us away from them, you know where they are, and as law-abiding citizens you'll tell us where they are."

"There is no law that justifies the ownership of one man by another."

"I don't know what law you may have in mind. I'm talking about the law of the United States. And that law says that escaped slaves are not to be helped in running away from their legal owners. That's the law I'm talking about. That's the law you're breaking. Now you tell me where those runaways are."

Sam said nothing.

Mr. Burritt climbed out of the buggy. He was not much taller than Eliza. "All right, Mr. Templin, you may not talk, but the nigger will. I know niggers. Swan, you're a freedman, I'm told. Now, Swan, you have got full freedom to keep the law and tell us where that pair is hiding. Or to break the law and let us knock it out of you. Where are they, Swan?"

Swan said nothing.

"Stir up his memory, Lafe."

In the half-light, Lafe, with his back to Eliza and facing Swan, did something Eliza couldn't see. Swan caught his breath in a whistling grunt, swayed, but stayed on his feet. Eliza felt a strange painful nausea, as if under her breastbone some organ more delicate than flesh had been twisted. She had never before in her life seen one man abuse another—a man lambasting a mule once with a fence rail, boys shooting arrows at an old hen—but not a man . . . Her gorge rose; she thought she might vomit.

"That help your memory any?" Lafe asked.

Swan's answer to that question was to hit Lafe twice. Lafe fell backward, and, in the narrow space between the two rigs, lay across Eliza's feet. Before she or Sam could say a word, Mr. Burritt hit Swan across the face with his pistol. Eliza heard the sound of metal on teeth and bones. Swan toppled away from the fallen Lafe.

Mr. Burritt stood for some seconds looking down at the two men. Then he kicked his own man lightly a few times, and Lafe stirred. "Get up," Mr. Burritt said, and Lafe floundered to his feet, arms outstretched as if clinging to invisible supports.

"Drag the nigger down to the river. A little water will bring him to. A little more will make him remember where those two runaways are."

When Lafe, dragging Swan by the heels, was halfway down the narrow sandbank that separated the two rigs from the river, Mr. Burritt gave Sam a little poke in the ribs with his gun. "Good Christian man like you, concerned for the welfare of his black brethren, you been baptized before, I reckon?"

"I'm a Quaker," Sam said. "We don't baptize with water."

"I'm a Baptist," said Mr. Burritt, "and we believe in total immersion. It might have a power that would surprise you."

Eliza took hold of Mr. Burritt's arm. "Mr. Templin's a sick man," she said. "He got up out of a sickbed . . ."

"Just to court you, ma'am?"

"He's not courting me. He's . . ."

"Helping runaway niggers? That's what I thought. You come on down to the river with us. We might have to give you the benefit of a little baptismal service, too."

At the first sick choking sound from Sam, face down under the water at the river's edge, Eliza sat and buried her face in her lap. She covered her ears and eyes with her skirt and finally closed her ears with her fingers. There were still sounds to be heard, but she found that she was able to choose what sounds to hear. An owl hooted near at hand, and a reply like an echo came from some distance. One of the horses whinnied. (It could hear what she couldn't.) The leafless limbs creaked in the rising night wind. Above all she heard in her blocked ears the pulse of her own heartbeat, and its rhythm took over the other sounds so that they all rose and fell together in a sound that was not any one person's, or even personal. Not personal. A night sound, rising and falling like the wind, or like the lap of river water; but high sometimes, like a kit fox lost down in the river bottoms and crying for its mother.

Finally she heard nothing, not even her own heartbeat. But when she began again to hear, she knew that she had awakened out of an unreal silence into a silence that was real. Now she heard nothing because there was nothing to hear. She rose finally to her feet and stood unsteadily on numbed legs. No voices. A mist was rising off the river. The owls were silent. The wind had died down. Then she heard a snoring sound, a sound of sickness, not of sleep.

Both men were at the river's edge, Sam the snorer. But it was Swan who, when she lifted his head, opened his eyes.

"Did they hurt . . . you?" Swan asked her. Eliza could scarcely understand Swan's words. With his broken mouth, he shaped his words peculiarly. "I couldn't . . ." he said. "I tried . . . but I couldn't help."

"No one hurt me," Eliza said, though she felt hurt. "Swan, how is thee?"

"Alive," Swan whispered. "Half-alive and half-drowned," he corrected himself, and smiled a little with his ruined mouth.

"Sam?"

"Sam's sick. . . . Could you manage to drive the carriage a little closer? The two of us together might get Sam in and home."

"Thee needs help thyself."

"You help me, then the two of us'll help Sam to his place."

Jess and Enoch were waiting for them at Templin's when they got there, but it wasn't until Jess and Eliza were going to bed that Eliza had any real chance to talk to her husband. After Enoch took Swan home, Jess and Enoch combed the river bottom until they found Burk and Lily. There was no rest then for either Jess or Eliza until Burk and Lily had been fed, given a change of clothes and a chance to wash, and were finally bedded down behind locked doors in the old sleigh bed in the attic. And Eliza hadn't felt easy until the highboy that usually stood in her and Jess's room had been placed against the door to the attic, more than half hiding the door.

"That highboy'd be a dead giveaway to any search party," Jess told her. "People have highboys in their bedrooms, not standing out in their upstairs halls where you'd have to walk the length of the house to get a clean nightshirt."

"I feel easier with it there."

"Well, it don't matter. Those two won't be back here. They left two men dead, for all they know. They may be able, where they come from, to do a little killing for the sake of getting back slaves. But up here it's a crime, and they know it. I guarantee thee those two are homeward bound at this minute."

Eliza, in her nightgown, was sitting on their bed braiding her hair. She didn't have the energy to comb or brush it, but she knew she couldn't sleep a wink with that black mane tumbling around her face. Jess, undressed down to shirt and drawers, was standing at the window that looked out over their front driveway. The wind had picked up again, and cloud shadows passed across the rag rug that covered their chamber floor.

"I hope thee's right," Eliza said. "I hope nobody comes here and asks me where they are. Because if they did, I'm afraid I'd tell them."

Jess didn't answer that, but he did turn to face her.

"I won't sleep, Jess, till I've told thee something."

Jess said, "What's happened the past few days can keep us talking all winter."

It was his way of saying that he'd just as lief wait till morning to hear what she had to say. "I know it's late, Jess, but I have to tell thee."

"Well, if thee has to," Jess said, "I reckon I got no choice but to listen."

"Get into bed," Eliza said. "At least thee can rest while I talk."

"No," Jess said. "I'd be asleep before my head hit the pillows."

"It's no long tale," Eliza told him. "Short and bitter," she said, marveling at her humor, never at the best of times in long supply. "This has come back to me since I've been home. I don't remember whether they hit me on the head the way they did Swan and Sam. Or whether they just threatened to. I just forget. And I forget what I told them, too."

Eliza finished with her long black braids, threw them over her shoulder, and came to Jess. "When they asked me if I knew where Burk and Lily were, I lied. I said I didn't know."

Jess acted disappointed. "Well, now, that wasn't much

of a lie. Who did know? It took Enoch and me the better part of two hours to find them."

"I knew they were down by the river. I lied about that."

"It's a good thing thee did. Would thee rather have told the truth, have a stainless conscience to go to sleep with, and Burk and Lily chained and plodding south?"

"I could've done what Swan and Sam did. They didn't deny they knew. They never lied. They wouldn't talk. If those men had done to me what they did to Swan and Sam, I would've led them to Burk and Lily. I know I would."

"Well," Jess said, "if that's true, I think thee better thank God thee had the courage to lie."

"Swan and Sam practice what I preach. They were willing to lay down their lives for their fellow man. I preach that but I don't practice it."

Jess laughed a little. "The course we're launched on now, thee may have another chance."

"The course?"

"I think we'll be taking Sam's place."

"Thee don't think Sam's going to die, does thee, Jess?"

"I don't think Sam'll do any more conducting for some time" was the best answer she could get out of Jess.

Sam remained very sick, out of his head, and convinced the runaways he should be meeting were crying and searching for him. Neighbors took turns at his bedside, holding him down when he struggled to get up, dress, and be on his way. Though there was no question of Sam's being able to take Burk and Lily to the next underground station, they would move out of the Birdwell attic exactly on schedule. The whole Templin tribe, to Eliza's surprise, appeared to be mixed up in one way or another with the underground. She supposed she shouldn't've been surprised in light of the strength of Sam's convictions and eloquence. Look what she and Jess were doing. Sam's son-in-law, Floy Oates, would take over Sam's job as conductor for Burk and Lily.

Eliza, on the afternoon of the evening Burk and Lily were to leave, climbed the steep attic stairs to say good-bye to Lily. She did not want to add to the emotion and confusion of the leave-taking that night. Jess had spirited Burk, for a change of scenery, out to the hayloft, and she could talk to Lily alone.

Burk and Lily had been in the attic for a week and two days. Eliza would have supposed that she would have been glad to have them on their way. In addition to the physical work of carrying all their food up and all their slops down two flights of stairs, there was the strain of secrecy; and the knowledge she had to bear of lawbreaking and of faithlessness to the Meeting.

Jess always said of her, for he was of a more gregarious turn than she, happy to spend an afternoon in chat with any passing pack peddler, that she enjoyed, when company left (even her own nearest and dearest), a "happy lonesome." And Jess hinted that the happiness outweighed the lonesomeness. In a way Jess was right. After the confusion of a visit, the constant talking and eating, she was happy to have the house filled once again with quiet and order. A little lonesome, of course, but too happy to have recalled, if a wish or a whistle could have done it, a single departed visitor.

So she had anticipated even more happiness than lonesomeness after Burk's and Lily's departure. Every rig that had turned in the driveway for the past week had sent her racing to a window. Every acorn that dropped on the roof had brought her heart to her mouth. And none of Jess's reminders that Quakers had been from the start lawbreakers had made her comfortable as a lawbreaker. She had been brought up to keep all laws, not to pick and choose among them, keeping only those that suited her fancy. So she didn't have Burk and Lily under her roof as the result of any conviction that Grove Meeting and Washington were both wrong. She had them there because she could not find it in her heart to turn away from her doorstep two such hungry, footsore, wronged, and hunted human beings. Meeting and state might be right in the main, but they were surely wrong about Burk and Lily. She was not defying the law, but loving persons. The law wouldn't die if she didn't look after it for a week or two; and Burk and Lily might.

As she climbed the last stairs, she thought that, contrary to what she might have believed about the labor and strain of sheltering the runaways, the work and strain had formed a bond which would make her less happy than lonesome when they left. A large part of that lonesomeness, of course, would be caused by who Lily was, not by what Eliza had done for her.

Lily unlocked the door when she knocked. She welcomed Eliza like one mansion owner to another. She pushed forward the best chair and turned it so that the late slanting light was not in Eliza's eyes.

The attic, though small and ringed around its edges with boxes and trunks, had always been a pleasant place. The two round windows in the gables gave it, for Eliza, the look of a sea captain's stateroom, something she had never seen, remote and strange. Eliza had kept it neat, but Lily, with broom and dustcloth, had burnished it. She had arranged its discarded chairs and tables in parlor patterns. It was, she said, the nicest place she had ever lived. She would never ask for better. She had an inclination to stand when Eliza was present. But Eliza would have none of that.

"Sit down, Lily, please. Thee has a hard night's travel ahead of thee."

Lily chose a straight-backed chair, one that had come all the way from Philadelphia with Jess's people. It had stood among like chairs around some polished Philadelphia dining-room table, and its owners had never dreamed of either Indiana attics or runaway slaves.

It had been Eliza's intention to speak calmly to Lily of practical matters. What she said was, "I am going to miss thee, Lily."

Lily smiled and nodded. Eliza didn't know whether Lily's silences were the result of the training she had received in the South or whether they were the natural expression of a placid nature. A good many things about Lily were beyond Eliza's understanding. To call a woman her color black was like calling a ball square or water dry. It was ridiculous for her, Eliza, a woman past thirty with three children, to feel in Lily, a girl of twenty-three, that same comforting assurance she had felt in her own mother. She had never told Lily about their loss of little Sarah at the age of five. She did so now. She didn't do it by way of saying to Lily, "Look, thee's not the first to have known sorrow," but because of Lily's strange motherliness; and because, when she spoke of Sarah to someone who had never even heard her name, Sarah seemed to live again in all her black-haired, round-eyed sprightliness.

"They're just about the sweetest at that age," Lily agreed. "You can still pick them up and hug them then— as if they were still babies. But they can talk to you then. Not plain maybe, but wise as a grandfather. Mine could anyway."

Eliza, who had never heard mention of children, had now to regard Lily in a different light. This girl was a real mother.

"Thee's never mentioned babies."

"They're not babies now. They're big boys. Mayhew's seven and Henry Joe is six. I maybe ought not to mention them now. Burk and I decided it was best not."

Eliza thought she understood that. Sorrows dwelt on became unbearable. But how could they leave them in the first place?

"Burk's going back for them," Lily said. "It's best no one know that."

"After what thee's gone through, would thee risk going back?"

"Burk will. That's one of the reasons we left. To learn the way, so Burk can bring the boys out."

"Where are the boys now?"

"My mother has them. My uncle bought her so he could help watch over the boys."

"Thy uncle?" Eliza asked.

"My father's brother. He was the one helped Burk get to Louisville when I was sold south."

"Is thy uncle against slavery?"

"No," said Lily. "He's a slave owner. But he's against the way my father treated my mother and me. He's against families being separated. And," Lily added, and she smiled a little, "he's against his new sister-in-law."

Eliza had pictured Lily to herself almost as if she were some graceful hunted animal, a solitary white doe, fleeing. And she had seen the entire South as one great band of hunters, all alike, pursuing, and pursuing for the same reasons. It was a childish picture. Lily was as entangled in family relationships as anyone; and more than most because of the added complexities of mixed colors and human ownership. And the South itself ranged all the way from men like John Shelby, who had taken his slaves north to freedom, to Lily's father, who bedded his slaves, then sold his own flesh, more inhuman than any butcher, through uncles who tempered the practice of slavery with human decencies.

Eliza leaned forward in her chair, under the pressure of all she had heard of Lily's past and all she imagined that lay ahead of her before she reached Canada, or even saw her boys again. And there Lily sat in a dress of sprigged blue calico, a lady's afternoon apron, beruffled and lace-trimmed, tied around her neat waist. Her hair was wheat-colored, her eyes gray. No Philadelphia Quaker had ever looked less a slave and a lawbreaker than Lily did, head bowed as she sat on that chair, spending her last hours under a roof before taking once again to swamp and river bed, or at best to an uneasy hiding place in somebody's attic or corncrib.

"Oh, Lily," Eliza said, "we can at least write."

Lily shook her head, smiling again. "I can't write," she said.

Eliza could only stare. A grown woman not writing. It was as strange as some malformation of nature, some affliction like deafness or dumbness.

Lily, when Eliza didn't speak, added, "I can't read either."

Eliza was still silent, trying to fathom the unfathomable.

"You know it's against the law to teach slaves to read and write?"

Eliza did know it. But she was like someone who, though he has heard of the law of gravity, has never in his life seen anything drop. The facts of slavery she could take into her mind. She could imagine herself owned, required to wash, bake, hoe. But to be deprived of the ability to read and write, that enslavement she could not imagine.

"Not the Bible even?" Eliza asked, finally.

"Not 'a, b, ab,'" Lily assured her.

"I should think, because of thy father . . ."

"Because of my father no one dared teach me. But Burk can read," she boasted. "There isn't a newspaper he can't make out. He's not a pretty writer, but you'd never be in doubt what he's writing. I've heard more than one person say that. He picked it out all for himself and took beatings for trying."

Eliza noted Lily's pride. Burk was nobody's idea of a handsome man, black, white, or any color in between. And he was a color in between, grayish, not black and shining like the handsome Swan. Burk fit exactly Eliza's idea of the part he'd been cast to play in his and Lily's escape: the burly handyman, his only talents in his muscles.

"Lily, thee could've married a white man."

Eliza could've bitten her tongue out the minute she said that. But if you think a thought often enough, sooner or later it will get said. What Eliza didn't like about the thought was that it suggested that somehow a white man was better than a black man. Eliza knew that wasn't true. Rascals came in assorted colors. The world had undoubtedly taken more harm from white hands than black. What she meant was, surely, only that if Lily had married a white man her life, in 1856, would have been easier.

Lily had no doubt been told this before. She answered mildly, "I loved Burk."

"What if Burk had been Burk but white?"

"That couldn't be," she said. Then she added, "I'd've missed him then, if it could be. I was brought up colored. I couldn't have married a white man."

"Thy father was white."

"In the South the child takes the mother's condition. That's the law. I was black and a slave."

Eliza said, "Then I'm blind."

Lily didn't argue with her. She said only, "I loved what Burk was like, the way he looked, and his good ways."

Eliza knew a wife was the judge of that in a man. It was nothing an outsider could say anything about.

She rose from her chair, went to Lily, and, leaning over her, clasped her head like a child's to her bosom. She felt thankful to God for sending Lily to her. She didn't for a minute think that God had sent Lily through bramble and bush for Eliza Birdwell's enlightenment, but she had been enlightened. Her heart had grown because of Lily's presence.

"Lily," she said, "I will pray for thy boys morning and night."

"Pray for Burk," Lily said. "If he don't get through, the boys are lost."

"All of thee," Eliza said. "Thee and thy family."

The tears Eliza had been afraid she would shed when they parted, she shed now. Not for the parting itself so much as for the world's sorrows and sins, of which Lily had more than her rightful share to carry.

That night when Floy Oates came quietly in his closed carriage, she was able to say good-bye to Lily and Burk without crying. She clasped Lily closely, sister, mother, daughter. She didn't know how to name her.

"I will never forget to pray," Eliza said, "for thee and thy husband and boys."

"Burk will write," Lily said. "I have asked him."

Burk said, "Soon as we get to Canada and shake the lion's paw, I'll send you word."

The two women kissed. Burk got in, closed the isinglass

curtains, and Floy drove out of the yard on the start of the long road north.

Jess and Eliza walked slowly back to the house together. Though Burk and Lily had never sat downstairs, even the downstairs, with the attic empty, seemed empty and lonesome. But Jess didn't say a word to Eliza about being able to have a "happy lonesome" now that their visitors were gone. Jess liked to poke fun, but he had some sense of what was seemly. The house without that endurance and courage in the attic was half a house.

Two days after Floy made his night trip with Burk and Lily, and ten days after Sam's baptism with water, Sam Templin, underground conductor, aged forty-seven years, three months, and two days, died.

Swan came over with the sad news. Jess was out in their berry patch, covering raspberry canes for the winter. Eliza, who hadn't seen Swan since they had parted at Sam's ten nights ago, ran out to greet him. He looked worse than he had that night. Most of one eyebrow had been replaced by a red ropelike scar. His fine teeth, smashed by the gun, were in worse shape than some old man's. There were stumps and vacancies, and the vacancies looked worse than the stumps. Swan's eyes, always bright and shining, were sunk back into his head like the surface of ponds during a drought.

"Swan," Eliza exclaimed. "Thee shouldn't be up and about."

"I'm all right," Swan said. "What I'm here to tell you is, Sam's dead."

Eliza couldn't say a word. She had hoped against hope, but since those first moans of Sam's by the river's edge she had known that his life was over.

"He's been terribly sick," Swan said, and added, "He wouldn't have been himself even if he had lived."

Eliza said, "Sam was such a good man."

"That's the reason he died," Swan said. "If he'd been willing to give up his goodness, he'd be alive today."

Eliza had a batch of light bread baking in the oven, and she asked Swan, who looked as if he needed feeding every two hours like an invalid, if he wouldn't come in for some coffee and warm bread and jam. Swan said, yes, if her light bread was soft enough to chew without teeth. They were on their way up to the house when Swan and Jess both turned at the sound of a horse spanking up the pike at a good clip. Both men were newly cautious of strangers. They stopped their talk of Sam, his quirks and humors and his proddings of those who didn't see eye to eye with him.

"Thee ever see that horse and rig before, Swan?"

"It's new to me," Swan said.

"This," Jess observed, "is getting to be the crossroads of the world."

"We may not know him, but he knows us," Swan said. Knew them by name even. "Mr. Birdwell?" the driver said, when he joined them.

"Jess Birdwell," Jess said. "My wife, Eliza. My neighbor, Swan Stebeney."

"Pleased to meet you, ma'am," the traveler said to Eliza, ignoring Swan. "My name's Yocum Tate."

"From the South, my ear tells me," Jess said. "What brings thee so far from home?"

"Business," said Mr. Tate. "I'm a lawyer. I represent Mr. Jefferson Choate, owner of two runaway slaves, a young man and woman, name of Burk and Lily. We have it on good evidence that you are hiding the two. I want to search your house."

Jess said, "Thee can't enter my door searching for escaped slaves without two things: first of all, proof of ownership; second, a search warrant."

Mr. Tate took two documents from his inside coat pocket and handed them to Jess. "First," he said, "proof of ownership. Second, a search warrant."

It didn't take Jess long to examine the papers. "Everything seems to be in order," he said, handing the papers back. "Thee's welcome to make thyself at home. Go anywhere. Upstairs, downstairs, and," he said with a little bow to Eliza, "in my lady's chamber. There's an attic at the top of the house. There's a fruit and root cellar underneath. Out here's the usual complement of farm buildings: chicken house, carriage house, smokehouse, hen house, springhouse, outhouse. There's a haystack, and I read recently of an agent from the South flushing a half-dozen runaways out of a haystack with a few jabs from a pitchfork. Killed a couple, but the other four weren't damaged much. There's a corncrib, too. That would make a tough hiding place, but desperate men'll take desperate measures, I don't doubt. The river bottom would provide some good hiding spots. That's about the best I can do in the line of suggestions. But the place is thine. Please feel free to turn it upside down and inside out."

Mr. Tate, sandy-haired and long-nosed like Jess himself, stood with thumbs in his vest pockets looking Jess over.

"The two are no longer here, I take it," he said finally.

"Now, Mr. Tate," said Jess, "after making the trip thee did, I wouldn't go jumping to any conclusions. I'd have a look around if I was thee."

Mr. Tate took his thumbs out of his pockets and regarded Swan closely. "Swan, you look like you run into bad trouble of some kind lately."

"Trouble is the name for it," Swan said.

"Mr. Birdwell," Mr. Tate said, "let's you and me not beat around the bush. Didn't you put up two runaway slaves here a week or ten days back?"

"I put up a young colored couple, man and wife. But I had no proof they were slaves."

"No proof," Mr. Tate said, getting red under his freckles. "Didn't they tell you?"

"They *said* they were slaves," Jess answered. "Dwelt on it, as a matter of fact. But thee knows as well as I do, Mr. Tate, a Negro's word isn't acceptable in any court. I had nothing but their word for it, and colored folks are well known for exaggeration. I didn't feel I was in any better position than the courts are to decide whose word to take and whose word to doubt. So—were they slaves or not? With only their word for it, I didn't feel I had any kind of admissible evidence. That's the court's stand, isn't it, Mr. Tate?"

Mr. Tate said, "Leaving the court out of it, it's my opinion I've run into another wily Quaker."

"Leaving 'wily' out of it," said Jess, "us Quakers have never been ones to stir up unnecessary trouble. They said they were slaves. I said to myself, 'That's as may be,' put them up, and didn't waste any undue sympathy on them."

Then was when Mr. Tate should have accepted defeat, said "good day," climbed into his buggy, and turned southward. Instead he said, "The loss of those two is going to set back my client some four thousand dollars. I'm not prepared to go home with the report that I found the man who put them up, but he talked me out of prosecuting."

The word "prosecuting" did it. Eliza saw Jess's face darken and his whole body stiffen. He sprang toward Mr.

Tate as if the earth beneath him had bucked up and thrust him forward.

"If there's any prosecuting done around here," he said, "it'll be of thee, and of thy employer, Choate, and of two agents of his who murdered one innocent man last week and mutilated another." He pointed to Swan. "Have a look at that and ask thyself who needs prosecuting. Now thee put thy papers in thy pocket and come with me to Vernon, and I'll provide thee with another set of papers charging thee with murder. Then thee can say 'prosecuting' out of the other side of thy mouth and see how thee likes the feel of it."

Mr. Tate was backing away from Jess. "I had no connection with agents hunting runaways here. And Mr. Choate can't control every man working for him."

"A man is dead. My friend is dead," Jess said. "Someone's responsible, and I hold thee, as legal representative of Mr. Choate, responsible. Thee come into Vernon with me and talk to the marshal there."

Jess had hold of Mr. Tate's coat lapel. And Mr. Tate made the mistake of defending the murderers. "When a man's making off with stolen goods," he said, "you can't expect to have him treated friendly."

Jess put a hand on the other side of Mr. Tate's coat, picked him up off the earth, then set him down again with so much force Eliza heard the change rattle in his pocket.

"The murdered man, when abused by thy agents until he died, was riding along a country road with my wife and with this freedman and twenty-year resident of this county. They mutilated Swan Stebeney, killed Sam Templin, and struck my wife. Now thee come with me to the marshal's and tell him thee wants to prosecute me. And when thee's finished, I'll tell him thee's a member of a pack of murderers hired to come into Indiana to threaten, kill, and abuse Indiana citizens."

"I have nothing to do with Mr. Choate's slave catchers. I'm a lawyer and I represent him on legal matters."

"Thee's representing him on an illegal matter now," Jess said, and, lifting Mr. Tate, once again jiggled his coins.

Enoch, coming up from the cornfield with a load of fodder, arrived in time to see Jess grappling with a stranger. Pitchfork in hand, he leaped to the ground.

"What happened?" he asked.

Swan, for Jess was too busy with Mr. Tate, and Eliza too busy with trying to separate them to answer his question, said, "Sam's dead. And this fellow's threatening to jail Jess for not helping his murderers."

"They killed Sam? Sam was my friend."

Enoch, pitchfork in hand, rushed toward Mr. Tate. With Jess in front of him, Enoch had no chance to spear Mr. Tate except from the rear. And some kind of chivalry evidently prevented him from such an attack.

"Jess, Jess," Eliza screamed, "look out for Enoch."

Either Jess didn't hear her or else didn't figure he had anything to fear from Enoch.

"Mr. Tate," he said, "if I wasn't prevented by religious scruples from using force, I would make thee pay here and now for talking of prosecuting innocent people while murderers go free."

Enoch jerked Jess loose from Mr. Tate's lapels. "I got no scruples," he said. "Why did you kill Sam Templin?"

Eliza cried, "Jess, one murder won't blot out another," and Jess, seeing someone else attacking Mr. Tate, appeared to come to his senses. He caught hold of Enoch's pitchfork arm. "Enoch," he said, "this man didn't kill Sam."

Enoch turned to Jess. "Why were you fighting him then?"

"I wasn't fighting him," Jess said. "I was impressing on his mind that if any prosecuting was to be done around here, it should be directed against him. Not me."

Enoch dropped his pitchfork. "Let's take him to town," he said enthusiastically, "and put him in jail."

"The fact of the matter is," Jess conceded, "that while morally we've got a case against him, legally we're on about as shaky ground as he is."

Swan, who through all the ruckus had been silent, spoke painfully and slowly. "Mr. Tate, if I was you I would get into that buggy and make the fastest tracks I could out of Indiana and across the border into Kentucky."

Jess nodded. "My friend's right. I don't want any more bloodshed, but I won't answer for what'll happen to thee in this neighborhood if thee hangs around here talking about what happened to Mr. Choate's slaves. Thee's bound to run into people who don't know the answer to that but do know what happened to Sam Templin."

Mr. Tate, while Swan and Jess were giving him this advice, was busy taking it. He ran to his buggy, climbed in, but turned around to face them—two Quakers, a hired man, a Negro—before he drove out.

"I'm leaving now. But I tell you, our patience is wearing thin. A little more of this interference with our rights and our property and we won't be up here by twos and threes, but by hundreds. And tens of hundreds."

"Who's we?" Jess asked.

"The South," said Mr. Tate.

Enoch picked up his pitchfork and made a run toward the buggy. "We'll be waiting for you," he said.

He gave Mr. Tate's horse a smack over the rump with the tines of his pitchfork, and Mr. Tate, who had been half standing, sat suddenly and departed swiftly. But when he reached the end of the Maple Grove driveway he turned around and drove slowly back. Enoch, lifting his pitchfork again, was preparing once again to drive him off.

Jess laid a restraining hand on Enoch's shoulder. "None of that," he said. "Mr. Tate's made no show of weapons. If talk's what he wants, he's got a right to ask for it."

Mr. Tate remained seated in his buggy. He sounded not so much belligerent or accusing now as honestly puzzled.

"I ask you men, and you, too, ma'am," he said courteously, including Eliza in his question, "are the North and the South parts of one single country?"

"They are," said Jess.

"Are they governed by the same laws?"

"In part," Jess said.

"Do the same laws as to the return of runaway slaves hold here as in the South?"

"They do," said Jess.

"But they are wrong," Eliza said. "They are un-Christian."

"Then change the laws," Mr. Tate shouted. "Change them. The North controls the Congress. Change the laws. But don't ask me, a lawyer, not to defend the law."

Then, with Enoch as quiet as the rest of them, they watched Mr. Tate drive out with all the law's dignity—and slowness.

After Mr. Tate disappeared around the bend, Eliza said, "There's a batch of light bread in the oven, if it's not burned to a crisp. I think we could all do with a bite to eat."

The bread was a little browner than Eliza liked it, but with fresh churned butter, black currant preserves, and hot coffee, it was passable. In the worked-up state they were all in, they could've eaten cold gravy and left-over griddlecakes with pleasure. They needed something to chew on, something to wash the unshed tears from the backs of their throats and to loosen the clotted blood around their hearts.

Enoch, who hadn't heard what Mr. Tate had to say before he put an end to the conversation with his pitchfork, now heard the full story, which Jess was not averse to telling. And in the telling he didn't forget anything and even added a frill or two Eliza, in the concern, must've missed. Enoch laughed out loud at that bit about not being able to accept a Negro's word. And Jess, hearing Enoch laugh, wore that look of surprise of his that made everything he said twice as laughable as it really was. Even Swan held his hand to his broken mouth trying to protect it from the grin that was threatening.

"Oh, I wish Sam could've heard you," Swan told Jess. "I surely do. Nobody liked a funny story better than Sam."

But Swan's appreciation wasn't enough for Jess. "What's thee looking so doleful for, Eliza? Every word I said to Enoch was the Gospel truth."

The truth of Jess's story, Gospel or stretched, wasn't what was troubling Eliza. Here were three men—Jess and Swan as good as any she knew, and Enoch, though he might win no medals for piety, no rascal either—and the three of them, their dear friend dead, rejoicing like any hardened campaigners around a campfire over an enemy routed. The routing had been done with words—leaving out that little flourish with the pitchfork—and the cause, she hoped, was a good one. Still, she thought that if words hadn't turned the trick, if Mr. Tate hadn't turned out possibly the most reasonable one of the lot, Jess himself might have been willing to use a pitchfork.

"It seems a poor time for laughing," she said, "with Sam dead."

Swan, still protecting his hurt mouth, said slowly, and with more deference to Eliza as preacher and woman than he usually showed, "A good time for laughing is when you can. I learned that when I was . . . a boy."

Eliza understood at once the change Swan had made in his sentence after he started it. He had intended saying, "I learned that when I was a slave." But that would be a reminder to those about him of what their people had done to his. He had been hurt enough not to want to hurt.

Enoch, with his own kind of courtesy, broke the silence that followed. "Seeing as it's so near noon, Mrs. Birdwell, if we had another loaf of bread, we could maybe call it dinner."

Nothing eased Eliza's heart more than heaping up plates of food for hungry men. If they were going to call it dinner, she would make it worthy of the name. She put sausage cakes in one frying pan and sliced boiled potatoes into another. While she was working she heard Enoch say, "This going to be an underground station now, Mr. Birdwell?"

Jess said, "Thee'd best ask Eliza about that."

"We have to help some way," Eliza answered when asked, "I see that. Putting up runaways here would be easier for me than wondering and worrying where Jess was. But Sam said it wasn't safe for a conductor to have a station. And I suspect Jess feels he ought to take Sam's place."

Jess nodded. "Try to take his place anyway. Yes, that's what I feel."

"So I reckon Jess'll be a conductor, and I won't have a chance to keep people here."

Swan said, "Well, Mrs. Birdwell, things'll likely work out so there'll be a little of both on occasion. So thee needn't feel left out."

The idea of feeling left out because she couldn't take any more wild rides through the night like the one she had shared with Swan and Sam made Eliza laugh. It was a very quiet laugh; only she and Swan heard it. Eliza knew Swan heard it because he smiled at her, not sparing his sore mouth. And she knew why he smiled: because at her age she was learning the lesson he had learned as a boy.

And she saw the time was coming when she'd learn it even better.

Fast Horseflesh

Eliza had supposed that Jess, when he took on the sorrows and responsibilities of being a conductor on the Underground Railway, would lose some of his interest in such worldly matters as music and fast horseflesh. She was wrong. When his dangerous and worrisome trips were over he seemed to relish the light and frolicsome more than ever before. And he had an excuse now for owning fast horses that he had never had before. He *needed* good horses for his own safety; and for the safety of his passengers. Eliza knew this was true. But she also knew that underground or no underground Jess couldn't resist a horse that could pick up his heels.

Once in a while as a sort of vacation from herself Eliza tried looking at a horse through Jess's eyes. She'd fold her arms across her Quaker shawl, half close her lively black eyes, and from a stance as manly as her small and swelling figure permitted, she would regard, for some seconds, a horse. But nothing, before Red Rover's day, had ever come of it. A horse had, for Eliza, three ways of looking only. It looked to be a good worker, or run-

down, or fractious. (Most horses looked this final way to
Eliza.) But these three categories did not, she knew,
exhaust the aspects of a horse. She could be done medi-
tating on a horse in a trice, while Jess, with a few like-
minded cronies, could perch atop a fence rail half a
morning in contemplation of what looked to her to be an
ordinary four-legged buggy horse.

She was at the churn the day Jess turned in the driveway with Red Rover. She stopped the dasher to listen:
somehow the sound was different from his usual comings.
She was outside, standing by the upping-block, round
and staunch in her neat percale, when he slackened the
big red horse.

"Jess," she asked, "where's Old Dolly?"

Jess lit down. He figured it would be easier to have
this talk standing on his feet. "I swapped her," he said
firmly. "She was getting on. She needed an easier job
than toting nursery stock about the countryside. She's
in clover now," he went on fast, trying to pin Eliza's
mind on Dolly's good fortune.

But Eliza's mind was too tough an organ to be held
down by any such feeble pinning. She looked the big red
horse up and down, and then and there she saw, as
clearly as if she'd been sitting on the top rail of a fence
and chewing tobacco, a fourth way a horse could look.

"Jess," she said somberly, voicing her new knowledge,
"this horse looks racy."

Jess gazed with pride from horse to wife. That was
just the word. That was what came of having a preacher
for a wife: she could lay her tongue to the right word
every time.

"Thee's got the right word, Eliza. Thee's practically
said his name by instinct. Red Racer."

Eliza looked at her husband, unbelieving. "Jess, what did thee say this animal was named?"

Jess appreciated his mistake. He changed the horse's name then and there and none too soon.

"This horse," he said, without answering her question about the "was," "*is* named Red Rover."

"Red Rover," Eliza repeated. "Sounds more like a dog's name to me."

"Does for a fact," Jess said agreeably, happy for the shift of interest. "Might have been the name of a favorite dog that died. Wouldn't say it was," he said in a sudden burst of truthtelling, "but," subsiding into safer conjecture, "it could've been. Horses always have been noted for their unusual names. Knew one once called Rocking Chair. Knew another called Custard Pie. Knew a third . . ." But somehow, watching Eliza's face, he got the feeling he was overdoing it.

"This a seed horse?" Eliza asked, avoiding the indelicate word.

Jess shook his head. Red Rover wasn't, but he kind of looked it. He was a two-ended horse, head up and tail over the dashboard. He had a neck heavy as an oak tree and curved like a hickory bow. He had the fine clean legs of a sprinter, had a chest that looked like it had built up fronting ocean waves, and a coat as satiny as where the wave bends smooth and unbroken before it crests.

Shaking his head and pawing the earth like a born fire-eater, he was a horse to rest your eyes on. He was a gelding, cut a little proud, maybe, and not completely reconciled to plow-pulling. And Jess thought he'd been named exactly right the first time: Red Racer.

Eliza seated herself on the second step of the upping-block, picked herself a pink from those that grew about its base, and sniffed it. "Jess," she asked, "was thee goaded?"

"Goaded," Jess repeated, uncomprehending.

"Was thee baited by the Reverend Godly?" she inquired cautiously.

Jess shook his head, and then, as if admitting it, said, "Well, there's nothing about that man I like. Godly," he said, "why, if thee asks me, it's pretty near to blasphemy to have a name like that. Worse for a preacher than anybody else. Looks like he's drawing comparisons. It's a wonder he can't call himself Holy Ghostly, too."

Eliza didn't smile. That was loose talking. Belittling a preacher was the least of it. "Friend Godly," said Eliza, "has the name he was born with, and for aught thee know, Jess Birdwell, it was the Lord's means of leading him to preach the Gospel."

Jess sniffed. "What about his other names? Marcus Augustus. 'Bout as well be Jupiter or Nero. Thee think they're suitable for a minister of the Gospel?"

Eliza didn't, but she was charitable, besides not wanting to leave her husband with the last word. "The Lord moves," she said, "in a mysterious way."

That was a statement not even Jess was prepared to debate, not with Eliza anyway.

"And," she continued, "he's the duly appointed minister of the Bethel Methodist Church."

"Duly appointed," Jess admitted, "he may be, but if that man's got a smidgin of Christian grace, I've never seen it. Not with my outward eye," he said, prepared to give the Reverend the benefit of what the outward eye could not see. "Nor enough humility to balance on a case knife."

Eliza sat silent, waiting. This was Jess's chance—but he wouldn't take it. It wasn't, Eliza knew, the Reverend

Godly's name, or his looks. He was a big pursy man, red in the face and smelling of Sen-Sen. It wasn't even his birthplace, Kentucky, home of Democrats and whisky. It was his horse, his big stallion, Black Prince—his cob, the Reverend Godly called him—that riled Jess. If the Reverend Godly had owned some spavined, broken-down, amble-paced mare with the heaves Jess would have found him a sight more spiritual.

The Reverend Godly had moved into the old Applegate place, up the pike a ways, and there he farmed six days out of the week like any able-bodied preacher, but on the seventh day he hitched up his cob and drove past Maple Grove Nursery to church, wife and children beside him.

The Methodist church was on the pike a quarter of a mile this side of the Grove Friends Meeting House where Eliza preached.

Every First Day morning the Reverend Marcus Augustus would manage to start late. Then he'd come pounding up the pike and pass the surrey full of Birdwells, swinging along behind Old Dolly, as if she were standing still.

Jess wasn't fine-haired about the Methodists. They were the Lord's people even if they had the misfortune here in Jennings County of having a Kentucky horse racer for a shepherd. But being the Lord's people didn't sweeten Black Prince's dust or make the Reverend Marcus Augustus's smile of triumph any easier to swallow; and it was this, Eliza felt, rather than any desire to put Old Dolly out to clover, that had suggested the trade to Jess.

Eliza had sniffed all the smell from her flower and had confirmed ten times over Red Rover's racy looks from where she sat on the upping-block; and still Jess wouldn't make a clean breast of it, say that cob up the road, Black

Prince, was the real reason for the transaction. Eliza knew her husband, a good man, but mighty set, as good men (and bad, too, Eliza surmised) are apt to be, and if he had no mind to open up to her about Black Prince, she certainly had no mind to waste an afternoon waiting for him to do so.

"Thee let Enoch put up that animal," she said. "There's warm bread and fresh butter. I reckon thee's not got so racy thee's past eating."

Spry as a girl, she sprang down from the upping-block and went up the path between the currant bushes to the house.

Jess wasn't past talking, though, when the hired man came up to have his look.

"Enoch," he asked, making no bones of the purpose of the trade, "this look like the ticket to thee?"

Enoch ran his crafty barnyard eye over the big red horse. "He looks the ticket, Mr. Birdwell. Question is, does he vote the ticket?"

Jess clapped his hired man on the shoulder. "Enoch, I tell thee he votes it. The straight ticket."

"Name of which," Enoch said, "is 'show his heels to Godly.'"

Jess laughed. "If this animal," he said, "will perform in a little brush with Godly the way he did just now, homeward bound from Butlerville and nothing at stake, we'll be so far up the pike from the Reverend that good man won't be able to tell heels from hocks." Jess curved an admiring hand along the shining neck. "I tell thee, Enoch, we got to traveling so fast the wind whistled past my ears with a sound like cyclone time out in Kansas. The pike just unrolled in front of us smooth as ribbon on a counter. Fence posts reeled by so often I got to feeling dauncy. I had to rein him in for my stomach's sake, not that he was in the least winded."

Enoch whistled. "What's the name of this masterpiece, Mr. Birdwell?" he asked.

"Up to thirty minutes ago his name was Red Racer. Since I got home it came to me Red Rover might be more suitable. Under the circumstances," he explained.

Enoch, who understood the circumstances, nodded. "Let us hope *he* don't pay any attention to the change," he said.

The following week, to Eliza's surprise, moved along smoothly enough in spite of the racy animal out in the barn. Jess didn't buy himself a peak-brimmed cap or a red silk shirt. He went about his nursery business as usual, no more given to horse talk with Enoch than before Red Rover's advent. To be sure, he appeared to have more call than usual to drive into town. He'd work all morning, but by afternoon like enough he'd run out of one item or another and have to drive into Butlerville. Plaguey thing, these shortages, interrupting the day's work, but he seemed to be getting low on every kind of gear a nurseryman needed to have at hand. And grumbling mightily, but not letting his reluctance for a minute stop him, he'd hitch Red Rover and drive off in the direction of town.

On Seventh Day of that week, a day colored like a fire opal, haze and sunshine mingling to produce that effect of milk and flame, Eliza sauntered in midafternoon down to the mailbox. Eliza was no child of nature, and her eye as she made the trip was housewifely; her thoughts, as she saw how pears and quinces were plumping up, were all of pear preserves and quince honey. With eyes still taking stock of what would presently enter her kitchen, her hand brought out the mail.

A disappointment. Nothing but the little weekly news-paper, the *Banner News*. She ripped the gray cover from it and, reading as she went, slowly mounted the gentle slope to the house. A quiet week, not much news. An oyster supper at Scipio. Good apple crop in the county. Hog prices up. Mrs. Tacey gone to Indianapolis to visit her sick daughter. "Poor girl," Eliza said. Under the star-ling cage which hung on the open veranda she paused to read, then reread.

"Jess, Jess," she called loudly. "Jess," she said again, this time weakly and to herself, "Jess Birdwell."

There it was in print, his folly and weakness, for all to note. It sickened her to read it. "Jess Birdwell," said the *Banner News*, "Quaker orchardist and nurseryman from out Rush Branch way, was clocked behind his Red Rover, Tuesday of this week, at a good 2.50 clip. Had Mr. Birdwell elected fauna instead of flora for his lifework, we have no doubt his knowledge of horseflesh would have made him one of the premier racing men of this state. Pull over, neighbors, when you see a cloud of dust coming up the pike and let Friend Birdwell pass."

"Jess," Eliza called again.

Jess came out of one of the nursery sheds, rangy, loose-jointed, quizzical, as inattentive as if still immersed in the day's timelessness.

"Thee call?" he asked his wife, who stood stock-still be-neath the starling cage, one arm extended, holding the paper.

"Thee speak?" he asked again.

If she had, she seemed unable again to do so; she feebly flapped the paper and inclined her head.

The *Banner News* was not the medium through which Jess had ever expected disaster to fall, and though Eliza's pose was tragic, still he walked unconcernedly between the rows of China asters up to the house.

"Something amiss?" he asked. "Thee taken aback by something?"

Mutely, Eliza extended the page and pointed.

Jess read in silence, Eliza watching. There was a look, though fleeting and fast erased, Eliza could have affirmed, of satisfaction on his face. More seemly concern instantly replaced it. He folded the paper gingerly, as if its touch were as distasteful to him as to his wife, and balanced it on the porch railing.

"*News*'s pretty hard up for news," he commented.

"Thee admits it happened then?" Eliza asked. "Thee don't deny thee's been racing on the public pike?"

"Oh, pshaw. Racing," Jess said, and tossed the word aside like a coin he'd bit and found untrue. His big nose wrinkled at the bridge; he ran his fingers through his carroty hair. "A little brush," he said. "A happenchance."

"'One of the premier racing men of this state,'" Eliza quoted. "And thee a birthright Friend."

"Racing?" Jess said. "Why, by sugar, it didn't last two minutes. Red Rover himself could tell thee it was no race. Just a little flourish, just showed the *Banner News* man the stuff he's made of."

Eliza wasn't reconciled. "Fast horseflesh." She repeated the *Banner News* headline and put into her saying of it the deeply hellish ring she felt those words to have. She gave them the full carnality of a good woman's imagining.

"Like any common . . ." There was a word for it, for a man who followed fast horseflesh, a word full of disapprobation and contempt, and for his soul's sake she would give it to him.

"Tout," Jess Birdwell said, "race-track tout."

"Thee even knows the word," she said.

Berated, Jess smiled fondly. "Horses," he mildly said, "are here to stay, Eliza, along with certain words about them."

Jess made his big mistake, he saw afterward, in pasting that *Banner News* item in his scrapbook. He could just as well have kept it in his wallet till Eliza'd got a little more accustomed to the fourth way a horse could look. But there was a space in his scrapbook that seemed to cry out for the clipping the way a hungry stomach cries out for a bite to eat. The fact of the matter was that that phrase "one of the premier racing men of this state" seemed to round off and complete some unfinished part of his life. Not that he was in any way a disappointed or unhappy man. He was living in the spot, with a whole continent to choose from, he'd elected himself: southern Indiana. His work, raising nursery stock, gave him his livelihood in so pleasurable a way that he pitied less fortunate men. He was married to the only woman he could possibly imagine being married to; without Eliza, marriage would appear to him to be an overrated state. Still, content as he was, full as his life was, there was a kind of alcove or niche in it that only horseflesh seemed to fill. And, not to beat the Devil around the bush, fast horseflesh.

It was not only the beauty of horses, the sculptured sheen of rounded muscles, the lively intelligence of liquid eyes, the steady power of a matched pair plowing a deep-bottomed field; it was, in fact, as Eliza had said, their raciness. The eager high-spirited flash of a natural runner brought tears to his eyes. If there was anything sweeter, he didn't know it. Not a bobwhite's whistle, or a spray of crabapple bloom, or the autumn sun coming up red and fiery over fields of shocked corn, silvered with the night's frost. And there was something closer to man in

a horse's raciness, less impersonal. The horse was trained
by man, answered his co-ee, nuzzled against his shoulder,
lifted food from his cupped hand. He'd been horse-struck
since boyhood, slipping away from the house when he
went visiting to get to the barns, sizing up the animals
on the road. There was nothing about a horse that didn't
please him—the pungent smell of a well-lathered horse,
the dancing look of a dainty stepper single-footing it
down a clean stretch of pike, the feel of their velvet,
pushing noses. He liked the names for their colors: claybank, roan, sorrel, chestnut, buckshot, piebald, skewbald,
mouse, dapple. He'd listened, boy and man, to the stories
of the great horses of his own part of the country:
Wrangler, Blue Dick, Big Sorrel, Ball, Red Jacket, Dancing
Rabbit, Grey Fox, Mohawk. He'd followed in the papers,
though as a Quaker he'd had to do this on the sly, the
accounts of the race-track winners. And up to now he'd
never owned an animal that would have merited any
such item as the *Banner News* had published. But opening his scrapbook for another peek, the day after the pasting, he saw that Eliza had put in under it an article from
the *Christian Convert* headed "The Race Track Evil." He
appreciated then the mistake he'd made.

He closed the book with a sigh and put it back in the
secretary. Then he went to the barn by the side door,
avoiding Eliza, who was out in the kitchen cutting corn
from cob for drying. In the barn he met Enoch, and the
two of them moved to Red Rover's stall like filings to a
magnet.

After they had silently feasted their eyes for a time,
Enoch said, "I saw Ed Arkell in town last night."

Arkell was editor of the *Banner News*, author of the
cherished item, and the man whose horse Red Rover had
bested. Arkell and the Reverend Godly had owned—up to

now, anyway—the two fastest animals in the county. Editor Arkell's little mare was no thunderbolt like Preacher Godly's big Black Prince. She was, to the untrained eye, no more than a pretty little chestnut carriage horse, a rounded ladies' pet and sugar-eater. She was a pet, all right, and she ate sugar; but let Arkell shake out the lines and say, "Come on, Maude," and the muscles you hadn't seen in her hindquarters and the reach of her great stride and the cleanness of her action came into evidence. Black Prince's appearance promised a little more than that fire-eater was ever able to deliver. Maude's appearance promised nothing; the only thing remarkable about that little mare was that she was faster than chain lightning. The two animals had never, to anyone's knowledge, met. The big black, by virtue of size and temperament, "ought" to win. But those back-country farmers were far too knowledgeable to be taken in by any "ought" to's. Crops didn't grow by ought to's, or deaths occur, or men and women marry. Contrariness, as much as ought to's, ran the world; and no bets had been laid on the outcome of a match between Black Prince and Maude.

"Mr. Arkell says," Enoch continued, "that he was taken advantage of in that little brush of yours and his."

"Advantage?" Jess asked, jarred from his imagining of the day when Red Rover would show his heels to Black Prince. "How's he figure that? Two animals, a stretch of empty road, and my horse pulls ahead—where's the advantage to that?"

"He says," Enoch explained, "that you flashed up on him from behind."

"Flashed! I overhauled him," Jess said. "That's a fact. He saw me coming, though."

"His story is you had a warm horse and a running start, while his poor little mare was cold and worn out."

"His poor little mare. By sugar," Jess said, "it can be one way or the other—but not both. A cold horse *or* a tired horse. But not the two together."

"I'm just reporting," Enoch said mildly, "the story as he tells it. Maude was tired from working the day before and cold from not having been on the road more'n a few minutes till you come along."

"She was a half-dozen miles from Arkell's place," Jess protested. "How d'thee account for that?"

"Mr. Birdwell," Enoch said, "try'n remember it ain't *me* speaking, but Editor Arkell. Furthermore, he says you were in your cut-down while he was in a regulation buggy. And to sum it all up, he was, as he says, taken advantage of."

"Why'd he print that piece then?"

"That you beat him, he says, was a fact. *That's* news. So he prints it. *How* you beat him is a matter of opinion, and he don't print that. He don't *need* to," Enoch confided, "the rate he's spreading it, word of mouth."

"Well, what's he want now? Me to write a retraction for the *Banner?*"

"What he wants, Mr. Birdwell, is a rematch."

Jess blanched a little at that word and, in spite of himself, had a quick look over his shoulder to see if Eliza, by some misfortune, had come up within earshot. "Rematch" was the nearest he'd come yet to race-track lingo. A little brush, two horses meeting by hapchance, was one thing, but a downright, bald-faced preplanned race was, so to speak, a horse of another color.

"Far as I know, Enoch, we had a fair match. But if Arkell don't think so and he can arrange what he thinks is, short of something public with paid admissions and side bets, I . . . I . . . reckon I'll meet his conditions. But thee do the fixing, Enoch, will thee?"

Enoch said, "You look on this as nothing more'n a warm-up for the Reverend, don't you, Mr. Birdwell?"

Jess nodded.

"Win or lose, a little brush with Maude can't do us no harm in that line?"

Jess nodded again.

"Any time suit you?"

"Eliza'd think it strange taking to the road in the morning."

"I appreciate that," Enoch said. "It'll be in the afternoon, late, and private."

He fixed it for the next Thursday at four on the new stretch of pike out beyond the Brush Creek School. He couldn't guarantee there wouldn't be spectators or other rigs abroad—after all, it was a public road—but Thursday was a quiet day and four a quiet hour. The "brush," and Jess was thankful for Enoch's delicacy in using this word, would start at the schoolhouse and wind up at the Sassafras Creek cemetery. He and the Arkells' seventeen-year-old boy would station themselves there in case it was horse and horse at the finish line.

Jess was satisfied with these terms, but by two o'clock on Thursday he was prickly-skinned and hot under the collar. Eliza hadn't said a word, but she appeared to know that something unusual was afoot. She sat at the noonday dinner table with her black eyes, ordinarily alight with plans, quiet and, Jess couldn't help but feel, accusing. He tried to reassure himself by remembering that the guilty flee when no man pursueth. He tried to put a good face on his departure.

"Is thee going into town, Jess?" Eliza asked as, lodged

in the doorway, he sought for some honest farewell word.

"I could go," Jess replied, "if thee needs anything."

"No," Eliza answered. "Nothing I need in town."

It was the minute to walk resolutely from the house, but still he lingered, deception weighing on his heart like lead.

"Thee just going out for a breath of air," Eliza asked, "so to speak?"

Going out for a breath of air was a silly thing for a man who'd been plowing since six. "More like for a little spin," he amended.

"Would thee like me to go with thee?"

Ordinarily, he was always urging Eliza to accompany him; a trip without her was half a trip, locomotion only. Now he had to say, "No, no, Eliza; I don't want to break into thy day," and quickly and unhappily closed the door behind him.

He and Enoch were silent on the way out to Brush Creek School. The day was mild and overcast, with the furry smell of goldenrod and the cellar dampness of decaying leaves. There was a threat of rain in the air, and sounds carried unusually well. They heard the ladylike clop of Maude's hoofs while the Arkell rig was still hidden from view where the road curved behind a woods lot. The voices of the two Arkells were pleasant and easy as they came to the meeting place. Jess envied them their good consciences.

By the time the two horses were aligned at the school, a good part of his uneasiness had vanished. His world had narrowed down to Red Rover, Maude, and the strip of road ahead. It was impossible, regarding the two animals, not to feel confident. He felt almost apologetic, matching a big powerful animal like Red Rover against a ladylike little contraption the shape of Maude. Only his memory of how that contraption could eat up the road made him loosen the reins and urge Red Rover on from the word go.

The road was empty and wide, the air heavy with harvest sweetness and the coming rain. This, Jess thought, is one of the glories of living, to fly across the surface of the earth, your challenger a half-length, a whole length behind you. It was a short-lived glory, however. A few drops of rain fell, and at that minute, whether it was the rain or not, Red Rover changed his way of going. Red Rover, who had the shoulders, the stride, the looks, for covering the ground, appeared not to have the heart for it. It was a race for another quarter of a mile. Then, as his horse slowed, and Jess began to push him, it was no race at all. Red Rover wouldn't be pushed. He could travel like a cannonball for his own pleasure, but he wanted to light the fuse himself. Something seemed to tell him that what had started as a frolic was petering out in hard work and weary going. He appeared to have a drop or two of Quaker blood himself, no more contentious than a lamb and wholly guided by the spirit; and the spirit didn't move him to do any further racing on that day.

Up to that point it had been a brush, short, to be sure, but pretty. After that it was nothing but a slow big horse eating the dust kicked up by a fast little one. Jess, short of stopping and pulling up a sapling to punish him with, urged Red Rover to the limit. Urging appeared to slow him down. Out of respect for the plow he'd set his hand to, Jess finished the course, more lengths than he cared to number to the rear.

At the Sassafras Creek cemetery, Enoch and the Arkells waited for him in the warm drizzle.

"What hit your horse?" Arkell asked.

"What hit him," Jess said bitterly, "was a sudden lazy streak. Combined with a mulish nature, laziness can't be coped with."

Arkell shook his head. "It didn't strike me as laziness. He didn't slow down; he stopped in his tracks."

"He's a quitter," Jess said, trying to keep the disappointment out of his voice.

"Don't be too hasty," Arkell urged. "He could've had an attack of some kind. Twinge in the liver. Spasm of colic."

"Twinge of laziness, spasm of mulishness," Jess insisted. "Ought to be a lesson to me. Handsome is as handsome does. Especially in horses."

Jess and Enoch were even more silent homeward bound than they had been on the outward trip. What can a loser say? And Jess's bitterness was increased by Red Rover's speed. Now that the brush was over, there was no holding him back. Half this willingness an hour ago would have bested Maude without trying.

"He sure is notionate," Enoch said finally. "First he will, then he won't."

"Well, he's been a lesson to me," Jess admitted, "if nothing else. Taught me that what a farmer needs is a plow horse, not a race horse. And I'll teach him tomorrow the lesson he taught me today."

Jess left the unhitching, when they got home, to Enoch. He felt he'd seen all of that big gelding he could stomach for one day. Eliza was putting supper on the table when he entered the house. She came over to him, a bowl of floating island, his favorite pudding, in her hands.

"Well, Jess?" she asked in a sympathetic voice.

Victory is a matter of chance; but truth, if a man so elects, he can have at any time. Deciding not to make defeat a hundred per cent, Jess told Eliza the truth.

"Eliza, I had another little brush with Arkell," he said, "and thee can put thy mind to rest about 'premier racing men' and matters of that ilk. Such things are all a matter of the past."

"Thee was bested then?" Eliza asked, not so much sympathetically now as knowingly.

"Bested is too mild a word for it."

"I thought thee would be," Eliza said pleasantly.

"Thought?" repeated Jess, thinking himself. "How'd thee know anything about it?"

Eliza went over to the table with the float. Then she turned back to Jess. "I didn't *know*," she said, "though thy actions were shouting it from the housetop; but I did have my suspicions. And, Jess, it came to me very strongly after thee'd been gone awhile to pray, for thy own sake, thee'd lose. I saw thee was getting far too taken with thyself as a horse racer for the good of thy soul. So I asked the Lord, if it was His will, to let thee lose this match. And I had the feeling, when I'd finished, that it *was* His will."

Jess was silent for a considerable spell. Then he asked, "Eliza, does thee recall about what time thee was making this petition?"

"Certainly not," Eliza said. "Does thee think I pray by the clock, Jess Birdwell? I did notice," she added, relenting a little, "that it had begun to rain when I opened my eyes."

"Eliza," Jess said, "I think I'd best go out to the barn and let Enoch know thee's a little forward with supper this evening."

Enoch was still rubbing down Red Rover when Jess got to the barn, and Jess stood for a while looking at his horse with changed eyes. Poor old fellow, he thought, what chance did thee have? Enoch looked up from his work, and Jess said, "Enoch, it might be we passed judgment on this animal a little too early."

"What do you mean, Mr. Birdwell?"

"Do you believe in the power of prayer, Enoch?"

Enoch came over to Jess, brush in hand. "Yes, sir, I do."

Jess told him what had happened. "At the exact moment Red gave up," he concluded.

Enoch ran the brush over his knuckles. "Mrs. Birdwell's such a good woman I don't suppose the Lord'd have the heart to say no to anything she asked. I know I don't," he said.

Jess nodded.

"Puts a different light on things, don't it?" Enoch asked.

Jess nodded again.

"I reckon we don't have to give up hope about the Reverend now?"

"I don't know's we'd have any better chance with him than we did today. Unless Eliza has a change of heart."

"Would she have to know about it?"

"She didn't know about today, far as anyone telling her goes."

"Mr. Birdwell," Enoch asked, turning the tables, "do you believe in the power of prayer?"

"If I didn't," Jess said, "today's demonstration would've convinced me."

"I don't mean Mrs. Birdwell's," Enoch explained. "I mean prayer in general, particularly yours."

Jess stared at Enoch. "Are you suggesting I start a praying contest with my own wife, Enoch?"

"No," Enoch said, "I ain't. It's no more'n natural to want your own horse to win, though. Is it?"

"It's natural enough," Jess conceded, "but under the circumstances it wouldn't be seemly. Besides being, under the circumstances, a waste of breath."

"Maybe so," Enoch agreed. He turned back to Red Rover. "Seems a pity, though. Got a man like Godly needs to be bested. Got a horse here could do the job. You don't think we could win Mrs. Birdwell over?"

"Thee mean get her to approve horse racing?"

"That's carrying it a little far maybe," Enoch admitted. "But get her not to pray, maybe? Leave it up to the horses?"

"I don't know," Jess said.

"She likes animals," Enoch argued. "If she knew Red, she might not have the heart to want to hold him back."

"She might not."

"What other chance have we got?"

"None," Jess admitted.

"I got your leave then? Leave to win her over to be neutral?"

"Yes," Jess said, "thee's got my full leave."

The two men walked up through the gusty autumn dark to the house.

The minute grace was over and the platter of tenderloin had started around the table, Enoch leaned toward Eliza and said, "Mrs. Birdwell, that new horse of ours don't feel at home here. He's restive and uneasy. You've always had a masterful way with animals. I wonder if you'd come out to the barn with me after supper and speak to him."

"Speak to him?"

"Big horse like that, people don't have no idea how sensitive they are. One that's been driven by ladies feels homesick for the petting he's been used to."

"Pet a racy-looking animal like that?"

"He can't help his looks. A few words from you and it

might make him more willing to settle down to a life of plowing and wagon-hauling."

Eliza looked at Jess. She was torn, he could tell, between her desire to make all persons—*and* livestock—at home and her reluctance to encourage any more road trials.

"It takes a woman to put heart in a homesick beast every time," Enoch said, in a voice suggesting that Red Rover was about the size of a sick kitten.

"There's no reason for not saying a word to him, I reckon," Eliza agreed.

Jess stayed planted right at the table when the two left for the barn. He didn't intend to do it, but the prayer welled up out of his heart in spite of himself. He didn't ask for much. He didn't think the Lord *ought* to concern Himself with horse races. But it would be a nice thing, he couldn't help suggesting to the Lord, if Eliza should develop some friendliness toward one of the Lord's own creatures.

Growing Up

In the South the war guns were thundering. Many men from Indiana were fighting; but the Quakers still planted their fields and minded their crops. Though it was deep in July the corn was neither so high nor so leafy that Jess couldn't see through the stalks and recognize who it was coming down the pike: Louella Mason, driving her splinter-legged old mare, in her buggy that rolled from side to side like a duck just emerging from water. Louella was a maiden lady of thirty or thirty-two, living with her old mother, and not a man on the place to align buggy wheels or to tell her when a mare had passed over the line that separates a carriage horse from crow bait.

Louella herself was, as usual, a sight to behold. She rose above the buggy seat bright and straight as a hollyhock, beruffled below the neck and beratted above. Louella was a seamstress, and she used her own person to exhibit her wares and demonstrate her abilities. She would don some of her latest creations, hitch her sorry mare to her unsteady buggy, and drive about the countryside visiting her customers. Or, as was often the case, Jess supposed, just visiting.

At the rate he and Labe were hoeing, they would reach the driveway to the house at about the time Louella turned in; if that was her plan, and Jess supposed it was. Eliza was probably Louella's most sympathetic listener. What had ever led Louella to believe that a strait-laced Quaker minister like Eliza would listen to her stories at all, Jess had no idea. Louella's stories were all about men. Jess believed that Eliza listened to Louella's tales with the same pleasure she would have had reading novels, had Eliza's conscience permitted her anything so worldly. As it was, her duty as minister and neighbor required her to hear Louella out—even though a novel couldn't have had more fervid accounts of dashed hopes, unsuitable avowals, and churning passions.

Eliza, while far too kindhearted to question Louella about the reality of these hopes and avowals and passions, did question Jess. She knew that Jess was no man of the world, but he *was* a man and thus better able than she to judge what was probable or possible in the conduct of men.

"Jess, does thee think a passing huckster, a grandfather, would act like that?"

"Jess, don't steamcar conductors have to keep regular hours?"

"Jess, what in the world would a boy of twenty see in a woman Louella's age?"

Eliza, marveling, pitying, sometimes laughing (though she said she was ashamed of herself for doing so, since Louella's stories, no matter how hopefully they started, all ended in disappointments), listened, except for suitable exclamations, in silence. And Jess listened to Eliza's retellings in the same way. If Eliza didn't think it kind for her to say to Louella, "Louella, if thee asks me, I think thee made up that story out of whole cloth," Jess didn't think anything would be gained by his telling his wife, "There's more goes on between men and women, Eliza, than thee has any notion of."

There was, and that was a fact. But if Eliza got to dwelling on this fact, she'd lose her pleasure in listening to Louella; and Louella would become uneasy about talking. Two people would be losers and for no good reason. So Louella told Eliza, Eliza told Jess, and Jess kept his mouth shut.

"Jess," Eliza asked, "does thee know what a gift of white roses means?"

"No," Jess answered, "that's something I've failed to learn."

"It means," Eliza told him, "'though the heart desires, duty forbids.'"

"Who figured that out?"

"Louella Mason."

"She give somebody white roses?"

"Don't make her out such a man-chaser, Jess. *She* was given white roses."

Jess whistled.

"Now don't scoff. Louella may make up stories, but she didn't make up those roses."

"How does thee know that?"

"She carries a white rosebud pressed in an old needlecase. It reminds her that though love calls, duty must come first."

"I'm glad she has a reminder," Jess said.

"Jess, does thee think that what Louella Mason needs is a good husband?"

That was a question Jess didn't mind answering. "A good husband never did anyone any harm," he said.

"The trouble with Louella," Eliza decided, "is she's too hopeful."

Jess couldn't find fault with that either. "Too hopeful by half," he agreed.

Though Jess had slowed down his own hoeing in order to avoid reaching the driveway at the same time as Louella, Labe kept right on at a 2.40 clip. It wasn't that Labe was by nature so work-brickel but that Jess had preached —and practiced—"hoe" so successfully during the past weeks that Labe appeared to have lost the hang of "slow down."

July was the growing month. There were those who said that on a hot still night they could hear the sound of the blunt cornstalks pushing their way upward through the loose loamy soil. Forty acres planted to corn sounded, on a hot still night, like a nest full of baby owls; a soft churring sound, they said, something halfway between cat purr and bird chirp.

Jess had never heard this sound himself. Even more awesome to him was the absolutely silent growth of weeds. They sprang up overnight, slimy and green as frog spit, between corn rows newly hoed the day before. All over southern Indiana, under the high-domed sky of July there was a heliograph sparkle of flashing hoes as the war against weeds was waged. Jess had his two big boys, Josh and Labe, and Enoch out in the fields by six in the morning. They stopped for dinner at eleven and paused in midafternoon for a rest and a pull on the switchel jug. Otherwise they hoed. Quitting time, Jess told them, was when it got dark enough for them to see the sparks when their hoes hit stone.

Jess stepped through the corn to the row where Labe was hoeing. "Thee can spare thyself a confab with Louella Mason," he said, "if thee slows down a bit."

Labe took a couple of chops like something wound up

and bound to go on until it runs down after Jess spoke to him.

"She the one coming down the pike?" he asked.

"She is, and heading for here or I miss my guess."

"I don't mind talking to Miss Mason," Labe said, and began to hoe again.

Jess let him hoe. He wasn't about to say to Labe, "I forbid thee to talk to Miss Louella Mason." There was no call for anything like that.

Labe was seventeen years old, a quiet boy whose quietness was sometimes mistaken for bashfulness. Labe didn't have a bashful bone in his body. Josh, his older brother, was the bashful one; ten times as shy as Labe and ten times as talkative in an effort to hide his uneasiness.

The buggy, as Jess knew it would, reached the end of the corn row as Labe did. Jess turned his back on the talkers and, stationary amidst the stalks, minced weeds he had already hoed up. His strategy didn't fool Louella.

"Jess," she called out, "what are you doing, hiding back in there?"

Jess, facing about, said, "I've reached the age, Louella. I can't keep up with my own boys any more."

It was a lie. He could still hoe Labe into the ground, and he resented Louella's forcing him into a lie—even a white one.

"That's just what I want to talk to you about, Jess."

Carrying his hoe and hoping to suggest that he could pause for a moment only, Jess walked down to the buggy. He and Eliza had had more than one discussion about why Louella Mason wasn't pretty. It seemed she ought to be. She had nice brown eyes, a good nose, curling auburn hair, and a smiling mouth. But they did not add up to prettiness, and her face was the more disturbing because of this. It was like concluding that two and two made three, something you knew well enough was less than right. Looking at Louella made you lose faith in your ability to see straight. She ought to be pretty. But she ain't, Jess thought for the hundredth time, she just ain't, and with those curling locks and big brown eyes she ought to be. And he felt he had a mean downgrading streak somewhere in himself not to be able to *see* Louella's prettiness.

Before he could say "Howdy," Louella was telling him what it was she wanted to talk to him about.

"Jess, how long's it been since you or Eliza's had a good look at this boy?"

"I don't know what thee means by a 'good look,' Louella. I see him every day of my life."

"That's likely the trouble," Louella told him. "What's right under our nose is what we miss."

Jess turned and looked at Labe as carefully as if he'd been a stand of corn. He had been heavier than Jess for some time. Now Jess saw that he was also a couple of inches taller. Time was when Labe, younger than Josh, had inherited Josh's clothes. That time had passed long ago. Lately, he had inherited Jess's hand-me-downs. That time, Jess now realized, had also passed. Labe's pants didn't reach his shoe tops, his shirt was split across the shoulders, and his collar couldn't have been buttoned without slicing off his Adam's apple.

"Well," asked Louella, "now you've had a good look, what do you see?"

What Jess saw was an oversized ten-year-old, a big fellow, but still his barefoot boy.

Louella didn't wait for Jess to find words for this.

"What *I* see, Jess, is a man."

That, Jess thought, is thy failing, Louella. But all he

answered was, "The boy does appear to be getting too big for his britches."

Labe, ordinarily unfazed by anything, flushed at this. "I better be getting back to work," he said, and left Jess exactly where he'd schemed not to be: alone with Louella.

When Labe was out of earshot, Louella said, "Jess, that boy's dressed like a scarecrow. I'm going to speak to Eliza about his clothes."

Jess, defending himself *and* Eliza, said, "Out here in the cornfield and in this weather we don't go in much for putting on the dog."

"He ought to have something that doesn't bind, even in the cornfield. And I've noticed him at box suppers. Pitiful! Alongside Josh, or even Enoch, he looks like an orphanage boy, someone you and Eliza took in for the work you could get out of him. Has that boy ever had an outfit firsthand since he was born? I venture to say even his didies were hand-me-downs from Josh."

"Thee better ask Eliza about that," Jess said, half turning away. "She's the one can answer questions like that."

"Jess," Louella said, "Jess, spare me a minute."

Jess refused to turn back toward the buggy.

"How long do you intend to keep reminding me, Jess?"

Jess paused. It went against all his training to walk away from a lady calling to him. But to talk to a lady on the subject Louella wanted to discuss went against his very grain, and that lay deeper than training.

"Jess, I didn't mean being so forward that time."

At that Jess turned to face Louella. If this was the tack she was now taking, he was willing to meet her halfway.

"It passed out of my memory long ago," he said—the second lie Louella had backed him into in five minutes.

Louella herself was not such an easy liar. "I didn't tell

you the truth, Jess. I meant it, every word I said. What I didn't mean was to let you know the way I felt."

"It's forgotten, Louella, long forgotten," Jess said, lying again. "Thee speak to Eliza about Labe's clothes. Now thee's called it to my attention I can see the boy needs a new outfit. Thee can tell Eliza for me I think she should commission thee to run him up a new outfit. Something more suitable to his age and size."

"Oh, Jess," Louella said, "don't go thinking I was trying to drum up trade. That's the last thing I had in mind."

"I know that," Jess said, taking pleasure in speaking, finally, the absolute truth. But he turned away resolutely from the buggy.

Labe waited for him to catch up. "Why don't thee like to talk to Miss Mason?" he asked.

Jess thought, I can't open my mouth about that woman without lying. "Midafternoon in July," he said, "and midst of the hoeing season is not my idea of the proper time or place for a little chat about sewing."

"Is that what she wanted to talk about?"

"That's what we talked about," Jess said, and hacked on up the row, easily outdistancing Labe.

In corn-hoeing weather, the pause between supper and bedtime is short. Except for Mattie, whose job it was to wash the supper dishes, the family was outside on the front porch. Little Jess, the child born after Sarah's death, was sprinting about catching lightning bugs in the grass. Jess, in the fading light, was squinting at a week-old Philadelphia newspaper. Eliza, beside him in a rocker, was crocheting edging for pillow shams. The two big boys, after a long day of hoeing, were stretched out on the porch floor, sound asleep insofar as the eye could see.

"Better get on upstairs to bed," Eliza said.

Neither boy stirred.

Jess looked up from his paper. "Let them enjoy the air for a while. Those upstairs rooms will be stifling tonight."

Eliza said no more. It was deep into katydid time, but from the banks of the stream that circled the knoll on which the house stood, frogs still remembered spring. Spring was long past, but frog croak and lip-lip of water against the limestone outcropping made April seem only yesterday. Eliza rolled up her crocheting and stuck her needle into her ball of thread.

"Jess," she said, "thee'll strain thy eyes trying to read in this light."

Jess knew what Eliza was asking. He could hear her perfectly well from behind a newspaper, but he had never been able to convince Eliza of this. The minute he folded his paper, Eliza said, "Louella Mason said she and thee had decided Labe needed a new suit."

"I told her to speak to thee about it."

"She did, and I agreed with her. Louella needs the money and Labe needs the clothes. I told her I'd send Labe over to be measured for a suit."

Josh, who had apparently been asleep, gave Labe a poke with his toe. "Thee hear that, Labe? Thee's going to a dressmaker to have a suit made."

Eliza spoke tartly to her oldest. "What does thee suggest, Joshua? We've got neither the time nor the money for a trip to Cincinnati to see a tailor. And I'm not enough of a seamstress myself to run up a suit for a man."

"Man," Josh hooted, "man!" He prodded Labe again with his toe. "Man," he said. "Thee hear that? Is Miss Louella Mason going to make thee a little outfit?"

Labe answered sleepily. "I reckon she could do it," he said.

"Is this going to have pink or blue? Ruffles or bows?"

"Now, Josh," Jess said, "no use running a good thing into the ground. Miss Mason can do tailoring, and Labe needs a suit."

Paying no attention to his father, Josh leaned over his brother and did an inchworm measuring exercise up and down Labe's outstretched frame. "Now we'll tighten it up just a wee bit here. And we'll let it out a lot here. Thee's a big boy for thy age, isn't thee, Labey? Shut my eyes and I'd almost think thee was a man."

Labe, who could have flattened Josh simply by rolling over on him, said nothing.

"Inchy, inchy-inchy," said Josh in what he took to be a seamstress's falsetto, knuckling and fingering his way up and down Labe's six-foot length. "Does thee want an old-maid dressmaker measuring thee, Labe?"

"I don't mind if she don't," Labe said lazily.

Josh jumped to his feet. "Well, if I felt that way I'd be ashamed to admit it."

"I know thee would, Josh," Labe said.

Josh ran inside, and they could hear his quick angry footsteps on the stairs and the slam of his bedroom door.

Jess felt as if he should rebuke Labe for something. But he couldn't think for what.

The time Louella spent on the suit would have been more noticeable if it had come at any other season of the year. But with harvesting going on, together with canning, drying, pickling, and preserving, suit-making was scarcely noticed.

Elderberries had ripened early, and Eliza had these, in addition to all the tame fruits of the orchard Jess maintained, to cope with. Combined with pieplant, elderberries made a fine sauce for the summer table. Dried, they made many a winter pie. Stone jars were packed with mango peppers. The house was filled with the smell of vinegar, spices, and brown sugar as Eliza prepared kettles of chowchow, piccalilli, and green tomato relish. It wasn't apple-butter time yet, but the summer apples had to be dealt with, dried or cooked up for early use as sauce. Daily, the baskets of Yellow Transparents, Early Harvest, Duchess, and Golden Sweets were brought into the kitchen.

In addition to pickling, preserving, and drying, Eliza had Mattie's buggy rides with Gardiner Bent to think about. Mattie was still a child to her mother, but the Bent boy had already started to pay her attention. Gardiner himself seemed a steady-enough boy in spite of his family. His mother was part Indian and would rather fish than keep house. And his father, whatever made up the other portions of his nature, was only part farmer. Weeds grew, fences fell down, cows went dry, while Silas Bent sat in his dooryard reading.

Labe's suit-making visits, with all these enterprises under way, seemed the least important part of the summer. After work he drove over for his fittings without being ordered to do so; he came home in good time and good humor, and ignored Josh's jibes. Eliza had spared the time to make a trip to Madison to buy the material for the suit. She had chosen a lighter gray than was absolutely practical because, when the merchant laid the cloth over Labe's shoulder, she had been unable to resist the way that color flattered his warm skin, tow hair, and gray eyes. Josh, when he saw the material's light color, said, "What's thee figuring on, Labe, a wedding suit?"

Eliza, who heard that, said, "Thee better bridle that sharp tongue of thine, Josh, or no woman'll ever have thee."

"I'm not figuring on asking any old dressmaker, when I do propose."

"That'll be enough of that kind of talk, Josh."

Josh continued to mutter, but Eliza, accustomed to the boys' bickerings, only half heard what was said.

When Jess spoke, though, she listened. One hot night in August, when the tailoring job had been going on for more than a month, Eliza took her time brushing her hair before bedtime. She was standing in front of the opened windows of their bedchamber, relishing the feel of air on her neck and shoulders as she lifted her heavy hair.

Jess, already in bed, said, "Eliza, how many fittings does it take to make a suit?"

Jess was always conjecturing; matters heavenly and earthly, foreign and domestic, interested him. Eliza was accustomed, at his prompting, to putting her mind to problems pretty remote from life at the Maple Grove Nursery. She answered this question with no thought of their own household.

"Why, there's no set number insofar as I know, Jess. Some people are easier to fit than others. Some materials are easier to handle than others."

"In that case," Jess said, "Labe is a caution to fit and thee picked some outlandishly hard material to handle."

"What makes thee say that?"

"Hasn't thee noticed?"

"Noticed what? I've noticed a good many things around here this summer. I've noticed that the blackberries need picking and that Mattie, every time I want her to do something, has to take a buggy ride. If thee's noticed something I haven't, tell me. It's too late at night and too hot for guessing games."

Jess, feeling he had possibly made a mountain of a molehill, said, "Mattie's not the only one taking buggy rides. Labe's been hitching up at least twice a week for the past month and driving over to Louella Mason's for a fitting. It just crossed my mind he was maybe being overfitted."

Eliza finished her hair and threw the heavy black braid across her shoulder with what was pretty near a snap.

"Overfitted? I never heard of such a thing. What does thee mean by 'overfitted'?"

Jess mumbled something about the material's being worn out before it ever took shape as a suit.

"Nonsense," said Eliza. "I know good material when I see it, and that's what I bought."

"I'm sure thee did, Eliza. It just crossed my mind Labe was calling on Miss Mason a little more often than was necessary."

"What's wrong with that? Is he getting his work done?"

"Oh, yes," Jess said. "No question about that."

"Does thee begrudge him the use of a horse and rig?"

"No, no," Jess assured her. "Won't do the horse and rig a mite of harm."

"Well, then, what's to complain about?"

"I wasn't complaining, Eliza. I was just noticing."

"Thee was noticing in a complaining way. And it isn't called for. Louella's a conscientious seamstress, and Labe's never to my knowledge had a new suit in his life. Nothing but hand-me-downs. Louella's taking pains. She's trying to get this suit done for Labe's eighteenth birthday, and I don't know anyone more deserving."

"Me either," Jess agreed meekly. And with that Eliza blew out the light and got into bed.

Jess, however, was unwilling to leave well enough alone. "Thee has to admit," he said, once Eliza had settled herself comfortably, "that Louella does have a kind of soft turn where men are concerned."

"So *that's* been troubling thee," Eliza exclaimed, sliding back against the headboard into a more conversational position. "And about thy own son, who is no more than a boy. Jess, I've always credited thee with having a nicer mind than most men."

"It's about average, I reckon," Jess said.

"All right," Eliza said. "I'll tell thee something I hadn't intended to tell thee. It'll just make thee more inclined to twit Louella. But it will set thy mind at rest about Labe."

"I got no desire to twit Louella. Got no desire to see her, even. It just struck me Labe was going over there pretty often."

"Louella's painstaking, that's all. Labe, except for getting the suit done, is the least of her concerns. A new happiness has come into her life."

"What's his name?" Jess asked.

"I said thee'd just twit."

"I'm sorry," Jess said.

"Does thee want to hear, or not?"

Jess wasn't extra anxious, that hour of the night and sunup threatening from the minute he put his feet under the covers, to hear another chapter in the tale of Louella's loves. But since he'd started this conversation, he felt honor bound to let Eliza finish it.

"A long time ago Louella loved a man, but had to give him up," Eliza said.

"She's had to give them all up, hasn't she?"

"This was her real love. And he loved her, Louella believes, as much as she loved him."

"What was the hindrance then?"

"He was married," Eliza said.

"Well, that'd be a hindrance all right," Jess said. "I see

that. What I don't see's how the memory makes her so happy."

"It's not the memory of the father," Eliza explained. "Louella's recently met the son."

"The son," Jess said. He threw back the covers, stepped out of bed, and went to the windows, which he tried to push higher.

"Those windows won't go any higher," Eliza told him. "Pushing will just jam them."

"It's mighty close in here."

"Thee'll just heat thyself fretting about it. So thee sees thee's being unreasonable worrying about Labe. Louella's mind is elsewhere."

"This son," Jess said, "ain't he a mite young for Louella?"

"The father," Eliza explained, "was considerably older than Louella. And there *is* a difference in age. But Louella is willing to wait."

"How about the boy?" Jess asked. "Is he willing?"

"Boy!" Eliza exclaimed. "Who said anything about a boy? He's a young man. What makes thee leap to conclusions the way thee does, Jess?"

"It's just a flaw in my make-up, I reckon," Jess said. "Where's this young man live?"

"Why," Eliza said, "I wouldn't think of asking Louella for names and dates and where people live. Does thee think I should?"

"No, no," Jess said promptly. "Certainly not. It'd be nosy and unfriendly."

"I just sympathize," Eliza said.

"Sympathy's the ticket," Jess said. "But I can't help feeling I ought to warn this boy."

"Stop calling him 'boy.' And what would thy warning be?"

"Blessed if I know."

"Thee never used to be a worrier, Jess."

"I'm getting older."

"Well, there's no use worrying about Labe. The suit'll be done Sixth Day evening. And there's no use worrying about Louella. Thee can't change her from being a dreamer."

"Thee think this business about first a father and then son is all a dream?"

"I might be able to swallow one or the other. But father *and* son. *That's* dreaming. Don't thee think so, Jess?"

"Dreaming?" Jess asked. "Sounds like a first-class nightmare to me."

On Sixth Day evening when Labe started down to the barn to hitch up for the trip to Louella's, Jess joined him.

"This the last fitting?" Jess asked.

"Louella said it should be done tonight."

"Well, I guess I'll just ride over to Louella's with thee. It's been on my conscience for some time, not calling on old Mrs. Mason."

"She's not home," Labe said.

"Not home?" Jess exclaimed. "I didn't know she was able to move about."

"Her son came and took her over to Scipio a couple of weeks back for a change. Thee could drive over to Scipio to see her."

"That's a pretty far step to see Mrs. Mason."

"It's a nice evening for a ride," Labe said.

There was no denying that. But a trip to see old Mrs. Mason wouldn't do Labe any good. And he didn't know what would: warn Labe, or get in the buggy and go with Labe, or tell Labe to stay home and he'd fetch the suit.

Labe's open face and candid eyes didn't encourage any
of these notions. What *could* he say? Labe had heard all
the family talk about Louella. There was not much sense
in telling him once again and at this late date that Louella
had notions about men. And he couldn't bring himself to
ask Labe if he'd come to like Louella's notions.

Jess had no intention of waiting up for Labe, like a
nervous mother worried about the length of her daughter's buggy ride. He'd just got interested in reading, and
by the time he had begun to feel drowsy, Gardiner Bent
brought Mattie home, and talking to them roused him
too much to think of bed for a while.

At ten o'clock everyone except Jess and Josh was in
bed and asleep. Josh was in his room, but Jess could see
by the light that shone onto the maple tree outside the
boys' room that Josh was not yet sleeping. At ten-thirty
Jess put down his book and went outside to wash his
feet. He had pumped a basin of water from the cistern
and seated himself on the wash bench when he heard
Labe turn in the driveway. Jess dallied with the washing,
but had soaped, rinsed, and dried before Labe finished
unhitching. He went inside, hung his pants over his arm,
and picked up his boots and socks. While he was waiting
for Labe, Josh came downstairs.

"Labe just now getting in?" Josh asked.

"I take it it's Labe," Jess answered.

Josh was the only one of the boys who slept in a nightshirt. Even Little Jess slept in his drawers. Jess privately
thought nightshirts pretty fine-haired for a farm boy; but
Josh fancied them and Eliza made them and Jess said
nothing. The two of them, Josh in his nightshirt and he in
his drawers, made a pretty strange-looking reception
committee, Jess couldn't help thinking when he saw Labe.

Labe was wearing his new suit. It fit him as smooth as the husk on an ear of corn. With his ankles and wrists covered, Labe had lost his look of a boy who'd outgrown his clothes. He looked like a large-bodied, full-blooded young man, at ease and confident.

"What's *thee* been celebrating?" Josh asked suspiciously.

Labe answered calmly, "My birthday."

"Thy birthday's not till tomorrow."

"I know that. But tonight was the night my suit was finished, so Louella cooked a birthday supper to celebrate."

Josh said, "Did thee change thy suit at Miss Mason's?"

"Yes, I did."

"Nobody but two ladies in the house?"

"One lady. Old Mrs. Mason's over at Scipio visiting."

"Just thee and Miss Mason?"

"Yes," said Labe.

"I'd think thee'd have more respect for a lady living alone than to strip in her house."

"I shut the door," Labe said, "and I kept my drawers on. Anyway, Louella was busy in the kitchen cooking." Then, to his father, "Louella wanted to see how the suit looked and for me to wear it to the party."

"Party," Josh exclaimed. "Thee just said there was no one else there."

"There wasn't. But she had it fixed like a party. And she was dressed like a party. So I dressed, too. It seemed the right thing to do."

"It was," Jess said. "It was the right thing to do. And the suit looks fine. A handsome piece of material and a perfect fit. And that white rose on thy lapel sets it off to a T."

"Where'd thee get that?" Josh demanded.

"Louella," Labe said.

"Now, boys," Jess said heartily, "let's all get on up to bed. It may be your birthday tomorrow, Labe, but the weeds don't know it."

Labe led the way, followed by Josh, nightshirt flapping around his thin shanks, and Jess, barefooted, carrying pants and boots. Halfway up the stairs Jess began to snicker.

"What's so funny?" Josh, always self-conscious, asked.

The thought had come to Jess that he and Josh, in nightshirt and drawers, were following the resplendent Labe up the stairs like the two ugly sisters after the ball in the fairy tale. But it wasn't a thought he could share with Josh.

"Life," Jess said, and without lying, "is funny."

"It don't seem any laughing matter to me," said Josh.

"Well," Jess added, still telling the truth, and this was a truth the young, for some reason, relished, "it's pretty sad, too."

This seemed to satisfy Josh. Arguing no more, he followed Labe into the room they shared and closed the door behind him.

Jess stood for a minute beside the closed door laughing silently. Then to his surprise he continued from what he'd said to Josh, "Sad as can be. Sometimes sadder than words can tell."

After the Battle

In the upstairs bedroom where Jess and Eliza slept the
July morning was already warm at five-thirty. Though he
hadn't roused her when he got up, Eliza knew before she
opened her eyes that her husband was no longer beside
her. She awakened and listened. "What do I expect to
hear?" she asked herself sleepily. The answer brought
her awake with a start: gunfire. She had been listening,
even in her sleep, for gunfire. Why, on a farm in southern Indiana . . . Then she remembered, all at once, not
piece by piece. The whole of the day before crowded her
mind. Yesterday there had been gunfire, and she and Jess
had listened with their very veins, not out of any fear
for themselves, but because their eldest was off with the
Home Guard, every one of his Quaker principles thrown
to the wind, trying to save Vernon from Morgan, the
raider.

As her memory of Josh and their fear for him came to
her, Eliza threw back the already too warm sheet and
hurried across the rag carpet to the windows. She felt
thirsty for the reassurance of the known landscape,

parched for it. The air outside the window was cooler than that inside the room, and she leaned as far out as she dared, grateful for the freshness. Rolling summer fields, wheat yellow, corn green. Cows, already milked, standing switch tail in the sycamore shade. Summer haze in the hollows mingling with morning mist off the Muscatatuck. Crows flapping by, early to work. An old hen, deceived by early warmth, letting off a premature mid-morning cackle. A few Juneberries escaped the children by some miracle, hanging drawn and dried like summer raisins on the Juneberry tree. Nothing changed. Nothing bearing the signs of disaster. And there had been a disaster yesterday, had there not?

It was odd for Eliza to ask herself such a question. It showed what the day before had done to her. You do not bear five children, become a recorded Quaker minister, and survive over twenty years as Jess Birdwell's wife without knowing a disaster when you see it. Yet she was uncertain as to the proper name for yesterday's happenings; yesterday, toward the end of the day, "picnic," instead of "disaster," had seemed as good a name as any. Labe had found Josh; and, except for a head cracked in a fall over a cliff, he was none the worse for the wear. None the worse physically anyway. Spiritually was another matter, for Josh was convinced that by his warlike valor he had singlehandedly saved Vernon from the enemy. And, for any outward indication, Jess believed the same. Jess had welcomed his prodigal home with a few prayers and many helpings of food. When she had rebuked Jess for giving Josh his best horse to ride off to war on, Jess had quoted George Fox to her. When Penn asked Fox what he should do, now that he had become a Quaker, with the sword he was accustomed to wear, Fox had replied, "Wear it as long as thee can."

259

That quotation had been a mistake on Jess's part. "Fox didn't," Eliza reminded Jess, "give Penn the sword. Or let him go off to a real war with it, telling him to lop off heads and arms as long as he could. That's what thee did, sending Josh off armed, on thy fast horse."

This conversation had taken place before Josh's return. And it had reminded both Jess and Eliza that lopping off was a two-way street. What Josh could do, he could also suffer. And being the boy he was, to suffer would more likely be his fate. Jess had turned away, sick at heart, she knew. But she had let him go without a word of comfort. There was no honest way for a Quaker to let his son go off to fight and at the same time be comfortable, and she wasn't the woman to try to deceive any man, let alone Jess.

But after Josh's safe return, Jess had become more and more comfortable. And when the children had finally gone to bed, every one of them was in a war fever of some kind: Mattie, proud of Gardiner Bent, her Methodist beau, who was a full-time soldier; Labe, resisting soldiering but banged up from a private fist fight he had won; Josh, with his cracked skull, evidence of his warlike courage; Little Jess, only eight, but in a swivet to land a blow somewhere on someone himself.

After the children were all asleep, she and Jess had stood on the back porch, breathing the cool and the peace of the evening—she with two minds about the day's events: rejoicing in Josh's return, but downcast that he had gone at all; and Jess, for all of his talk of how bright the stars were and how well the peaches were ripening, was not, she could tell, completely easy in his mind either. Jess, when happy, never lacked for a subject for conversation, particularly late at night when everyone else was ready for sleep. But last night he had finally found nothing to say. And it was in this silence that he had heard the sounds down by the springhouse, and, investigating, had found the poor Southern boy.

Jess had carried him into the kitchen. The boy had been hurt several days earlier at Dutch Ford and since then had been hiding, living off the country and trying to catch up with Morgan. He had been trying to find something to eat in the springhouse when he had fallen down the steps and reopened his wound. It was this fall and the moans he had tried to stifle that Jess had heard. In the beginning the boy was in too much pain and too hungry to worry about being caught by the enemy. And after Jess had bound up his leg, and Eliza had fed him, he was too worn out and too sleepy to care. They had half led, half carried him to the spare room, and before Jess could get him undressed he was already sound asleep.

The arrival of the Rebel boy had done wonders for Jess's peace of mind. After he had put him to bed, Jess had become as talkative as ever, his qualms about the day's events washed away in the flood of his happiness at being able to care for one of the enemy. That proved, didn't it, that he was free of hate? Eliza didn't know what it proved. But Jess, cleaning up the kitchen after the bandaging and feeding, had hummed as carefree as if the morning's gunfire had been nothing more than the sounds of an Independence Day celebration. Or real gunfire, but of no consequence, because he didn't hate.

He had stuffed the last of the soiled bandages into the cookstove, and had momentarily paused in his humming. "I'll set some buckwheat batter for breakfast," he said. "We'll have a hungry crew on our hands in the morning. How about my bringing up a crock of sausage meat from the springhouse? Buckwheat cakes and sausage gravy? How's that strike thee, Eliza?"

It struck Eliza as something she had no heart for. If Jess was in a picnic mood, she couldn't stop him. But she couldn't pretend to share it either. She went upstairs to bed leaving all the breakfast preparation to him.

These were the events of the day before. Thinking about them, it took her a half hour instead of ten minutes to dress. It was six when she came downstairs. She opened the kitchen door and saw that the picnic mood of the day before was still in full swing. Jess, in one of her checkered aprons, motioned to her with the griddlecake turner to come in and to be quiet. When she had closed the door behind her, he said, "No use rousing up all the others. Jimmy and Little Jess are keeping me busy as it is."

"Jimmy?" she asked, and Jess, like a schoolmaster with a backward pupil, pointed to the soldier boy.

Little Jess and Jimmy were seated at the end of the table next to the stove. The gravy bowl was already half empty and the sorghum-molasses pitcher needed refilling.

"Good morning, boys," Eliza said.

Little Jess, who was in his own home, and, besides, had a mouthful of buckwheat cake and gravy, didn't reply. The boy, Jimmy, said, "Good morning, ma'am."

He looked worse to Eliza than he had the night before. In morning light she could see that the rising above his left temple was big as a turkey egg, but less solid, discolored and wobbly. She looked away quickly.

"I thought thee'd like to sleep late this morning," she told him.

"I'm out of the habit of sleeping after daylight." He appeared to think this over. "Out of the habit of sleeping, you might say. Anyway, I was hungrier than I was sleepy this morning, ma'am."

"Thee could've had thy breakfast in bed."

The boy looked at Eliza, amazed. "I ain't sick, ma'am."
He had lifted his head quickly, and the rising trembled.

Eliza, courteously ignoring the ugly rising, motioned
to his leg. "I been hit," he said, "but I ain't sick."

"Doesn't thy head hurt?" she couldn't help asking.

"I know that bump don't look nice, ma'am," he said,
"but it's a real good sign. I got a shell splinter in there,
and it's working its way out. It's just like a splinter in
your thumb you can't dig out. It's got to fester its way
out. Don't cause me no pain. It did at first, but it don't
any more. My leg hurts. That's a good sign, too," he said.
"It's beginning to draw. That's a sign of healing."

"Did a doctor tell thee all this . . . about your head and
leg?" Eliza asked.

"Doctor?" He repeated what she had said as if she had
spoken in a foreign language. Then he understood. "I was
with Morgan, ma'am, and we been riding real hard. If
you get hit, Morgan don't get off his horse and fetch you
to a doctor." He laughed, and in spite of herself Eliza
looked again at that soft-shelled egg-shaped rising. "No,
not Morgan," he said quietly. "No, ma'am, you ain't with
Morgan for your health. That's a dead-sure cinch."

Eliza didn't need any argument to convince her of that.
If Jimmy had ever had any health, he had lost it a long
time ago. He was rawboned, though the bones he had
were small. Under his tan was the yellow of fever. His
blue eyes were back in his head like an old man's. His
hair, which in health had been black, was as dingy and
matted as an old worn-out buffalo robe. Eliza didn't know
where he got the energy to eat and talk as he was doing.
From fever, probably. But back of the courtesy and the
conversation, the "yes, ma'ams" and the apparent willingness to answer all questions, Eliza saw a constant wari-
ness. He was practicing half-forgotten parlor tricks. A

sudden sound of movement and his sunken blue eyes were hard as stones. The skin would tighten across his sharp little jaws. Then he would go back to his eating, spooning sausage gravy onto buckwheat cakes, like a mannerly fox or stoat.

"How old is thee, Jimmy?" Eliza asked.

"Nineteen." He saw her surprise. "I know I'm kind of runty," he admitted. "Two years with Morgan's kind of shook me down in the saddle. A good thing. You ain't such a good target down low." Then he laughed again and touched his forehead. "Sat up too high once, though. I sure did."

"We'll get thee to a doctor this afternoon, Jimmy."

Jimmy, all fox now, put down his fork quickly. "No," he said, "I don't need any doctor. I'll stay right here if it's all the same to you."

Jess, who had been keeping the supply of griddlecakes coming, intervened. "Eliza, I've got a cake here for thee."

"I'm not hungry," she said. "I'll bake while thee eats." She poured herself a cup of black coffee and managed it with one hand, the cake turner with the other.

At the table Jess began, and Jimmy unbelievably continued, to eat. Little Jess, a knife-and-fork winner himself in lesser company, gave up, pushed back his plate, and settled down to a steady stare at the Johnny Reb, a man, Eliza knew, that Little Jess had expected to carry some sign of the nether regions upon him: a brimstone smell, or even horns. Maybe he thought that Jimmy's rising was horns beginning to sprout.

"Can thee give a Rebel yell?" Little Jess asked.

For a minute Eliza saw that the boy thought Little Jess was making fun of him. Then he said, "Is that what you Yankees call it?"

"What do you Rebels call it?"

"We don't call ourselves Rebels."

Little Jess wasn't interested in the names for things. "Can thee give the yell?" he persisted.

"Sure," Jimmy said.

"Will thee give it now?"

"Now? No, it wouldn't be right, here in the house."

"Couldn't thee give a quiet Rebel yell?"

"You can't give that yell quiet . . . any more than you can shoot a quiet cannon."

This gave Little Jess ideas about an even more interesting subject. "Did thee ever . . ." he began, but Eliza stopped that question before he could finish it.

"Fill up the woodbox, Little Jess," she said. "Now, this minute."

Little Jess, no soldier, still knew a command when he heard it. He left the table promptly. Eliza, when Jimmy had finally pushed back his plate, urged him, if he wouldn't see a doctor, to go back to bed. But he refused to budge, too proud perhaps to show any weakness before his enemies. All his signs were good, he said again, head easy, leg drawing, belly tight as a drum. He tilted his chair against the wall and looked at her and Jess and the room: house, furniture, and civilians—all curious and faintly ridiculous to him after two years on a horse's back. He answered Jess's questions, though plainly puzzled by many, without hesitation. Jess wasn't as simple as Little Jess. Rebel yells didn't interest him, but Rebels did. Where was he from? What was he fighting for? He was from Plum Tree, South Carolina. And as to what he was fighting for, Eliza had heard the same story word for word from Josh a dozen times in the last two months: honor and freedom and self-preservation. The Mason-Dixon Line hadn't changed that story a whit.

She cleared the table, washed the dishes, swept the

floor around the two men. Jess lifted his feet to make way
for the broom, but didn't pause in his talk. By midmorn-
ing she had fresh peach pies in the oven. The heat from
the cookstove, which she was keeping fired up, would
surely drive the two of them out, she thought. Jess gave
no sign of feeling it. He was making a day of it, celebrating something, peace or victory or Josh's return or the
enemy made welcome. He was waiting for the surprise
the children would have when they finally got up and
saw who had spent the night with them. He was antici-
pating the love feast they'd all celebrate at dinner, North
and South united around his table. Eliza, stringing green
beans for a mess of succotash, listened to the talk and,
through the opened window, to the summer sounds: the
regular creak of the windmill and the papery ruffle of
the big-leafed maples. Over the smell of the baking pies,
she caught whiffs from the Prairie Rose now in full
bloom, and, over that, all the mingling of scents of fruity
ripenings from Jess's orchards. She could see the big cannonball clouds at the horizon and above them the arch of
deep summer blue. Stretch her senses in every direction,
there was nothing but felicity. Nevertheless, she could not
manage happiness. Children at home and in health;
enemy routed; Jess in high fettle. She counted her blessings, and, like women at weddings, had to squeeze back
her tears, for at the heart of the tulle and the orange
blossoms there is a core of sadness: the fairer the bride,
the higher the wedding cake, the greater the cause for
sorrow; for life, which is going to contradict these things,
will be, by contrast, the darker.

As if to tell her how silly tears were on such a day, she
heard singing. The trees hid arrivals from her sight, but
Little Jess brought in the news with his armload of wood.

"Enoch," he announced in great excitement, "is bringing home a prisoner."

Enoch hadn't been, insofar as Eliza knew, mixed up with the fighting.

Jimmy, at the word "prisoner," brought his chair down on all four legs. Jess, stopping his talking to listen, said, "Mighty happy prisoner, sounds like."

Eliza, who could see the porch, said, "It's no prisoner. It's Clate Henry."

Eliza often thought Jess could have a hired hand a little less talkative and self-assured than Enoch. But Enoch came in now, meechin' as you please, holding Clate Henry up with one hand and quieting him down with the other.

"You folks know Clate Henry, don't you?" Enoch asked. "From over Sand Creek way? He's been in the Guard for the last couple of days."

Clate Henry was a straw-colored, pudgy little man. Eliza didn't know a thing about guard duty, but she'd think twice before she'd give Clate a job of egg-hunting after dark. Clate sat down suddenly and looked surprised.

"What's the matter with him?" Eliza asked Enoch.

"He's a little under the weather at the minute," Enoch, as slick with words as Jess when he wanted to be, answered.

Clate, as if embarrassed by the silence that followed this, lifted his round face, shut his round eyes, and began to sing.

> "Oh Lily up and Lily down,
> And lay them on the side wheels."

He delivered the two lines loudly but plaintively, then stopped suddenly, as if he'd received an order.

There followed another silence, which Little Jess finally took care of. "That don't make sense," he said.

Ordinarily, Eliza would have rebuked Little Jess for such discourtesy. Under the circumstances, it seemed a mild observation. She said, "Enoch, Clate Henry is drunk."

At the sound of his name, Clate Henry roused up for an encore.

> "Oh Lily up and Lily down
> And lay them on the side wheels."

He kept his eyes shut. For a man as small, round, and pale as he was, he had a resounding voice.

"Is that all he knows?" Little Jess asked Enoch.

"No," Enoch said shortly, "it ain't." He turned, as if fearful that the question would refresh Clate's memory, to Clate himself. "Hush up, Clate," he said. "Hush up your noise."

Clate opened his eyes and looked at his friend as if he couldn't believe his ears. Eliza looked at Jess, waiting for him to take charge. Jess didn't say a word, he didn't make a sign. So she herself spoke.

"Enoch," she said, "thee knows I won't have a drunkard in the house."

"Clate ain't a drunkard, ma'am," Enoch protested. "He's a farmer and not used to fighting—or drinking either. If I turn him loose, he'll just do himself harm. He was lost for the last two nights as it was."

"Lost? How could he be lost? He's lived around here all his life."

Clate roused himself to answer Eliza. "The first night," he said, "I was lost because I was scared and running and hiding. Then somebody offered me a jug of corn likker to get me over being scared. From then on I was drunk and scared. But I was lost both nights. Where am I now?" he asked, looking around wildly.

Eliza would have nothing to do with such play-acting. "Thee knows where thee is, Clate Henry. This isn't the first time thee's been here. Thee's drunk."

There was no arguing with such a man. He agreed with, then enlarged upon, her accusation. "Drunk," he repeated. "Dead drunk and sick to boot. I ain't real stout, ma'am. Fleshy, but that's not the same. I've never slept out of my own bed a night in my life—let alone on the ground. There was a heavy dew the last two nights. I've got a weak chest. They say summer nights are short. They're long. Longer than any winter night I ever knowed."

Eliza didn't feel melted by his story. Her boy had been out those nights, too, one of them spent at the bottom of a cliff with a cracked skull. He hadn't taken to corn likker.

"Why did thee join the Guard," she asked, "in the first place?"

"I didn't know my own nature, ma'am," Clate said sadly. "I wasn't prepared for what I'd see and hear. I wasn't prepared for the screeching."

"Screeching?" Eliza asked. "Josh didn't mention any screeching."

"He's deef then. Or calloused. Them Rebs kept up ascreeching like hoot owls fresh from Hell. Excuse the bad language, ma'am. But they're bloodthirsty. They're white Comanches."

Without warning, Clate Henry cut loose with a couple of terrible screeches. Hoot owls and Comanches would've turned tail at the racket he made. Eliza would never have guessed the pursy little fellow had such sounds in him. She felt as stunned as though he had struck her a blow.

Clate appeared well satisfied. "Bloodcurdling, ain't it?"

But Jimmy wasn't stunned and his blood wasn't curdled. He leaned forward in his chair, his rising livid. "That's no Rebel yell," he said.

"How do you know?" Clate asked.

"He's a Rebel," Little Jess said. "That's how he knows."

Clate stared at Jimmy for a few seconds, then he closed his eyes and began once again to sing.

> "Oh Lily up and Lily down
> And lay them on the side wheels
> And every time the wheel goes round . . ."

Enoch took his friend by the shoulders and shook him out of harmonizing. "What he needs," he told Eliza, "is a pot of strong coffee, hot and black. Hush up," he told Clate, who was showing signs of continued melody.

Before Eliza could get the pot on the stove, Clate had collapsed, head on his arms and arms on the table. At that minute Labe, still tucking his shirt in his pants, appeared in the doorway, blinking around at everyone sleepily.

"A diller-a-dollar, a ten o'clock scholar," Jess greeted him.

Labe smiled. It was no trick to make Labe smile. He had a mop of curly two-colored hair, a black eye, and a dingy unwashed look. He was big-framed, man-sized, but his eighteen-year-old face showed that he hadn't met any man-sized troubles yet.

"I thought I heard something," he said.

"If thee's up," Jess said, "thee heard something."

"It was a Rebel yell," Little Jess said.

"No," said Jimmy.

"Who's he?" Labe asked, staring at Jimmy.

"A Rebel," Little Jess said proudly.

"He give that yell?"

"No," said Jimmy.

"Where'd he come from?"

"He come from falling down our springhouse steps."

Labe was much too polite a boy to say, "What was he doing on our springhouse steps?" Instead, taking in head and leg, he said, "Must've been a pretty bad fall."

"He got them in the war," Little Jess explained. "He's one of Morgan's men."

"Was one of them," Enoch corrected him.

"Am," Jimmy said. "I'll catch up with him. Men are away a month and catch up. I've only been away a week."

"And every time the wheels go round . . ." Clate muttered.

Labe turned his attention to Clate's collapsed figure. "Who's he?"

"Home Guard," Little Jess replied promptly.

"That's Clate Henry from out Sand Creek way," Jess told him. "You've seen him before."

Clate moaned or snored.

"What's the matter with him?" Labe asked. "He hurt?"

Little Jess was happy to give him the answer. "He's soused," he said.

With that word, Eliza ended the picnic. Picnic was one thing, but circus was another. She was not going to have a circus in her kitchen. Drunkenness was no subject for fun. Wars, simply because they had moved from your neighborhood to someone else's, were no cause for rejoicing. Under her roof were three men who had been ready to kill: Josh, spared that evil by falling over a cliff; Clate, saved by cowardice; and Jimmy, maybe not saved at all. If you wanted a picture of war and death, she thought, take Jimmy. His own mother, like as not, wouldn't recognize him. He had shed his humanness. He was shrunk down to bullet size. He carried a thing on his head that looked like the grave. The bones of his head were saved by the thinnest of coverings from being a skull. Yet he was a boy. She tried to find in the back of his sunken eyes the boy he had been before he rode off with Morgan. She turned on him every bit of motherliness and love she had. She had as well have said "son" to a rock. She was an enemy, a part of a household whose people had been out to kill him and who called him "Reb."

"Get out of my kitchen," she said to all of them but Jimmy. Jess turned to her in surprise, but she cut him off before he could say a word. "I need room for cooking."

It wasn't true. She could cook in a nest of them. Rebelling against ugliness and blindness, she had lied. So far as she knew, none of them was a liar.

"It's not true," she said. "You're not in my way."

But Jess herded them out. She and Jess were as divided as the states, but she let him go without attempting to explain. Jimmy rose with the rest of them, but some weakness in head or leg made him hang on to the chair back. Outside, Eliza could see the others settling down in the side garden where there was a lawn swing and a hammock slung between two cedars. There, on the hottest days, the air in the clumps of cedar needles moved with a mountainy sound and smell. Clate was singing again. The picnic was not much interrupted.

Eliza did not make the mistake of saying "bed" again to Jimmy. "If thee stays inside, thee might help me later," she told him. "Come on into the dining room. Thee'll be out of my way and handy for table-setting later."

She went to him but didn't offer to help him. A pulse was beating in his rising like a misplaced heart.

"This way," she said, and went, without looking behind her, into the dining room, which opened out of the kitchen. It was a long narrow room, papered green, and dark now, with blinds pulled to keep out the sun and discourage flies.

She turned, and Jimmy was on her heels. "Thee can sit there," she said, pointing to a narrow black-leather lounge with a built-in hump at one end to support the head. She said "sit," but no one could sit on that narrow leather thing, and Jimmy, once seated, lay back against the bulge of the built-in pillow.

"You let me know if there's anything I can do to help you," Jimmy said, as if this readiness excused his stretching out.

"I will," Eliza said.

The voices of the picnickers could be heard. "I hope you didn't think that yipping was the real thing," Jimmy called to her.

"It scared me," Eliza said. "I suppose that's what it's supposed to do."

"No," Jimmy said. "We ain't trying to scare anybody." In the gloom Eliza could see the little fox skull part at the mouth, and yellow teeth, whiter than yellow skin, show in a smile. "We don't need to, once they know Morgan's around."

"Why do you do it then?" Eliza asked.

"We do it," Jimmy said, "because it's what we feel like doing. We feel better doing it."

He would have talked more. Eliza, however, didn't want to hear any more about it. She went back to her work, but Jimmy called after her, "That's why I wouldn't do it. You can't do it except then."

"Then" was what Eliza wanted to forget. She went up-stairs and wakened Josh and Mattie. Josh came down to breakfast, his shame at blundering over a cliff less, and his pride in being one of the defenders greater. Fear had sent Josh toward the enemy and Clate Henry away from them. But fear was the master of both. Mattie came downstairs, hung, uneating, over her cakes, her throat too thick with worry about Gardiner Bent to swallow.

"There's a wounded Southern boy in the dining room," Eliza told her children. "He's lost from Morgan. He stumbled in here last night. Maybe you'd like to talk to him."

Neither one wanted to. Josh felt embarrassed at the idea of sitting down and talking to someone he'd spent a couple of months screwing up his courage to take a shot at. He felt funny enough already, falling over a cliff, without finding out that he'd taken all his trouble and done all his shaking because of some poor, starved, done-in, bunged-up Johnny. This was the very reason Eliza wanted him to see the boy. It would take some of the false pride out of his sails; make him see how big Goliath really was, this poor boy of bones and festerings. But Josh wouldn't budge. He didn't want to see any Rebs who weren't fire-eaters. And Mattie wouldn't go either.

"If Gard gets home safe," she said, "I'll see him."

"All right," Eliza said. "Outside, both of you. Out with the picnickers."

"Picnickers?" Mattie asked.

"Look," Eliza said, and she pointed to the side garden. There they were, spread around under the cedars amid the phlox and the snowball bushes, the lawn swing creak-ing, the hammock swaying. "What's thy name for them?"

Josh looked at his mother and left. Mattie put a hand on her mother's arm. "Come on out, Mama," she urged.

"Isn't thee glad Josh is home? And that Vernon's saved from Morgan?"

"Morgan's in some other town today."

"But, Mama, thee can't be sad for every town in the county."

"I don't know why not," Eliza said.

There was sorrow in her, though whether enough for every town in the county she wasn't sure. But she didn't want to make any claims. Mattie made a pitcher of lemonade and took it outside, but Eliza stayed in her kitchen working, halfway between Jimmy and the picnic, able to see one and talk to the other. She took her pies out of the oven and put her light bread in. She scoured the case knives with brick dust and scalded all the milk pans and put them in the sun to sweeten. Blackbirds were at the cherries. White butterflies hovered over the little cabbage heads. The Dominique rooster's colors were faded in the heat. She picked enough Summer Sweetings for a dish of applesauce.

Little Jess came in for more lemonade. When she had made it, he said, "Can I take a glass to Jimmy?"

Eliza poured the glass. "If he's asleep, let him sleep. He needs that more than lemonade."

Little Jess tiptoed in, and Jimmy must have been awake.

"I brought thee a glass of lemonade."

There was a silence, followed by, "Does thee want another?"

"Why do you folks say 'thee'?" Jimmy asked.

"We're Quakers."

"What's Quakers?"

"A church."

"Like Baptists?"

"Is thee a Baptist?"

"Yes."

"We don't believe in being baptized."

"What do you believe in?"

Eliza waited.

"God."

"So do Baptists. You're no different from us."

"We're different," Little Jess said. "We don't believe in fighting."

Jimmy hooted. "Who don't? Your mama?"

"Father don't."

"He didn't keep his son home from fighting."

"Labe don't believe in it."

"How'd he get that black eye?"

"That was a private fight, not war."

"What was your hired man doing?"

"Saving Vernon from Morgan."

"Same as me. Saving the South from the Yanks. If I say 'thee,' I reckon I'll be a Quaker. Little Jess, will thee bring me some more lemonade?"

Little Jess brought the glass out to Eliza to be refilled. "He said 'thee' to me," he complained.

Eliza was short with him. "He can if he wants to," she said.

After Little Jess went outside with his lemonade, Eliza took a piece of warm peach pie to Jimmy. The boy was lying back, flat as the hump would let him, one hand picking at the nub of the rag carpet. "I'm too full of lemonade—to eat any more right now," he said.

Eliza shooed a couple of big black flies away from him.

"Those buzzards have smelled me out," he said.

"It's my pie they smell," Eliza said. She apologized to him. "I'm sorry thee had to get in a house that's so mixed up with the war."

"That's what you got to expect in wartime, ma'am."

"Not in a Quaker house," she said.

She decided to give the family their dinner outside. It was hotter out there, and succotash, light bread, and peach pie could've been served easier at a table. But if she set the table, Jimmy would get up, and she didn't want to disturb him. Besides, in serving the meal picnic-style there'd be so much running back and forth and waiting on, she'd have an excuse not to sit down with them—and no excuses to make, either, for not doing so. She was disturbed by her reluctance to break bread with her own family, but she had it; and once they were attended to she sat down with Jimmy.

"You got some kind of an old rag I could have?" Jimmy asked. "This here thing's begun to run."

She brought him clean cloths, saved from worn-out pillow shams, and would have brought him a basin and water, too, but he wouldn't hear of it. "Don't want to get in the habit of washing again," he said. "I'd just have to break it. I'll be well in no time now, soon as the corruption drains off. That's what's been making me dauncy. It's been poisoning my system."

There was a smell now, and Eliza would have liked to shut it away from her kitchen. "Does my clattering out here bother thee, Jimmy? Could thee doze if I closed the door?"

"No, ma'am," he said. "Leave it open. It sounds good. I ain't heard anybody stirring around in a kitchen for quite a spell."

After a while he called to her, "What's that click-clack I hear?"

Eliza went to the dining-room door. "That's the wind-mill," she said.

"I don't feel any wind moving."

"The windmill catches it when we can't feel it."

As they listened to the windmill, the voices of those on the side lawn came through the opened window, still eager and rejoicing in midafternoon, recalling each incident, real or reported, of Morgan's routing.

"They sound happy," Jimmy said. "All safe at home and happy."

"Yes," Eliza said.

"Like a party."

"That's what it sounds like."

"I could watch your cooking if you want to set outside for a spell."

She felt more at home with Jimmy, with his wounds and dirt and bad smell, than with those high-spirited ones out there.

"No," she said. "I feel like cooking this afternoon."

"What's for supper?" Jimmy asked.

"What strikes thy fancy?"

"Corn bread," Jimmy said, "greens, and custard pie."

"This time of year, I can't manage greens, but the corn bread and custard pie I can."

"I forgot what time of year it was," Jimmy said.

She was glad of the need of cooking, of keeping the stove going, of stirring and peeling, mixing and washing. Sometimes she stood at the back door and looked at the view which for sixteen years had sustained her as much as food. Jess was in it. Jess had made it, except for the rise and dip of hills beyond the farm's boundaries. Apple orchard, berry patch, vegetable garden, snowball bushes and syringa, and a graveled path edged with bleeding heart and sweet alyssum. She couldn't take joy in what she saw without taking joy in Jess, too. Maybe what made Jess such a good nurseryman made him a man not easily separated from the joy of others—even when they were wrong. When she wasn't with Jess, she imagined conversations with him. Now she could hear him in defense of himself quoting more George Fox to her; reminding her of the time when George, no smoker, had put a proffered pipe in his mouth to show "he had unity with all creation." "That's all I'm doing, Eliza," she could hear him say, "out here with the returned warriors showing them I have unity with all creation." In her imagined conversation she was able to have, what wasn't always so easy when she was face to face with Jess, the last word. "What thee's showing them thee has, Jess Birdwell, is unity with all destruction."

She felt better after that, the way Jimmy said he did after he gave the yell. It wasn't said to put Jess in his place, but it did tell her something about hers. Behind her, the kitchen clock struck five. The afternoon was ending. A wind out of the southeast had sprung up, changing the windmill's tune and spattering the pathway with the green-white litter of broken snowball blossoms. Away off westward past Jess's handiwork, where the joining of Sand Creek and the Muscatatuck showed in a thicker mounding of sycamore green, the sky was murky, gray-yellow, like some old fire opal in need of a cleaning. The wind that was turning the windmill, scattering the petals, banking the clouds was strong enough to feel now. Eliza turned back the collar of her gray dress—but there was no refreshment in warm sultry air.

It must have been around five-thirty when Gardiner Bent trotted into the yard, tied his lathered horse at the upping-block, and got a hero's welcome from everyone on the side lawn.

Mattie flew into the house for more lemonade and to ask if Gard could stay for supper.

"Won't he want to go home to his own folks?"

"He's been there already."

"It'll make quite a crowd."

"That Clate Henry won't want anything to eat. He's been sick and now he's asleep."

"He'll wake up the hungriest of all."

"Please, Mama. I'll help."

"I don't need help," Eliza said. "Tell Gard he's welcome. Everyone else is. I don't see why we should draw the line at him."

Mattie turned to go, then stopped. "How's the boy?"

"Don't pretend thee's given him a thought all afternoon."

"I haven't," Mattie said. "I'm not pretending. It was Gard I was thinking about. This boy might take it in his head that he ought to keep on fighting."

"No matter what he takes in his head," Eliza said, "he's too sick to fight. Thee just see to it that Gard stays peaceable and we'll have nothing to worry about."

One outdoor meal a day, Eliza decided, was enough. She was not going to carry fried chicken, mashed potatoes, corn bread, and custard pie outdoors. She'd have a sit-down meal at the table. But instead of moving Jimmy upstairs to the spare room—where he'd be shut away from everything, and refuse to go, anyway, probably—she'd move him out to Enoch's room. That was only a step away, off the kitchen, a part of the porch roofed over and sided up. It was nothing but a hired man's room, nothing fancy. But Jimmy wasn't in shape or practice for enjoying anything fancy.

He surprised her by being perfectly willing to move. He sat up, holding the cloths she had given him wadded against his head.

"Who was that rode in a while back?"

"A neighbor boy," Eliza told him.

"He had on a uniform."

"He's a soldier," Eliza admitted.

"He's a Quaker, too?"

"No," Eliza said, "he's a Methodist."

"I reckon it don't make much difference," Jimmy said.

Jimmy followed through the kitchen, across the back porch, and into Enoch's room. He walked as if the floor under his feet were uneven, and as if Enoch's door shifted from left to right. But he was in good spirits. When he saw the custard pies lined up to cool, he said, "If some of them turn up missing, you'll know where to look for them."

Eliza, after she had settled him, unresisting, on Enoch's bed, brought him a half-pie on a plate and a supply of clean rags.

"Thank you, Mama," he said.

Eliza was at first pleased; then, after she went back to her work in the kitchen, puzzled. Had he spoken jokingly? Or in a minute of lightheadedness did he think he was back in Plum Tree with his own mother? But she was too busy frying chicken with one hand and mixing a batch of corn bread with the other to worry about it.

Jimmy asked to be excused from going to the supper table. "I ain't a very pretty sight for eaters. Besides, I spoiled my appetite with pie."

Eliza was glad he felt that way. Apart from his looks and his smell, something might be said he would take exception to.

She got them all down to the supper table before lamp-lighting time, all hungry after the pick-up dinner, the fighting, and the talk of fighting; and Clate Henry, just as she'd guessed, was the hungriest of them all. Eliza served them like a woman working in a stranger's house. She knew that this day of estrangement would pass, that it signified nothing but the dying down in her of a spirit of perfect sympathy which would rise again and would embrace them all. But she accepted the lull and the separation, fought neither it nor them—and moved back and forth silently with platters and pitchers to be refilled.

She had brought the supper plates from the table and gone to the porch for the pies when she saw Jimmy—who had seen her first—standing on the steps below her, immovable. He had the rations bag he'd arrived with over his shoulder, and one side of his face, for all that he had tied up his head with a bandage torn from one of her pillow shams, was covered with the bloody outpouring from his rising.

"Jimmy," she said, "what's thee doing?"

Jimmy didn't stop to argue. He hurried down the step with his hobbling, stiff-legged gait.

"Jimmy, thee's not fit to travel."

Fit or not, he traveled, his gait uneven, his hands to his head as if afraid it might, in spite of the bandage, split open. He took off down the pathway littered with the false snow, under the green-yellow Summer Sweetings, heading for the main road. He was running, but weaving and stumbling as he ran.

"Jimmy," Eliza called, "Jimmy, let me help thee."

With skirts lifted she was far fleeter-footed than he. He barely missed trees, stumbled over hummocks of grass, lost his bandage, and kept going.

At last Eliza understood that he was running away from her and stopped. "Jimmy," she called. "I'm not following."

It was too late. The boy tripped, fell over, and lay where he had fallen. When Eliza reached him, he struggled to sit up, and, kneeling beside him, she supported him. Half of his head seemed to have fallen away. From the brain-deep cavity where his rising had been, blood and pus covered his face. Eliza cradled his head against her shoulder and rocked him a little before it occurred to her that this might be bad for him.

He appeared to be trying to say something. An indistinguishable sound filled his throat, and Eliza thought, when no words took shape, that he might be trying to give that yell, the one he believed the others had mismanaged and that made him feel good. She hoped he could do it. But it wasn't a yell he had in mind. He said, perfectly clear and quiet, "Be good to Jimmy," and underneath the blood he closed his eyes.

Eliza sat flat on the ground under the apple trees with the boy in her arms. She felt guilty, as if she had killed him herself. Not by running after him, which might have hurried things, but no more than that. But because when the others came down from the house, as they would in a few minutes, and found her here with the boy dead in her arms, he would say to them what she had been saying all day, "Don't rejoice so much." And they would listen to him as they hadn't to her. He would be her "I told you so." With all her heart she wished him a live boy and no sign. But he was both: a boy and a sign, and she couldn't separate them—and shouldn't try. Whatever message he had for those who found him, he'd earned the right to say.

A Family Argument

The war finally came to an end, as all wars do. But Mattie knew that for all that it was over, peace treaties signed and proclamations made, there were divisions still existing within her own family. Because she had married a soldier and a Methodist, these divisions were more inclined to come out into the open when she and Gard were at home for a visit.

They were home now to celebrate her father's birthday; and Mattie was determined that the occasion *be* a celebration, not a prolonged political debate. She had been on tenterhooks all evening trying singlehanded to steer the conversation away from such subjects as impeachment and Southern favoritism and did or did not the President drink.

For an hour she had been willing her father and mother to go to bed. At last they went. She had also been willing her husband and three brothers to stay where they were—at least until her parents were out of earshot.

Little Jess made a motion to rise from his chair, but

Mattie, risking being overheard, hissed at him, "Little Jess,
I have something to say to thee."

"What?" asked Little Jess, but Mattie put her fingers
to her lips and shook her head.

"What's thee got to say to me?"

When she heard the bedroom door upstairs close, she
said, "It's not just thee. It's everybody."

"What's thee got to say to everybody?" Little Jess
asked, yawning. Mattie stared at him until he put a tardy
hand over his already-closed mouth.

"You all know why we're here."

"Papa's birthday. Thee don't need to keep me up to
tell me that."

"Nobody seems to be remembering it." She was beating
the Devil around the bush and she knew it, addressing
this to Little Jess. It was her older brothers, Labe and
Josh, and her husband, Gard, who needed to be reminded.
She had agreed with every word Gard and Josh had to
say; but her father hadn't agreed with them, and Labe
hadn't agreed; and Little Jess, though he of course didn't
know what he was talking about, had put in his oar at
every opportunity.

"I remember it," Little Jess insisted.

"Let's not argue, Little Jess. That's what I want to talk
about. Arguing."

"That's what thee wants to argue about."

"That'll be enough, Little Jess," Gard said, coming to
his wife's defense, and suffering the fate of a husband
who tries to discipline his wife's relatives for her own
good.

"Little Jess was only joking, Gard," Mattie reproved
her husband.

"Oh, forgive me for interfering," Gard apologized, and
turned away, miffed, from wife and in-laws alike.

Everyone's nerves were on edge. They were lined up on opposite sides of the political fence—Andrew Johnson's impeachment—and had been tossing barbed words back and forth across it all day. They had been very near to downright quarreling before Jess and Eliza went to bed, and had certainly passed over the demarcation line between talking and shouting sometime earlier.

It was this Mattie wanted to speak about.

"Mama has planned this celebration for a long time. She's had her heart set on all of us being here at the same time. It wasn't easy for Gard and me to get away from the farm. Or for Josh to leave his work in Philadelphia."

"Work?" jeered Labe. "All he's doing is studying."

"Studying is work, Labe. As thee would know if thee had ever done any."

"Let's not *argue*," Mattie repeated. "The point is, we're all here and it wasn't easy to get here. Now let's not spoil the day for them tomorrow by carrying on the way we did this evening."

"Carrying on?" Labe asked. "Who was doing the carrying on? Thee and Josh and Gard! All I did was to put in a word now and then to support Pa when thee started shouting 'Impeach Andrew Johnson!' and 'Hang Jeff Davis!'"

"'Hang Robert E. Lee,' too," Little Jess said. "That's what Josh was saying."

"May I ask," Josh said, in his most Philadelphia tones, "if thee has followed the career of that eminent Quaker legislator George Julian?"

There was silence.

"I am speaking to thee, Little Jess."

"I ain't stopping thee," Little Jess said.

"I admit it was a silly question to put to thee," Josh said. "But I will tell thee what George Julian said. He said, 'Hang Robert E. Lee. And stop there? Not at all. I would hang liberally while I had my hand in.'"

"Hand in what?" Little Jess asked.

"Blood," said Labe.

"Since when has punishment of crime been considered bloody?" Gard asked.

"Thee heard Pa's answer to that," Labe said.

Gard wasn't so far gone in anti-Johnsonianism as to attack his father-in-law. Or so foolish.

"Your father is an old-line Quaker and naturally against violence of any kind."

"And thee is a new-line Methodist and naturally for it."

"Labe," Mattie said, "please remember that Gard fought against these Southern traitors. And was wounded protecting us. Does thee want him to have to go back to war and fight them all over again?"

"Fight who all over again?"

"The Rebs," Josh said. Josh had never forgotten having his head broken open falling off a cliff when the Home Guard, mistaking cattle crossing a creek for Morgan's raiders, had made an unfortunate charge.

"The Rebs! Why, the Rebs are busted. No guns, no horses, no money, no supplies," Labe said.

"That's what they'd like us to believe. And I can see thee's swallowed their story hook, line, and sinker."

"Andrew Johnson," Gard explained in a patient, reasonable voice, "is a Southerner himself and he is soft on Southerners. With his help they'll soon be rearmed. There's plenty of signs of Johnson's favoritism. He's vetoed every bill to punish the leaders of the South. He's leaving them free to foster another rebellion. That's why he must be impeached."

"Well, apart from politics," Mattie said, believing what

she said, "Johnson is not the kind of man we can be proud of in the White House. He is a very common-looking man. Sometimes he looks out of his mind."

"That's because he drinks so much," Josh explained. "He's sane enough when he's sober. That's not saying he's right, but he's sane. But two drinks and he's a mad dog."

"Is that what thee's learned studying medicine in Philadelphia?" Labe asked. "Two drinks makes a mad dog?"

Little Jess, seeing that Labe had Josh on the run, decided to bark at his heels. "Did thee ever see Andrew Johnson take a drink, Josh? Did thee? Does thee go to drinking parties with the President in Philadelphia, Josh?"

Josh ignored the question and attacked Little Jess's geography. "The President does his drinking in Washington, Little Jess. The capital of the United States. The drink is rum, I believe."

"What does thee drink in Philadelphia, Josh?" asked Labe. "Embalming fluid?"

"Yeh, embalming fluid," Little Jess hooted. "Two drinks and thee's a dead dog."

Mattie jumped to her feet. "This must stop. We're here to make Father happy, not to fight and squabble."

"Thee hasn't set us the best example in the world," Labe said.

Mattie admitted it. "I'm ashamed of myself. Does thee know what Papa said when I followed him outside? When you boys were quarreling so?"

Jess had left the room earlier after something Gard had said. That was one reason Mattie felt responsible for restoring peace now.

"We shouldn't forget how Andrew Johnson came to office," Gard had reminded everyone.

"Why, he came to office like any other candidate," Jess

had replied. "He ran on the ticket with Abe Lincoln and was elected vice-president when Lincoln was elected president."

"I'm not talking about how he got to be *vice*-president. I'm talking about how he got to be *president.*"

"Everybody knows that. He succeeded Lincoln when Lincoln was shot."

"Andrew Johnson was a friend of the man who killed Lincoln."

It was then Jess went outside. But not before he gave Gard a piece of his mind.

"I wouldn't permit gossip of that kind in my house about the worst rascal in this community. And I certainly won't put up with talk like that about the President of the United States."

As he opened the door of the sitting room, Mattie said, "Papa, where is thee going?"

"Outside, where the air is clean."

After a few minutes Mattie had followed her father. She saw him down by the edge of the creek, pacing back and forth, arms folded. It was her intention to apologize, not so much for what Gard had said, as for all of them forgetting why they had come home. But Jess didn't want to talk about what had been said by Gard, or his children's behavior. He was solemn, taken up with the night, musing about old times.

"Thee takes all this for granted, don't thee, Mattie?"

She wasn't sure what he meant.

"White house. Cornfields. Cisterns. Rag rugs. Organ from Philadelphia. Swinging lamp from Cincinnati."

"I can remember the log house."

"Before that there was a wilderness here."

"And thee has tamed it, Papa."

"I wasn't asking thee to say 'What hath Pa wrought,'

Mattie. I was thinking that I see a different world from my children. And no help for it. I see a different Andrew Johnson. I see that poor boy, bound boy he was, to a tailor, who never learned to read or write till he married. I've got a weakness, Mattie. It's bothered me since I was young. Once, they were lambasting a man when I was ten years old or so, and I said, 'Mort Clark whistles real well.' I never lived that down. And I don't suppose I've changed much either."

"Thee should be proud to see the good in men."

"Seeing the good don't win thee any praise nowadays. It's the downgraders and the backbiters and the underminers and the faultfinders who get the praise."

"Papa, Gard doesn't . . ."

"I'm talking about myself now, not Gard. The world suits me to a T, Mattie. That's my trouble. Why, sometimes I think the Lord made it especially for me. I like its colors. I don't see how the flavor of spring water could be improved on. I'd hate to have to try to invent a better fruit than a Grimes Golden. Yellow lamplight on white snow. Thee ever seen anything prettier? Out here alone, this quirk of mine seems a blessing. I feel downright joyful. Inside, with the boys, I feel downright simpleminded. I'd sooner say the words 'Hell and damnation' to them than 'joy.' Is that something they don't know anything about, Mattie? To hear them talk thee'd think they had some special little bird whispering nothing but bad news in their ears. It grabs me in the throat to hear those two boys, ignorant young farmer and ignorant young student, so quick to put the worst meaning on any happening. Generosity of soul. Looks like they were both standing behind the door when that commodity was passed out."

"Papa," Mattie cried, "I didn't come down here to listen to thee call Gard names."

"Call him names?"

"Mean-souled."

"I never said that, Mattie."

"Thee had as well. Thee thought it."

She turned on the run for the house, but not before she heard her father say, "I hope Andrew Johnson appreciates me. I ain't got too many other friends left."

It was this she repeated to her husband and brothers. Mattie was big-souled enough to leave out what her father had said about the souls of her husband and brother and tell them only of the sorrow she had heard in his voice when he said, "I ain't got too many other friends left."

"Think of that," she told them. "Think of being a father with thy children home for thy birthday, and feeling without friends. Feeling that the President of the United States was a better friend than thy own children."

"And what a president!" Josh said.

"Stop that," Mattie ordered. "Stop it. There's not going to be any more of that kind of talk! There's going to be a change tomorrow."

"Now I honor Father, and thee knows it. But I'm not going to change my opinions for him, and he wouldn't want me to," Josh said.

"Me either," Gard said. "I'm no turncoat."

"Turncoat," Mattie flashed at her husband. "Who's asking thee to be a turncoat? All I'm asking thee and Josh is to hold thy tongues tomorrow about politics."

"Is thee going to hold thy tongue tomorrow, Mattie?" Little Jess asked.

"Yes, I am, Little Jess."

"Pa's not going to think it very friendly, everyone sitting around mum on his birthday," Labe said.

"Who said anything about mum? Be mum about politics. That's all I ask. There's plenty of other things we can talk about besides Andrew Johnson and impeachment."

"What?" asked Josh.

"What? Why, just about the whole rest of the world. All the things we did together as children. All the things they'd like us to remember."

"Once we get to talking, we're likely to stray onto politics in spite of ourselves," Gard said.

"I won't let it happen. At the first sign of a slip I'll bring up a subject we can't quarrel about. Thee help me, Gard, and thee'll see. We have to do it for Pa's and Mama's sake. We'd never forgive ourselves afterward if we didn't."

Mattie's plan worked like a charm. Breakfast was nothing but "Happy birthday, Papa," "Happy birthday, Pa." Eliza and Mattie served buckwheat cakes and sausage gravy, and words like "lynch" and "impeach" seemed as foreign to that table as Choctaw.

Mattie steered the talk to subjects that were safe: snowstorms of yesteryear, horses dead and gone, neighbors who had moved to the plains states. Somebody said "carpetbagger," but the word was said once only. Mattie immediately asked her father what kinds of apples he had brought with him from Ohio. That was the kind of a question Jess liked to wrestle with.

"The oldest trees here are Rambos and Ben Davises. My guess would be that they came from the home place in Ohio. I wouldn't swear to it, though."

"Rome Beauties," Josh said flatly. "There was a Rome Beauty out by the corncrib, till it died."

"That was a Rambo," Labe contradicted him.

"We have a strange apple up around Noblesville," Mattie hastened to say. "Strange name, I mean. Willow Twig. It's really a very nice little winter cooking apple."

"Willow Twig's a new name to me. But in Mount Pleasant, I remember, we had an apple called Spring Strawberry."

"Early Strawberry," Gard corrected his father-in-law. "That's what my father always called it."

"I'm a nurseryman," Jess said, "and I never heard anything but 'Spring.'"

"I reckon Gard knows the name of his own father's apple trees, Papa," Mattie said.

"Oftentimes," Eliza put in, "the same apple'll have different names in different parts of the country."

"In Noblesville, it's 'Early,' not 'Spring,'" Mattie persisted.

"How does thee know so much about apples, Mattie?" Little Jess asked.

"She knows because Gard tells her," Labe answered. "And Gard's a well-known apple authority."

"Pancakes!" Mattie exclaimed. "Who wants more pancakes? I'm frying more this minute."

They ate breakfast in the kitchen, but the birthday dinner was served in the dining room. Mattie thought that she had never seen a more festive table. The cake itself, on a pedestaled cake stand, occupied the center of the table. It was iced in white, and Eliza had outlined on it in red sugar the word "Jess." Around the base of the cake stand was a circle of bridal wreath and pink phlox. The cut-glass pitcher usually reserved for bridal parties was filled with pink lemonade. The best of everything was on the table. The spoons in the spoon-holder were newly polished, and the celery in the celery vase was as pretty as a bouquet. The men had worked as usual all morning, but for dinner they had changed out of their work shirts. Mattie and Eliza had put on their light afternoon aprons, each fancy with ruffles and crocheting.

Mattie prayed, when heads were bowed before the meal in silent grace, that she would be able to hold her tongue. And be able to help everyone else to hold his. "Dear God," she prayed, "save us from politics for at least two hours. In Thy name's sake, I ask it."

God seemed to have heard her prayer. Gard, Josh, and Labe were passing food, filling their plates, and praising what they ate as if it couldn't matter less who was in the White House, or how long he stayed there. Little Jess, who had drained his lemonade glass without pausing for breath, didn't say a word when Eliza refused him a second glass.

Jess was beaming. "Well, here I am," he said, "arrived at being a patriarch without ever having noticed the way I was traveling."

"We're the ones who are making thee a patriarch, Papa," Mattie said proudly, for she and Gard were expecting a baby.

"I kind of thought thee might be the ones to do that the day thee rode over to Gard's aunt's place."

"I'll never forget that ride. I was barefoot and on Old Polly."

"Old Polly?" said Labe. "It was Old Fox thee was riding."

"Old Fox! Thee was just a boy. What does thee know about it?"

"Thee was just a girl."

"What color was Old Fox?" Gard asked Labe.

"Blood bay."

"You're mistaken about the horse Mattie rode then. She was on a white horse. Was Old Polly white?"

"Of course she was white. Labe's developed a contrary streak lately."

Labe gave Mattie a good long hard stare. "Who's developed a contrary streak, Mattie?"

"I have," Mattie said, all contrition. "I have. Now the horse I like to remember is the one Papa brought home from Kentucky. She gave Papa great pleasure. Didn't she, Papa?"

"Lady," Jess said fondly. "She was a real traveler."

"Such a nice mild name," Eliza said, "for a horse who'd take the bit in her teeth and run the way she did."

"Papa won lots of races with Lady," said Little Jess.

"Races!" Jess protested. "Why, I never raced a horse in my life."

"Thee maybe wasn't racing," Labe said, "but Lady was. She just naturally outpaced every horse on the road."

"Didn't she ever come up against any good trotters?" Gard asked.

"Reverend Godly's," said Labe.

"Prince was nothing but a preacher's Sunday trotter. I mean a real trotter—one that can give any side-wheeler fifteen yards and beat him by fifty."

"She came up against them all right," Labe said. "And she side-wheeled right on past them like they were standing still."

"That's hard to believe," Gard said.

"Anatomically," Josh instructed his brother, "pacing's not a natural gait."

"I guess nobody ever told Lady that," Labe said.

"Every record for speed in this county's held by a trotter," Gard said. "How do you account for that?"

"There's a hundred trotters to every pacer."

"Labe," Josh asked, "did thee ever give any thought as to *why* there's so many more trotters than pacers?"

Labe fired right back. "It don't take thought. People are in a rut. The pacer got a bad name, and nobody looks beyond the name."

"Like Johnson," said Little Jess.

"Hush up," Mattie said. "We're talking about horses."

"A pacer," Josh repeated, "has an unnatural gait. Two legs on one side. Two legs on the other. A horse isn't supposed to move that way."

Mattie couldn't resist agreeing. "A horse is supposed to rock, head up, head down."

"Who told thee that, Mattie?" Labe asked. "God or Gard?"

"Now let's leave the Lord out of this," Gard told his brother-in-law. "There are places suitable to call upon His name and places unsuitable."

Labe, usually calm, roused thoroughly when he did rouse. He stood now at the dinner table and glared down at his brother-in-law. "I don't need thee to tell me what's suitable to say and what ain't."

"Thee needs someone," Josh agreed with Gard.

"Is it against the law to prefer a pacer to a trotter?"

"It's not good sense."

"Don't thee tell me I ain't got good sense, Gard Bent."

"It's Gard's duty to speak the truth," Mattie said.

Little Jess stood up to join his brother. "Does Gard know what's the truth?"

Josh shoved his younger brother back into his chair. "One thing's certain, and that is thee don't."

"Take thy hands off Little Jess," Labe shouted.

"My hands aren't on him."

Little Jess stood up again. "Mama had a pacer."

"Mama never had a horse in her life."

"She had Samantha. Samantha was a pacer."

"Samantha was a *goose*. That's the whole story of pacers," Josh said.

"What else can a goose do with only two legs?" Labe asked. "A goose paces. But not all pacers are geese. That's the argument of somebody who ain't got a leg to stand on."

Josh reared up from the table, rocking the china and glassware. "Don't thee call me names, Laban Birdwell."

Labe gave the table a smart rap. "I didn't. But if the shoe fits, wear it."

Three boys were now on their feet. Gard was red in the face, and Mattie unnaturally white. The birthday cake, from all the table-pounding, the jumping up and sitting down, was off center: the cake not squarely on the cake stand, the cake stand not squarely in the center of the table. Mattie was thinking about running out to the barn to cry, when her father began to laugh. He had a big booming laugh at all times, and now he laughed so hard that the cutlery, agitated by the boys' table-pounding, began to quiver again. When finally he got his laughing fit under control, he said, "You boys can sit down now."

The boys sat.

"Now I've got something to say to you. If we're bound to quarrel, let's be honest about it and abuse Andrew Johnson, not horses. There's just two things you can't do at this table or in this house.

"The first is, I won't put up with any talk of hanging anybody from Robert E. Lee on down to the lowliest Reb in the South. That understood?

"The second is, no slander. Talk impeachment all you like. Nobody, so far as I know, is arguing the President's a teetotaler, or a polished orator, or got his education very early. You can't impeach a man for such things, but if you like to talk about such things, it's a free country and I won't try to stop you.

"But anybody here who wants to talk treason or assassination or plots or Southern favoritism will have to produce proof. Now is that clear?"

If it wasn't, no one was willing to say so.

"All right, now who wants to speak first? For or against, it don't matter which—so long as you keep these two rules in mind. Josh? Labe? Gard?"

The three were silent.

"Mattie?"

"Happy birthday, Papa."

"Little Jess?"

"Please pass the chicken."

Home for Christmas

Everyone home for Christmas! Jess stood at the front window of the sitting room on the morning of the day before Christmas relishing the fact.

It had snowed the night before, and though the bright sun threatened the whiteness, there had been no melting yet. Wet snow still clung to cedar and maple trees, to the snowball bush, bare of leaves. The flat-topped upping-block had a curved white roof like an igloo. The slope from house to the county pike was unbroken except where the spring branch crossed it like a black snake, live and moving. A snowy landscape made Jess feel the way liquor, he supposed, made a tippler feel: lightheaded, happy, ready for anything.

His three boys were out at the barn doing the few chores a winter day provided. Behind him, still visiting, were Eliza, Mattie, Gard, and the young folks' two-year-old Elspeth. Mattie and Gard had driven in at dusk the night before, all the way from their farm in Ripley County; and mother and daughter hadn't yet exchanged half the news they had to tell each other. The sounds of their voices joined the sound of the wind blowing through the big blue cedar in front of the house to form a wintry sough.

"It's a good thing I don't have any power over snow," he told his family. "I'm such a snow fancier I don't know as I'd have the good sense to let well enough alone. If I had my say, I'd have another flurry right now. With the sun as bright as it is, what snow we have will be melted by nightfall, I'm sorry to say."

"Sorry because of Christmas?" Mattie asked.

"Snow looks good to me any day—Christmas, washday, or Washington's Birthday."

"I'd like to have it white tomorrow for Elspeth's sake. I'd like her to have *something* Christmasy tomorrow."

"What does thee mean, 'Christmasy'?" Jess asked.

The preparations Eliza had made were just as Christmasy as any Mattie had ever known. Old hens dressed for roasting. Pies filled with venison mincemeat, baked and waiting. The whole family safely gathered under the home roof. What more did it take to make a Christmas?

Mattie, who didn't enjoy arguing with her father any day, let alone the day before Christmas, said, "Thee knows what I mean by Christmasy, Papa."

Well, come to that, he did know.

Christmas had never been a problem in their Quaker household until Mattie, read out of Meeting for marrying a Methodist, had become a Methodist herself. Now she had begun to pick up Methodist ways. Christmas, for as long as Jess had known it, in his own home and, before that, in his father's home, had been just what Eliza or his mother had planned for tomorrow. There had never been on Christmas the feasting of Thanksgiving or the excitement of Independence Day. If the twenty-fifth fell on First Day, they all went to Meeting, of course. There was

a little more food and a little less work than usual. Otherwise the twenty-fifth was a day like any other, no more
or no less holy. There had been a birthday in the world.
It was marked on a calendar no one was very certain
about; and it was certainly meaningless except as it was
celebrated in the heart. The bigger the celebration in the
world, Jess feared, the less chance the heart had for its
celebration. There had never been in his or his father's
home trees or stockings or gifts. And in spite of this, or
more likely because of it, a quiet as soft and enfolding
as snow had always settled across the day.

Mattie joined her father at the window.

"Papa," she asked, "does thee think it right to make
such a to-do over Independence Day and let Christmas
Day go by without so much as a nod?"

"I nod," Jess said.

"Don't joke, Papa. Does thy country mean more to thee
than thy religion?"

"Less, less." Jess spoke sharply. "My country's where I
live. My religion's who I am."

"Thee shoots off a gun for the Fourth. Hangs up bunting. Listens to speeches."

"Guns and bunting and speeches would belittle Christmas."

"Nothing could belittle it."

Jess saw that he had a sharp thinker in Mattie as well
as a little mother and a new Methodist.

"We can belittle ourselves by what we do, Mattie."

He had more to say, but Elspeth, unaccustomed in
this household of doting grandparents and young uncles
to being ignored for so long, pulled at her mother's
skirts.

"I want a Christmas tree, Mama. I want a Christmas
tree."

Jess waited for Mattie to speak to her daughter. When she didn't, he did. "Elspeth, when thy mother and I are talking, thee keep quiet."

Elspeth hid her face in her mother's skirt.

"Elspeth's not used to being talked to like that, Papa."

"I can see she isn't."

"Papa, times have changed since thee was a boy."

"Thee's right about change, Mattie. Times *have* changed. And not always for the better."

Elspeth, who knew whose side her mother was on, repeated, "I want a Christmas tree, Mama."

"Yes, petty, Mama knows. *Children* have changed, too, Papa. They're not brought up with nothing the way we were."

"Did thee ever miss a Christmas tree, Mattie?"

"I couldn't miss what I'd never seen. But Elspeth's seen them."

"Tell her they're nothing but baubles."

"Why is thee against Christmas trees?"

"I don't know's I am."

"Thee's not *for* them. Thee hasn't said, 'Put it up.'"

That was a fact. Out in the woodshed stood a six-foot spruce. Gard and Mattie (as if he had been some old miserly farmer, chary of putting an ax to a tree of his own) had fetched it over in the back of their buckboard all the way from Gard's one-horse farm in Ripley County. Though it had been seen by all, this was the first time the tree had been mentioned.

Jess hadn't said when he saw it, "What's this?" Nor had Gard said, "Father Birdwell, we've brought you a Christmas tree." The tree might've been invisible or indelicate, for all the mention there had been made of it. Jess had looked at it—and held his tongue. Gard had carried it to the woodshed—and had remained silent. Jess was glad to have Mattie speak up, calling a tree a tree.

"Does thee think Christmas trees are wicked, Papa?"

"Wicked? How can a tree be wicked?"

"I read the heathen worshiped them once."

"My guess would be there's nothing in the world's not been used for heathen purposes one time or another."

"Is it because thee don't want Christmas to change from the way it was when thee was a boy?"

"I'm not against change."

Gard, who had cut the tree, at Mattie's request, didn't relish arguments about it. He put his hand on his father-in-law's shoulder and directed his attention to the lane.

"You've got company coming," he said.

A good horse, hitched to a weathered splay-wheeled buggy, was spoiling the untracked snow on the driveway.

"Jasp Clark!" Jess said.

Jasper Clark, a man with an almost-grown daughter, Jenny, and a son, Clarence, a fair-sized boy, still kept a buggy for his own use, like a young fellow sparking. For family use he had nothing better than a spring wagon. If his wife, Clara, had been another woman, that mode of travel, jouncing around unprotected from the weather, might not have seemed so undignified. But Clara was a stately dark-haired woman who deserved a better vehicle than the wagon Jasper used to haul manure in.

"What's Jasp Clark doing here this time of the day?" Eliza asked.

"He's not delivering Christmas presents," Jess said. "That's one thing thee can bank on."

"Jess, if it's money he wants, don't give it to him."

"Thee think that's the proper Christmas spirit, Eliza?"

"For Jasper Clark, I do. Thee knows for a fact that any money thee gives him will go for liquor."

"I don't know it for a fact," Jess said. "Though I admit it's a likely possibility."

Jasp said it wasn't a fact.

God had given Jasp Clark a handsome face, and Jasp had run it downhill straight from the cradle. He stood in the Birdwell sitting room and held that face up to them all the way a hunter holds up a used and valued gun: nicked, scarred, dropped on stones, storm-soaked, still the finest weapon a man ever had for bringing down game. Jasp ought by rights to be a meechin' fellow. He had, excepting Clara, a raggle-taggle family. He owned a side-hill farm, and had spent more days lying down drunk than standing up sober. There wasn't a thing the man had done, barring his marriage to Clara, that Jess approved of; yet he couldn't help admiring the way Jasp was able to make his seamed and surly face shine now with Christmas neighborliness.

It was money he wanted, all right, but not for liquor. Never at this season for liquor. His whole thought was for his family. He was on his way to Vernon to buy a few delicacies for the Christmas table; and now, halfway there, he had discovered that he had left his money at home. Money he had earned cutting railway ties all fall up around Scipio. The rail-tie story was true. That much Jess knew. That Jasp had left any money at home, or had had any idea of spending it on table delicacies, he doubted. Still, he was unable on the day before Christmas to tell him to turn back home to fetch his forgotten money. He loaned him two dollars and a half. Jasp, who had suggested five, put the money in his pocket as carelessly as a bandanna. The Christmas sheen, as soon as the money was in his pocket, disappeared from his old rifle-barrel face.

"I'll see you get the money back day after tomorrow," he said. His face was cocked like a gun ready to go off at the first sound of a word of disbelief.

Jess doubted it, but kindness kept him quiet.

When the door was shut behind Jasp, Eliza said, "We don't have money to throw away, but I'll be content if that's the last we ever hear of that two-fifty."

It wasn't the last. About midafternoon, the snow by this time half-melted, so that the ground was blotched and scaly, Jasp's boy, Clarence, bareback on his father's buggy horse, came into the yard at a hard trot. Clarence, a lightweight, bobbled about on the chestnut's broad back like a fisherman's float on a riffle.

Clarence was an earnest, snaggle-toothed boy with a hayrick haircut. His summer freckles were so faded they looked on his bleached face like elderberries under cream. He had left home coatless, and his lips after the fast ride in the raw December air were blue.

Jess stood him up with his back to the sitting-room fire to thaw.

When the boy stopped trembling, he said, "Pa's sick."

"Did he send thee over?"

"No. Mama."

"Thee's got nearer neighbors."

"Mama said to fetch you."

"How's thy pa sick?"

"He's shooting."

"Well, that's sick, Clarence. What's he shooting at?"

"People coming to see Jenny."

"Why are people coming to see Jenny?"

"No one is coming. He's shooting to scare the people off who might come."

Jess chewed his underlip awhile. Then he said, "I reckon I'll have to ride over."

"Thee'll just get thyself shot, Jess," Eliza protested.

"Clarence said his pa was shooting at nothing. I ain't nothing."

"You soon may be," Gard said, "if you ride up to a house where a man's drunk and shooting. Let Josh and me and Labe ride with you. We can surround the house."

"Gard, this isn't a war."

"A man shooting. That's what it takes to make a war."

"Thee's only half-right, Gard. It takes two men shooting to make a war, and I'm not going to shoot. Thee heard what Clarence said. His father's sick. I'm not sick."

Mattie, her wits sharpened by a morning's arguing, said, "Good health won't turn a bullet."

Jess couldn't help but laugh at that. "It'll make me a better dodger."

Jess looked down from his big gelding at Clarence on his father's buggy horse. The boy had been well toasted on both sides before the fire, and Eliza had bundled him up in one of Little Jess's coats. Still he looked peaked and drawn, his lips still blue and the rims of his eyes red.

"Clarence," Jess said, "there's no need thee making this trip back with me. Thee could spend the night at our house and go home tomorrow when thy father's feeling better."

"Ma needs me," Clarence said.

"If thy father's shooting . . ."

"Pa won't shoot me. He's got nothing against me."

"What about me? He got anything against me?"

"He oughtn't to."

"Clarence, where's thy father doing his shooting?"

"The upstairs bedroom window."

They were riding along the top of a ridge where the sharp wind burned their faces. The road dropped down to follow the river, and there, where the shade of the riverbank growth had protected it, the snow was still white. Jess's nose watered with the raw smell of snow and the aromatic wintertime scent of the evergreens on the slope above them.

The Clark house, like his own, stood on a knoll, and from the upstairs window Jasper Clark would be able to take pot shots at anything moving on the quarter-mile land that led up to his place.

"Thy pa at the front upstairs window?"

"There ain't no back window."

"Thee sure he won't shoot thee?"

"Not if he knows me."

"He'd know thee, on his own horse, wouldn't he?"

"He always has."

"I'm going around the back way to thy place, Clarence."

"There's no road into the back."

"I know that. I'll leave the horse and walk across the field. Nothing to be hurt at this time of the year. Thee take it slow, so thee'll be riding in up the front road at the same time I come in at the back. Thee sing out as thee comes up the road, so thy father won't mistake thee. Thee understand?"

Clarence nodded his head.

"Maybe thee ought to take off that coat."

Clarence unbuttoned the top buttons, but at the first touch of cold he buttoned them up again.

"Pa'll know me," he said.

Jess knocked lightly at the Clark back door; when no one answered, he walked in. There was a fire on the kitchen hearth and something savory-smelling bubbled away in the pot that hung over the fire. A trestle table was laid for a meal. A pendulum clock wigwagged on the mantel. There was a sink, but the pump was outside on the porch. The room took Jess back in time to his and Eliza's early log-cabin years, before they built the clap-board house. Eliza had a cookstove now, but nothing would ever be as homey as an open fire on a kitchen hearth. He had no hankering to return to past times. A cookstove beat a fireplace all holler. And who would go out onto an icy porch to pump water when he could have water right at hand in a warm kitchen? Still, he felt regret for the passing of things he had once known and used and which were no more.

For a couple of seconds, recalling old times, he had forgotten where he was, and why he was where he was. Clara Clark recalled him. She entered quietly from the adjoining room.

"Jess," she exclaimed, "I didn't hear you come in. I was with Jenny."

"Is Jenny sick?" Jess asked.

Clara hesitated. "There's no way to put a good face on this. Jenny'll be sicker before she's better."

"Thee should have let us know."

Clara looked at Jess squarely. "There wasn't anything you could have done."

"We might've understood Jasp better."

"He didn't know it himself till this week. We both kept it from him. Jasp talked about shooting Jenny. Or shoot-ing himself. Then today he took it into his head that this fellow might come back, so he got himself fixed to shoot him. He's drunk now and upstairs, shooting for the sake of the noise."

"Where's the stairs?"

"Let him alone, Jess. He'll run out of bullets or whisky pretty soon. I likely shouldn't have sent for you. But for a while I didn't know what he might do, or where to turn."

308

"Clarence and I've got a way figured out to grab him. Clarence's due to come riding up the lane in a few minutes. While Jasp is trying to make out who Clarence is, I'll step up behind him and take the gun away."

"Drunk as Jasp is, he could fire without knowing or caring who Clarence is," Clara said. "He's been aching for someone to take a shot at ever since he got back from town."

"That being the case, I'll make some noise as I go upstairs. While Jasp's figuring out who's coming up the stairs he won't be taking shots out of the window. And he sure's not going to pepper me."

"That's nothing I'd bank on, Jess."

Jess didn't linger to argue. If someone *had* to be shot, it had better be him than Clarence. But his plan was for both of them to escape. The stairs that led up to the attic bedroom passed through the front room where Jenny lay stretched out on a sofa and covered by a quilt. She had her mother's dark eyes, and she looked full at him, musingly, it seemed to Jess, as if pondering the question "How did I ever come to this pass?"

Jess had told himself to make a noticeable clatter as he ran up those stairs. The best he could manage was his natural clump, though faster than usual, fearful as he was that Clarence might turn into the Clarks' lane before he had a chance to direct Jasper's attention to himself.

The stairway opened directly into the bedroom. At the front window, its only window, Jasp Clark, gun on window ledge, knelt. Beside him was a jug of whisky. Jess, as he entered, saw, through the raised pane above Jasp's head, Clarence turning off the country road to head up the Clark lane. The bulky coat made a man of the thin boy.

The second Jess saw Clarence, he shouted, "Jasp, Jasp."

As he ran forward, he noted, out of the corner of his eye, Clara in the yard below. She was also shouting, waving a dishcloth or something that size, and jumping up and down.

Jasp fired as Jess shouted. Not at anyone, Jess thought, not even seeing Clarence, likely, and possibly not even Clara; a reflex action, the result of the sudden hullabaloo. He hit what his gun had been trained on, a cone hanging from the evergreen at the front gate. Jess saw the cone fall, wondering that he was able to notice it while in the midst of his arcing leap across the room onto Jasp. Jasp was a younger man than Jess, wiry, and heated with alcohol. Jess exerted all his strength, pushing Jasp backward, with the gun between them. He had his own need to succeed. His conscience hurt him. It was his money that had bought the liquor; it was his plan that had endangered Clarence's life. Jasp, with unexpected suddenness, let go the gun and fell back against the window. Whether it was the thump he took or the liquor, Jasp closed his eyes and stretched out on the floor as slow and easy as a baby dropping off to sleep.

Clara, panting from her run up the stairs, came into the room as Jess, gun in hand, stood over Jasp. "You didn't shoot him?"

Jess could scarcely grasp the meaning of that.

"No one shot anyone," he said. "But thee took a great chance, calling up to a man drunk and with gun cocked and ready to fire."

"What else could I do, with Clarence coming?" She knelt beside her husband. "Jasp would never harm a hair of my head anyway. Never has, never would. Help me get him to bed, Jess. Let's put him under the covers before Clarence sees him."

Jasp was boneless as a snake. They stripped him down to his underwear and covered him over snugly.

"He'll sleep it off now."

"That was a pretty smart crack he took on the head," Jess said. "A poultice might be in order."

"Nothing hurts Jasp but drink. He's strong in every way but that one."

Jess said nothing.

They were downstairs in the kitchen by the time Clarence came in.

"How's Pa?"

"Napping," his mother said. "Go up and have a look."

Clara wouldn't hear of Jess's leaving without having a bite to eat.

"Stay and have a little taste of the burgoo," she insisted. "Clarence shot the squirrels for it himself. You don't need to eat enough to spoil your appetite for supper. Just enough to take the sharp edge off the wind on your way home. And to please Clarence. And me. I got a good do on it."

While Jess spooned up the burgoo Clara had dished up for him, Clara said, "Excuse me. I want to go tell Jenny what's been going on."

When she came back she said, "How was the burgoo?"

"I never ate better, Clara."

Clara nodded. "I made it special for tonight. The ham gives the squirrel a good smoky flavor, don't it? Have some more. There's plenty for all. We won't eat till Jasp wakes up. He'll come out of it by dark. He don't drink much, Jess. It's just he can't hold what he does drink. Jasp's got presents for all, and we'll wait supper for him."

Clara proudly moved some packages from the side mantel to the front. "He remembered every last one of us."

Clara spoke as if Jasp had a dozen or more kinfolk to keep in mind, not three. But Jess was surprised at Jasp's remembering any one of them.

"I figured he spent the money I gave him on that jug."

"That jug was a present to him from a man who calls himself a friend. Jasp bought us presents the way he said he would. Jasp's no liar."

"I didn't say he was, Clara. What can we do to help you with Jenny?"

"Not a thing I know of. Do you? She's a good girl, but her head's easily turned. I prayed she'd be spared this, but she wasn't and she'll live through it. We all will."

Clara changed the subject as Clarence came in. "Your pa still asleep?"

Clarence nodded.

"Take your borrowed coat off, son, so Mr. Birdwell can take it home with him."

"It's a good fit," Jess said. "He's welcome to it."

"No, no, Jess. We're well provided for around here. Clarence rode off in a hurry without a jacket."

"Well, bring it some other time. I don't want to ride home with it tied to pommel."

"There's two things I want you to ride home with, Jess, burden or no burden. The gun and the jug."

"I'll take the gun. But there's no point carrying the jug. We can empty it here as well as at my place."

"It's a pity to waste it. Except for Jasp, I'd flavor my mincemeat with it. The spirits boil away with the cooking anyway and nothing's left but the flavor. Why don't you take it home to Eliza?"

"Clara, thee knows Eliza would never put up with anything like that."

Clara laughed a little. "I don't suppose it's likely."

"But I will take the gun. Clarence, thee ride over in a

few days and hunt squirrels on my place. Thee's got a natural talent for hitting tasty ones, and I got more fat fellows than I need."

It was getting on for dark when Jess came in sight of his own well-lit place.

The first thing they noticed, of course, when he stepped into the sitting room, was the gun.

"Jess, was anybody hurt?" Eliza asked.

"Not a soul," Jess said.

"That Clark's gun?" Gard asked.

Jess nodded.

"How did thee get it away from him?" Josh asked.

"I had a little help from Clara. Jasp was leaning out an upstairs window looking for someone to shoot at, and Clara ran around in the yard below calling to him. While she took Jasp's attention, I came in from behind and grabbed the gun."

"Wasn't that dangerous for Clara?"

"She was risking her life, in my opinion."

"He spent the money for liquor," Eliza said.

"Thee's wrong there. He was drunk all right, but he'd spent the money he got from me for presents. He bought presents for everyone."

"With two-fifty? That wouldn't have gone very far. What can we send over?"

"Send over to the Clarks'? When it comes to sending things to the Clarks', the shoe's on the other foot. They've got all they need over there. Enough to be making hand-outs themselves. They've got God's plenty for Christmas."

"With a man drunk and shooting?" Gard asked.

"What have they *got*, Papa?" matter-of-fact Mattie asked.

There wasn't any answer to that question unless he said

"love"; but that was a hard word to say right out. Besides, it seemed a reflection on those about him, as if they lacked something the Clarks had, and he didn't think that.

"For one thing," he told them, "they've got the finest kettle of burgoo over there I ever tasted. Mattie, does thee still want to put up that tree of thine?"

"Not if it'll make Christmas unhappy for thee, Papa."

"A tree," Jess said, "won't cut that much ice with me one way or another. Having or not having it."

It cut some ice though. More than he had expected. Mattie couldn't wait until after supper to get started. And she'd come over fully expecting her father to give in, with baskets of trimming: tinsel, strands of popcorn, gilded nuts, popcorn balls, candles, all ready for the decorating.

"The only thing I ask," Jess said, "is put it in the parlor. I don't want to be tromping round it in the sitting room for a couple of days."

Jess had to admit to himself that though a six-foot tree set indoors, festooned with edibles, and lit with candles was an outlandish sight, it was also, in a strange way, pretty. It had not a thing, insofar as he could see, to do with Christmas. It went against nature and made him feel a little uneasy, the way he might feel seeing an oak tree sprout blossoms. A tree in the house was an oddity to begin with; then set the tree to drooping with what a tree was never made to carry! Unnatural or not, it worked on all the children like a tot of hard liquor. Maybe there *was* some magic in them. Voices were getting louder, gestures more violent. It wasn't necessary to say anything funny to get a laugh. Little Elspeth, running in circles and screeching like a Comanche, was admired by all.

Jess himself stepped outside to see how his house looked with a tree in it. And to get away from the noise and heat.

He was in the driveway, across from the bay window in which the tree stood, when Eliza joined him. She threw one end of the shawl she was wearing across his shoulders, and together they gazed in at what was theirs, but from which so much separated them.

Beyond the parlor and the tree, they saw room after room, face after face: log cabin, farmhouse in Ohio, Eliza's parents in their brick house in Philadelphia; lost Sarah, Jess's father's stern prophet's face, Eliza's mother's secret smile, the soldiers who died. And now this roomful of young people for whom the vanished rooms, the faces that would be seen no more, meant nothing, except as part of some tale of "olden times" their parents might tell them.

Jess added the day's experiences to these memories of the past. There had been drunkenness and shooting, he supposed, when he was a boy. Girls had had babies without husbands since the beginning of time. Christmas trees, however, were certainly a new wrinkle. Nothing made to hold presents had occupied the center of attention in the days when Christmas had been celebrated at Mount Pleasant. And presents! If the day meant anything else to Elspeth, he'd seen no signs of it. "What's my present, Grandpa? What's my present, Grandpa?" He blamed Mattie for letting her daughter grow up that way, centered on getting, not giving.

"I don't know, Eliza," he said. "I just don't know."

"Well now, Jess," Eliza said, "it's not like thee, making an admission like that."

But Jess wouldn't be lured into lightness.

"I don't know what the world's coming to," he went on. "People getting more worldly every day."

They turned away from the parlor window. Jess held his hand in front of him. It had begun to snow again.

315

"Except for me and thee, Jess," Eliza corrected him.

"Me and thee what?" Jess asked, engrossed in the thickening eddies of snow.

"Getting more worldly."

Jess had an answer to that on the tip of his tongue, thought better of it, and said instead, "Let's walk up to the barn. See if the boys got the animals bedded down all right. We're in for a cold blustery night."

Halfway up the already whitening slope Jess stopped, put an arm about Eliza. The parlor noise had grown faint. In the barn he could hear the munch and stomp of drowsy feeding animals. Overhead, the winter stars were hidden by the falling snowflakes.

"Except for me and thee," he repeated. And he wasn't thinking of worldliness at all, but of the life the two of them had shared.